CHASING SHADOWS

A Psychic Justice Novel

ERIN RICHARDS

I0629187

www.ErinRichards.com

CHASING SHADOWS
Erin Richards

Print ISBN: 978-0991126446
Digital ISBN: 978-0991126439

Cover Designer: Robin Harper @ Wicked by Design

First Print Edition: July 2012
Second Print Edition: April 2015

PRAISE FOR
CHASING SHADOWS

Night Owl Reviews Readers Choice Award Nominee for best romance in Mystery and Suspense

EPPIE Award Finalist in the Mystery / Suspense / Horror romance category

"Oh my god I loved this book and it never faltered from its action and suspense. The story line not only kept my attention but each chapter was suspenseful trying to find out what the kidnapper was going to do and how Juliana would deal with it." ~*Night Owl Reviews* (NOR 5-Star Top Pick)

"A whirlwind of emotions, twists, turns and rediscovered love will keep you breathless!" ~*Fresh Fiction*

"The suspense will keep you turning the pages... The characters are complex and well-developed and there is never a dull moment in the story. If you love your romance with suspense, this is one book you need to read! 5 stars all the way!" ~*The Romance Reviews*

"This story was masterfully written and illustrates just what a frightfully good imagination the author has to work with." ~*Fallen Angel Reviews* (5-Star Recommended Read)

"This book has so many twists and plot turns that a seatbelt should be required. One of the best romantic suspenses that I have read this year and I heartily recommend to any fans of this genre. This book is just incredible." ~*Love Romances & More*

Books by
Erin Richards

Psychic Justice Series
Chasing Shadows, Book 1
Twilight Rising, Novella
Stealing Twilight, Book 2

Wicked Paradise

Young Adult
Vigilante Nights
Dragonfly Nightmare

CHASING
SHADOWS

CHAPTER ONE

Hardly a kidnapper's friend, the moon floated round and luminous in the ebony sky. At least it could never reveal his secrets.

Stifling a chuckle, he slipped into the peaceful backyard, leaving the gate unlatched. Bushes and trees created ghostly shapes undulating along the dark fence in the slight breeze. He scanned the tiny yard until he found his entry point.

Honeysuckle teased his senses and disgust pinched his gut. Grimacing, he disregarded the childhood memories the familiar reek evoked. Such distractions were a waste of time, a hindrance to critical concentration on his task at hand.

The window beckoned, inviting him through the pink, frilly curtains framing the panes. Innocent and unsuspecting, the young girl slept inside the darkened bedroom beyond the window.

He stared at the silent house, his body vibrating with the hunger flowing hot through his veins. Could he climb in and out through the window with his prize in hand without disturbing the tranquility? Oh yeah. He grinned. Nothing would stop him now. Not the moon, not the dancing tree shadows waving him onward.

Like a lover whispering his name, his treasure inside

lured him closer to the window. His pulse quickened. The full moon—his sole witness—illuminated his prey. He gazed at the tiny girl through the lacy curtains. Another tremor of anticipation warmed his gut, adding fuel to his fire.

Three months of preparation would soon culminate in his final triumph. Excitement rolled through him as he touched his gloved palm to the window.

Soon she would be his.

An anguished cry escaped Juliana, jolting her awake. She bolted upright in bed, her breath caught thick in her throat. Clutching at the sheer scarves cocooning her bed, she parted them to let air flow inside the suffocating space. A throbbing started in her temples, then raced behind her eyes. After what seemed an eternity, Juliana's heartbeat steadied and her lungs synchronized. She tugged the satin sheet over her breasts and massaged her temples.

There would be a kidnapping soon.

She had endured enough psychic visions in her past to know this one was real. Juliana quivered as the kidnapper's intentions invaded her. Already a strong psychic connection to the unknown assailant spiraled through her mind. She knew his thoughts, felt his emotions, and fought the dreaded invasion for a few seconds.

Quickly, she racked her brain to recall the details of her precognitive dream. Even though she felt his excitement and desire, she didn't feel one grain of his fear. He was too confident. More so than any other.

What interest did he have in the child? Why her? Who was she? Would he hurt her, kill her? And who was he? Juliana wanted to scream in frustration at the lack of answers. There were too many shadows obscuring the details. But the truth would surface soon enough. Now that the connection was made, more dreams would follow, like waves crashing on the beach, just as briskly receding, leaving fear and hope in the wake. Fear that the dream would become reality. Hope that she could glean enough clues to stop the kidnapper before he acted.

Juliana sighed heavily. The purple and gold scarves billowed gently. She flung aside the sheet and hopped out of bed. Grabbing her cell phone from the night table, she headed downstairs to look up the number to police headquarters. This would most likely be the first of many such phone calls to the San Jose Police Department. Time to key in the number in her contact list.

She raised her eyes heavenward, closing them for a brief moment. *God, couldn't you have given me some time to settle in first?*

∞

Juliana walked toward the SJPD building, and the fragrance of summer lilies eclipsed the downtown smog. Her gaze drifted to the golden flowers growing in profusion around the stark façade of the building. She sighed and swallowed her apprehension. The flower garden was her last slice of heaven before she succumbed to the barrage of questions from a typical skeptical detective. Another detective she'd have to convince she wasn't a nutcase vying for attention. She assessed her appearance, smoothing the wrinkles in her silk skirt and straightening the matching short-sleeved blazer.

Juliana entered the glass and concrete building and approached the counter separating the lobby from the squad room. The expansive work area beyond the counter hummed with voices, computers, and phones. Uniformed and plain-clothed personnel moved briskly about their duties.

A uniformed policewoman at the reception window glanced at her impatiently. "Can I help you?"

She dug her fingernails into her black leather portfolio. "Juliana Westwood. I have an appointment with Captain Hayes."

The officer frowned and looked over her shoulder. A man's voice rose from behind a cubicle wall. "I got her."

The grubby brown door leading into the squad room creaked open. Juliana turned toward the attractive, lanky man who stepped through.

"Captain Hayes had an emergency." He flashed a lopsided smile. "Detective James O'Malley." His russet crew cut and freckled face gave away his Irish ancestry as much as his name did.

She handed him her business card. "Juliana Westwood."

He took the card and shook her hand, his grip firm. She returned his charming smile, despite the renewed nervous stirring in her stomach. For some reason, she always had good luck working with Irish cops. The Irish seemed to have a higher respect for paranormal activity due to the rich folklore of Ireland with its fairy folk and restless spirits.

Without warning, Juliana's heartbeat accelerated and an ache raced behind her eyes. Strange and incomprehensible thoughts flitted through her mind. Thoughts from someone else. As quickly as the sensations assaulted her, they dissipated. Juliana wiped dots of perspiration off her forehead and rubbed her fingers on her bag. Something wasn't right, and she suspected the looming abduction would be problematic, more so than any other case.

Shoving the forewarning aside to deal with later, she followed O'Malley to a cramped, bleak interrogation room.

Four chairs and a gray-speckled laminate table occupied the lion's share of space. A closed-circuit surveillance screen dangled from the ceiling in the farthest corner. A two-way mirror on the opposite wall rounded off the furnishings. Typical cop shop. Juliana wrinkled her nose as harsh pine cleaner clashed with O'Malley's citrus and amber cologne.

Her wary gaze dallied on the two-way mirror. "There's no one behind the mirror I take it?" She skirted the table and sat in a battered chair on the other side, her back to the mirror. Juliana stifled a groan as her bottom made contact with the worn seat cushion that did its best to mimic a cement slab.

"No." O'Malley shrugged. "Why?" He dropped in a chair next to the door and pulled it closer to the table. He squared her business card in front of him, a small white blip on the blank expanse of gray table.

Relief began a slow, tortuous crawl up her spine. "Just wondering." Juliana smiled and shifted in her seat, futilely seeking a comfortable position. The concept of two-way mirrors hit too close to home with her telepathic abilities. She'd hate someone unobtrusively watching her, even though she was capable of doing the same in an even more intrusive manner. It was absurd, but it wasn't as if she could severe her ability and become normal.

"Your message was mysterious." O'Malley smiled his friendly crooked smile.

His melodious voice soothed her and her muscles loosened up another notch, despite the new presentiment.

She didn't have any experience working with the SJPD, so she wasn't sure how tolerant they were of psychics. "As I informed Captain Hayes on the phone, I'm a psychic. I have information regarding a possible kidnapping."

O'Malley squinted, his mouth a straight, tight line. He

pushed away from the table. "Hayes didn't tell me you were a psychic."

Juliana crossed her ankles, her calf brushing against a cold steel table leg. Shivers raced over that crawl of relief. "Is there a problem?" She kept her voice impassive, confident. Cool objectivity afforded her the only means to maintain her sanity while engaged in a criminal case.

"Policy." He glanced at her business card. "A senior officer has to sit in on first-timer psychic interviews." Annoyance roughened his voice and he flicked his pen on his pad. "Do you belong to the Psychics Guild?"

Her pulse quickened at the mention of the über secret group of psychics with factions on both the East and West coasts. Her former doctor tried to get her to join it for her own protection during her cases. "You know about them?"

"I have a healthy respect for their management and protection of their psychics. We stay out of each other's business for the most part. I just don't want to run up against your Guild guardian, protector, whatever they're called. Those dudes usually get in our way."

"Guardian," she murmured. "No I don't belong."

After a moment of deliberation, O'Malley rose to his feet, pocketed her business card, and opened the door. "Hang tight." He took one last, assessing look at her over his shoulder before the door slammed shut behind him.

CRSO

Alex heard a presence in his open doorway before he sensed one. He was so engrossed in his work that his normally astute senses had betrayed him. Glancing up from the cold case homicide files burying his desk, he saw James filling the doorway.

"What's up?" He leaned back in his chair, stretching his arms behind his head, relieved to abandon the endless research and analysis.

James leaned his shoulder against the doorframe, shoving his hands in his pockets. "Hayes dumped a psychic on me."

Alex laughed and tossed his pen on the desk. "And you want me as your senior officer? You're full of it. Take a hike."

"Yeah, man. I know how you *love* psychics." James flipped him the bird.

"Why me?"

"Take a guess." James snickered. "You're top of the dung heap today."

"Damn Hayes. He did this on purpose."

James grinned and jangled his keys in his pants pocket. "Not that you give a rat's ass, but she looks legit. Professional, serious, nervous."

"Is she Guild?"

"Nope."

Alex grumbled and shoved his chair back from the desk, bumping into the window frame. He made no bones about his dislike of psychics, but he trusted James' judgment before anyone else's. "Shit." He sighed and stood, stretching his cramped legs. "Let's get it over with."

Stepping around his desk, he grimaced at the files that seemed to multiply as the clocked ticked. But he needed the break, if only for the amusement factor. If he analyzed one more report on homicidal killing sprees, he'd have to drink his lunch.

The walk to the interrogation room remained silent, and a bad feeling seeped into Alex's gut. He halted before the closed door and slowly turned to face James. "What's her name?"

"Juliana." James plucked a business card from his shirt pocket. "Westwood. Financial planner."

Alex stiffened. *No. Fucking impossible.* He clenched

his hands into fists, then slowly unclenched them. Memories surged forward. Long-buried pain rose to meet the anger he thought he'd relinquished years ago.

"Man, you okay? You look like you've seen a ghost."

"And she just waltzed over my grave." Alex took the card from James and studied it. "Damn." He shrugged back his shoulders and opened the door.

Juliana Westwood sat across the table in the flesh.

Her widening emerald eyes brought back vivid memories of her gazing at him with absolute love and adoration. Once again, he could feel her silky blonde hair between his fingers. He could feel her slim, soft body molding itself against him, her arms around him, holding him to her as if she'd never leave him.

What the hell? He curled his fists. A loathing he hadn't experienced in a long time anchored him in the doorway.

Juliana Westwood was back from the dead.

CHAPTER TWO

Juliana froze in her seat, unable to move a muscle, ice and cement meeting as one. Perspiration wet her face like a balmy mist before turning into snow as blood rushed downward. "Alex?" she managed to croak out. "Alex MacKenzie?"

Her heart thumped against her ribcage and she thought it might burst through her chest. A key turned the rusty lock on the box where she'd stowed away memories of her first eighteen years.

O'Malley glanced from her to Alex, speculation dancing in his eyes. "You two know each other?"

"Yes," Juliana whispered.

"Hardly," Alex bit out, cold enough to freeze her skin. He pulled out the chair James had vacated earlier and sank down, back rigid and face a granite slab. A very dark and lethal granite.

Juliana let Alex's barb slide. After all, she deserved it. In that moment, she just wanted to run back to New York, but she couldn't tear her gaze from Alex. Never in a million years did she envision he'd become a cop.

Despite Alex's authoritative air, he looked the same. Mature, bulked up, still undeniably gorgeous. Unforgettable azure eyes glared at her in a face darkened by the California sun. A four-inch scar along his left jaw-line marred his otherwise perfect face. The scar's ivory ridge on his blank mask reminded her of the dangers of law enforcement. *Perfect cop face.* Frowning pensively, she strained to read his eyes, but they remained unfathomable.

Some things had changed. Once, she could read him as well as her own soul.

O'Malley shut the door and sat next to Alex. "Now that we have that out in the open." He chuckled in an attempt at levity to wade through the awful tension.

Alex sat motionless, looking as menacing as the gun protruding from his shoulder holster. The earlier feeling of déjà vu expanded in Juliana's stomach. No wonder she felt as if this case would be tricky. *Alex MacKenzie? What the hell is he doing here?*

His gaze traveled leisurely from Juliana's eyes to her mouth, her pulse skittering as his perusal dipped lower. Something close to desire flickered in his eyes before quickly dimming to a glower.

Juliana pressed her hands against her stomach, trying to ward off the thoughts and emotions attacking her. Did she imagine the way he looked at her? As if time had spun backward and they were eighteen, inseparable, and in love again. No. She must have mistaken the look. After all, she deserved his hatred, and more.

Her back muscles twitched when Alex crushed the silence with a soft and level, "Hello, Juliana." His expression mellowed, but the softening didn't spread to his flinty eyes. "What can we do for you?" He leaned his elbows on the table, fingers steepled under his chin.

Juliana tugged together every loose strand of her being to manage the impact of seeing Alex for the first time in twelve years.

The only man she'd ever loved.

Get through the meeting and escape this hell before Alex lunges across the table and beats answers out of me. She painted on a cool veneer and straightened in her chair. "I'm here on official police business." She felt compelled to add, "This isn't personal."

"Why would it be personal after all this time?"

Alex's question squeezed her heart so hard it skipped a beat. Ignoring his dig, she reached inside her leather portfolio. She pulled out a sheet of paper and slid it across the table toward Alex. Even though he'd experienced her psychic abilities firsthand a long time ago, he would need major convincing now.

"My references." She tapped the paper. "You should speak to Captain Jamison at NYPD first."

Alex pushed her references aside. O'Malley lounged back in his chair and watched them, amusement crinkling the corners of his eyes.

If she weren't honor-bound to help save an unsuspecting family a world of grief, she'd walk out and pretend that day had never happened. But the premonition refused to let go, and duty prevailed.

Juliana rushed to continue, "Have either of you worked with psychics to solve any cases?" Their reactions and receptiveness would tell all. She'd worked with enough cops to expect cynicism and derision from the best of them. Such attitudes made for a thorny working relationship. If that were the case here, she wanted to know upfront.

"We work with a couple freelancers now and then," O'Malley replied. "Once and a while with the Guild psychics, like I said."

"No. *You* work with them," Alex corrected, his voice unyielding. "The few I've worked with were pain-in-the-ass nut jobs craving the limelight."

A frisson of anger sliced through Juliana at Alex's

depiction of paranormal science, but she held her tongue. She'd heard it all before. But it still stung stemming from someone who'd once believed in her abilities. In *her* completely.

"Why are you just now coming out of the woodwork?" O'Malley glanced at her business card as if it offered further clues to her identity.

"I keep a low profile or use a pseudonym. Few people are aware of my particular talents." She avoided looking directly at the sparks in Alex's eyes and fixated on a reddish brown smudge on the wall behind the two detectives. "I was born and raised in San Jose. Twelve years ago I moved—" Her voice wavered at the recollection, and she rapidly buried the memory. "To New York. I worked with the NYPD for several years solving missing persons, rape, and homicide cases. I moved back to San Jose a few weeks ago."

Before either man uttered a response, she gave her standard recitation. "I have ESP, which occurs as visions while I'm asleep." Absently, she toyed with her braid, laddering her fingers in it the way Alex used to do. "Sometimes I experience premonitions first. Other times, I see the actual event as it occurs."

She breathed in the scent of Alex's spice and musk cologne. It drove her batty with unexpected familiarity and long ago, but not forgotten memories. She rubbed her nose, smelling her own freesia perfume, and forced herself to ignore his haunting cologne.

"Certain dreams are warm and fuzzy, others are horrible, evil." She glanced at Alex's face to weigh the impact of her words. A boulder boasted more expression than he did.

O'Malley nodded and flicked a hand at her to continue.

Relief flowed through her. She loved a receptive cop. They were much easier to work with. "This morning I had a premonition." She related the details of her dream, including the presence of the illuminating full moon, giving voice to a timeframe.

O'Malley scribbled in his notepad, while Alex's dark gaze remained riveted on her face, disconcerting in his intensity.

"I don't believe the kidnapping has happened yet. I didn't sense or see completion, only anticipation." Her heart wrenched again in sympathy for the unwary child and family. In case her senses were wrong, she asked, "Has such a kidnapping been reported?"

O'Malley gave her a measured stare, tapping his pen on the table edge. "No."

"An abduction *will* occur, and it will happen nearby."

"Because you dreamed it? Do you know the girl's identity? The kidnapper?" Alex jabbed the tabletop with his index finger after each question. "Didn't your dream tell you that?"

She expected the grilling. The NYPD had put her through dozens of similar interrogations. But she wasn't prepared for the niggling doubt Alex dumped in her mind. "I wouldn't recognize either one of them if they sat next to me. I wish I could."

Alex folded his thick, muscled arms across his chest. "Then how can you help us?"

Juliana averted her gaze from Alex's tanned arms, exposed beneath the rolled-up sleeves of his blue heathered dress shirt. Desire surged at the thought of those strong arms around her, and she batted the insane feelings down. She brushed clammy palms on her skirt, hating her nervousness. Hating that Alex caused it.

Why Alex? Why now? Every police case she'd ever assisted with flipped her life upside down while she dreamed her way through it. She certainly didn't need this complication or the attendant distractions.

Sweeping her thoughts aside, she shifted her attention back to the detectives. "I've connected with the kidnapper's mind. I may have encountered him somewhere, touched an item he touched, saw his picture, or heard his voice. When I experience this sense of invasion, the criminal's thoughts, emotions, and feelings will surface in my dreams. I'm ninety-nine percent sure I'll dream of the actual kidnapping."

"Are *all* your visions about strangers?" Alex's calculated question pushed the long-locked door to her buried memories open another inch.

Bastard! Anger surged through her once again. She swiped away the perspiration tickling her forehead, hating that Alex had reduced her to this state. "Sometimes I dream of things and events happening to people I know. I don't *only* dream of crimes happening to strangers."

Another thick hush blanketed the room. O'Malley's sudden scrawling on his small notepad drowned out any other sound.

Juliana peeked at her watch before her gaze darted to the slate-blue door behind the two men. She cut through the silence in a rush of words. "The kidnapping will happen soon. When it does, I'll provide as much assistance as I can. Check my references. I am *not* wasting your time."

Alex's eyebrows arched and he gave a curt nod. "Fine."

O'Malley quit writing and lifted his head. "We'll be in touch."

"Thank you for your time." She stood, clutching her bag to her middle and adjusting her purse strap over her shoulder.

With brisk steps, Juliana walked out of the conference room and down the empty hall, surprised that they just let her go without an escort. She gave an inward shrug and kept walking. Halfway through the squad room, she felt a touch on her arm from behind. As abruptly as the touch landed, it vanished. Electricity tingled along her arm, and she knew without turning that Alex stood behind her. She knew his touch and would always know the burn of it in her mind.

Noise in the squad room decreased to an oppressive stillness. She sensed a dozen pairs of eyes watching her as if she held a live grenade.

She turned slowly. "Detective?" It was difficult to remain coherent when he stood mere inches away.

"You appear out of thin air and drop a bombshell on me." His voice lowered for their ears only. "Just like that."

"What more do you want me to do?" she whispered through clenched teeth.

"By the way, it's *Lieutenant.*" His mouth tugged at the corners.

"What?" She blinked rapidly.

"Forget it." He scowled.

He stood so close, her gaze was bound by the magnetism of his extraordinary eyes. His eyes didn't mask his inner fire, but the rest of his face was as unreadable as the worn and stained carpet under his feet.

Without thought, she skimmed her fingers over the whitened scar on his face. "What happened?"

"Busted up a street gang fight."

"I'm . . . sorry." She dropped her hand and stepped back.

The spell dissolved and regret zigzagged through her. "Alex, call Captain Jamison. He'll verify my work with the NYPD."

By tacit consent, they both turned and walked away.

"You know how to reach me," she tossed back as she practically fled the confining squad room.

Under the bright August sun, she forced herself to

walk with calm, purposeful steps to her BMW. Once inside the car, long-hidden guilt crashed into her full force. Pain washed over her heart, seeking a crevice, pinching and prodding. The premonition took a backseat as the nightmare from twelve years ago swamped her.

Juliana and Alex had been eighteen years old, nearing graduation and the road to college. They'd been in love, ready to tackle the world together. Instead, two weeks prior to graduation, they stood dressed in dark funeral clothes, staring at each other across a six-foot-deep hole in the ground. A pine coffin housing Johnny Cates' mangled body sat next to the dark cavity. Alex's best friend. The result of a premonition she'd screwed up.

The funeral service had reached a dismal end, grieving family and friends had departed. Without warning, unusual and puzzling thoughts collided with hers. Something had clicked in her psychic awareness. For the first time in her life, she'd been able to read someone's mind.

Alex's mind.

What she'd interpreted shocked her more than the confusing looks his pain-shrouded eyes hurled at her. He'd directed resentment, anger, and uncertainty at her. The array of emotions had devastated her.

She'd buried a large part of her heart along with Johnny that horrible afternoon. It had been the last time she'd seen Alex, when events out of her control forever altered her life.

Wiping away a lone tear, Juliana corralled her drifting thoughts. She concentrated on the short drive to her office tower downtown.

She would deal with the merciless premonition like all the others she'd experienced. But how could she expect to cope with Alex, the pain, and the memories at the same time?

CHAPTER THREE

Juliana sank into the high-backed chair behind her desk, the plush comfort soaking up her mixed bag of emotions. She tapped her laptop on and glanced at her day's schedule. Back-to-back appointments would keep her busy through lunch and her mind off the events of that morning.

An acquaintance and prospective client from New York was first on her agenda. He could potentially bring her several high-dollar referrals. Plenty of money flowed in the high tech world of Silicon Valley, and her solo practice would get its share. Having the right clients upped the ante. She couldn't let the day's events distract her from establishing essential business contacts.

A sigh escaped her as the busy workday loomed ahead. She swiveled her chair around to gaze through the glass wall behind her desk, a moment's respite before getting down to business. Juliana pried her mind off the premonition, the police, and especially Alex. The rare moment of procrastination was blissful while it lasted.

The rolling foothills surrounding the valley were golden from summer's heat. The bleak landscape matched her mood perfectly. Exhaustion already threatened her, and her blood sugar was dropping in response. *Damn!*

She'd love to erase the morning from her life.

The dream weighed on her like a dropped anchor; there was no escaping it. "Not another child," she whispered.

"I'm sorry. Should I come back later?" A silky, deep masculine voice arose behind her.

Shoulders stiffening, she spun her chair back around. Her gaze landed on the second most striking man she'd seen that day. How could she have forgotten that Nicholas Hastings resembled a Greek god?

She rose, right hand extended, mentally slapping down the grasshoppers in her stomach.

Brazen blue eyes swept over her. He shook her hand, his palm cool and smooth. "Juliana, it's wonderful to see you again," he said in his smooth, eloquent voice.

His grin flashed dazzlingly against coppery skin, leaving her unusually disconcerted. Heat crept up her neck. *What is it with this day and gorgeous men?* Her composure was running on overtime, otherwise, charming and handsome men wouldn't normally affect her so.

Putting on a business face, she said, "Nicholas. It's wonderful to see you on the West Coast." She swept her arm toward the two client chairs. "Please, have a seat."

"I'm sorry I intruded. There was no one at the front desk." He set his briefcase on the floor and dropped with ease in a deep-cushioned chair facing the expansive glass-topped desk.

Juliana dismissed his apologies with a flutter of her fingers and a cheery smile she didn't feel. "I was taking a mental break. You merely startled me."

She assessed the elegance of his custom cut suit. It certainly fit his financial profile, a profile she wanted to get her hands on for the commissions brokering his money promised to earn her.

She clicked open his Client Intake file on her laptop,

notes taken from their recent telephone consultation. "Okay. What can I do for you?"

His grin turned into a seductive smile. "I'm sure I've mentioned before that you're an incredibly beautiful woman." He crossed his legs and rested his forearms on the padded chair arms.

Nicholas Hastings was a man accustomed to getting whatever he wanted, and arrogance practically oozed from his pores. How could she have forgotten about his inflated ego? Despite his bank account and after the morning's events, she didn't have the time or the inclination to indulge him as she would under normal circumstances.

"Nicholas, are you here to plan your finances?" Juliana raised an eyebrow.

He chuckled, haughty, irritating. "All business," he said nonchalantly. "You're a woman after my own heart."

She tapped her manicured fingernails on the keyboard and smiled at him, tongue in check.

Fortunately, her impatience spurred him on. "I want you to invest half a million in whatever way you think will earn me the biggest gain in a sixty-day period." He drew several sheets of paper from his briefcase and slid them across the desk. "Next, I want you to invest another half-million in this stock and pull the funds out after the stock triples." He rested back in the chair, challenge written across his smug face.

Juliana leaned forward and glanced at the prospectus. Unable to restrain her disbelief, she blurted out, "You're kidding." She quickly realized how unprofessional she sounded and gave an apologetic smile. "I mean, are you aware of the turmoil inside this company?"

Head crooked to the side, he stroked his chin. "Are you afraid of losing my money?"

Is he for real? "I'm sorry, but you'll accomplish that on

your own." Juliana kept her tone guarded. "Altz is going down. Unless you know more than the business and financial world, I strongly urge you not to waste your money."

No one wanted to invest in a company knocking at bankruptcy's door. Her old boss in New York had referred Nicholas to her, and he gave high praise for Nicholas' business acumen. She trusted that connection, but this proposal landed precariously close to the edge of lunacy.

"I've done my research." His shoulders squared and his chin jutted out.

"Is your research based on insider information?"

A breeze of condescension accompanied his deadpan look. "No."

Liar. "How did you arrive at your conclusions?"

He smiled. "I have significant faith in their new product line."

The company did have a respectable product line, but a sorry management team. She sighed in resignation. She'd conduct her own due diligence and make him sign a release. "What about a financial plan? Long-term financial planning is my focus now."

He winked. "Let's start with the first million and work our way from there."

"Give me a few days to prepare a proposal." She punched in several keystrokes on her laptop. "I'll have my assistant schedule a follow-up for next week."

"Join me for dinner tonight." His eyes twinkled.

The invitation, a command really, caught her off-guard. He was an attractive catch. Another day and she would've jumped on it just for the fun of it. "Rain check?"

"Of course." Flashing a Cheshire cat grin, he rose. "I'll set up that dinner party with those high flyers I mentioned during our call last week. They're dying to meet you now that you're on the West Coast." Full of confidence, he added, "Then we'll have our dinner," before turning and swaggering out.

Arrogant bastard. However, if he produced referrals with fat wallets, she'd let him charm her. Another day.

Adrenaline kicking in, a small smile tugged at her mouth. This was the sort of day she lived for. One rich new client and several more on the horizon. She geared up her mind for her next appointment.

CR&SO

The desk phone jangled several times before Alex interrupted his report writing and answered. "MacKenzie."

"Hey, it's me."

His twin sister's singsong voice sparked life in his tired body. "What's up?"

"My idiot father-in-law." Ire slipped into her voice.

Disgust began to build inside Alex. "Now what?" His gaze settled on the folders that threatened to topple off the file cabinet in the corner. Anything to avoid the work on his desk, even listen to what he knew he wouldn't like.

"They want more visitations. He's harassing me again through that stupid butler, Bremley. Ugh, that man creeps me out."

"What—" Alex cut in.

"Get this." She continued as if Alex hadn't uttered a sound. "That trollop they hired to babysit is leaving the estate when she's not supposed to. I found out today that Sharon saw them at the park on Saturday. With Bremley in tow." She sucked in a breath. "Alex, I don't like what's going on."

That didn't make sense. Sharon and Andrea not only lived next door to one another, they worked together. They talked about everything and were best friends.

"Today's Thursday and Sharon just told you?" The scar on his face twitched, but he resisted rubbing it. It had been driving him crazy ever since Juliana had touched his face earlier.

"Yeah, well, she's on a space trip with her own problems. Fertility treatments." Andrea paused for a half-second. "Alex, what am I going to do?"

His niece disliked her paternal grandparents. But they were "encouraging" Lisette to visit them regularly by giving her anything she wanted.

Alex's gaze shifted to the mounds of paperwork on his desk demanding attention. He groaned and rubbed his eyes. He didn't have time for this now, and it wasn't so important that it couldn't wait.

He sighed heavily. "Let me think about it. Can we talk tomorrow?"

"Oh. Sure." She exhaled a loud, frustrated breath mimicking his own. "You're still coming over Saturday to fix the screens, right? Dinner's on me. We'll barbecue and go swimming." Her voice turned bubbly again. "Bring James."

"Where else would we be?" His gut clenched as he considered if he should mention Juliana. Andrea had missed Juliana as much as he did. After an indecisive moment, he asked, "Guess who I ran into today?"

Silence fell on the line. "Beats me," she finally said.

"Your old best friend." He set the phone away to avoid the expected ear-splitting screech, but none met his ear.

"Huh?"

"Juliana Westwood." He balled a few pink phone messages and tossed them through the basketball hoop hanging on the wall to join the other paper balls littering his floor.

Another pea-soup hush landed on the line before Andrea cut through the silence. "What? Are you kidding?"

"Hell, no."

"God, Alex. I can't believe it! Where has she been?"

"New York." Alex slid a pen end-to-end between his fingers.

"When did she get back? What happened? Did she tell—"

She'd ask a million questions if he let her. "Andrea?" He shook his head, wishing she'd take a breather or two.

"Is that Alex? Tell him I said hello." Alex heard Sharon's familiar chirpy voice in the background. "Let's go, Andrea."

"Oh crap. I've got a nurse association meeting," Andrea said in a rush. "Ask Juliana to dinner on Saturday. I really want to catch up. Love you."

The line dropped dead. "Love you too," he muttered, returning the receiver to the cradle. He rotated his chair around and stared out at the illuminated parking lot.

He hardly believed that twelve years had flown by since the nightmare day Juliana had disappeared. No goodbye, no note, no nothing. One part of him always wished she'd never come back. The other part hung onto the hope that she'd return someday.

He'd felt as if time had stood still when he saw her sitting in the conference room. More beautiful than he remembered. Brilliant emerald eyes. Long honey-blonde hair. Perfect angelic face. His groin tightened in vivid recollection of the mere sight of her. Her five-foot-seven frame was firm and slim like an eighteen-year-old. The silken tan skin of her bare legs made his blood surge.

The door banged shut, and Alex caught James' reflection in the window. He swiveled his chair around and glanced up at his best friend. "That's twice you've done that to me today."

"Deal with it." James grinned and threw a manila folder on the desk. He leaned forward and rested his fists on the cushioned back of a steel-legged chair. "Going home?" Alex had invited James to live with him temporarily after James split with his wife, and they kept tabs on one another's whereabouts.

"Later."

Undeterred, James twisted the chair around and straddled it. He nodded at the file on the cluttered desk. "My report on the psychic."

Alex rubbed his eyes, glanced at the clock, and then at the file. Slowly, he picked up the folder and opened it. He wasn't in the mood to read the contents, but paperwork came with the territory. Alex scanned the computerized report, inked his signature, and laid it aside.

Drained and boneless, he settled in the worn leather chair. "Another kidnapping. Just what we need."

"Nothin' we can do without more intel."

"No shit. Can't panic the city over a psychic's premonition that may never pan out." Alex hated his own words. He wished they could do something to forestall Juliana's premonition. But he knew her potential all too well. She'd been wrong only once that he remembered.

The folder caught his gaze. "Don't file it yet."

James nodded. "She's legit." He crossed his arms over the top of the chair. "Off the record, Jamison at NYPD called her his 'dream chaser.' He said we might as well put her on payroll, we should be so lucky to have her."

Alex grunted at the praise. He always figured Juliana would leave a mark on the world somehow, somewhere. Once upon a time, he never figured she'd leave his side to do it.

"One warning." James paused for a beat. "Jamison said to keep the media away from her or we'd lose her. Her terms. Wouldn't tell me anymore."

Alex grabbed a half-full cola and guzzled it down. The warm, flat liquid cut through the sourness in his mouth.

He set the can next to two cups of stale morning coffee.

James' face was sober as he looked at Alex. "Who is she?"

Alex stood and faced the windows. "Every boy's fantasy girl at Mission City High."

"Oh, man." James let out a low whistle. "The one who split on you? That fucking sucks."

"Tell me about it." Alex skimmed his hands through his thick hair and rubbed his scalp. Weariness claimed his body, numbing his mind.

"What happened between you two?"

Alex turned around. "I need a drink."

"Just one?"

"As many as it'll take."

CHAPTER FOUR

Quiet as the dead, he climbed through the window into the small room. The old saying "quiet as a church mouse" sprang to mind, and he suppressed a chuckle. The bedroom door to the hallway was closed, and warm satisfaction pooled in his gut.

The faint amber glow of a nightlight lit a corner of the dark bedroom. Wraithlike, he picked his way through the toys scattered on the floor. He eased to a seat on the bed beside the sleeping child. Cupping his palm over the girl's mouth, he caressed her baby-smooth cheeks with his thumb.

He withdrew a juice box and straw from his windbreaker pocket and plucked the tape off the hole he'd enlarged on the top. He plunged the straw into the box and set it on the nightstand. Tightening his hand over the girl's mouth, he nudged her leg with his knee. The bed vibrated as her small body shook awake. Her eyes opened wide with a mix of fear and surprise.

"Hi," he whispered. "Shhh." He rested his index finger on his lips. "We're going to surprise Mommy. Will you be quiet if I take my hand away?" he asked with what he hoped was a warm smile.

Recognition crossed her face. The fear in her eyes

subsided and she nodded. He removed his hand, still smiling at her.

A heavy whiff of honeysuckle wafted through the open window, cloying, hateful. He nearly gagged on the smell.

"Why are you here?" Her whisper held more curiosity than fear. She pushed aside the vivid floral comforter with the smiling sunflowers and knelt next to him.

He brought his finger to his lips again. "Remember how we play the hush-shush game?"

Grinning, she nodded. Fervent eyes flitted to the juice box on the pink-painted nightstand.

He lifted the box and handed it to her. "Drink it all so you don't get thirsty later."

She eagerly took the juice box and began sucking on the straw. Delight rippled through him at his foresight. The mild sedative in the punch would make her compliant without sending her completely to sleep.

He stepped away from the bed and grabbed her sweatshirt hanging on a chair in the corner. Snatching a pair of sneakers off the floor, he waited for her to finish the drink. "Put these on, it's chilly outside."

Her eyes rounded, large as quarters. "Where are we going?"

"It's a surprise. Mommy will follow us soon."

She scooted to the edge of the bed, and he helped her slip into her shoes and sweatshirt.

"I know how to tie my own shoes," she whispered, proudly displaying her double knot.

"You did a fine job," he said. "Now let's keep quiet so we don't wake Mommy."

He scooped her into his arms and shoved the empty juice box into his pocket.

Her tiny arms wrapped around his neck. The fluffy bunny she gripped in one hand felt almost weightless against his back. He decided to let her bring the toy. After *all, she never slept without her favorite stuffed animal.*

"Okay. Don't make a sound or you'll spoil the surprise."
With a fluid movement, he stood before the open window.

She giggled. "Are we going through the window?"

"Shhh." He drew his forefinger and thumb across his
lips and uttered a faint zipping sound.

She copied the act, struggling to contain a grin.

The only sounds audible were the faint rustling of their
clothes and their excited breathing.

Exultation wrapped around him as he climbed out into
the moonlit night. His triumph overwhelmed him when he
joined his silent witness watching from the star-filled sky.

After a twenty-five minute unimpeded drive, his
triumph knew no bounds. "Perfection," he whispered.

He awoke his prize and shuttled her out of the car.
Adrenaline surging, his hands shook as he unlocked the
front door. The girl's grip tightened on his hand, and her
back stiffened as they stepped into the dark house. They
walked into the living room, and he hurried to flick on a
couple lights. The girl glanced furtively around the
meagerly furnished room.

In a small, distressed voice, she asked, "When will
Mommy be here?" He crouched down. Tears welled in her
eyes. "Where's my mommy?" The tears trickled unchecked
down her cheeks.

"She'll be here soon." His lies came easy. "You'll go
back to sleep. When you wake up, your mommy will be
here."

Had he given her enough sedative? The next dose
would definitely be stronger. The last thing he needed was
a loud, distraught child.

He lifted her into his arms and carried her down the
hall into a small, softly lit bedroom. A dresser, matching
nightstand, and bunk beds with dragonfly bedspreads
furnished the room. Coordinating wallpaper covered the

walls, and a thick pink curtain hung over a portion of one wall, pulled open to expose wallpaper where the window used to exist.

Juliana tossed and flailed about on the disheveled bed. The sheets tangled around her, binding her like a mummy. "No, no!" The uninvited words jolted her awake.

Her head throbbed with the intensity of a full-blown migraine. The malevolence permeating the dream sank deep into her soul. Goosebumps broke out over her body as her skin crawled with *his* exhilaration and satisfaction.

The kidnapping had happened.

She'd managed to claim a few hours of sleep before the vision played through her head. Juliana had witnessed the crime along the fringes of the kidnapper's mind.

Morning sunlight streamed through her bedroom window, seeping through the sheer bed enclosure. The warm summer rays offered a sliver of relief. But she knew she wouldn't have a moment's peace until the child was returned to her home, safe and sound, however long it took. Even though yesterday she'd known the actual kidnapping promised to follow her premonition, the reality never ceased to fill her with sorrow and dread.

Juliana leaned against the carved headboard, tugging at the entwined sheet and shoving it off. She grabbed the TV remote from the night table and punched the *on* button. After flipping through several satellite channels, she found a local news program. A commercial break ended, and the news team returned with the day's top story. The abduction. No surprise there.

Her cat jumped on the bed, craving attention. She absently hugged his silky, fluffy body to her chest, engrossed in the unfolding news.

The newscast reported the details of the crime before proceeding to the child's identity and background. "Lisette

Chamber is the six-year-old granddaughter of billionaire Grantham Chamber II, founder and chairman of GC Media Corporation."

Juliana could barely concentrate on the victim's name and family as the kidnapper's leftover taint dissolved. Her headache receded, but ice flowed in her blood. She squeezed her cat to her chest until he squealed and squirmed for freedom.

"Sorry, JB." She set him on the bed. He arched his raven-black body and rubbed his head against her bare thigh, purring madly. The unconditional love of her cat relaxed her for a heartbeat, until she began searching her mind for details of the crime, particulars from the kidnapper's mind.

The more deeply she delved, the more she realized he possessed strong electrical currents in his brain. He'd connected easily with her powerful and receptive mind. It wasn't unusual for her to think or to see everything a perpetrator did while in an excited state, when his transference was the strongest. But it was rare that she felt his emotions, felt what he felt. This man reached out to her in *all* ways possible—the strongest psychic connection. She didn't like it one bit. Fear chilled her down to her bones, and she pulled the comforter back over her.

Juliana wished she could determine the kidnapper's identity from the puzzle pieces trickling into her mind. At least she could appease herself with the fact that consistency patterned her premonitions and visions. She'd eventually dream enough to ID him. Will it happen in time to save the victim?

An unwelcome thought surfaced, and she rolled on her side to the edge of the bed. Pushing her hand past the bed skirt, she groped on the floor until she felt cold, hard steel near the bed leg. She pulled the gun out from under the bed and examined the .38 revolver. It was loaded, safety catch on. Frowning, she returned the weapon to its hiding place.

Exhaling deeply, she expelled the taint from inside. She hated guns, hated the reasons she possessed one.

⊂Ձᔕᗞ

The phone's jarring ring scarcely registered in Alex's brain. As much as he willed it, the sound refused to stop. His head throbbed and molten lava spread through his gut. Three beers and a night obsessing about Juliana had reduced him to shambles.

Muttering, he fumbled for his cell on the nightstand, knocking the lamp against the wall. "Shit," he groaned. His mouth tasted like moldy sawdust, his throat scratchy.

He grabbed a bottle of antacids off the nightstand and dumped a couple in his mouth. The phone continued to ring until he finally clicked it on, not recognizing the number on the display. The antacid bottle dropped out of his uncooperative hand. He cursed as the multi-colored tablets scattered across discarded clothes carpeting the floor.

"Better be damn good," he managed to say between bites of the bone-dry tablets.

"Alex?" a familiar high-pitched female voice questioned.

Gravity pulled at his lethargic muscles, and his arm refused to cooperate with his brain. "Yeah?" Alex reclined back on the bed and wedged the phone between the pillow and his ear.

"It's Sharon Douglas." Urgency vibrated in her voice. "You need to get over here. Lisette's missing. Andrea—"

The words shoved Alex fully awake. He leaped from the disheveled bed, stumbling on a pair of jeans pooled on the floor. He caught the nightstand with his free hand, preventing a head-first crash into the wall.

"What do you mean, missing?" Cold iron edged his words. Terror gripped him. He grabbed his rumpled pants and pulled them on one-handed.

"Andrea woke up this morning and found Lisette's bed empty and her window wide open. Matthew and I heard her screaming and rushed over."

The last vestiges of sluggishness cleared from Alex's mind. Andrea's hysterical crying in the background on Sharon's end nearly crushed him. With fierce determination, he forced the experienced cop in him to take over and grab the reins.

"Listen to me, Sharon," he said in a level, authoritative voice. "Don't let anyone inside the house or backyard. Stay out of Lisette's bedroom. Don't call anyone. Can you stay with Andrea until I get there?" He waited for her affirmative response, then shoved his phone in his pocket and shouted for James.

"I'm up, man." James sauntered out of the hall bathroom, hair wet and a towel wrapped around his waist. "You look like shit." He laughed, but stopped when he caught sight of Alex's grim expression. "What—"

"Lisette's gone." Alex snatched a clean black polo shirt off the top of his laundry basket, not bothering to waste time dressing in his usual suit and tie.

Color drained from James' face. "What?"

Alex wasn't going to sugar-coat it, knowing that James harbored a crush on his widowed sister and loved Lisette almost as much as Alex himself did. He seized his service revolver tucked in its holster from his headboard shelf.

"Andrea found Lisette's bed empty, window open." Surprisingly, he managed to maintain his cool. His sister would need to depend on his ability to remain the composed professional, despite his overwhelming desire to torture the SOB who'd snatched Lisette.

"Juliana Westwood's dream came true." James' voice sounded far away.

CHAPTER FIVE

Yellow police tape secured the perimeter of Andrea's condominium. Shaken beyond belief, Alex did his best to console his frantic twin in the living room.

The forensics team searched for evidence and dusted for fingerprints. The crime scene investigators discovered a footprint in the recently watered flower garden below Lisette's window. The otherwise summer-parched yard offered no additional clues.

Outside the condo, neighbors and onlookers milled in excited and anxious groups, watching the crime scene with a mixture of curiosity and fear. James interviewed neighbors and studied onlookers for anything out of the ordinary. Sometimes perpetrators returned to the scene of their crime if they knew they could mingle with the crowd and remain unnoticed. Alex left an undercover detective mingling with the crowd to study the swarm of people.

Dane Christensen, the lead forensics technician, entered the living room. "Lieutenant?"

Alex gave Dane a hopeful look. "What did you find?" he asked in a strained voice.

"Nothing new. We've dusted and searched the bedroom. Snapped photos and made a plaster of the footprint."

"Keep looking," Alex snapped. Andrea's heart-rending sobbing shook him to his soul. Muttering soothing words, he rubbed her back, providing little comfort.

Dane pushed his gloved hands into his coat pockets, jiggling loose coins. "I'd like Mrs. Chamber to tell us what's missing in the bedroom."

Alex glanced down at his sister's head. Her auburn hair was limp and messy from a night in bed and from his fingers sifting through the long locks. He'd give his life to strip away her pain and bring Lisette home safe and sound.

"Andrea, sweetie." Alex kissed the top of her head and handed her a clean tissue. "Do you think you can do that?"

She took the tissue, her hand falling in a limp heap on the pile of crumpled tissues in her lap. She sniffed and lifted her head off Alex's chest. "Yes," she said roughly.

Alex grimaced at the pain and horror that dulled the usual vividness of her blue eyes. A raw and primitive grief overwhelmed him. He wanted to lash out at the person who threatened to destroy his family. As a cop, he'd vaguely understood what drove crime victims or their families to violence while protecting their loved ones. He now experienced the same feelings at a gut level.

Arm around Andrea's waist, Alex led her into Lisette's bedroom. She slumped down on the twin bed and described the missing clothes and shoes. When finished, she began crying with renewed vigor.

"Enough for now," Alex said through the lump in his throat and made a dismissive gesture.

Andrea suddenly swung around and frantically rummaged through the tousled bed covers. "Her bunny's gone. It's her favorite." She dabbed at her eyes with the tissue. "At least she isn't alone."

Small consolation. Alex jotted down a description of

the stuffed animal. He'd given the white bunny to Lisette the day of her father's funeral a year ago. She never slept without it.

Alex carried Andrea into her bedroom and made her lie on the rumpled bed. He whispered more calming words that did little to defray her grief. Sharon's husband Matthew, a doctor at the local hospital, had sedated her. She refused to swallow the pill at first, but Alex convinced her that Lisette needed her strong, clear-headed and calm. Finally, Andrea's best friend arrived to relieve him and he felt confident enough to leave his twin for a while.

He joined the other detectives in the living room and wrapped up the crime scene investigation. They installed a wiretap on the phone as the final task. The media swarmed outside like killer bees, waiting for a chance to interview the lead detective and the victim's distraught mother. An officer remained at the front door to keep the horde away.

Alex strode out to James' truck and jumped into the passenger seat. He felt strangely detached, as if this crime hadn't happened to his sister or his niece. Reality hadn't set in entirely. The terror hadn't completely seized him.

James slid into the driver's seat. "Westwood's meeting us at HQ."

Alex stared out the windshield, his body strung tighter than a guitar. Rage simmered below the surface of his control threatening to break through with a vengeance.

"You don't have to be there when I question her. Best if you're not."

"Best for who?" Alex asked with deceptive calm before he slammed his fist on the dashboard.

CR80

Juliana parked in the visitor lot behind the SJPD. She glanced out the windshield at the red-gold sun blazing in the periwinkle sky. A breeze chased away the coastal overcast that had blanketed the city overnight. She closed her eyes for a moment, unable to block out the evil blemishing the glorious day.

She accidentally bit the inside of her bottom lip as she got out of the car. The pain mercifully overshadowed her mounting apprehension for a few seconds. Tendrils of hair escaped her hastily fashioned braid and tickled her face in the light wind.

Detective O'Malley had instructed her to enter through the rear door since the media scavenged for their next meal in front. She appreciated his forethought and hoped it continued throughout the case. She'd quit posing as shark bait for the media years ago.

Juliana shuddered at the memory of reporters waylaying her. In her early twenties, she'd been the reluctant subject of a public paranormal study. For the short time the medical and science community courted her, she'd lost her independence and privacy. Worst of all, they'd treated her like a one-person circus act.

It took years and a new pseudonym to achieve her yearned for anonymity after that fiasco. Then, two years ago, she'd unwillingly faced publicity again after a leak at the NYPD divulged that she was assisting them on a headline-news homicide case. It ended in a tragedy she wanted never to experience again.

She'd make damn sure the SJPD knew how much they needed to keep a lid on her involvement. One slip and she could wind up the next victim. One blunder and she'd permanently lose the tenuous tie to the kidnapper's mind.

Juliana shooed her unwelcome thoughts away as a

uniformed officer identified and cleared her at the back entrance. Another officer left her alone in the same interrogation room used the day before. She eyed the digital recorder added to the laminate table. The scent of burnt coffee lingered in the room, making her nose itch. She wished she had a fresh cup of coffee to clear her head.

Would Alex tag-team with Detective O'Malley? She saw no reason for it. The SJPD website listed Alex as a lieutenant in the homicide division. If luck were on her side, she wouldn't have to see him throughout this ordeal. Especially when his mere presence set her blood on fire. He was a distraction she could do without for the time being.

The steel door swung inward, and Juliana nearly jumped out of her seat. O'Malley stepped into the room—alone. Relief fluttered in her stomach. No Alex. *Thank you, God.* She set to flogging down the butterflies.

Nodding at the lean red-haired man, she said, "Detective O'Malley."

"Call me James." His ruddy face was pinched tight, forehead creased. An odd grief shadowed his hazel eyes. Rigidly, he sat in a seat near the door and threw a manila file folder on the table.

O'Malley gave off a distinct feeling of angry fear and distress. Juliana suspected he treated his cases too personal, too close to the vest. Not good for a cop in Missing Persons. She knew from experience how abductions debilitated the parties involved. A cop needed to remain objective and unemotional.

O'Malley turned on the recorder and recited the standard who, what, when and where.

He straightened in his chair and folded his long arms across his wiry chest. "You saw the news?"

"Yes." She hesitated. "Before we continue, who's behind the glass?" She tilted her head toward the two-way mirror behind her.

His eyes narrowed. "Room's empty."

She didn't miss his nearly imperceptible fidgeting in his seat.

Juliana didn't make a habit of using her telepathy to read minds. She'd hate it if someone intruded upon her mind without her knowledge or consent. In the past, hiding her thoughts from others offered the only privacy afforded her. Throughout the years, she'd finessed her telepathic abilities to a fine art. Only in extreme circumstances did she allow herself an excursion into another's head. One of those rare moments landed upon her. O'Malley lied.

"I need to make one thing clear." Juliana pitched her voice as insistently as she dared. "I can only help if you promise to keep my involvement under wraps." She leaned forward and tapped a fingernail on the table for emphasis. "If the media gets wind of my involvement, your case is done from this angle. And you need to keep my identity a low profile in the PD, with only necessary personnel involved on a need-to-know basis."

"Jamison said the same yesterday. He didn't tell me why." Judging by the questioning slant of O'Malley's eyes, he expected her to pony up to the table.

Perfect. He'd verified her authenticity with Jamison.

"Please, Detective—James. Remaining anonymous is crucial to my ability to help you." Her cool gaze fixated on his face, ever watchful for changing expressions, clues to his thoughts without digging into his mind. She leaned back and clasped her hands loosely in her lap. "When you chase out the suits behind the glass, we'll proceed."

James hesitated, as if to gauge her plea, and then flicked his wrist in a dismissive half-circle. He lifted the receiver off the wall phone, punched in a number, and issued the order to clear the room. A few long seconds followed, then he replaced the receiver on the hook.

"Done."

His mind was an open cavern, and she read him easily. The officers behind the wall had complied and emptied the room. He didn't like it, but he grudgingly accepted her demand.

She smiled gratefully. "Thank you."

"I know from an investigative standpoint why we'd want to keep your involvement secret. What's your agenda?"

"Simple. It's devastating to my mental and emotional state when I'm hounded and dubbed a lab rat." She gave him a measured look. "That's how most psychics are treated when they've been exploited." James nodded. "And I'll become a target." She accepted the commiserate understanding on the detective's somber face.

"Once my head is clouded with such annoyances, the dreams will stop." Juliana swallowed the lump in her throat. "And I want to help find the girl, not play showpiece for the police or the media."

His face reddened, and he shifted his gaze away. Hurt and frustration rolled off him in waves. Confusion twisted in her mind. James sat too close to the case. Why? Did he know the child?

Imposing a rock-hard control, she broke the uncomfortable silence. "Shall I tell you about my dream?" Nervously, she fiddled with her braid, laddered her fingers in the weave.

Spine ramrod-straight against the chair, James faced her again, his expression grim. "What were you doing from midnight to five this morning?"

She expected his insinuation. Any good cop must ask the question. He didn't know her from Eve.

As soon as she opened her mouth to speak, the door flew open, forcing her gaze past James. With a loud thunk, it slammed into the doorjamb on the interior wall, and Alex dominated the doorway. The top of his head missed the frame by several inches and he froze in a powerful stance. The charismatic animal magnetism he exuded struck Juliana mute.

But she sensed more. Without looking at his face, she discerned rage and an odd hint of helplessness ready to burst from him. Sudden panic skipped across her heart. *Surely, after all these years, he can't hate me that much. He can't loathe psychics so passionately.* A fiery sheen of perspiration glazed her forehead. She forced herself to draw several deep breaths of the cold air blowing from the ceiling vent.

Alex slammed the door shut. The closed-circuit monitor in the corner vibrated, its shaky hold in jeopardy. He eased toward the table across from Juliana. Emotions ranging from anger to confusion colored his face.

The silence crumbled with Alex's iron-edged voice. "Lieutenant Alexander MacKenzie joining the interview, oh nine twenty," he announced to the recorder. He sat, leaned forward, and planted his elbows on the table, glaring at her from eyes burning like a rampant fire.

Juliana's gaze dropped to her lap. *Don't let him rattle you.*

What seemed eons later, she lifted her head. Pain glimmered in Alex's eyes before he shifted focus to James and asked about their progress. While watching the covert eye play between the two cops, she waited for a prompt. Finally, Alex leaned back in his chair.

James slipped back to his interrogator mode. "Where were you between midnight and five A.M.?"

Juliana gripped her purse and cleared her mind. "I was home asleep between midnight and five. I live alone and have no witnesses who can verify it." Her knuckles whitened, and she released her vise grip on her purse.

James and Alex exchanged another one of their shuttered looks and Alex nodded.

"We'll return to your whereabouts and activities later. We'll also want to search your house. For now, tell us again how your ESP works."

Several bangs on the wall outside the door startled her, and muted laughter followed. James and Alex ignored the ruckus and waited for her response.

Heart beating erratically, she gathered her inner strength. "This morning, I experienced a vision of the actual kidnapping. I felt the kidnapper's thoughts, feelings, and actions. I knew the kidnapping had occurred when I woke up.

"I saw the crime happen as if I sat on the edge of the kidnapper's mind." Or in his body. Nervously, she bit the blossoming bump on her inner lip again as she recalled the kidnapper's emotions creating physical manifestations in her body. "I can't tell you who he is, since I couldn't see him through his own eyes. Things he did were automatic to him, so I couldn't see or feel them unless he specifically focused on them."

She crossed her ankles, shifting in her seat for a more comfortable position to wake up her numb butt. "He has to be in an extremely excited state for me to connect with his mind. Even then, things aren't always clear."

Underneath the memorable scent of Alex's cologne, fear emanated from him. Fear of what? *Why is Alex involved in a missing person case if he's a homicide cop? Why is James so distraught too?* She needed to dig to the bottom of their odd behavior before her curiosity drove her batty. Unless . . . the horrible thought entered her mind. Was Lisette Chamber dead? Her mouth gaped open and she clamped her hand over it.

Waves of alarm engulfed her. "No," she moaned and wrapped her arms around her abdomen as the blood drain from her face. The warmth that had infused her since she'd entered the room turned to an arctic chill.

"Jewel!" Alex bolted out of his chair and crossed the distance around the table in a few steps. He knelt beside her, leveling his face to hers. "James, water!"

His voice sounded miles away. The door opened and shut in a narrow vacuum.

"Look at me." Alex lifted her chin.

His touch was soothing and gentle. Heat radiated off him, throwing her out of whack. The warmth contrasted sharply with the frigid Alex who'd first entered the room.

She looked deep into his eyes. "Why are you involved if you're a homicide detective?" Juliana managed to ask. "Is she dead?"

Alex's mouth stretched in a tight grimace. "Lisette Chamber is my niece."

His tender fingers dropped from her chin, and Juliana suffered a twinge of loss.

"Alex, I didn't know. I'm so sorry." She reached out and caressed his cheek. The rough stubble of a two-day-old beard prickled her fingers.

He laced her fingers with his, both lost in the emotion in the other's eyes. James returned to the room, breaking the spell. They jerked back from each other as if burned. James slid a bottle of cold water across the table, and Juliana threw him a weak smile.

"No, I guess you wouldn't have known," Alex muttered. Movements lethargic, he stood and returned to the chair across the table.

Small relief washed over Juliana in the realization that she hadn't missed a key element in her dream. She'd confronted many grief-stricken parents in other abduction cases. But she was always the outsider, having no previous bond to the victim, so the impact wasn't as great on her. But this! Poor Alex. She couldn't even imagine what he was suffering.

Juliana sipped her water and let Alex's hot and cold attitude toward her slide. The kidnapping of a loved one was enough to turn anyone into a raving lunatic, let alone being confronted with a past he probably wanted to forget.

"You okay?" James patted her hand from across the table.

"I'm fine." She forced a smile to her lips.

Concern simmered in Alex's eyes as he eagle-eyed her every movement. Her throat narrowed as he continued to stare, and her body betrayed her in response. Her nipples tightened under her silk blouse, and it wasn't from the frigid air. She crossed her arms over her chest to hide her annoyingly inappropriate reaction.

James sagged into his chair. "Let's move on. What did you see in your dream this morning?" He picked up his pen and scribbled on his notepad.

Thankful to resume the interview, she counted to ten in her head to steady her nerves. Then she proceeded to describe the dream in vivid detail.

When she finished, Alex leaned forward, his large hands splayed on the table. "You're positive Lisette knew him?"

"Absolutely. There's no way she'd have willingly gone with him if she didn't."

"Could you pick his face out of a mug book? Or his voice from a recorder?" Alex asked in desperation.

She wished she possessed the ability to do what he asked. "Not right now. And I've already gone through my contact list and searched my memory for people I've met lately. No one rings a bell. When I have another dream, I may distinguish his features, but there's no guarantee."

"What do you mean?"

Juliana's heart fluttered at the curiosity in Alex's

voice. "If he looks into a mirror or if I see his reflection in glass or water, I might see his image." She tightened her arms to ward off the chill refusing to leave her extremities alone. "I might get an idea of his features, his own thoughts about himself. I may see things about him." She paused and studied James' chicken scratches on his notepad. "For instance, I might see his height in relation to the height of an automobile. A scar on his hand. If he's thinking about his eyes, I may see that they're blue or green, whatever. Or I might see him wear certain pieces of clothing."

Alex sat back and tipped his head. "Okay."

A missing detail lodged behind a wall in her memory. She struggled to recall the elusive element.

James asked, "Did Lisette take anything?"

Again, she concentrated on the vision. The evasive detail surfaced as if one of the detectives had transmitted the thought. "Lisette took a white stuffed animal with her. A bunny, I believe. Her favorite."

Alex sprang from his seat. He spun toward the door, his fists clenched loosely at his sides. James stood and laid a calming hand on Alex's shoulder, but Alex shrugged him off.

"Alex. If you didn't believe in psychics, you have to now. You know in your gut *Juliana* didn't take Lisette," James said, but his voice wasn't in an "I told you so" tone. "For Lisette's sake."

Alex sighed heavily, and his shoulders sagged.

Why couldn't this have been a normal case? Her mouth felt like old, dusty paper. She drained half the water and gripped the bottle in her already frozen fingers, not even feeling the coldness of the liquid.

Long seconds dragged past while Alex reined in his emotions. When he returned to his seat, his face was expressionless.

Almost afraid to upset the balance, Juliana burst the tense hush. "Knowing it's your niece . . ." She threw Alex a compassionate look. "I'll do *anything* to help you find her."

Long ago, she'd learned to disassociate herself from the crimes to avoid as much of the agony suffered by the victim's families. However, this case was so close to home that it would levy a hefty fine on her emotions. And she would give her all for the investigation. She owed Alex that much.

"Let's get back on track." James looked from Alex to Juliana, a hard sober look to counter any defiance.

Alex crossed his arms over his broad, muscled chest. "Do you think he'll go after Andrea?"

Juliana realized her queasy nervousness and headache were gone, and she said a silent prayer of thanks. "He lied to Lisette about Andrea joining them soon. I felt it—interpreted it." To her surprise, Alex nodded. She dug deeper into her mind for additional clues, but the search bore no fruit.

"You didn't see what model car he drove, street signs, what the house looked like?" James rapped a ballpoint pen on the laminate table, the sound startling in the small room.

Sadness bore down on her. "I'm sorry. The dream was fuzzy after he left Lisette's room. He was less excited until he arrived at his destination."

"What else can you tell us?" James implored.

More than a causal work relationship linked James O'Malley to Alex. Such a connection explained the forlorn look in his eyes.

Alex threw her thoughts off kilter when he asked, "Why do you insist on no publicity?"

Juliana traced a spot of ink on the table. "Do you really want the kidnapper knowing a psychic's involved?

Don't you think it might jeopardize your case?"

Alex reached for the untouched file James tossed on the table earlier. "Yet, you have no problem publicizing your prowess on Wall Street, *Ms. Gold Maker.*"

She knew her successes on Wall Street would eventually find their way into the conversation. She'd earned the nickname in the financial world several years ago when she couldn't pick a loser investment if her life depended upon it. "I keep those two parts of my life separate. I don't care to parade my private life to public scrutiny."

"Your psychic abilities didn't earn you the nickname?" Alex's eyebrows quirked.

"I didn't say that."

"So why your terms about no publicity?" He scratched at the scar on his face. The slash reddened from the rough contact and Juliana yearned to soothe it. "What do you hope to gain in the end?"

"A good night's sleep." She met his gaze, challenging him. "If I have to put up with reporters and doctors hounding me, *and* if I have to spend my life fearing the kidnapper may come after me, my psychic dreams will turn to dust. I won't have the ability to help find your niece."

The sobering effect of her words triggered the fear that flitted across Alex's face. He needed her, and he knew it. Precious little consolation coated that reality.

James cleared his throat loudly, as if to wade through the mud-thick tension. "Have you ever been wrong about your premonitions and visions?"

Another anticipated question. She looked directly at James and replied, "Once." Mistaken through her own misinterpretation, and her guilt would die with her. Juliana forced her mind off her past. She couldn't afford the interference, not when she needed to focus on Lisette's abduction.

"There's one more thing I'd like to add." The most difficult skill to confess. Something even Alex didn't know about her. Juliana lowered her head and weaved her purse strap through her fingers. The reactions she'd received in the past varied from awe to flagrant derision.

Alex nodded for her to continue, and James stared at her in anticipation.

She grabbed the water bottle and downed a few gulps, the liquid like rain in a dry creek bed. "I've been able to help the police in interrogating suspects and witnesses. Under the table-type stuff, since it's not quite legal."

She stirred uneasily in her chair. "I'm telepathic." Ready for their best shots, she raised her head proudly. "I can read minds."

CHAPTER SIX

"What the hell? You've been sitting here fucking reading *our* minds this whole time." Alex shoved away from the table and jumped to his feet, the metal chair clattering on its side.

James nodded and smiled at her. "I like a psychic with multiple talents."

A chill swept through Juliana as she looked at Alex and formed her response. She opened her mouth to speak, but Alex cut her off.

"Have you?" he demanded.

She clenched her lips tight as her tolerance of Alex's attitude wore tissue-thin. "What are you hiding?" she egged him on.

Alex's lips twitched with a tight smile. "What goes on in my mind is none of your damn business."

James rapped his pen sharply on the table. "Let's get back on track. We're wasting time we don't have."

Alex ran a hand across his face. "Shit. I can't deal with this right now." He moved toward the door. "James, finish up and meet me in my office."

"Alex," Juliana said. When he turned around, she continued, "I'd rather throw myself off the Golden Gate Bridge than read your mind."

Alex left James to complete Juliana's interview, and called to check on Andrea. Nothing he said consoled her, and he hung up the phone, misery stabbing at his heart. He gazed lovingly at Lisette's colorful artwork pinned helter-skelter on his office walls.

An unwelcome voice from the corridor intruded upon his reflection.

"Too bad about your niece." A raspy laugh followed his archenemy's arrival in the doorway.

"Son of a bitch," he muttered. Why did that loser ex-detective from Internal Affairs have to be in his face every day? IA was the last thing he needed. "What do you want, Shelby?" Alex's jaw clenched.

"To say how sorry I am."

Alex glared at the smirk on Shelby's face. Forcing extreme self-control, he kept his tongue. Last thing he needed was more trouble from his number one ass-buster.

"Maybe I'll stop by and console my *ex-girlfriend.*" Shelby's smirk curled into a wicked grin.

"Ex-girlfriend, my ass. You had *one* lousy date. Stay the hell away from my sister." Disgust reached the roasting point inside him, and he wanted to drown in a bottle of antacids or a bottle of whiskey. "And get the hell out of my face."

After a two-finger wave, Shelby stalked off, not a moment too soon.

Racehorses ran the Kentucky Derby in Alex's head. He palmed a handful of antacids, threw in a couple of aspirin, and downed them with yesterday's cola. The flat, tepid liquid burned as it went down his throat.

Focusing on the abduction, he skimmed the list of potential suspects, which included family, friends, neighbors, teachers, and any other person who may have connected with Lisette over the last few years. He pounded on his keyboard, listing questions in preparation for the interviews. Only a few minutes elapsed before James barreled through the doorway and banged the door shut. Alex met his friend's stormy eyes. James made a rotten poker player—his face showed every mood. His shirt hung halfway out of his khakis, his tie askew, hair sticking up in spikes, the way they both looked at the end of the day after a particular hard case.

Lisette's case would have an enormous emotional impact on both Alex and James. It was already a top priority for the entire police department, which rallied together to find their own kin, related by the fellowship of law enforcement.

"Tag Shelby, but don't tip our hand," Alex barked out, in no mood for civility.

James dropped onto the visitor chair and frowned. "You think he did it?"

"He has motive. I wouldn't put it past him."

James' frown turned to a deep scowl, dragging down the corners of his mouth. "You didn't bang him down from detective to desk flunky."

For the most part, Alex hated Internal Affairs, and his opinion worsened when Shelby joined the team. "He's digging for any excuse to bust my ass to cover up his own fuck-ups."

"Man, he was responsible for the murder of that witness. He shouldn't even be on the force in any capacity."

Alex threw James an impatient look. "Forget that stupid ass. We'll work on him later. Forensics update?"

James flicked his fingers across his tablet device. "No fingerprints anywhere in or outside the bedroom. The footprint outside the window belongs to a man's size ten-and-a-half athletic shoe. The tread revealed no worn spots. Forensics is working it to determine the perp's weight."

James leafed through a couple more screens. "Standard latch. Jiggled open with a knife or similar object. Andrea removed the screen last week for you to fix." James held up his hand and rushed on. "Don't blame yourself, man. Anyone could have bypassed the screen. And the lock on the window's the same as the others in the complex."

"I was supposed to fix the screens and install new locks on the windows this weekend." Alex slammed his fist on the desk. A stack of closed case files careened to the floor in a jumble. He kicked them aside, carpeting the floor with loose papers.

"He knew what he was doing." As usual, in a crisis or an intense case, James' voice remained steady. Alex didn't know what he'd do without James taking the lead. "Appears to be premeditated." James leaned back in the chair and laid his tablet on the desk. "The guy would've found a way in no matter what kind of lock. Or he'd have snatched her some other way."

Alex rubbed his scar. Who took his niece? And why? His gut continued to churn with the lack of evidence.

"I've divvied up the interviews. Sterling and his team are on the people at her school, neighbors, and others. We'll take the principals."

Alex studied the list again. The first names at the top: Grantham and Samantha Chamber, Lisette's paternal grandparents. His grimace hardly displayed his loathing adequately. He didn't savor the prospect of speaking face-to-face with the man who'd wanted custody of his niece since her father had died a year ago. Not that day. He'd tear Grantham's head off. James might have to do that interview alone.

Alex's body ached as if he'd just run a cross-country marathon. He lifted a fresh roll of antacids from his desk drawer and shoved it into his pants pocket. "Let's do it."

Alex and James agreed to play by the rules and interview Lisette's grandparents without Juliana as she'd suggested. They would include her for a second round of interviews, if warranted.

After compromising on the division of work, Alex wound up at Juliana's house while James conducted the first interviews. Grimly, he took in the huge two-story home that dwarfed his own forty-year-old ranch-style house. If not for his foul mood, he might even have appreciated the beautiful and sparkling new Mediterranean-style house.

The idea of seeing and working with Juliana again after all these years, when he could do without the distraction, caused apprehension, confusion, rage, and an array of other emotions to war within him, leaving him jittery. James had coerced Alex into taking Juliana to Andrea's condominium to examine Lisette's bedroom. In her interview, Juliana had suggested to James that she might recall more if she viewed the room in person. She assured the detectives that she wasn't a touch telepath, but she sometimes recalled new details at the crime scene.

Two ulterior motives compelled him to pick up Juliana. First, he wanted to see if she really had moved back to San Jose. He'd believe it when he saw it. Second, he wanted to snoop around her house even though the police had searched it earlier. He wasn't taking any chances, especially after her vanishing act twelve years ago. Not that he thought she was involved in the kidnapping.

To his surprise, Juliana opened the door before he jabbed the doorbell. His heart did a double beat as he took in her slim capris and silky T-shirt. Her intoxicating, trademark perfume intrigued him still. His eyes raked her from her blonde hair to her pink toenails, his heartbeat quickening as a tiny smile lit her beautiful face, a face that had hardly changed since she was eighteen.

She inclined her head, dainty hand resting on the doorframe. "Hello, Alex."

"Juliana." His frosty businesslike nod belied his internal upheaval. It was the only way he could think to get through being around her and deal with Lisette's disappearance.

She ushered him into the large, airy house, and he strained to hear any unusual sounds as he scanned the entryway and beyond. He searched for any clue that might disprove her dream and produce Lisette alive and well. A vise seized his heart at the thought. He wanted Juliana to be clean with him almost as much as he wanted to find his niece.

Juliana's eyes widened. "Have a look around. I've nothing to hide from the police, or you."

Damn. She'd always known his thoughts, without resorting to reading his mind. They'd been in tune in a way he'd never experienced, not even with his twin sister.

"I'll wait in the family room." She swept her hand toward a large room to the left, and with a provocative sway to her hips, sauntered away from him, her sandals click-clacking on the stone floor.

Too damn distracting, and he wanted to kick himself for looking. And thinking. And feeling.

He blew the cobwebs out of his head and began his exploration in the roomy, sterile kitchen. His methodical search of each room proved futile, and relief sluiced over the perpetual acid in his gut. Despite the small amount of furniture in the house, it appeared Juliana was home to stay.

CHAPTER SEVEN

Andrea's condo resided in an older, centrally located neighborhood. Meticulously landscaped grounds surrounded the slightly worse-for-wear condominiums. Lawns were freshly mowed, and the pungent smell of cut grass wafted up in the summer heat. The brilliant sun caught Juliana's eye and she stifled a sneeze.

How had Andrea ended up in such a humble neighborhood after marriage to the son of one of the richest men in the world?

When Alex parked his SUV in the guest parking spot, strange perceptions that escaped meaning ratcheted up a thumping in her head.

To her relief, no reporters skulked around. Despite the lack of media, the case had prompted plenty of airtime. Children snatched from their homes under their parents' noses tended to create vast tension and fear. Certainly, in any abduction case, a parent wanted all the public exposure they could generate. Nonetheless, Juliana was glad she wouldn't be accosted going into Andrea's home.

As soon as Alex and Juliana hopped out of the SUV, Andrea's front door opened. His twin ran out and flung her arms around Juliana as if she'd found a long-lost relative. *Or a long dead friend.* Juliana stifled her pleasant surprise at her high school friend's welcome. She didn't deserve the warm and fuzzy feeling that she belonged in Alex and Andrea's world again.

She eased out of Andrea's arms and regarded her with a mixture of sadness and welcome familiarity. Still tall and slender, Andrea seemed like the same girl Juliana remembered from high school, despite the worry lines fanning her eyes, creasing her otherwise smooth forehead, and giving her exotically beautiful face a fatigued look.

Andrea clasped Juliana's hand and they entered the condo. The instant Juliana stepped across the threshold, the strange sensations that had assailed her in the driveway intensified. They nearly smothered her with the impression that she'd been here once before.

"Juliana, I'm so grateful for what you're doing." Andrea attempted a smile, despite the tears glimmering in her eyes. Eyes that looked exactly like Alex's.

She swallowed hard and gently squeezed Andrea's hand. "I'll do what I can to help find Lisette."

Alex coughed, impatiently clearing his throat. "Juliana. Do whatever you need to do."

She nodded and breathed deep. The foreboding had moved into the pit of her stomach, and the pounding in her head increased.

What was happening to her? Off-key didn't begin to describe the odd sensations.

Juliana followed Alex down the short hallway to Lisette's bedroom, with Andrea bringing up the rear. The closer she approached the room, the more Juliana's heartbeat accelerated. Perspiration broke out on her forehead and she felt feverish.

Alex stepped through the second doorway on the right at the back of the condo. "Lisette's room."

Juliana pressed past him, her hand brushing his thigh. Heat flared up her arm, shaking her already frazzled nervous system.

Alex jerked away and leaned against the closet door. He yanked his notebook and pen out of the back pocket of his jeans, avoiding eye contact.

Hooking a tendril of loose hair behind her ear, she scanned the room, taking it all in. She neared the bed in the middle of the small room, her dream crystallizing in her mind. Smiling sunflowers patterned the comforter in jewel-tone colors, just as she'd pictured in her dream. She leaned over the twin bed and lifted the stuffed penguin from atop the pillow.

A sharp pain shot through her left temple, and the stuffed animal dropped to the floor. Suddenly, a wave of nausea convulsed her and she instinctively clutched her stomach. Her mind's eye glimpsed the kidnapper touching the penguin. Juliana jerked upright as if yanked by a marionette string.

"Jewel, you okay?"

Alex's strong arm snaked around her waist, and she leaned into his warm, so familiar body.

He gently coaxed her to sit beside him on the end of the bed. "You don't have to do this right now," he said tenderly. Concern paled his handsome bronzed face, and her heart melted.

"I've never experienced touch telepathy. I think it just happened." Excitement masked the pain in her head. She'd just reached a new level of psychic ability, a talent that had toyed with her for years but had always eluded her. It was little wonder she'd been feeling strange since she'd arrived.

Alex eased his arm from around her waist and stood. The loss of his comforting touch left her confusingly bereft.

He stared at her as if he'd seen an apparition and resumed his stance in front of the closet. "Can you continue?"

"I think so."

Andrea lowered plaintive eyes to Juliana from her position in the doorway. "What did you see?"

Juliana focused on her vision. "The kidnapper pushed the penguin aside while he covered Lisette's mouth with his other hand."

Alex smoothed down the chaotic spikes in his hair and threw her a guarded look. "You didn't mention the penguin earlier."

"I told you everything I remembered at the time." Juliana gave him a measured stare. "It's no different than you waking up in the morning and remembering bits of dreams you'd had that night." She fingered her braid, then flipped it over her shoulder. "That's why I'm here," she added, defending herself. "This is new."

She glanced at the toy penguin lying on the plush carpet. "The stuffed animal evoked my memory. Touch telepathy works when you touch an item someone else has touched. Or touch a person. You see visions surrounding that person."

Juliana sat for a moment and regained her composure, cleared her mind. Once steady, she wandered around the room, searching for other memory triggers, touching toys, clothes, furniture here and there. Peering out the window, she glimpsed the wooden box to the left of the window the kidnapper had stood on to climb through the window. Telltale honeysuckle vines crept along the back fence. She retraced his footsteps in her mind as she paced from the window to the side of the bed. Juliana examined a small blue stain on the earthtone carpet next to the penguin.

"There's something missing here." She pointed at the floor between the window and bed. "He stepped over a small obstacle to reach the bed, toeing it aside after he sat down."

Andrea returned and pushed his hand away, placing a wet cloth on Juliana's forehead.

Juliana flinched and cried out, uttering a few incomprehensible words. Narrowing his gaze, he strained to decipher them.

"She's dreaming." His pulse accelerated.

"Do you think she's dreaming about Lisette?" The hopeful look in Andrea's eyes sunk his heart. She hung onto a conviction that Juliana was their savior. Any disappointment, however small, would devastate her. Sitting cross-legged on the floor, she stroked Juliana's arm as if she was stroking a beloved child's head. "Tell me where you are, Lisette."

"Andrea, don't." He hated to see his sister caught up in too much psychic paranoia.

"Alex, she has a link to Lisette. James said—"

"James isn't an expert." His exasperation exploded in his words. "Juliana has a connection to the kidnapper, not Lisette." What did James know? Why had he filled Andrea with potentially empty hope? Just because James worked with psychics and the Guild didn't make him the Pied Piper of ESP.

Andrea ignored him and continued whispering reassuring words to Lisette.

Yet Alex couldn't deny what he'd witnessed himself. If the innocent sentiments brought comfort to his grieving sister, he wouldn't refuse her. He tightened his grip on Juliana's cold hands, transferring heat from his body to hers.

"Alex, she came back for a reason," Andrea said with undeniable certainty. "To find Lisette. To make us whole."

He felt the truth in her words deep in his core. Could he stow away the past when he had no clue about Juliana's life over the last decade? Or why she'd deserted him—them—in the first place? Did he even want to know?

Juliana twitched, jerking his mind back to the present and to the beautiful woman causing his thoughts to wander. First things first—he had a niece to find. Juliana wasn't going anywhere anytime soon. He'd make damn certain on that score.

 catalog

He unlocked the bedroom door. The pastel lamp on the otherwise bare dresser contributed a faint glowing pool. The light barely penetrated into the corners, but it was all he needed. The scent of baby powder lotion wafted to him, eclipsing the faint odor of fear in the airless room.

Lisette bolted upright on the bottom bunk bed. Alarm darkened her face, fresh tears shimmering in her eyes.

Revulsion crashed over him in waves. She no longer listened to him, and it angered him more than the tears revolted him. Nothing had prepared him to deal with such childish behavior. Her sobbing sounded like the wail of sirens grating on his ear drums.

"Where's . . . my . . . mommy?" Lisette formed the question through her blubbering.

"Don't ask me that again!" He couldn't suppress the anger from his voice. When he'd failed to produce her mother as promised, he'd destroyed her flagging trust. But the lie had served its purpose admirably.

Lisette's tears streamed faster, and she clutched her toy animal to her stomach.

Fury beat down his disgust. He'd lose control if he didn't escape the room soon. "Do you need to use the bathroom?" He forced restraint into his tone.

As she shook her head, the cell phone clipped to his pants sang a welcome song. Finally! He jerked the phone off his belt loop and stabbed it on with his index finger.

"It's about time," he shouted into the speakerphone.

"What do you want me to get for lunch? Has Lisette eaten?"

"I don't care what you get. You know what she'll eat. She won't touch anything I've prepared." He punched the phone off and backed out of the stifling room.

"You'll eat if I have to cram it down your throat," he muttered, before his mind moved to tempting thoughts of revenge.

Juliana awakened on her back. Unfamiliar crushed velour rubbed the back of her legs, and the air smelled faintly of fear, as if Lisette's fear was a palpable thing smothering the room. Or was it Alex and Andrea's fear? Everything blurred as she tried to focus her sight. When she finally recognized Alex and Andrea crowding around her, the day's events snowed her.

"What happened? The last thing I remember, I was sitting on the bed with a horrible headache." Shock suffused her as she realized she'd fainted. She'd never fainted before.

She remembered delving into the kidnapper's mind through touch telepathy, far different from her night dreams when her mind was already open and receptive. The intrusion felt like he'd used a can opener to pry the lid off her mind and sucked it into his. Her head still reeled from the force.

Unwavering, Alex stared down at her. Worry creased his forehead. "You okay?"

"I think so." She pressed her fingertips to her temples.

An insistent thought reached the surface of her mind. "The doll box! I remember what bothered me about it."

She struggled to rise on the couch, and Alex helped her to sit. Her thick braid had unraveled completely, and her hair tumbled around her shoulders.

"Do you need aspirin?" Andrea asked. "Water? Anything?"

"No. I'll be okay." Juliana forced a confident smile, keeping her hands clutched close, fearing to touch anything further.

Alex examined her beneath hooded eyes. Apparently satisfied at what he saw, he snatched his notebook and pen from the glass-topped coffee table. "What about the doll box?"

The scene from her early morning dream sprang to mind as if suddenly unearthed by a shovel. "The kidnapper sat on the side of the bed and he kicked the doll box. Then he pushed it away with his hands." Juliana sorted through her memory, rubbing her fingertips over her face. "When he bent over it, I heard the clink of something dropping inside the box."

Lines of concentration deepened across Alex's forehead as he scrawled his notes. Juliana remembered how he'd get those lines when he'd struggled with his homework and how she used to smooth them out until they disappeared.

"That's not what you dreamed, is it?" Andrea rose off the floor and sat beside Juliana on the couch. She picked up the damp washcloth, twisting it with both hands.

"No," Juliana said in a soft voice.

"Is she okay?" Andrea cried in alarm.

"Yes." Without a second thought, she squeezed Andrea's arm, bracing herself for a jolt of memory that never hit. Her heart pulsed in empathy, unable to fathom how Andrea dealt with her fear and worry.

Hesitant, Juliana said, "She's alive and well." She glanced at Andrea's slender fingers fisted around the red-striped washcloth. "He hasn't hurt her. She's locked in a bedroom and now knows he lied about you joining her, Andrea. She's upset and won't eat."

Andrea hiccupped and wiped her nose on the washcloth.

Juliana continued, "Someone's bringing a meal. She seems to know what Lisette will eat." She didn't want to divulge the rest to Andrea. Lifting her eyes to Alex, she arched a brow and winked twice. Would he remember their old eye signal? Instantly, she recognized his return flicker.

He stepped behind Andrea and rested his hands gently on her shoulders, massaging beneath the mantle of her thick, auburn hair. "I'll take a full statement in my office."

"Yeah. I could use a breather." Juliana smiled, hoping to alleviate the tension smothering the room. She attempted to rise to her feet, but a flash of vertigo overwhelmed her, and her knees collapsed, depositing her back on the couch.

Alex skirted the sofa and crouched in front of her. Concern shifted across the hard planes of his rugged face. He stroked her cheek.

"Give me a minute," she said. A jolt from his touch invigorated her, and she shook off the lethargy, willing strength back to her body and mind. Willing strength to her disintegrating walls blocking Alex from intruding upon her hormones.

"Don't move." A glimmer of tenderness reached his eyes.

◌⸿⸾◌

Alex settled Juliana and Andrea in the living room and returned to the bedroom to examine the doll box.

The emotions he experienced when Juliana fainted stunned him. He wanted to protect her, care for her, and never let her out of his sight. For the first few years following her vanishing act, he'd waited for her to come back, never wanting to snuff out the flame of hope. As time dragged by and there was no word of her, the fire burned into embers until cold dry ashes remained. And an epic fear of love. Now, back in his life, she'd reignited that spark.

A small yappy dog barking in the neighbor's yard returned him to the present. Leaving the past behind, he locked his thoughts away and concentrated on his job.

Using evidence bags as makeshift gloves, he lifted the doll box off the closet shelf. All evidence pointed to the fact that the perp had used gloves, but Alex wasn't taking any chances. Doll accessories stuffed the box to the rim. He tipped it on its side and spread the contents on the bed. After a few seconds of sorting through the tiny toys, excitement swamped him.

"Son of a bitch." He picked up a half-dollar-sized gold disk and dropped it inside an evidence bag, careful not to contaminate it with fingerprints. Raising the object to eye level, he fingered the jagged edge. It was a broken Scottish clan medallion soldered to a keychain fob.

He cleaned up the pile of tiny shoes and clothes and returned to the living room. "You were right." His eyes locked with Juliana's, appreciation spilling from his voice. Respect for her psychic talents jumped several rungs on his ladder of trust.

When Alex showed them the evidence, Juliana edged back, afraid to approach the keychain. Fear wove through him as he recalled her fainting spell. If she suffered similar trauma during each case, he wondered how she'd managed to survive all those years.

"Do you recognize it, Andrea?"

She peered into the clear bag. "Never seen it."

Juliana maintained a wary distance, her eyes inquisitive.

"It's a piece of a Scottish clan medallion—"

"Scotland Forever," Juliana blurted out. "The ring tone on the kidnapper's cell phone. I knew it sounded familiar."

Alex's jaw dropped. "You sure?"

"Positive."

He pulled his own intact keychain from his pocket. "These are sold at Celtic stores and festivals. They make them into Celtic heritage wear—pendants, cap badges, brooches, keychains." Alex flipped it over, revealing the smooth backside. "Most are sold in pewter or silver. Gold pieces are usually custom-made."

He pointed out the design on the two keychains. The name *Campbell* was engraved above a boar's head logo on the one he just found. "The coat of arms and motto are different for each clan. Clan MacKenzie has a stag's horn, and this is a boar's head."

Andrea's expression turned doubtful. "What if Lisette found it somewhere?"

"Does she put her treasures in with her doll things?" Alex asked.

"No." A spark animated Andrea. It was enough for all of them to hold onto.

"It's his." Juliana clutched her throat. "I sense it." After a tense moment, she removed her hand from her throat and held out her open palm. "Let me touch—"

"No." Alex shoved the evidence bag in his pocket. No way would he let her go through that again. At least not yet.

She rolled her eyes. "Alex, it won't kill me."

"We have to dust it for prints. Come on." Alex strode toward the front door. "I'll take you home."

"Please stay, Juliana," Andrea pleaded. "I really want to catch up. You can help shift my mind off . . ." Tears pooled in her eyes.

It devastated him knowing that Lisette was out there at the mercy of the bastard who'd abducted her. And it tortured him to see his sister so distraught and helpless. If Andrea wanted Juliana to keep her company, why should he object?

If Juliana stayed, she might tell Andrea why she'd disappeared for twelve years. He desperately wanted to know. Yet, on the flip side, he feared the truth. Feared what it might do to his jacked emotions. And because of what had just happened, he wanted Juliana to work with him at the PD. He wanted her insight on the case as an impartial party.

Who are you kidding? You just want her there.

He left the decision to Juliana.

CHAPTER EIGHT

A cooling breeze stirred the balmy summer night. Palm trees swayed, fronds rustled. Stars winked at them, and a full moon shed light on the parking lot as they walked toward the building. Appreciative of the extra illumination, Alex couldn't take his ravenous gaze off Juliana.

James met them outside Alex's office. Alex dangled the plastic bag holding the Scottish keychain for James' perusal. He pointed out the engraved markings on the reverse side, hoping the symbols would provide evidence as to the creator. Alex gave James a quick rundown on the night's activities.

James turned speculative eyes on Juliana. "You said you weren't a touch telepath."

"I wasn't." Exhilaration lit up Juliana's face in the twinkling of her eyes and the slight smile tugging at her lips.

Alex wanted to devour her full, tinted lips. Wanted to feel the softness of them under his. *Shit. I'm losing it.*

Ripping his pen through a piece of scratch paper, he scrawled a deli order and handed it and the evidence bag to James. "Take this into forensics, and it's your turn to order up dinner." He took Juliana's elbow and guided her into his office. A tremor surged up his arm from contact with her silken skin. He hated removing his hand from her arm to shut the door.

As soon as Juliana entered his office, her gaze flitted to the Scotland posters covering his walls. Their Scotland dream vacation after college had evaporated the day Juliana disappeared. The posters served to remind him of their ruined fantasy. Dismally, he realized he should have removed them ages ago.

"Spill it." He eased behind the desk, folding his arms across his chest. "What else did you see in your vision?" Alex dropped into his chair, relieved to take the load off his dog-tired body.

Juliana sank into the visitor chair near the door, silent and stiff. "I wasn't sure how much to reveal to Andrea."

A spasm knotted his gut. Did he even want to hear?

She fiddled with her braid, twisting it around her slender fingers. The action brought back painful memories of combing his fingers through the glossy gold tresses. He quickly shook the memory off. She'd always played with her hair when nervous. It didn't look like that habit had changed.

Her emerald gaze was transfixed on his face. "At first, he was gentle with Lisette, earning her trust. Now she fears him." Juliana set her purse on his desk and clasped her hands in her lap. "He's impatient and obviously not used to children and their emotions."

Alex expelled an anxious breath he wasn't aware he held. He expected worse. "What else?"

"He received a phone call. He's angry because Lisette won't eat. The caller's apparently someone Lisette knows, because he told the person to bring what she likes to eat." She halted and looked down at her lap. "He's out for revenge." Juliana lifted her head, her face pale.

Alarm traced a thin, icy line down Alex's spine. "He hasn't hurt her?"

"Not that I could tell. But he's angry, vengeful."

He rose and turned to stare out the windows. Several uniformed officers stood by a row of marked police cars, bantering and laughing, preparing for a night patrolling the streets.

Moments later, Juliana's warm hand touched his arm, coaxing him around.

"I'm so sorry, Alex," she said softly. "I know how this hurts."

He turned around, fists clenching. "Do you really?" he snapped.

She flinched, and he instantly regretted the words. She'd been through enough criminal cases to know how they affected the victims and their families. Despite his harsh words, she stepped closer and wrapped her arms around his waist.

Instinctively, his arms encircled her, and he rested his cheek on top of her head. Her light berry-scented shampoo smelled heavenly, and he breathed in deeply. His initial embrace was unforgiving. He didn't loosen his hold until Juliana made a small sound in her throat, and he realized he was hugging her too tightly.

She unfolded an arm from around his waist and ran her fingers through his short hair, smoothing the chaotic spikes. Her touch was almost unbearably gentle, and her hug settled him more than he should allow.

Regret flashed inside him. He hated that Lisette's kidnapping was the reason that had brought Juliana back into his life. Alex cupped her face, and he lost himself in the depths of her sultry eyes. Sighing, he drew her closer still until her breath grazed his mouth. With growing insistency, his lips met hers and her matched hunger. The kiss deepened as control melted, and they abandoned themselves to the fever that had lain dormant for over a decade.

Stroking his back, her hands seared his skin through his shirt. Her breasts crushed against his chest, kindling a desire he raged against. The heady scent of her familiar floral fragrance created mayhem with his senses, and he began falling into a drowning pool.

Not until his tongue slipped between her soft, luscious lips did her arms wrap around his neck, pulling his mouth harder onto hers. Her mouth tasted of mint and simply Juliana as his greedy tongue probed and danced with hers. When his hands moved to cup her firm, rounded butt, reality whacked him upside the head. What the hell was he doing?

Abruptly, he broke off the kiss and jerked out of her arms. The ties that once bound them were racing back with such velocity that his tightly-held control had slipped.

Uncertainty tinted her rosy cheeks, and she just stood there, arms dangling at her sides.

"I'm sorry." He stared at the posters on the wall, the files stacked on his desk, at the carpet, anywhere but at Juliana.

The energy between them proved volatile. He feared breaking the fragile bond if he moved, yet he needed distance from her.

As if she felt the same need, Juliana eased back, and the tension-laden air stirred around them. She bumped into his leather chair, caught the back with her hand. "I . . . it's okay." Her voice was thick, husky.

A dense silence loomed and Alex experienced an intense desire to read her mind.

As if on cue, James flung the door open, dispelling the sexual edginess pervading the room. Renewed focus on the case provided the welcome diversion Alex craved.

From Juliana. And from what once was.

James stopped mid-stride into the room and flashed Juliana his trademark crooked smile.

A seed of jealousy sprouted inside Alex. Grimacing, he tossed off the unsettling mood and motioned for James to take a seat. "Let's go over the interviews."

He let Juliana have his chair as he sprawled in the other visitor chair next to James.

James plowed right in. "Do you think the perp's name is Campbell?"

"Campbell's a Scottish clan name. Under each clan, there are various named septs." Alex adjusted his chair so his line of sight included both James and Juliana. "He may be a Campbell, or not."

He ignored the interrogation list James shoved at him, and James dropped it on the desk. "No one has a clue who could've snatched Lisette."

Alex rested his elbows on his knees, chin in his palms. "Give me the short list."

"Grandparents. Jasmine, the twenty-year-old they hired as a part-time nanny—"

His perpetual disgust of Lisette's grandparents exploded from his voice. "Lisette's supposed to spend time with her grandparents, not some damn babysitter." He slammed a fist on the desk. "They have her one damn weekend a month."

A clerk pushed the door open, delivered dinner, and fled the squirrelly atmosphere. Thankful for the diversion, Alex dug into the bag and produced deli sandwiches and bottled sodas. Juliana stretched across the desk to grab the sandwich he offered.

She unwrapped the turkey and cheddar cheese sandwich. Her eyes widened in hunger and awe. "You remembered my favorite."

His mouth twisted in a wry smile. He didn't know if

she hungered for the sandwich or for him. And why the hell did he care? He massaged the nape of his neck.

"This is heavenly," she said after a couple of bites.

"Best deli in town," James agreed, his mouth full as he tackled his own hefty sandwich.

Alex's stomach flip-flopped at the sight of his untouched meal. "Where were we?"

"The list," Juliana replied.

James chugged down half a soda and continued, "The ultra-rich grandparents, nanny Jasmine, Sharon and Matthew Douglas, and Bremley."

"Who's Bremley?" Juliana sat back and rubbed her stomach.

"The Chambers' butler," James mumbled through a mouthful.

Alex tore the wrapper off his hoagie and bit off a large bite. The normally superb roast beef was tasteless. He swallowed roughly and set the sandwich down, pushing it aside. "Andrea hates that bastard."

"He's a tough nut to crack," James said. "Icy, sarcastic, knows nothing. I get the impression he'd do anything for them, above or below the law."

Alex smirked. "Wouldn't all butlers? Isn't that their job?"

"Like I'm supposed to know?" James snorted. "Do I look like I can afford a butler?"

"Put a tail on him."

"Wouldn't hurt to put a tag on them all, man. But Hayes won't bite without more evidence."

Alex fingered his scar. It always itched like crazy when a time bomb ticked in his pocket. "What'd Bremley say about taking Lisette and the nanny to the park?"

"Chauffeur was sick that day, so he filled in."

Alex flipped open the interview file. "Did you interview the chauffeur?"

"He's not full-time. Got his phone number, left a message."

He skimmed the grandparents' interviews. Grantham and Samantha Chamber were perfect targets. They had millions of dollars and owned a dozen businesses. They couldn't escape the disgruntled masses with those bucks. Probability was high that they were involved. Somehow.

Alex tossed the file across the desk and studied James. "How did old man Chamber come across?"

"A cold, arrogant SOB. Hard to figure where he's coming from. All business. Need to do background intel on the whole family."

The Kentucky Derby that had pounded through Alex's head earlier had dwindled to a greyhound race. Despite the alleviation of pain, Alex snagged the aspirin bottle off his desk and washed a couple down with his soda. "Samantha Chamber?"

"Distraught, knows nothing. Says she loves Lisette and would never hurt her." James' voice hardened in anger. "They have an airtight alibi, not that it matters. With that kind of money, they could've paid for an alibi without cracking open the checkbook."

⟨⟩

Listening with one ear, Juliana's gaze wandered around the room. She examined the overflowing bookcase behind the visitor chairs, the dented file cabinet shoved in the corner. She smiled at Lisette's artwork tacked to the wall behind Alex and James. The framed photograph of Alex and a laughing Lisette perched on his shoulders entranced her.

Several moments of contemplative silence passed before Juliana said, "It wasn't Grantham Chamber."

Alex lifted his eyes in an assessing stare. "He could've

hired someone."

Juliana shook her head. "Maybe, but I don't think so." She flicked her hand dismissively. "Lisette was comfortable with the kidnapper and trusted him at one point. If she only spends one weekend a month at her grandparents', and most of that time with the babysitter, she probably isn't real comfortable with her grandparents. It could've been the butler if he spent time with Lisette and the nanny. Or Grantham could've hired the butler to do it, in that case." Juliana studied her soda bottle, deep in thought. "How long has this nanny arrangement been going on?"

Appreciation flickered across Alex's face, and her heart fluttered.

"Long enough." Alex shrugged. "Lisette's afraid of her grandfather. She was glad she didn't have to see him much." He rubbed his jaw. "If Grantham hired someone to snatch her, Lisette would've gotten to know him at the estate." He rose and paced the cramped room. "James, did the household staff indicate if Lisette befriended anyone else?"

"No. They keep Lisette on the estate with Jasmine at all times."

"Not true." Alex scowled. "We know Bremley took them to the park last week. Sharon Douglas saw them."

"Right." James made a notation in the file. "On the interview list for Sharon."

Juliana wrapped up the rest of her sandwich. "Did Jasmine foster a relationship for this purpose? With Bremley?"

James knocked down his soda and slam-dunked his bottle into the recycle bin. "During the interview, Jasmine was antsy, said cops made her nervous. Her grief seemed real. She said she loves Lisette like a little sister. But I have a gut feeling she's holdin' out."

Juliana leaned forward and crossed her arms on the desk. Theories and fatigue made her head reel. "What did Jasmine say about the park outing?"

James stretched out his long legs. "Same as Bremley. Pre-arranged play date with Lisette's friend from daycare."

Alex halted his pacing and stared at James. "Did Andrea verify the play date?"

"It was legit. Andrea was pissed 'cause Jasmine didn't clear it with her first. Lisette didn't mention it either."

Juliana spotted a picture of Andrea and Lisette halfway hidden behind a stack of files on the corner of the desk. Andrea shared Alex's auburn hair and blue eyes, which boosted the natural beauty of her smooth skin, high cheekbones, and tanned complexion. The smiling, happy person in the picture belied the distraught, terrified mother she saw earlier that evening.

"This sounds like a cliché, but what's the butler's story?" Juliana pinned her gaze on James. Alex scrutinized her as if she sat buck-naked, leaving her feeling disconcerted. She folded her arms across her breasts.

"He's not off the hook. He wears the same shoe size as the print found in the garden. Evasive, no alibi." James' face hardened and an angry light gleamed in his eyes. "He forked over his one and only pair of athletic shoes for inspection. They're brand new, never been worn."

"So he dumped the old pair and bought new ones?" Juliana raised her eyebrows.

"You've got it." The desk phone rang and Alex jabbed a button on the console, sending the call to voicemail. "What else?"

James checked his notes again, then slapped the pad against the desk. "As far as Lisette getting comfortable with another man, it would've been on the estate, and that's a virtual fortress. Jasmine denies any knowledge of Lisette befriending anyone. They never left the estate, except for the one play date."

"You think she's lying?" *Easy to determine if they let me at her.* Her telepathy would definitely benefit the investigation. But how much credence would Alex and James attach to her mind-reading ability?

James shrugged his hands midair.

A hard, vigilant look touched Alex's eyes. "We'll have Juliana meet Jasmine and the Chambers tomorrow for phase two interviews." He leaned his back against the tall file cabinet. A dozen or so stuffed folders toppled onto the floor and he booted them aside. "What's the story on Andrea's neighbors?"

"They can't have children and they're desperate. Andrea says Sharon tries to mother Lisette." James shifted in his seat and propped his foot on Alex's abandoned chair. "A few weeks ago, Andrea went to get Lisette at Sharon's one day and found her wearing clothes she got from Sharon. When Andrea asked Lisette about it, Lisette said Sharon has a room full of girl's toys and clothes."

"Shit," Alex groaned. "Yesterday Andrea told me Sharon's been acting weird." He began prowling the room again. "Get a search warrant."

Juliana drank her soda and cleaned up the dinner debris. "How could they hide Lisette so close to home?" she asked. A risk for the Douglases, but not impossible. Nothing floated out of the realm of possibility at this stage of the game. *Hell, people hide kids in walls nowadays.*

"Sometimes the least likely place or person is the one to fear the most." Alex gave Juliana a meaningful look.

A hot flush crept over her at his implication. Her eyes held his until his gaze broke away.

"Man, you know we can't get a warrant yet." James sighed. "They're first up tomorrow. They both work at the hospital with Andrea, and we haven't been able to reach them yet. We'll ask if they'll consent to a search. Andrea can probably get them to agree."

Juliana stifled a yawn. She was exhausted and past ready to sink into bed.

Alex's gaze strayed to the wall clock hanging at a crooked angle above the door. "A few more minutes and I'll drive you home." He returned his attention to James. "Give me a quick run-down of the rest."

James ticked off each item from memory. "A public plea aired on all major networks during the evening news. Volunteers are distributing and posting flyers, combing the city and vicinity. A volunteer center's up and running." James' face grew red with anger. "Get this, man. Grantham Chamber donated space and equipment for the volunteer center in his office tower. Showing his concern."

Alex threw his uneaten hoagie in the trash. A heavy thud resounded in the room. "Generous guy."

"We're following all leads and phone calls. Searching the databases for like crimes. Liaising with other agencies for similar MOs." James tossed his list on the desk.

Alex opened the door, voices from the squad room drifting a dull roar into the office. "I'm taking Juliana home. Then I'll be at Andrea's."

Juliana and Alex left the office in silence. The thought of being alone with him jostled the sandwich in her stomach. *Why does he leave my nerves twisting in the wind? Because we haven't discussed the past? Because he's still gorgeous and twists my insides into knots? Because of a kiss that makes me want to surrender everything to him?*

They drove along the darkened streets, long minutes dragging past. Juliana rested her head on the headrest and closed her eyes. She was done for the night. Her ESP dreams always exacted a huge chunk of energy. The secondary visions that evening sapped what little stamina she'd managed to preserve throughout the day.

Reaching her house, Alex parked in her driveway. Annoyed, she noticed her dead porch light and dark porch. Her first-ever new house suffered from numerous growing pains, the porch light the least of them.

A coastal breeze cooled the night, and stars twinkled brightly in the moonlit sky. The faint scent of roses wafted in the air. Alex's arm brushed against hers as they ascended the two steps to the porch, and he stiffened.

"Wouldn't hurt to keep a light on around here."

"I wish." She flicked her hand at the dead lamp. "That stupid thing's automatic, if you can believe it. The builder was supposed to fix it last week, along with a dozen other things."

"Such as?"

Juliana sensed he sought a discussion topic other than the past or the investigation. Heat blossomed across her flesh. Being alone with him outside the arena of the case terrified and excited her at the same time. It was even more rattling than their earlier kiss, which stirred her like no other man's kisses did. The kiss that played trick-or-treat with her heart.

The glow from the streetlamp at the side of the house yielded enough light to insert the key into the deadbolt. Turning the key was another problem in itself.

"Like this blasted lock!" She exhaled in exasperation. Too tired to deal with the inadequacies of her new home, frustration wearied her even more and she sagged against the door.

"Let me."

Alex reached from behind and his large hand closed over hers. His touch spun her senses. He easily opened the lock, and she resisted pressing herself into his too-close-for-comfort hard body.

Don't go there, she screamed in her head. *Keep your distance. You don't need the complications a man brings to your life. Now or ever.*

The door swung inward, and she barely noticed until Alex flicked on the foyer light.

"You need to get these fixed." His voice was gruff.

"I will. Thank you." Juliana stepped inside, away from him. He stood motionless, filling the doorway.

Their eyes met, captivated with each other for what seemed an eon. Alex was first to break contact, and backed down the two steps.

He stopped as his feet landed on the slate walkway. "Thank you. For your help."

Better than a kick in the teeth. The words warmed her, and she smiled. "You're welcome."

Alex stood his ground, indecision tingeing his face. "Why did you leave?" he finally asked in a strained voice.

She knew the subject would eventually surface. But her stomach felt like a bowling ball had suddenly slammed into it.

Hands shoved in his front pockets, he waited, looking like a lost little boy.

She gripped the door until her knuckles turned white. "It wasn't my choice."

"You were eighteen. An adult," he stated almost accusingly.

Leaning her head on the doorframe, she regarded him ruefully. "I was also the eighteen-year-old daughter of Daniel Westwood." No explanation was necessary. Alex knew what that meant.

He grunted an acknowledgment, and his expression softened.

"Alex, we really need to talk. You need to understand

what happened."

"Not now." He shuffled his feet, looking down, up, around, anywhere but at her. "Answer one last question and I'll let you go." His intense and expectant stare settled on her face once again. "Why did you stay away?"

A sob climbed up Juliana's throat, and she swallowed it with difficulty. She felt a wretchedness of mind she'd never experienced before. Even though he wouldn't understand her reasons any more than she'd accepted them, she gave him the truth.

"Because it was for the best. For both of us."

CHAPTER NINE

The scent of star jasmine drifted through Juliana's upstairs bedroom window and prodded her awake. Sunbeams streamed through the blinds, dawn long gone. She glanced at the alarm clock with sleep-blurred eyes. In less than an hour, Alex would arrive.

She planned to assist with his interviews of Lisette's grandparents, babysitter, and Andrea's next-door neighbors. They hadn't established how he'd introduce her to these people. But if it came to it, she'd resort to tactics she used at the NYPD as a bogus assistant profiler with a fake ID.

Juliana stretched her arms and legs, waking her muscles. No dreams, no nightmares had plagued her. Lisette should be safe or else she would've dreamed about it. Fortunately, there was small chance at this stage that she'd lost touch with the kidnapper. She'd never lost touch in any other case.

Surprisingly, she'd slept soundly and hadn't lain in bed half the night with the tumultuous day playing over and over in her mind like a bad song. She relished the solitude and reflected on Alex and her life. When he'd stalked off last night, she'd sensed his acceptance of the fact that her life hadn't entirely been her own to chart.

During the twelve lonely years in New York, she'd shied away from trusting anyone. She'd fought for her independence, knowing her sanity hinged on making a life for herself—alone. Her controlling and oppressive father had conspired to suppress the family's psychic curse in her. He hated her abilities and tried to control every facet of her life after her mother had died. Once he'd finally released his hold on her, his only child, she'd won her freedom, but there was still an empty hole deep inside her.

A heavy sigh welled up. There'd be enough time to dissect Alex and her life after they found Lisette. She didn't intend to ever leave San Jose again.

When the doorbell chimed an hour later, eagerness mixed with nervousness pulsed through her. She'd experienced similar feelings whenever she worked on a criminal case. However, this case included the unexpected—in the guise of a gorgeous detective and a history between them that spanned the continent. Not to mention Alex's connection to the victim.

A man off-limits because of a stupid family curse, she reminded herself as she opened the door to see Alex's haggard face.

She arched her eyebrows at the steel box in his grip. "Do you always travel with your toolbox, or is that a new style of briefcase?"

"You've retained that witty banter I remember so well." His words were cool, but the smile crinkling the corners of his eyes warmed her.

She eased aside to let him in the foyer. He set the toolbox on the travertine floor near her hand-painted bombe chest.

Alex returned to the door and tested the deadbolt. "I'll look at your porch light and deadbolt later."

She blinked rapidly. "Okay." *Whoa, the day promised*

more than anticipated.

Alex locked the door behind them, and they walked in companionable silence side-by-side to his SUV, as if going on a really weird and long-overdue date. When he opened the passenger door, Juliana realized her fashion mistake of the day.

"I'm glad I wore pants," she teased, eyeing her mid-thigh skirt. Not waiting for a response, she hiked her leg up to climb into the SUV in a very unladylike fashion.

"I don't know about that. I like the skirt," he drawled behind her.

A few seconds slipped by before Juliana realized what he'd said. "Nice try." She settled into the seat, tugging down her skirt. "And I thought you were a gentleman."

"I'm human." He closed the door, sprinted around the front of the vehicle, and eased into the driver's seat.

She smiled to herself, pleased he'd managed to maintain his humor. *The Alex I remember has come home. To stay, or just for a visit?*

Juliana rubbed her arms, wishing she'd thought to bring a sweater. Fashion mistake number two—short sleeves.

Alex looked exceedingly comfortable in his dress shirt and black slacks. *Exceedingly edible,* an elusive thought whispered in her mind. A shiver ran through her, but it didn't stem from the cold air assaulting her from the vents.

Juliana waited until he maneuvered out of the neighborhood before asking, "How's Andrea?"

He must have sensed her physical discomfort, because he turned the air-conditioner to low. "Hanging in there. She's looking forward to seeing you tomorrow."

"Does that bother you?"

"I don't want her upset any more than she already is." His grip tightened on the steering wheel as he drove the

SUV onto the expressway.

She glanced at his profile, his face inscrutable. "I won't go if you don't think I should."

Alex shook his head. "It's not up to me. Andrea wants you there. She wants to be close to Lisette."

Juliana's heart jerked at the break in his voice.

"Look, here's how I want to operate." Alex's voice turned hard, controlled again. "News hounds are everywhere. You're an old family friend. I don't want you going to Andrea's or to the PD without my approval first." Alex pulled a business card out of his shirt pocket and handed it to her. "Don't use the PD phones. Use my cell number."

"No problem." She noted the number jotted on the back of the card before she slipped it in her purse.

"There are a couple of jerks at the PD who'd love to see me fall on my ass with this case. Especially if they find out a psychic's involved."

"Got it." Her contained voice contradicted the indignation abrading her insides. "Is Internal Affairs on you for something?"

Alex turned his head, raising an eyebrow. "How'd you guess?"

She offered him a tight smile. He'd forgotten the intuition that had played a large part in the connection they'd shared years ago. "What's the scoop?"

Alex opened his mouth, hesitated, then said, "Chad Shelby. He thinks I'm responsible for his demotion to an IA desk flunky. We tested for lieutenant at the same time, but he screwed up a homicide case, which I ended up solving."

He paused as if deciding how much to tell. "One of the murder victims was a witness he was protecting. They were engaged."

"How were you involved?"

He swerved to avoid a traffic jam in the right lane. The shrill horn of an economy-car blared at him. Juliana squeezed the armrest, pulling on the seatbelt locking her in place.

"Sorry 'bout that," he muttered. "I got wind of a hit on her and warned Shelby. He didn't believe me, thought I wanted to sabotage his case. Now he blames me for everything wrong in his life, and he's digging for any excuse to put the screws to me."

"So if I botch your case, he'll use it against you?" Juliana feared nothing. After years of experience, confidence sided with her on this one.

"Bingo."

She longed to soothe the ragged scar pulsing on his face. "Then you have as much to gain as I do by keeping my involvement secret."

"You'll use a fake name."

"Leigh Duncan." The pseudonym slipped out before she could stop it. She'd used hers and Alex's middle names. "I used that name with the NYPD," she felt compelled to add.

Alex shot her an assessing sidelong look. "Whatever."

Jumpy silence enveloped the cab. She smoothed imaginary wrinkles in her skirt. The pine-scented air freshener dangling from a stereo knob suddenly caused her nose to prickle, and she scrunched her face to fight back a sneeze.

"Why didn't you tell me you were telepathic at our first meeting?" A muscle jumped in Alex's jaw.

She lifted her eyes to the pain flickering across his handsome face. She reached out to caress his cheek, but he grabbed her wrist in a steel grip before her fingers made contact.

Sighing, she said, "It's hard enough being a clown act in my own mind, let alone in the eyes of every cop I meet.

I wanted to prove my abilities first."

"Have you read my mind?" he demanded hoarsely.

Her skin smoldered where he grasped her wrist. She shook her head.

"You expect me to believe you?"

The words stung. "It's the truth."

He released her wrist. The air-conditioner cooled the inferno his touch kindled.

"Alex, I rarely let myself read people's minds. If I did, I'd go crazy. Literally." She drummed her fingers on the armrest. "You have no idea what it's like to be around people whose thoughts range from stupid to outright criminal. My brain overflows to the point that I can't even figure out what *I'm* thinking."

"*Can* you read my mind?" Alex's voice softened.

"If I want to, and if your mind isn't blocked. I can't read everyone. Some people can even block their own transmissions if they know how."

"Have you tried?"

"To read you? No."

Alex's eyebrows lifted in disbelief. "Why not?"

"Because your thoughts would scare the hell out of me." Her voice trailed off in a whisper.

He stopped at a red light and turned to stare at her. The intensity in his eyes bored into her, thrusting into her soul. His scrutiny was familiar and somewhat frightening.

"Have I been that awful?" Contriteness wasn't a normal state for Alex, proven by the challenging yet awkward timbre of his voice.

"What do you think?" She laughed to defray the unease.

Alex groaned in mock annoyance and stared out the bug-splattered windshield. Suburbia enveloped them as they continued past neighborhood shopping centers and entered a maple-lined street of older boxy houses.

"Can you really read minds? No joke?"

"After this conversation, you still don't believe me?" Juliana laughed softly and crossed her arms under her breasts.

"I'm still ticked at you." His lips edged up.

She suppressed a grin. "Gives me something else to look forward to. Along with the mistrust."

Unable to resist opening Pandora's Box further, she asked, "So what do you have against psychics?" *Or is it just me?*

Alex's shoulders stiffened against the seat. "Let's just say I haven't had any good experiences with them. And it's old news to anyone who knows me."

Did he only remember the negatives? Juliana let it drop. She'd soon disabuse him of his pessimistic attitude. And his forgetfulness.

He pulled his SUV into the bare driveway of a small tract home in south San Jose. She glanced around in dismay as they left the vehicle. Grass browned in spots and weeds choked the flowerbeds. The cracked and uneven walkway was a lawsuit waiting to happen.

"Is Jasmine expecting us?"

Alex shrugged. "Couldn't reach her."

He rang the doorbell several times until a sleepy female voice from inside grumbled unintelligibly at them. The door opened, and an attractive, curvy woman in her mid-twenties faced them. She wore a tight tank top and boy shorts sleepwear. Her short platinum-blonde hair was bed-tousled. "Yeah, what'd ya want?"

Alex flashed his badge. "Jasmine Webley?"

"Jaz," she yelled, her raspy voice grating on Juliana's ears. "Cops are here again." Her eyes razed them. "Damn, they know how to grow 'em in San Jose," she said in a sultry burr, eyeing Juliana suggestively. "And you're definitely my type."

Juliana stifled a gasp. Alex shifted his head and arched an eyebrow, chuckling under his breath.

"Jaz!" The young woman flung another shout over her shoulder. "Bet she spent the night at her sugar daddy's." She flounced away, leaving the front door wide open, giving them a peek inside.

"See anything?" Juliana squeezed between Alex and the porch wall. He moved aside to allow her full view through the doorway.

Craning their necks, they peered into the sparsely furnished living room. "Probably college girls pooling their money to pay the rent."

Juliana stepped a foot over the threshold.

Alex seized her arm, shaking his head. "Can't enter without an invite or warrant."

His fingers danced on her bare skin before he dropped her arm. Heat skittered down her spine to her southern parts.

"Receiving anything?"

"Nothing useful." Other than the blonde having interesting sex acts with Juliana on her mind, she'd read nothing helpful. The blonde woman barely tolerated Jasmine and had no clue whom Jasmine knew or what she did away from home.

The woman reappeared in the entry, eyes rolling. "She didn't come home last night."

Juliana struggled to keep her telepathy centered on the woman. Any slight hiccup and Alex's thoughts would fly into her mind.

"Do you know where she is?" Alex asked.

"Beats me." Her gaze raked Juliana from head to toe.

"Who's the sugar daddy you mentioned? Grantham Chamber?"

"That old windbag?" The blonde woman snorted. "Wrong weekend of the month."

"Someone else?"

"Yeah. New guy she's doing. Don't know him, never met him, don't even know his name." She yawned wide. "Now, can I go back to bed?"

She started to push the door shut, but Alex inserted his foot between the door and the jamb.

"What?" Her twinkling eyes once again strayed to Juliana. "Care to join me?"

"No thanks, honey. Another time." Juliana threw the woman a teasing smile, unable to resist flirting.

Alex thrust a couple business cards at her. "Give one to Jasmine and tell her to call me. Keep the other for yourself. Call if you hear from her."

She held out her palm toward Juliana. "Where's yours?"

"Fresh out, hon."

A pout spread across the woman's face before she whisked the door shut.

Juliana's laughter held until they were inside Alex's SUV. To her astonishment, Alex's familiar deep laugh joined hers.

"'Another time'?" he mocked.

She loved to hear him laugh, and the way his face lit up. If she could keep him in a good mood, life would be awesome.

"I couldn't resist. She's too cute." Juliana giggled.

"Is that why you stayed away for twelve years?"

"No!" She burst out in a fresh peal of laughter.

"Good." The word must have slipped, because Alex's face sobered and he hastily turned away.

Wings of apprehension fluttered in her stomach. She knew exactly what he meant. She couldn't allow them to grow close again. Nor could she forget the kiss they'd shared in the heat of the moment. The kiss indelibly stamped on her mind next to the imprint of their first kiss from years ago. But no future existed for them together. Her heritage saw to that. Or was there a future? Did she dare dream? No! She couldn't risk putting him through a life with a crazy psychic. Couldn't risk buckling herself onto that rollercoaster life.

Her thoughts whirled uncontrollably, and she blurted out, "Feels like old times, doesn't it?" She tossed him a tenuous smile and absently straightened her skirt as if it were mangling her insides into knots.

"It's not." He stared at a crack in the windshield, his face a mask of winter's ice.

She watched a vein pulsing on his neck, willing it to stop. "We still need to talk about us."

"I just want to find my niece," he said in a tone that matched his expression. "We can talk later."

"I need you to understand." She rested her hand on Alex's thigh in a comforting gesture. The tensing of his leg sent a jolt through her arm, and she yanked her hand back as if burned.

"Why, so you can alleviate your guilt?"

"So I can concentrate on finding Lisette," Juliana whispered.

"Later, okay?"

She slumped back in the leather seat. "Yeah, sure."

A reckoning was around the bend. She'd always known someday she'd bump into Alex, even in a city as large as San Jose. And she'd even planned to contact him one day—to explain what had happened.

But not this soon. Not this way.

CHAPTER TEN

The quiet half hour drive into the foothill homes of the valley's elite was barely tolerable. They didn't speak until Alex stopped outside the tall wrought-iron gate in front of the Chamber estate and punched the intercom button. After verbal identification, the gate slowly slid open.

Alternating purple plum and watermelon-colored crepe myrtle trees flanked each side of the driveway. The drive ended in a circle surrounding forest-green grass. A huge gargoyle fountain sprayed and splashed in the center of the verdant lawn. The Gothic-style house nestled beyond the expansive lawn and ornamental shrubbery.

Alex parked in the circular driveway by the front door. He joined her on the passenger side, and they walked to the stone-pillared porch together. Juliana gazed in fascination at the mansion's medieval turrets and gray and taupe stone exterior. What kind of people lived in a castle in California?

Alex clanged a dragonhead knocker on the black walnut door. Seconds later, an impeccably dressed butler in a black and white suit swung the door wide. Alex flashed his badge. The snooty butler gave them the once-over, his dark, impenetrable eyes lingering on Juliana.

In his mid-forties, the tall, attractive man sported burnished brown hair shot with strands of white. His muscular build surprised Juliana—not the typical English butler.

Unease slipped over her as if someone had wiped cold, muddy feet on her naked skin. She clutched her purse to her stomach and studied the mansion's Gothic architecture.

"Jeeves." Alex handed the butler a business card.

Gingerly, Bremley grasped the card as if ink still dripped from it. Or blood. The Englishman sniffed disdainfully. "The name is Bremley, Lieutenant."

"Yeah, whatever," Alex said. "We're here to see Mr. and Mrs. Chamber."

Bremley looked point-blank at Juliana, interest lighting his dark eyes. "Who else shall I say is calling?"

"My associate, Leigh Duncan."

Juliana flashed Bremley an engaging smile, which disarmed the pretentious butler into flustered action. Red-faced, he knocked the mail from the mahogany console onto the black and gold marble floor.

Ignoring the fallen mail, he waved them into the foyer, eyeballing them as if they might slip priceless antiques in their pockets. He spoke into a house phone with a degree of distaste, "Madam, Lieutenant Alexander MacKenzie and associate Leigh Duncan are here to speak to you. Would you like—" He paused, adjusting the sword on a suit of armor in the corner of the foyer. "I'll show them in."

"Mrs. Chamber will see you in the sitting room." He moved with a panther's grace into the mansion's interior.

They slipped through double doors into a bright, spacious room. The room featured pastel yellows, corals, and apricot decor. Floral paintings in watercolors and oils patterned the walls. The room, so out of character with the medieval charm of the manor, pleased Juliana's senses.

A delicate scent of fresh-cut flowers offered a temporary remedy to Juliana's unbalanced emotional state. She wandered around the room, touching furniture and art objects. Large windows overlooked sweeping gardens, and sunlight danced on her bare arms. The cheery room welcomed her and harbored no evil.

"Alex. Have you found her?" A cautious but excited voice carried into the room.

Juliana spun on her heels and gazed upon a beautiful, elegant woman of Scandinavian descent rushing into the room from a back hallway.

"No." In typical fashion, Alex crossed his arms over his broad chest.

Despite the distinguished bearing of the petite, blonde woman, lines of anxiety creased her troubled face. Fatigue settled into dark pockets under her iris-blue eyes.

"Oh dear." Mrs. Chamber sank in a desolate heap on the overstuffed sofa in the center of the room. Tears spoiled her impeccably made-up face. She waved a handkerchief at them. "I'm sorry. I simply can't seem to control my emotions."

"Mrs. Chamber." Juliana sat beside her. "There's no need to be sorry."

The woman's thoughts buffeted her with their severity. Her mind was an open vault. Juliana winced as the thoughts overwhelmed her.

"Jewel . . . Leigh, you okay?"

The slip of her old nickname crashed into her. She realized he'd used the nickname yesterday also. How had she overlooked it? This case and Alex had her as confused as a drunk playing Twister.

"I'm fine," she lied, not wanting to upset Lisette's grandmother. "That annoying headache's hanging on."

Alex continued to study her, concern grooving his forehead. Juliana held her hand out to Mrs. Chamber, who grasped it and clung. "Leigh Duncan."

"Heavens, where are my manners?" Her lips formed a tight smile. "Samantha Chamber. Please, call me Samantha."

Alex strode to the far side of the room, scanned the backyard through the floor-to-ceiling windows, then pivoted around to face them. "I have a few follow-up questions." Samantha nodded. "Do you remember anyone becoming friendly with Lisette at any time while in your care?"

Samantha searched her mind. "No one I'm aware of, except the staff members Detective O'Malley interviewed yesterday."

"Who do you think would abduct her for ransom?"

Samantha's slender fingers flew to her throat. "Has there been a ransom demand? Grant didn't mention it this morning."

"Not yet."

Dropping her hands, she seemed unsure what to do with them. She plucked at her silk dress, clasped and unclasped them on her lap. "As I told Detective O'Malley, I don't know anyone who'd do such a horrible thing to Lisette." Samantha folded and unfolded her handkerchief. "She's here one weekend a month, and we don't leave the estate."

Juliana blanked out the verbal questions and answers. Instead, she concentrated on the thoughts tumbling in Samantha's head. The woman told the truth. Her frantic appearance was definitely genuine. She loved Lisette and respected and admired Andrea for being a good mother.

Alex switched his interrogation direction. She didn't have to hear his questions, given the way Samantha's trains of thought collided with one another. Samantha was terrified her husband might have done something stupid. He'd once threatened to keep Lisette instead of returning her after a weekend visit. Samantha verbalized none of this.

Alex completed his questioning. Juliana pulled herself back from the words echoing around her and quickly and efficiently rebuilt the mental block in her mind.

"Thanks for your time. Contact me if you remember anything helpful." Alex patted Samantha's shoulder and squeezed gently.

"Of course." She dabbed at her renewed tears. "Don't hesitate to call if you need *anything* from me. Anything." Samantha clutched Alex's arm before dropping her hand in her lap.

Alex and Juliana left, followed at a discreet distance by Bremley, guardian of Castle Chamber.

Once outside the closed front door, Juliana said, "That man gives me the creeps."

Alex halted mid-stride and turned to stare at her. His eyes darkened, slivered. "Andrea said the same thing. Did you try to read him?"

"Yeah." She rolled her eyes to the hazy blue sky. "You don't want to know what he was thinking."

Alex closed the distance between them and brushed away a loose tendril of hair stuck on her eyelashes. "Try me." His fingers trailed off her cheek, leaving heat rising in their wake.

"He . . ." She paused. "He'd like to rip my clothes off and—"

Alex held up his palm and scowled. "You're right."

Juliana lightly rubbed her face where Alex touched it, as if to capture his essence. "I thought we were interviewing Mr. Chamber too." She was eager to read his mind after hearing Samantha's thoughts.

"He's not here." A muscle flicked in Alex's jaw.

"Weren't you listening?"

"No. Did you forget why I was here?"

A tentative smile curled his lips up. "Sorry. You'll have to clue me in on *your* side of the conversation."

He opened the passenger door and waited for her to climb in. But she stood her ground in an affronted stance.

"What?" His shoulders moved in a half-shrug.

"Can you exit stage left?" She gritted her teeth. "I'm having a fashion calamity." Again, she wished she'd worn something that didn't hike up to her butt while climbing into the towering SUV.

Eyeing her damnable skirt, he leaned forward and drawled, "Need help?"

His breath fanned her ear and her heart palpitated. "I can manage." She sent him a withering glare that belied the havoc his nearness created.

Alex's triumphant laughter echoed as he strode to the driver's side. She hopped into the passenger seat and straightened her skirt before he even shoved a leg inside the SUV.

The engine roared to life and he headed off the estate. "Did you pick up any visions or vibes from the room?"

"No, and Samantha Chamber was honest. She loves Lisette and respects Andrea." Juliana buckled her seatbelt and adjusted it from cutting into her shoulder. "She's glad you're working the case and confidant you'll find Lisette."

"What else?" Amazement and wariness weighed Alex's voice.

Cool air circulated in the vehicle, and Juliana breathed in deeply. "She's afraid her husband's hiding something." She glanced around the interior and spied a beanbag toy nestled against a gym bag on the backseat. "He alluded to wanting to keep Lisette after a weekend visitation. She's afraid to ask him about it."

"What do *you* believe?"

"It's what she thinks, but she's cautious." She stretched back and snagged the beanbag kitten. The soft black fur against her skin subdued her ragged thoughts. "Apparently he's secretive about everything."

"What a guy, huh?" Alex tossed her a grim smile. "Anything else?"

"I wish." Juliana smoothed her fingers through the black fur of the tiny black cat. "Is this Lisette's?" She held the toy at dash level.

The muscles in his arms tightened as he gripped the steering wheel. "She collects them. I buy her a new one every month or so. I haven't had a chance to give it to her."

The engine's thrum eclipsed the silence. Alex guided the SUV onto the highway, his body visibly relaxing. Juliana set the stuffed kitten on the dashboard.

Alex steered around a slow-moving sedan, his corded arms flexing as he shifted the wheel. "Do you have other psychic talents I should know about?"

She laughed dryly. "None that I'm aware of. I'm still working my way around this new touch telepathy."

Her gaze shifted to a couple of tree squirrels frolicking in the wooded pines. They drove through the exclusive hillside area on the edge of suburbia. The fragrant evergreen forest filtered into the interior, overpowering the pine air freshener, refreshing and diverting.

Her former doctor, Brian Miller, had explained to her that she might have the capability for touch telepathy since her psychic makeup was powerful and diverse. He also told her it would take a major blow to the system for the skill to manifest itself in her, if then.

Was bumping into Alex and linking with a kidnapper who had a strong psychic transmitter a big enough trigger? And finding out the kidnapped child was Alex's niece? She couldn't imagine a greater whack to the system.

CRR80

Alex banged on the Douglases door and rang the bell several times. Palpable tension oozed off him. Juliana placed her hand on his forearm, and he turned toward her, a questioning slant to his eyebrows.

"Hey, relax." Juliana locked eyes with his and held until his expression softened.

Breaking the spell, she dropped her trembling hand, and peeped through the mini blinds on the window beside the door. "Looks like no one's home."

"Are you looking for Sharon or Matthew?" A gravelly woman's voice called out.

They turned simultaneously. An elderly woman hunkered down in her walker across the courtyard waved at them.

"Yes, ma'am. Have you seen them?" Alex asked.

"Not since yesterday mornin' after that little girl was taken." The woman shook her head. "Such a sweet thing. I can't imagine why anyone would want to hurt the darlin'."

Her voice drifted off as she shuffled around the corner faster than Juliana considered possible at her age.

"Not since yesterday? Not good." She chewed her lower lip. "Can you get a search warrant?"

"Only for probable cause." Alex called the PD and ordered an investigator to dig deeper and faster into Sharon and Matthew's background and whereabouts.

A short drive later, Alex once again parked his SUV in Juliana's driveway and left the engine running. She reached to unlatch the passenger door, but his relentless words halted her.

"When did you start to read minds? You never did

before."

"Selective memory?" Juliana chided, knowing he forgot next to nothing.

"Hardly." He scowled. "Answer the question."

He really is still mad at me. No less and no more than she'd anticipated.

"You don't want to know." She averted her gaze.

"Try me."

Juliana screamed in frustration. Only the scream never left her head. "At Johnny's funeral."

His expression altered, as if someone had smacked him from behind. He faced away from her, shifting the SUV into reverse. "I'll call if I need you."

Juliana seethed. *Damn him. Two can play that game.* Wordlessly, she left the edgy atmosphere in the vehicle and watched him drive away.

"Thanks for the help today, Juliana," she mocked as she strode toward the porch. Prevailing over the tricky deadbolt, she stepped through the front door, almost tripping over Alex's tool chest.

"Possession's nine tenths of the law." She tapped the box with the side of her foot. "You're mine now." Satisfaction curved her lips. He'd return for his toolbox, and she wasn't sure she didn't want him to.

The old Alex was emerging in bits and pieces. Part of her wanted to push him away and keep him at a distance, solve the case and move on with their separate lives. She'd survived twelve long years believing she'd always live alone, her psychic burden keeping her company. Telepathic ability played a major deterrent to any normal relationship. That fact had been ingrained in her all her life.

But another part of her longed to wrap her arms around Alex and kiss away the bad memories, and the pain of Lisette's abduction. She yearned to bury her head on his shoulder and weep for the pain and misery she'd caused him. And she ached to have him kiss away the heartbreaks and nightmares she'd suffered, along with the loneliness, the fear, and the Westwood family curse.

She knew without question she couldn't do either. She was stuck in an ocean so deep, it would take a deepwater drill to tug her out.

CHAPTER ELEVEN

Alex returned to the precinct, a black cloud hovering over his mood. He slammed shut the door to his office, glowering at the clanging of his window blinds. His world had tilted off its axis, and he struggled against unknown assailants to right it again. What more would this week pile on him? First he'd had to deal with Juliana's reappearance, then Lisette's disappearance.

He threw his messages on the desk where they spread like pink Pepto Bismol across the paper-strewn surface. He shut the blinds and adjusted his air-conditioner vent, closing off the warm, chaotic exterior world.

That morning, he'd started reconnecting with Juliana, the way they'd connected in high school. His reserve had slipped, and he'd accepted her as a necessity in his life, at least until he found Lisette, and maybe even longer. A fraction of him wanted to erase the past and pick up where they'd left off the day before prom. Yet the past hindered him. By not allowing Juliana to fess up about her desertion, he protected himself from getting too close to her. He hadn't healed from loving her all those years ago. And he'd never stopped loving her.

Dragging his fingers through his hair for the umpteenth time since dawn, Alex hauled in a sobering breath. When he'd first confronted Juliana on Thursday, he'd vowed not to get close to her again. Yet he couldn't forget the hunger in the kiss they shared in his office. He loved the taste of her ripe lips, the soft, lush feel of them under his. The kiss had made him want more, until sanity prevailed. She was too damn intoxicating. He wished he could hate her intrusion into his life. But he couldn't.

Scowling, he shoved Juliana out of his mind and focused on finding his niece and the bastard who'd abducted her. Lisette was his top priority, not a resurrected fantasy.

Alex spent the next few hours working on leads and searching the Internet for information on Grantham Chamber and family. The entire Chamber estate dripped platinum. It wouldn't surprise him if thousand dollar bills sprouted instead of leaves on their trees each spring. How much of that wealth would belong to Lisette after the old man nose-dived into a six-foot hole?

Chamber possessed enough money to bankroll any criminal activity. However, no evidence pointed in his direction yet. The man and his family looked like saints in the public eye. They made a great show to the press of their concern and support. They'd offered a substantial reward for information leading to the kidnapper's arrest and the safe return of their granddaughter.

They appeared innocent and helpful, when they were probably as guilty as Bonnie and Clyde. He doubted they cared much for Lisette, except to use her for whatever ulterior motives the rich played in the game of life. They'd never cared about her before Lisette's father had died last year. What had changed?

A knock sounded at the door, and Alex tossed the last of his introspection out, along with a stale bag of vending machine pretzels he'd tried snacking on the last hour.

James poked his head in. "Safe to enter?"

"When did that ever stop you?"

James handed him a cup of coffee. Thankful it wasn't squad room brew, Alex lifted the lid off the large cup and sniffed the welcome elixir. "Thanks."

Sinking into a seat across the desk, James unfolded his lean legs and propped them on the desk. "City's got their drawers in a twist over this case. Press is chomping our ass."

Alex clenched his jaw. The media had skipped past thirsty and raced straight to ravenous. "Any new leads?"

"Nothing that means a shit." James slammed his half-full coffee cup on the desk, hot liquid sloshing over the rim. Shaking his hand, he said, "Team's following up on the calls pouring in. Usual crap, people claiming to have seen her. A couple of confessions. Nothing's panned out."

Callers always inundated the police after an aired public appeal—people who claimed they saw the victim or the perp in every crevice of the city. They usually received a few confessions, which were sick jokes ninety-nine percent of the time. They investigated all leads in hopes of one bearing fruit.

"Pedophiles? Megan's Law?"

"No matches."

"Any other cold cases?" Alex sipped at the steaming black coffee. The rich aroma energized him as much as the caffeine.

"No similars in the area."

Alex drummed his fingers on his computer keyboard. He pushed aside case files and set down the coffee cup. "Ransom?" They were in a race against the clock; every hour counted in a kidnapping case. The first day was critical, and death often took victims during the initial hours. Already on day two, they should've received a ransom—if ransom was the kidnapper's goal.

"Grandparents might have received a ransom and

been warned not to reveal it or the kidnapper would . . ."

Alex sensed James' discomfort. He couldn't say the words any more than Alex wanted to think them.

"Wouldn't put it past them. I've done background intel on them." He stabbed at the keyboard and scanned through his computer notes. "A few hostile takeovers that might have pissed off a couple of business people, but we're talking major corporate players. No known disgruntled employees. He fired the first architect who designed that freaky house five years ago. The architect lives in Houston now."

"What about the older son?"

"Hasn't been in the States in years. He was seen jet-setting in Barcelona, Spain just this week. The hotel where he leases a penthouse confirmed his lease. Guess he splits his time between Barcelona and Monte Carlo." Alex shrugged. "I've left messages. And I've contacted Barcelona law enforcement."

James stretched his arms until his shoulder bones cracked. "How'd it go with Juliana?"

Alex filled James in on his day.

James' freckles flushed red, his eyes gleaming excitedly. "She's the real deal."

"Why were you so sure of her?" Alex asked, despite the fact that Juliana had always been as honest as a nun.

"Gut instinct. I saw no reason not to."

Alex grumbled in response, rubbing at the crick in his neck. He was living on borrowed time, every nerve chewed raw.

James rolled his eyes and smirked. "What went down between you two, anyway?" He crossed his ankles as if settling in for the long haul.

James knew Juliana had disappeared without a trace, but not the events leading up to it. Alex couldn't hold out any longer. He owed his friend the story.

He leaned his head against the chair-back and exhaled heavily. "Andrea and I switched schools senior year, and we hooked up with Juliana right off the bat. You already know that everyone treated us like white trash. They ostracized Juliana because they thought she was a witch. So we hit it off perfectly." Alex's scar throbbed miserably. "Fast-forward to senior prom. By that time, we planned to spend our lives together."

"She's hot." James gave him a mock leer. "I can see why you'd want to bag her."

"Wasn't like that." Alex frowned as he toyed with a roll of antacids. "We never even had sex."

James' jaw dropped. "You're kidding me."

A suffocating sensation tightened Alex's throat. He and Juliana had possessed a connection deeper than mere sex.

James laughed. "Went through a lot of shorts, huh?"

"Asshole." Alex threw the roll at James, bouncing it off his shoulder.

James' face grew somber. "Shit, man. I'm sorry."

"How do you think I felt? We were in love, then out of the blue, she splits on me, no explanation, no nothing," Alex continued in a gruff voice. "A couple nights before prom, she had a premonition my car would be involved in an accident on prom night. She convinced me to rent a limo."

"The accident that left Andrea in a coma?" James' back went rigid.

Alex nodded. The horrible memories rushed back. "After we left the prom, we drove around in the limo. The next thing I knew, Juliana was screaming at me that Johnny and Andrea just passed us in his truck and we had to stop them. She was incoherent, saying the dream was wrong." Alex gave in to the incessant itching and massaged his scar. "We caught up to them, yelled at them to stop. But Johnny blew through a red light. A semi slammed them cross-traffic. It killed Johnny instantly and left Andrea in a coma, with cracked ribs and a broken leg." Alex swallowed hard. "They were both drunk."

"Damn." James shook his head. "Why did Juliana split?"

"The million dollar question." Alex drew a ragged breath. "Johnny's dead, Andrea's in intensive care, and Juliana's father snags her from the emergency room. The last time I saw her was at Johnny's funeral. She didn't say a word to me.

"She never returned to the hospital to visit Andrea. Then she was gone. I called and went to her home a hundred times, but her father told me she didn't want to see me anymore." A vein pulsed in his forehead in sync with his throbbing scar.

"Her father was an asshole, over-controlling and over-protective, big bad CEO of a major high-tech corporation. He hated me for no good reason." Alex had been forbidden fruit to Juliana, but it hadn't stopped them from falling in love. "Her mom died from cancer when she was ten; Juliana was all he had left."

"You have no clue what happened?" James gulped his coffee.

Alex shook his head. "She never once tried to contact me after she disappeared."

The room quieted as their gazes met, flickered, and dropped.

James slashed the silence with his words. "We'll have to keep on Grantham and Samantha like flies on a dead man. And Juliana's gonna sit in on every interview."

Glad to bury the past, Alex replied, "Track down Sharon and Matthew Douglas and Jasmine ASAP. Who else should Juliana meet?" He was relying on James to keep the facts straight and the ball in play. He didn't have the mental capacity or the time for the mountain-load of paperwork and details. Not for this case.

"Bremley." James shrugged. "We've got pictures of people who've connected with Lisette. I want Juliana to look at them." James threw an envelope on the desk and thumbed on his tablet.

"The footprint in the garden was on the approach to the window. Forensics estimates it was made between two and four A.M. The perp weighs one-eighty-five to two hundred pounds."

Alex tried to concentrate on James' words, but concern for Lisette scraped him raw, leaving little room for comprehension. "What else?"

James swiped through his notes. "No discernable prints on the keychain."

"Wonderful." Alex slammed his fist on the desk.

A quick rap on the door interrupted them. The door slid open and Alex glared at the intruder, swearing under his breath.

Chad Shelby lounged against the doorframe, a brown envelope clutched in his hand. The wiry man's close-cropped blonde hair and an evil smirk accentuated his thin, bronze face.

"What the hell do you want?" Alex settled back in his chair, his scar now twitching uncontrollably.

"Thought I'd see how a *homicide* detective solves a missing person's case."

"Get out, Shelby." Disgust charged James' voice.

"Surely, you're not afraid of IA breathing down your back?" Shelby snickered, a sound not unlike a Chihuahua sneezing.

"Did I forget to cross a 't' somewhere?" Alex didn't turn a hair.

"Something far better. Here's my report on the Rodriguez bust. Originals are filed with HQ." Shelby tossed the sealed envelope on Alex's desk.

Alex pulled a crumpled dollar bill from his slacks, unfolding it with slow deliberation. He extended it toward Shelby. "Thanks for the delivery, mail boy."

Shelby's cloudy gray eyes blazed angrily. "MacKenzie, you'll get yours someday." The ubiquitous threat rolled off Shelby's tongue, and Alex mentally filed it away with all the others—in file number thirteen.

"Just like you did?" James threw in, sly menace in his voice. "Hit the road and let the real cops fight crime."

Another smirk twisted Shelby's compressed lips. He straightened against the doorframe, crossing his arms over his lean chest. "How's your niece, MacKenzie?"

"Get the hell out before I kick your ass to China." Alex's self-control teetered on a jagged edge.

The asshole's smile widened as he pivoted in the doorway and disappeared down the corridor.

Alex called out, "Hey Shelby, what's your shoe size?"

James stretched behind him and shut the door, cutting off Shelby's response. "That idiot's eleven bottles short of a twelver."

"You think?" Alex's fury simmered and he quickly put a lid on it. He flexed his hands, as if readying himself for battle. "Do we still have a tag on him?"

"Yeah, man." James rose, then stiff as a board dropped back into his seat. "No unusual activity."

Alex gave him a double-look. Something was up. "Problem?"

"We're gonna get major flack if Hayes or IA finds out we're tailing him without authority."

"That's the least of my worries. I'll take full responsibility. Find out his shoe size."

"You're serious?"

"He has motive."

"No opportunity. He didn't befriend Lisette."

"James, don't go stupid on me." Alex stood and paced to the filing cabinet. One of Lisette's drawings of his house fell from the wall, and he bent to pick it up. He ran his finger lightly over her signature and tacked the picture on the wall. He turned around and stared his friend down.

"What are you talking about?"

"Andrea dated him a couple of months ago," Alex replied.

"She what?" James' eyes widened, his fists clenched.

"Guess you didn't know." Alex's shoulders lifted, fell. "My quirky sister and Lisette met him at the department picnic in June. The one you missed because you were dealing with your ex-wife." Alex gave his bud a pointed stare. "He didn't reveal his true identity to her. I didn't find out about it until afterward."

"You told her who he was and she broke it off, right?" James' cool voice belied the anger that seethed on his mottled face.

"I didn't have to. She figured it out after a couple of dates."

"Lisette never got friendly with him, did she?"

"How the hell do I know? She loves everyone." Alex slammed a fist into his open palm. The pain did little to relieve the ravaging ache in his gut and heart.

CHAPTER TWELVE

Juliana's afternoon was as quiet and peaceful as the clear cerulean sky. She used the opportunity to unpack moving boxes stacked in her garage. The task provided her mind a welcome breather from dwelling on Alex and Lisette. Until Alex called for further assistance or she experienced another dream, she could do little to help.

Dismayed, she frowned at the boxes as endless as an ant trail. Where had she put all this stuff in her New York loft? To top it all, she still needed to sort through a storage unit full of her mother's belongings—all she wanted from her father's house except for her own childhood mementos. She'd kept few reminders of her father. He'd been dead to her for years.

His death six months ago had been her catalyst to return to San Jose. The only thing left to handle was his substantial estate. Thankfully, the lawyers managed the probate matters, leaving a stack of papers to sign that made the Library of Congress look small.

Done-in after unpacking and organizing for hours, Juliana sat down at the kitchen table to eat a late dinner of leftover pizza. She worked on investment proposals for her newest clients in preparation for next week. An irritated grunt escaped her when she looked at her research on Altz Corporation.

"Hastings better have a solid lead on the company or he'll lose every dime if he doesn't heed my advice," she muttered. He might as well throw the cash out a high-rise window downtown. The street bums would get better use of the dough.

She was deep into analyzing Altz's financials when the doorbell chimed. Startled, she jostled the hardcopy file off the table. Loose pages spilled across the tile floor. "Dang it." She glanced at her watch. Eleven P.M.?

The habit of living alone in New York forced her to grab her phone before heading to the front door. She poised an index finger on the emergency button.

When she glimpsed the familiar rugged profile through the peephole, her eyes widened. "Alex?"

"Yeah." His unforgettable voice was tired and flat.

"What's up?" Juliana twisted the stiff deadbolt, but it didn't budge. *Why do I bother?* She glowered at the lock, yanked again, and it clicked open.

"I was in the neighborhood, saw your lights on." He craned his neck to peek around her. "You could light up a city block with the power you're burning."

In the neighborhood. Right. "I like light." Stepping aside, she let him into the foyer. "It keeps me company."

Alex's dark eyebrows peaked and a smile tugged at his full, sensuous mouth, causing her heart to flip-flop.

Juliana closed the door, leaving the deadbolt unlocked. "Why are you really here? Arresting me for exceeding my electricity quota?"

"I promised to look at your porch light and deadbolt." His eyes probed hers, gripped, and reached into her core. She forced herself to look away before she drowned in the twin blue lakes.

"It's a little late." Juliana stepped away from him and set the phone on the bombe chest. She ignored her fluttering heartbeat.

"You're awake. I'm awake." He shrugged his shoulders in a leisurely manner.

"You shouldn't be. Go home, get some sleep."

Alex scrubbed his scalp. "Sleep? Never heard of it."

Juliana loved to see his fingers tease his thick hair and the fluctuating effect. She longed to sink her own hands into his dark hair, to feel the satin softness she'd once loved touching. Her hands nearly lifted of their own accord. *Stop,* her mind howled, and she locked her arms to her side.

"Go keep Andrea company."

"James is with her." He scrubbed his face and sighed. "I can't face her right now."

Juliana nodded slowly. Until he had concrete news to report to his bereft sister, she could only imagine that bearing witness to Andrea's grief was excruciating.

Her curiosity piqued, she changed the subject to one she hoped was less distressing. "What's the relationship between you and James?"

"We were recruited at the same time and were partners until I made Lieutenant in January." Alex crossed his arms over his chest and leaned against the kitchen archway. "He's roomed with me since his divorce. It was supposed to be temporary, but it's been eleven months. Now," he laughed dryly, "he's hot for my sister."

Surprised by his cool admission, she asked, "You okay with that?"

"He's my best friend. There's no one I trust more." An indefinable expression skipped across his face.

"I'm glad. For them." If she couldn't experience blossoming love, at least she could watch it happen from a distance. Juliana brushed past him through the archway, feeling his body heat shoot through her, compounding her newly-minted misery. *Damn it all to hell!*

He followed her into the dining nook. Kneeling to gather the papers strewn across the floor, she felt his eyes scour her.

"Do you always treat your files so well?"

"Only when the doorbell scares the crap out of me."

A few pages rested against the far wall, and Alex bent to retrieve them. "Altz? You're kidding, right?"

Obviously, his own investment knack still shadowed him. "I take my work seriously," she teased with a mock glower.

"Then maybe you ought to quit your day job and become a psychic full-time." He stacked the loose papers on the table and regarded her with wry amusement. "Don't you know what's going on at Altz? The company should never have gone public. They're weak; the stock will never rise."

"It's a solid company. Why shouldn't I invest in it?"

"Gold Maker, huh?" He laughed, shaking his head.

His hearty, unguarded laugh made her heart soar. She so missed his incredible deep, full-bodied laugh and the way it lit up his face.

He flashed that slightly crooked, devastating grin she adored. "Don't tell me you had a vision the company's on a turnaround?"

Her own laughter bubbled out, and she fell back on her butt, fanning her warm face with the retrieved papers. "It's a dog, isn't it? I have a client who thinks he has a crystal ball." Juliana hesitated. She'd convinced herself earlier in the day that she wouldn't allow her heart to intimidate her mind where it concerned Alex. "You've kept up with the investing world?" she asked tentatively, forcing her heart to shut up.

They'd finished first in a high school investment contest together. Their plans following graduation had been to earn their finance degrees, hers at Stanford and his at San Jose State, where he'd won an athletic scholarship. They'd planned to work at a brokerage firm together for the experience, then eventually start their own company.

Foolish dreams. *Damn you, Dad! I hex you, Westwood curse.*

He moved closer, towering above her. "I follow the market. Made enough to buy a decent house when the housing market took a dump."

"Good for you." She accepted his extended hand, and electricity zinged up her arm and down her back. He nearly pulled her into his arms.

Their fingers twined and he looked down at her, his eyes smoldering. "I'm glad you followed your dream," he said, his voice like a sultry breeze. He caressed her cheek, leaving her knees shaky, her heart defying her mind.

She reached up to stroke his face, but he gently caught her wrist in his large hand. He bent his head, and she sucked in her breath when his lips brushed her palm so provocatively, her entire body trembled. She would have melted to the floor if he wasn't holding her up.

"Alex, please." The whispered words escaped. Her mind screamed at her to run for the hills, while her heart told her to cave in.

As well as she knew it was dark outside, she knew she'd never stopped loving Alex. The realization slammed her hard, and her heart jolted against her chest. She pulled free and backed away from him. Crescent fingernail holes in the papers she clutched diverted her attention as she smoothed them out.

Alex cleared his throat, edging past her. The sexual tension followed him to the foyer as if handcuffed to him. She battled to keep her feet rooted to the floor, not follow him and jump him on the spot.

"Call me if you need help." Her emotions roared inside

with no door, no window, no outlet. Whipping her emotions in line, she focused on arranging her files into a semblance of order.

A few minutes later, Alex called to her. "Jewel, come here."

There he goes with that nickname again. The memories the name summoned disconcerted her. She loved hearing him call her Jewel *too* much.

She slid past him and stood in front of the door. He moved so close, the heat emanating from his muscular body burned into her already boiling core.

Inching the door shut, he showed her how the lock didn't line up with the doorjamb. "That's your problem."

Her eyes absorbed the misalignment. "I suppose the builder will have to fix it?" She looked up into Alex's face. Eyes hooded, he was all business again. A silent cry of relief blared inside her head.

"More than I can handle tonight. You should get it fixed before it gets worse. It's easier to lock if you lift up on the door." His demonstration looked effortless with his strength. "You try."

He stepped back, and they deliberately avoided touching each other. But the air sizzled around them, along her bare skin.

Following his example, she found less pressure on the lock. "I can deal with it until it's fixed."

With a familiarity of long-time friends, they began diagnosing the porch light. Juliana held a flashlight to illuminate the dead lamp while Alex dismantled it.

Curiosity about his past torched a hole in her brain, and he seemed open to conversation. She couldn't forego her first chance to grill him. "Alex, did you ever marry?" Her throat held her breath hostage.

"What?" The muscles of his extended arms tightened.

A screw dropped to the porch and pinged down the

steps, landing among the multi-colored petunias and lilies.

"Just making small talk." She swallowed the stagnant air in her throat. "Do you mind?"

Alex handed the glass lamp globe to Juliana. "Only if I can ask the same."

"Deal."

"No. Never been married."

"Anyone serious?" She set the lampshade on the porch and illuminated the guts of the porch light.

"No."

The flashlight silhouetted his profile, and Juliana couldn't see his expression. "Why not?"

"Because no one—" He paused, as though to say something else, then appeared to change his mind. "Because cops and wives don't mix."

"Oh." She sensed what he wanted to say, but shied away from that dangerous line of questioning.

"My turn." Alex dangled the light's electrical wires, his eyes fixed on the repair job.

She made it easy on him. "No, I've never been married, and no, there's no one serious." The wistfulness in her heart steered clear of the words that slipped from her mouth.

"Why not?" Intense skepticism marked his expression as he glanced down at her.

"Because psychics and husbands don't mix."

Wariness registered on Alex's face, as if he expected a seasoned liar's lamest excuse.

It's now or never. Juliana took a deep breath, inhaling Alex's familiar musky scent. She lowered her arm to her side, the light beam bouncing off the slate landing. Alex ceased working, and his eyes probed for hers from the dark porch.

"I didn't leave you of my own free will." Air became

thin and her heart beat wildly. "My father had me committed." Her voice sounded strangled to her ears.

But she clearly heard Alex's sharp intake of breath. "What the hell?" The screwdriver clanged on the porch and followed the screw into the flowerbed. He advanced toward her as if in slow motion.

A tremor rolled through her from the horrible memories. She dropped the flashlight on the slate tiles and it landed with a crunch. The beam died, giving way to the darkness. Nothing prepared her for actually uttering the truth to Alex in person. The impact and release were so great, her knees buckled.

In a blur, Alex caught her to him, and her arms wound around his neck of their own volition. She clung to him while he carried her to the couch in her family room. He sank into the thick cushions and cradled her on his lap.

"Jewel?" Alex tenderly swept loose hair off her face.

Gazing into his eyes, she recognized pain—and guilt. "Alex, let me up, please." Instead, he cuddled her closer and she let it slide. Bound by his arms and his heat, sitting on his lap felt exquisite.

"Look at me." He tilted her chin up, forcing her gaze to latch with his. "Your father did what?" His voice faltered.

"You heard me correctly," she whispered.

"What the hell do you mean he had you committed?" Alex's steely arms stiffened around her.

Face flushed hot, Juliana's heart beat as rapidly as a jackhammer. The day of reckoning had arrived. One, two, three . . . The calming count to ten was maddening.

"Answer me," Alex demanded through clenched teeth.

A blade of snow defined his scar. With a tentative finger, Juliana traced it, gaining strength from the pulsing edge. He dropped his fingers from her chin and twined them tightly with hers.

She exhaled, then seized a deep breath. "My father

had doctors shoot me up with sedatives after the prom night accident until he shipped me off to New York." She nestled their threaded hands on her lap, giving a gentle squeeze. "Our housekeeper helped sneak me out of the house between doses so I could go to Johnny's funeral."

"That son of a bitch," he growled. "Shit. Did the tranquilizers start your telepathy?"

"No. The shock of witnessing the accident did."

"Where did he send you?" A vein in his neck jerked in sync with his twitching scar.

"To the Paranormal Scientific Institute of New York, where he had me legally committed. Half the time I didn't know who I was, for almost a year." Alex knew what her father had been capable of doing. However, he might not understand about the years after she broke contact with her father.

He slid her off his lap and set her gently on the couch. She curled her legs underneath her in a tight ball. The loss of his touch and warmth hit her with a resounding blow. She hated deriving such comfort from him—a temporary need that would disappear with the tides.

But would it? Did she really want it to?

He stalked the large, nearly empty family room, pacing back and forth, his face as expressionless as the bare white walls. Juliana waited for him to say something. Anything.

Finally, he said in a strained voice, "I always had a feeling that that bastard was responsible."

She sensed he wasn't being completely truthful. "Did you think otherwise?"

Guilt wove lines across his forehead. "I need a drink."

Juliana started to rise from the couch, but Alex held up a forestalling hand.

He left the room and returned a few minutes later with a freshly opened bottle of wine and two wineglasses.

"Do me a favor and buy some beer. This stuff puts me to sleep."

Her eyebrows arched. "You plan on visiting often?"

Alex poured the wine, and she took a full glass, taking a large swig of courage.

Rigid, he sat in the recliner across from her. "Tell me what happened. All of it." He gripped the stem of his wineglass, engulfing the fragile crystal in his curled hand.

"I misinterpreted my dream about prom night, and you saw what happened." She peered at him through the rosy liquid in her glass. "After the accident, I freaked.

"My father decided he couldn't stand to watch my life deteriorate like all the other Westwood women. He thought it was the beginning of the end for me. Had me convinced it was." Juliana swirled the wine in her glass and then propped it on the couch arm. "He watched his own mother go crazy and commit suicide. His grandmother was diagnosed insane and was committed. All the other Westwood women—all psychics—suffered similar fates."

A tangible hush descended. Alex frowned into his wineglass, seeming to digest her words.

The Westwood women all possessed ESP, and none of them had been lucky at love. She saw a similar fate for herself—the biggest bane of her existence.

"Westwood?" Alex raised an eyebrow in a questioning slant. "Why did they all have the Westwood name? Didn't any ever marry?"

"What does that tell you?" She threw him a tight smile. "Few married. My father's mother bore him out of wedlock. She knew life was better off alone, without putting a husband through the paces of living with a loony-tune."

"You're not crazy," he said softly.

"Not yet." Her eyes misted.

"Never."

The conviction and tenderness in his voice ignited hope in her heart. Her family heritage and a lifetime of believing the worst were hard to overcome. She'd been on the edge of insanity several times before Dr. Miller taught her how to control her telepathy.

She blinked back the tears in the corners of her eyes. "My father didn't want the same to happen to me. Or if he couldn't stop my life from a psychic meltdown, he didn't want to be around to witness it. He made arrangements to send me to the Institute for observation and training."

Alex's eyes blazed. Scarlet fury replaced the golden tone of his face. "Fucking monster."

She shrugged. "He figured he was protecting me from losing my mind. The prom night trauma caused latent telepathic ability to surface at the funeral. I thought I *was* going bonkers." She coughed to clear the sadness from her throat. "You have no clue how horrible it was to suddenly start hearing the thoughts of everyone around me. For a while, I welcomed the drugs."

"Why didn't you talk to me at the funeral instead of running away?" He couldn't cloak the sorrow and remorse in his voice. He stood and resumed his pacing with steps determined to beat a path through her new carpet.

"I was scared, confused, half out of it." A tear escaped, and she wiped the back of her hand across her face. "Your thoughts frightened me." *And broke my heart.* "You were angry, you blamed me for Johnny's death. And the hatred—"

In a blur, Alex knelt in front of her. He lifted her chin with light fingers. She wanted to kiss away the agony on his face. His musk and spice cologne smelled heavenly and warmed the hollow places the wine didn't reach.

"I was angry, confused, and hated what happened. But it wasn't directed at you." His gaze softened. "How could you even think that?"

"You hated who I was. You were angry at me because of it."

He released her chin and scoured his face with both hands as if he could erase the past with the motion. "I hated the fact that you were Daniel Westwood's daughter. I was pissed off because you had such awesome talents, yet you couldn't prevent the accident. The thoughts were stupid, but they didn't change what I felt for you."

Juliana circled the rim of her glass with her index finger. "Well, that's beside the point now."

"Jewel, you have to believe me. I never meant to hurt you. I was devastated, then you disappeared." He gained his feet and continued stalking the room.

"I believe you," she said softly.

"Thanks." His face eased, alleviating the guilt and anguish. He exhaled a frustrated groan. "What happened next?"

"I spent a year at the Institute, a human pincushion, while they turned me into a druggie. I was an anomaly. Research reports were produced by the dozens." She sipped her wine. The fruity Zinfandel tickled her nose as she leaned her head back and stared at the ceiling. "They'd never seen anyone with the depth of psychic talents I exhibited." She snorted.

"A year went by. Dr. Brian Miller arrived and took over as the research director. He stopped the drugs and experiments." Juliana lowered her head. "He told them that *they* would drive me crazy at the rate they were going." She sipped her wine, swishing the liquid in the glass.

"Miller obtained a court order releasing my father as guardian, lifting the commitment papers. He and I worked to control my visions and interpret them better. He taught me how to block telepathic thoughts." Juliana sighed. "He gave me my life back. I owe him so much."

Alex halted in front of her. The disbelief in his eyes launched waves of compassion through her. Juliana couldn't begin to imagine what he'd endured, wondering about her. She wished she'd had the guts to contact him sooner, to allay his concerns, if nothing else. She grew languid from the wine. Alex backed away and slouched in the recliner, incredulity painting his face.

She was glad for the distance between them; the fury and shock rolling off him unnerved her. "My father was angry, since he loved to control every facet of my life. But we came to an agreement. He agreed to pay for my college and housing if I stayed in New York, got my degree at NYU, and continued training with Dr. Miller. After what I suffered, his offer was a gift from God."

"Why didn't you contact me at that point?"

She spread her hands, shrugged. "Alex, I was a basket case. All I wanted was to concentrate on college, Dr. Miller's therapy, and regaining my life. Another year raced by, and life got easier to manage." Juliana unfurled her cramped legs and leaned into the couch arm. "Then one night I dreamt about a child being abducted. When I read about it in the paper, I contacted the police, and that's when I began working with them.

"I found a great job at a top financial firm on Wall Street. By that time, my father stayed completely out of my life." She drained the last of her wine. The alcohol created a slow throb in her head, and she rubbed her temples. "I was making money right and left for my clients, and assisting the police. Before I could blink, twelve years had gone by and I received word my father had suffered a massive coronary and was dead."

It relieved her to know her father no longer controlled her life. But knowing he had died without ever patching the wall between them still hurt like a flaming arrow in her heart.

"Was I just a blip on your radar?" Alex asked with weary cynicism. He leaned forward, snatched the wine bottle off the coffee table, and topped off his glass. He held the bottle toward her, and Juliana shook her head.

"You've seen up close who and what I am. Can you honestly say you could've handled it, or handled me, for that matter?"

Alex glowered. "You never gave me the chance."

"Not a day goes by that I don't think about you." Juliana inhaled the mild fruity bouquet wafting from her wineglass. "I thought it best, considering we had no future. I knew I'd only hurt you again."

Alex scratched his scar and leaned forward, elbows on his knees. "Why did you come back?"

Juliana noticed a flicker of movement on the patio. "My father was gone. It was safe. And I missed California." She set her wineglass on the marble table and rose from the couch. "I was tired of New York. And Dr. Miller retired last year to Oregon, so he's closer."

Juliana moved to the French doors, looking out into the inky blackness. She caught a shimmer of black on black. Her cat, JB, was stalking the little creatures of the night.

"Didn't you think you might run into me?"

"Eventually." She watched Alex's reflection in the glass. Tugging on her braid, she worried the thick plait between her fingers. "I wanted to contact you, but only if you were receptive. I didn't want to interfere with your life. I even put together a package for you once."

Abruptly, she sprinted past him and ran to her office. Centered on her desk lay the sealed envelope she sought. She returned to the family room and handed him the brown padded envelope. Curiosity whisked across his face.

"I tried to mail it a few years ago and chickened out

after the postal clerk put the postage on."

With a reverent touch, Alex held the envelope, but didn't lift a finger to open it.

"It's full of research reports and a book Dr. Miller wrote."

"Dr. Miller again?" Jealousy narrowed Alex's eyes.

She suppressed a smile. "He was more of a father to me than my own." His eyes softened at her words. "We still have phone consults as needed. He's been wonderful."

"I'm glad you had someone to rely on."

A fractured silence descended upon the room, and Juliana grew uncomfortable under Alex's steady gaze.

He drained his second glass of wine and set the crystal flute on the end table. Tipping his head back, he closed his eyes. "I could have helped you."

"No, you couldn't, Alex." She slipped to the floor at his feet. As soon as she propped her chin on his knee, his hand slipped under her braid, stroking her neck.

His tender touch comforted her. Unsettled her. She didn't want his fingers to stop the dance upon her skin.

"How would you feel being around someone who could read your every thought? Or live with someone who could freak out on you one day?" She pressed into his hand warming her neck. "I couldn't put you through it. There was no future for us." She whispered the last words.

That awkward fractured silence swathed them as the night wore on. Her muscles relaxed from the wine, from Alex's closeness. The caresses on her neck stilled and his hand rested on her shoulder. Tension eased down his arms, loosening the knots of his muscles.

"Did I ever tell you I'm sorry your father's dead?" Alex's mellow voice pierced the exhaustion settling over Juliana.

"No," she murmured drowsily.

"Good."

CHAPTER THIRTEEN

Alex awoke disoriented, his neck stiff from sleeping upright. He felt pressure on his knee and peered through slit eyes at Juliana's head resting there, his grip locked on her braid. The horrible truth she'd revealed last night felt like an anvil on his heart. He'd never imagined anything like that happening to her. He fingered her hair, reveling in the silky strands.

A faint scratching sound in the backyard prickled his senses, and he realized the front door was still unlocked. The lights in the house blazed as dawn's gray glow leaked through the glass doors.

He swept Juliana into his arms. Her head lolled on his shoulder and her arms encircled his neck. Desire coursed through him, and he was acutely conscious of her soft perfumed flesh touching his arms.

"Alex?" she mumbled.

"Taking you to bed," he whispered and planted a light kiss on her temple.

"Ummm, bed? Sleep is good," she murmured.

Her heartbeat synced with his. The unshakable sensation that they were two halves of a whole filled him with such a longing he almost dropped her from the impact.

Straightening his spine, he carried her up the stairs and through the double doors off the landing. He fought his way through layers of what looked like mosquito netting surrounding the bed. Tenderly, he laid her on the mattress. The box springs were stiff, silent, and Juliana slept on. Caressing her cheek, he touched her lips with his thumb before he moved away.

Trudging downstairs, he secured the house and stretched out on the couch in the family room. Staring up at the vaulted ceiling, remorse hung over him like a thundercloud. He'd spent too many wasted years imagining the worst. Despite the pain her disappearance had caused, he wanted her more than ever. That realization struck him harder than the blow her reappearance had caused him. No woman had ever replaced her in his heart because Juliana had never left it. She would always sit firmly under his skin, in his soul.

Alex ached to touch her with a ferocity that terrified him. He couldn't deny he was helplessly in love with her. Always had been, always would be.

Minutes ticked by, and he knew sleep wouldn't claim him again. He flexed his stiff muscles, and found his way into the kitchen for coffee. Waiting for the coffee to perk, he peeked inside the cupboards and drawers, frowning at the emptiness. Dishes and glasses were stacked neatly, the counters uncluttered and spotless. Frozen dinners crammed her freezer, a few canned goods in her pantry.

Final coffeemaker rumblings drew his attention back to his task. With a large cup of instant breakfast, he returned to the family room. Spying the discarded envelope, he set his cup on the table and snatched up the package. He returned to the recliner and pried open the seal on the envelope, sliding the contents onto his lap.

A hardback book caught his eye first, and he scanned the back cover description. The book was a compendium chronicling research conducted on several ESP subjects. Juliana's doctor, Brian Miller, M.D. and Ph.D., had authored it. He opened the front cover, eyes drawn to a handwritten note half obscured by the jacket flap. His heart galloped as if after a vigorous gym workout. Juliana had inscribed the book to him, dated three years ago.

Alex drank a large swig of courage, gripping the cup. He dared himself to read the meticulous script.

> Alex,
>
> I have always loved you and will continue to love you until the day I die. My life was never completely mine to lead. But what part I controlled, I want you to know everything I did, I did for you. To protect you and allow you the life you deserve.
>
> I hope you can forgive me someday.
>
> Forever,
>
> Your Jewel

His hand tightened around the mug, sloshing coffee over the rim, burning his hand. Ignoring the sting, he muttered, "Damn."

They could have salvaged the lost years. If only he'd known. If only Juliana had accepted the fact that he would never leave her, no matter what she believed about that damn Westwood family curse.

Fingers twitchy, he skimmed through the scientific mumbo-jumbo and honed in on the sections about Leigh

Duncan. He no longer needed to be convinced of her capabilities, nor how she'd suffered over the years. The evidence shouted at him in black and white.

A rage burned low in his gut as he contemplated her bastard of a father, and how those quack doctors had violated her under the pretext of science. Alex slammed the publications down on the coffee table, the urge to set fire to them strong. He desperately needed to feast his eyes upon Juliana. The moment he stood upright, a scream pierced the early hush of dawn. He clanked his coffee cup down onto the marble table.

"Alex! Nooo!"

His heart clenched as he raced up the stairs and stormed into the master bedroom. He attempted to slice an opening in the netting around her bed, but it was useless. He tore the ring from the ceiling and tossed the endless, flowing material across the room.

Juliana's face was pasty, her breathing labored. She shuddered forcefully enough to jiggle the king-sized bed. Calling her name, he gripped her shoulders. Her eyes flew open, and a tear spilled from the corner of one.

"Sweetheart," Alex murmured. He stretched full-length on the bed and gathered her in his arms.

"Alex? What are you doing here?" She tried to push him away, confusion and fear in her foggy gaze.

"We fell asleep last night."

Her struggles ceased as she grasped his words. "You carried me up here. Then you were gone."

"Slept on the couch."

"Sorry I woke you."

"Fat chance." He smiled as she lifted her gaze to his. "The wine put me to sleep, but it didn't keep me there."

She caressed his chin, her fingers rasping over his stubble. "You look tired."

"Was it bad?" Fear and hope fought for equal footing

in his heart. "Another vision?"

"Just an old-fashioned nightmare," she said. He gained strength from her stroking his face as color returned to her own.

"I guess talking about the past gave free reign to my recurring nightmare."

Her trembling subsided, and he savored the feel of her body against his, wanting never to let her go again.

"You called my name." He tightened his arms around her.

"The nightmare was about you." Heat radiated from her palm on his chest.

"Tell me."

She sighed quietly. "I've had the nightmare off and on since the prom night accident. Not only was Johnny killed, but you and Andrea died, hit by the same truck."

Alex winced. "Not a premonition, I hope."

"No!" Juliana shivered. "Doc Brian said it was my way of grieving over losing you when I left."

He smiled at her. "You haven't, you know."

Her warm, soft body tensed against him. Warily, she asked, "Haven't what?"

"Lost me."

She started to pull away, but he held tight. "Alex," she pleaded. "Please."

"Stay with me a few minutes."

Her resistance ceased, but she remained wrought-iron stiff in his arms. "What'd you do to my bed scarves?"

"What's up with that mosquito netting?"

"The *scarves* are—were—my safety net." A hard edge darkened her green eyes.

He couldn't help but chuckle. "Let me get this straight. Lights keep you company and gauze makes you feel safe. How about a Rottweiler and a nine-millimeter?"

"Ha ha ha," she mocked. "That's not what I meant. A

gun and a big dog won't chase away the demons in my mind."

Alex became all too aware of what stupid felt like. "Sorry." He rubbed her bare arm, loving the velvety feel of her skin under his hand. "I wasn't thinking."

She placed a finger over his mouth. "No one could know what it's like."

The barest hint of her evocative touch turned him on, and Alex shifted to hide the stiffness in his groin.

"You haven't lost me, you know." He brought the paramount subject back around. "You only misplaced me." He grinned.

A heavy sigh escaped her, and her breasts rubbed against his chest. His erection bulged and begged for release. *Maybe this wasn't such a good idea.* He pulled away a fraction, but not enough to tease her into thinking he'd release her.

He drew in the scent of heaven—sweet, flowery. The same perfume he'd bought her on her eighteenth birthday. It was all she'd ever worn when they were together.

"I thought I'd come back and find you a stockbroker, married, three kids." She rested her cheek against his chest. "We'd put the past behind us and move on with our separate lives."

"It didn't happen that way."

"That's what terrifies me." Her breath seared his skin through his shirt. "You know who I am and what I can do. Can you honestly say you're comfortable around me, knowing I can read your mind?" She drew imaginary pictures on his chest. "Or see me go from an independent, self-reliant financial planner one minute, to gelatin the next time a vision hits? I'm a freak of nature."

None of that mattered to him, yet she wouldn't believe him any sooner than she'd believe a psychopathic liar.

"You can be my little freak," he chided, kissing her head.

"Alex." She slapped his arm in frustration.

"Can we take it one day at a time?" The pained lines fanning her eyes were excruciating to behold. He squeezed her tightly, as if to bind her flesh to his.

"No promises?" Apprehension laced her voice. "No regrets?"

"Deal." He kissed her head again, her silken hair tickling his lips. "How 'bout another hour of sleep?"

A smile curved her lush lips. "Like this?"

"Like this."

Juliana wrapped her arms around his shoulders and pressed her cheek to his chest. Her warm breath fueled the bonfire that had been buried far too long.

No promises, no regrets. *Like hell.*

Too many past losses gave rise to a huge void of love, trust, or reliance on anyone except Andrea, Lisette, and James. His father had left when he and Andrea were five, never seen nor heard from again. His mother remarried a man Alex adored, who then divorced his mother when Alex and Andrea were fifteen. Never seen nor heard from again.

Then Juliana disappeared.

By the time his mother had died from breast cancer days before he entered the police academy, he was afraid to love anyone. Afraid to become intimate with another woman.

Juliana was the first loved one to return.

Those threads of life that had bound them from the day they'd first met were twining back together, tugging on the connection deep inside him. Juliana was his soul mate—he'd always known that. The bindings holding them as one would never break, no matter where she was or with whom. He'd draw his last breath before he let her go again.

CHAPTER FOURTEEN

An annoying ringing noise blasted in Juliana's ear, her mind straining to grasp the sound. Her limbs were languorous, unmovable. The bed shook and she realized why she couldn't move. Her eyes flew open and she stared into Alex's startled face.

He whipped his wrist around to look at his watch. "Shit. It's almost nine."

They disentangled from each other as if the bed were on fire. She snatched her cordless phone off the night table and fumbled with the *on* button.

Alex scrambled out of bed. His eyes sparkled from the sunlight streaming through the windows and other things she could only imagine. He perused her as if they'd done more than snuggle. The awakening left a flush blanketing her more fully than her clothing.

Juliana breathed out, "Hello."

"James O'Malley."

"Hey, James."

"Have you seen Alex?" James asked, frustration dripping from his voice.

"He's here." She handed the phone to Alex, crawled out of bed, and ran downstairs.

When she entered the kitchen, she noticed Alex had

already brewed a pot of coffee. But the auto-shutoff had activated and the coffee was tepid. Nervous, confused, her hands shook as she prepared a fresh batch of her morning drug of choice.

Juliana returned to her bedroom as Alex replaced the cordless on the night table. "What's up?"

"Douglases are on the run." His gaze crawled over her wrinkled appearance. "James is getting a search warrant. We'll meet him in an hour."

"How do you know they're on the run?" Juliana crossed the room and began straightening the bed covers.

"Their condo's staked out." Alex reached over to help her with the comforter, but she shooed him away. "No one's seen them since Friday morning."

She squinted at him sideways, brows arched.

"Jasmine came home earlier. We'll pay her a visit." Alex's hungry eyes continued to devour her every movement. "Then we'll track down Chamber. You'll have to shelve your tea party with Andrea."

She had planned to spend the afternoon with Andrea and catch up on old times, and keep Andrea's mind off Lisette. "I hope she's not too disappointed." Juliana patted the toss pillows in place.

"You're our link to Lisette. She wants you to do whatever it takes to keep the link."

"I know." Juliana twisted her messy braid, wanting to twist clues into her mind.

An edgy silence ensued. Juliana grew uneasy under Alex's scrutiny and turned away.

His gruff voice yanked her gaze back to his face. "Do you mind if I take a shower? I have my gym bag in my SUV."

Her lips curved. "You can use the shower downstairs."

"Draw me a map?" He gave her an amused grin.

Her fingers twitched to touch his face and smooth

away the worry lines his devastating smile didn't erase.

"Funny." She waved him off. "Bathroom's past my office."

Another vibrant moment followed, two pairs of eyes gripped, neither flinched. Her breaths grew shallow and she tried to relax but her limbs refused to move. She ached to have his arms around her again, to lie in his embrace. Her mind was so congested with doubts and fears, she didn't know which way was up. Despite the mixed bag of emotions, an overwhelming joy danced in her blood.

Alex regarded her intensely for a moment longer, and then strode from the room. Juliana sheathed her inner turmoil and hurried toward her bathroom to soak in an ice-cold shower.

Uncertainty ruled her. That morning was the first time in her life someone was present to alleviate her fears upon waking. She hated to admit her life was lonely, but the alternatives promised little better. She could be with Alex, then eventually drive him away with her psychic craziness. At least she'd get a slice of time with him. Or they could go their separate ways and forever deal with the fact that she allowed him to twine around her soul and steal her heart. Either way she was screwed.

Refreshed from her shower, Juliana crept into her kitchen. Alex leaned against the counter, so sexy, so masculine. He looked fresh, relaxed and smelling amazingly of his musk cologne. Their eyes locked; his spoke of an indefinable emotion, and she wanted to wallow in his being, his presence in her house.

She approached him, impelled by an internal passion that was useless to control. She touched his cheek, his fresh-shaved skin warm to her touch. Blood rushed to her cheeks and she averted her face. She backed up a few steps, but that didn't stop him from following.

"Stop." His voice was husky as he hand-combed her loose hair.

Anticipation zipped up and down her spine. His fingers were still magic. "That's not a good idea."

Alex ignored her and lovingly fingered her hair, drawing strands to his nose and inhaling deeply. "Your hair feels better than I remembered. Don't braid it." A satisfied grin crossed his mouth. He drew away and snagged two cups of steaming coffee off the granite counter. "One teaspoon sugar, dash of cream."

"Do you forget anything?" She returned his adorably shy smile.

Careful not to touch him, she took the hot cup. She was melting, and one touch was all it would take to consume her. He was moving at racecar speed, repairing the wide rift between them, and her defiant body refused to obey her head and slow down.

"Have you seen JB, my black cat, skulking around?" She spread her hands basketball-size, careful not to spill her coffee.

"No." His eyebrows peaked up his forehead. "JB?"

She giggled. "A Christmas present. 'Jingle Bells'." Backing out, she headed toward the family room, Alex close on her heels.

"He's probably on a foray into the great unknown." She shrugged. He had food and water in the garage and a cat door in the kitchen to squeeze through whenever he craved a place to sleep. He was the epitome of a self-sufficient pet. Perfect for her long workdays.

Alex eased a hip on the back of the green floral couch. "If you wanted a huge house, why didn't you just move into your father's place?"

The emotionally charged question was as taut as the currents flowing between them. At least it was easier to talk about her father now.

"I love Mediterranean houses." She blew on her coffee and took a fortifying sip. "After living in oppression for eighteen years under my father's roof, the last thing I wanted was to live with his ghost in that sprawling Tudor." She grimaced wryly. "I needed to spread my wings after years of living in dinky New York apartments and dreary hospital rooms."

His fingers alighted on her arm for just a soothing moment. "Was the Institute that horrible?"

She didn't want his pity. It was easier to tolerate his anger. "It wasn't a home." Juliana picked up the empty wineglasses, gaze drifting to the contents of the envelope spread across the coffee table. He didn't have to tell her he'd read the inscription in the book.

Momentary panic fluttered in her chest before her mind jumped onward. "We'd better hit the road."

"Right." He gathered the publications, shoved them inside the envelope and under his arm.

CRSO

Without knocking, Alex pushed open Andrea's front door. After witnessing his error in judgment, Juliana hid a grin.

James lounged in a recliner near the door, with Andrea nestled on his lap. They jumped apart as if they were teenagers caught in the act.

Alex shot Juliana a meaningful smile and her own widened.

A scowl traversed James' scarlet face. "Where the hell have you been?"

The tables had turned perfectly. A warm flush crept over Juliana's face in remembrance of her morning.

"Taking care of business." Alex's cool dodge brooked no further discussion. "You have the warrant?"

James pulled a crumpled piece of paper from his back

pocket. "Key too."

Alex's eyes widened. "How'd you score that?"

"I watch their place when they go on vacation," Andrea interjected, stepping closer to Alex.

Alex rubbed his sister's back and kissed her cheek. "How are you holding up?"

"I'm okay." Her puffy red eyes refuted her answer.

Juliana crossed the room and gave Andrea a hug.

Alex's questioning gaze met Juliana's own. "Ready?"

"Yes." *About as ready as I'd be facing a murderer.* Her preparation was merely a focused and lucid mind. But this investigation taxed her ESP to new extremes. She didn't know what to expect or how she'd react anymore. She followed his brisk, long-legged steps to the condo next door.

Her pulse accelerated when Alex drew his gun outside the Douglases front door. He projected an energy and power that attracted her beyond reason. *Damn!* Her eyes had never feasted on any NYPD police officers the way they consumed Alex. She wrenched herself away from her ridiculous preoccupation and focused on the task ahead.

Juliana and Andrea waited on the porch while Alex and James entered the residence. A few minutes later, Alex called for them.

The floor plan duplicated Andrea's condominium. The tidy living room overflowed with mismatched furniture and knickknacks. It oozed warmth and a well lived-in charm. Juliana and Andrea went directly to the bedroom that mimicked Lisette's in the floor plan next door.

The stunned expressions on Alex and James' faces mirrored Juliana's shock.

"Oh, God." Andrea's hand flew to her mouth, smothering a sob.

Sharon Douglas had decorated the room for a girl Lisette's age. Toys littered the dresser and wall-shelves.

Clothes of Lisette's size hung in the open closet.

Juliana caught Andrea's hand in her own. Lungs constricting, she looked around in dismay.

James and Alex paced past each other, searching, absorbing. "Did Sharon or Matthew tell you someone was visiting?" Alex asked his twin.

Andrea shook her head. "No, and Sharon usually tells me everything. But she's been evasive lately."

"Adoption? Didn't you say they couldn't have children?"

"Sharon told me the fertility treatments were going well."

"The other day you said she was acting strange." Alex stopped before her, his expression dark.

Titling her head, Andrea said, "Yes, when she mentioned seeing Jasmine and Lisette at the park. She seemed like she wanted to tell me something, but she brushed it off when I asked if everything was okay."

"Bremley was at the park too?"

Andrea frowned and shivered. "Yes. Ugh, he freaks me out. His eyes . . ." Her voice trailed away.

"According to the hospital, they're scheduled for two weeks off." James halted and jangled coins in his pants pocket.

"I didn't know that." Shock registered on Andrea's face. "Sharon would've told me. They would've asked me to watch their place if they'd gone on vacation. They've never been secretive about their plans." Her voice frantic, she clutched Alex's arm. "Could they have taken Lisette?"

"Doesn't make sense," Juliana piped in, perplexed. "They fit up a room, then take off?"

Alex glanced at James. "Did you put out an APB?"

"You bet."

Juliana wandered around the room, picking up a toy here and there. She touched the lavender and white painted furniture and smoothed her hands over the twin bed. A rainbow-colored comforter eerily similar to Lisette's bedding covered the bed. Dancing cartoon animal pictures decorated the walls. The situation was bizarre, but she felt no discomfort, no psychic awareness. Nothing unusual.

Alex and James searched the other rooms, finding no evidence Lisette had ever been there.

They locked up and returned empty-handed to Andrea's place. Alex continued his tense pacing in the living room. "Andrea, why didn't you suspect something odd, even after Lisette told you they had toys and clothes her size?"

"You know Lisette exaggerates." She raised her hands, dropped them. "They're great people, everyone at work loves them."

"Yeah, well, Ted Bundy was a nice guy," Alex snapped before contrition zipped across his face.

"I'm sorry." He reached for his sister, but she backed away and moved into James' outstretched arms.

Andrea's muffled sobs against James' chest deafened the room. James glowered at Alex as he whispered pacifying words to Andrea.

"Let's go." Alex seized Juliana's hand in an unyielding clasp. "We're off to interview Chamber and Jasmine." He kissed Andrea's head. "Sweetie, I'm sorry. I'm such an idiot."

"Just go, Alex," she said dejectedly.

He snatched a tablet and the evidence bag containing the keychain off the coffee table and passed them to Juliana.

CRISO

"Brilliant, maestro," Juliana chirped once seated in his

SUV, driving toward the foothills. "What do you do for an encore?"

"Put a lid on it, will ya?" Alex's tone wasn't as stern as his words made out. "I feel like shit as it is." Stopping at a red light, he punched buttons on the tablet and handed it to her. "Take a look at these photos, see if you recognize anyone."

Silence chilled the interior as she viewed the police snapshots. Only Mrs. Chamber and Jasmine's roommate looked familiar.

Cracker-box houses disappeared as they left the suburbs. The winding, tree-lined road leading toward her father's private estate drew Juliana's gaze. The huge house stood empty, waiting for its new owners to move in, now that it had finally sold.

Alex must have seen her glance up the hill. "Why didn't you go to your father's funeral?"

She contained a shocked gasp. "How did you know I didn't go?"

"The DA mentioned what a huge turnout there was. He said you were noticeably absent."

"Oh." For a second, she'd wondered if Alex were a tad psychic himself. "Do you blame me for not attending?"

"Hell, no." He scowled, jockeying the SUV onto the highway. "If I'd known what he did to you, I'd have gone to make sure the bastard was dead and in the ground."

Juliana wound a strand of hair around her finger. "My father's been dead to me for a long time. When I broke ties with the Institute, he never once tried to contact me. It was if he'd written me out of his life." She gripped the armrest, fighting the loneliness embedded deep in her heart. "He paid my college tuition, established a trust for my living expenses and that's it. After I graduated, I accepted no more from him, even though he kept dumping money in the trust account." She hesitated, sighed. "I saw no sense in reburying a man I'd buried years ago." No love, no trust, no family. All the things she'd missed out on for such a long time.

Alex turned down the street leading to the Chamber estate. "I'm sorry, Jewel. Does it hurt to talk about the last twelve years?"

A bitter laugh edged out. "Oddly enough, telling you makes it seem like someone else's life."

He tossed her a quick smile. "Glad to help. I think."

Juliana laced her hand with his. "You are. Thanks." She gave him a tentative smile, and then turned her head to stare at the redwood and pines littering the verdant foothills, realizing how much she'd missed California redwoods in the cement and steel jungle of New York.

CHAPTER FIFTEEN

That creepy-crawly sensation she'd experienced previously emanated from Bremley again as his dark, unfathomable eyes bore into Juliana. Silent, he escorted them into the colossal study where Grantham Chamber waited behind a mahogany desk fit for a giant.

On the edge of sixty years old, he looked closer to fifty. He sported a full head of salt and pepper hair. He was slender and fit, most likely from days at the country club golf course.

"MacKenzie." Grantham tipped his head before his severe gaze nailed Juliana to the spot.

Her gaze caught his and she blinked briskly. His slate-blue eyes were like glacial ice, memorable in their intensity, yet unknown. She noted his frank and admiring appraisal and defiantly returned his stare.

Alex nudged her elbow. Trapped within her thoughts, she hadn't heard Alex's introduction. She quickly held out her hand. "I'm sorry. Leigh Duncan." Grantham ignored her extended hand, and she quickly dropped her arm and rubbed her palm against her pant leg as if slime coated it.

Nice guy. Little wonder Andrea didn't want her daughter involved with these people.

Alex pulled out a chair for her and whispered, "You

ready?" His breath tickled her ear, his lips so close to kissing her neck before he stepped back.

Despite the frogs croaking in her belly, she nodded. She opened her mind, tuned Alex out with a mental flip of a switch, and changed the channel to Grantham Chamber.

She couldn't have slammed into a granite slab any harder. She consciously switched gears and attempted to read Alex. That time a mountainside hit her. Both minds were impenetrable.

A gasp mounted in Juliana's throat, and she tried to stifle it, but started to choke. The conversation abruptly halted, and both men glared at her.

"I'm sorry," she sputtered. "Can I ask your butler for some water?" To clear her mind, Juliana focused on the leather-bound books crammed in the floor-to-ceiling bookcases behind the desk.

Grantham punched the intercom on his desk phone and barked the request into the speaker. He glared at Juliana as if she harbored a contagious disease.

If Bremley's mind was closed, then her psychic abilities were going haywire. Another milestone in the life of Juliana Westwood. She'd definitely have to squeeze in a sanity-checking call to Doc Brian.

Appearing in the room like a ghost, the butler nudged her shoulder and proffered a bottle of spring water and a glass of ice on a silver tray. Juliana made a show of thanking him in a flirtatious voice. Detaining him further, she asked him to pour the water. He complied with discreet pleasure. Too much pleasure.

She could easily read his mind. The man had the audacity to think she could thank him by kneeling and giving him a kiss. *Of all the freaking nerve.* Indignation fumed inside her.

"A word with you." Alex sent her a measured look. He

gripped her elbow, maneuvering her from the room. The door closed on a seething Grantham and Bremley wringing his hands.

"What's wrong?"

"I can't read him."

"What? I thought—" Alex scratched his scar. "Why not?"

"I'll explain later." Firmly, she clutched his arm and steered him around to the door. "Finish up and ask him if we can inspect the grounds. I want to visit the areas where Lisette's been." She coughed. "Oh, we need to interview Bremley. Ditto Andrea's opinion." A disturbing quake rippled across her shoulders, emphasizing her point.

He moved closer, dropped his voice. "What was all that with Bremley? You probably gave the guy a hard-on."

"I did." She grimaced. "His mind's an open book."

Alex rolled his eyes. "Come on." He playfully slapped her butt.

"Don't write checks your hand can't cash, Lieutenant." She couldn't resist the tease.

"Yeah, well, when the bank's closed, it's a little tough."

On that note, they re-entered the room, and Bremley sauntered out, both heads erect.

Juliana restrained the laughter threatening to erupt. There were some fun and games to reading people's minds. Sometimes.

CR80

Alex pulled out his notepad and pen. At least the old man remembered him. Their one and only previous encounter occurred at Ethan's funeral last year. It was also the first time Lisette had met her paternal grandparents.

"Why do you have visitations with Lisette, now that

her father's dead?"

"Samantha and I don't see her nearly enough."

Grantham's nasally, aristocratic voice grated on the one live nerve left in Alex's body. "Isn't that because you never wanted to see her before Ethan died?"

Grantham scowled. "Her father forbade us to see her."

Alex had anticipated the lie. He scrutinized a photograph of Grantham and Samantha on the desk. They were about twenty years younger. Curiously, he noted the absence of photos of their sons and Lisette. "Did you arrange to have her kidnapped?"

"No."

"Do you know where she is?"

Grantham steepled his fingers under his chin. "Now, if I knew that, don't you think I would've informed the police?"

Alex stood to his full height and stepped behind his chair. "Do you know of anyone who'd kidnap her? To get back at you for some reason?"

"No and no."

A stone from the mansion's walls showed more emotion than the man inside the architectural eyesore.

"Why do you hate Andrea?"

"No offense to you, but the MacKenzies' status is quite beneath the social status of my family." A cruel smile twisted Grantham's lips. He picked up a crystal paperweight, balancing the small pyramid on his palm.

"How did you get along with Ethan?" Alex drummed his pen on the richly padded leather chair, his eyes fixed on Grantham's face, looking for any sign to glom onto.

"He's dead. I don't see how it matters."

"Answer the question." Instincts warned Alex that the old man was hiding something. Probably a lot of somethings.

"We didn't see eye-to-eye on most matters."

"Did you disown him when he married Andrea?"

"You certainly are a smart one, Alexander."

Alex took the response as a yes. "Why do you care about Lisette? Is she a pawn in your game of life?"

"I love my granddaughter. She's all we have left." He said the last words with a small choke.

Amusement flared briefly in Alex. The man could fake a heart attack if he set his mind to it.

"If you care so much for family, why did you cut Ethan out?"

"We would have mended fences in due time." Grantham's face frosted over, lips pinched tight for a moment, eyes sub-zero. "He would have straightened out his act and come crawling back."

"Where's your oldest son, Grantham Chamber, the third?"

"The last I heard, he was living in Monte Carlo, squandering his trust fund." Grantham peered into the paperweight, eyes now flat, bored.

Alex shifted his stance. A renewed urge to flee the stifling house bolted through him, and his gut churned. Grantham was as cold and useless as the paperweight he held. "Have you received a ransom note, phone call, message of any sort?"

Grantham gave Alex a calculated stare. "Don't you think I would have called the police if I had?"

"If Ethan hadn't shot himself up with heroin and cocaine, would you have asked him to divorce Andrea and bring Lisette here to live?"

A sardonic smile played on the jerk's lips. "I see why you made Lieutenant so quickly."

Alex gripped the back of Juliana's chair. Her heady scent renewed his lagging spirits. "If you receive a ransom note or call, or know anything else that may help find your granddaughter, you know how to reach me." Alex tossed a business card on the nearly bare desk.

Bremley opened the door before Alex and Juliana reached it. Alex swore the man must have held a glass to the door to hear the conversation end.

He just saw why Junior Grantham and Ethan steered clear of their father. He wouldn't have traded places with them for his own poor, broken childhood if he'd had to live with that jackass with the personality of an iceberg.

ೞ೪ಬ

Bremley's interview traveled along the same vein, adding no useful evidence. Juliana and Alex wasted little time with him before heading out to the gardens.

Juliana walked at Alex's side onto the estate grounds behind the mansion. Trepidation filled her when they left the shade of the main house.

"What did you think of Bremley?" Alex asked.

"Creepo kept his mind on the mundane, almost as if he was trying to mask his thoughts." They walked along a flagstone path leading to a gazebo in the middle of the lush, formal gardens. "There was little to no byplay between his verbal and non-verbal responses." She paused and glanced ahead at the meticulous rose garden surrounding the gazebo. "He's extremely devoted to Samantha. He'd do anything for either Samantha or Grantham."

"Kidnapping?" Alex's heavy boot treads on the stone walkway drowned out the click-clack of her sandals.

"That's my impression." They stepped into the gazebo. Juliana wandered around the small octagon-shaped space, touching the green *verde* patina chairs and glass-topped table. Alex remained on her heels like a puppy.

Nothing sparked a vision or memory. "When you mentioned Jasmine and the trip to the park, Bremley thought she was heading for trouble. He was afraid for her." Juliana stopped and gripped his arm. "You need to find her fast. I really think something's going on between them. But I can't sort it out."

"From a gut feeling or from his thoughts?"

"Both." She sighed and released his arm. "I don't know why he bothers me. Andrea gets a weird feeling about him, too, so you can't discredit it."

Alex fingered the roll of antacids in his pocket, his forehead furrowed. "Damn it." He hopped down the gazebo steps and strode a short way along the path before stopping to wait for her.

She followed him. "Can you get a warrant?"

"Not without more substantial evidence," he said tersely.

They continued to stroll around the yard, halting at areas where Lisette had played. No additional visions arose.

Walking toward the rear of the estate grounds, Alex grabbed her arm and tugged her to a stop. He released her and toyed with the hair billowing around her face in the gentle breeze. "Why couldn't you read Chamber?"

Unsettled, she continued walking along the path. "People have walls in their minds." Alex caught up beside her on the wide walkway. "Caused by trauma or injury. Certain people can learn to build walls, like I did." A blue jay's riotous cry startled her. A second one followed it. She watched the flutter of blue wings through the trees bordering the gardens filled with a mass of colors from flowers to shrubs to trees.

"It's difficult for non-psychics, but not impossible." The birds hopped and danced on the lawn, then flew off, chasing each other into the copse of trees. "Either Grantham has had some sort of trauma, emotional or physical, or he's learned to build walls in his mind. It was sealed tighter than a sarcophagus."

"Can people have half-walls or cracks in their walls?"

"Sure. For example, take a child whose father abused her. She grows up and suppresses the memory. She blocks that part of her mind from herself, and from others."

"Would the suppressed memory ever open up?"

Excitement centered Juliana, loving an eager and tolerant pupil for a change. "Yes, either all at once, or in bits and pieces."

"Can you read what I'm thinking?"

"Alex, don't." She halted and studied a fiery hibiscus bloom, afraid to travel that dangerous and dark highway.

Easing in front of her, he touched her chin and lifted her head. Determination set his eyes sparkling. "Do it."

"I can't."

"Play along, will ya?"

"No, really, it's impossible." She groaned in frustration. "When I hit the roadblock on Chamber, I tried to read your mind and it was just as blank. Why do you think I wanted to scope out Bremley? I wanted to be sure I wasn't having a problem."

"Try again. Concentrate." His face relaxed, and he clasped her hand in his.

"Alex!" He tapped her head. "Oh, fine." Juliana closed her eyes and cleared her mind.

I'm glad you're back. I missed you more than you'll ever know.

Her eyes bulged. "How in the world did you do that?" Strange and unsettling ideas crisscrossed her mind. Doc Brian was definitely on the agenda that evening.

The warm breeze blew hair across her face, and she pushed it behind her ear. "One minute your mind's a blank sheet of paper, the next it's filled with words."

He grinned mischievously, his thumb caressing her cheek. "I wanted you to read my mind."

"If it were only that simple." She absorbed the words she read from his mind and blushed. "Did you really mean—"

"Yes." He bent his head, and his lips touched hers like a whisper. A delicious sensation scudded through her before shock at her eager response eclipsed it. She pulled back and spun on her heels.

"Come on, we have work to do." His reluctant tone grounded them. He weaved his strong, safe fingers through hers and led her toward a towering fountain. Water cascaded in layers into a pool filled with lilies and koi.

Juliana spied Bremley approaching at a fast clip, as cool-looking in the summer sun as he appeared in the air-conditioned mansion. She subtly untangled their hands, and they halted at the fountain to wait for Bremley.

"Lieutenant. Ms. Duncan." He gave them a terse nod.

She painted on a seductive smile, turning his sedate bearing to red and flustered dust.

"Mr. Chamber specifically requests that you examine the guesthouse at the end of this path." Juliana's eyes followed the direction he pointed out. "Jasmine resides there when she's on duty." Bremley didn't wait for a response, just turned and glided away.

"Thank you, Bremley. You're a doll," Juliana called to his retreating back, her voice as sweet as a candy-cane.

"Stop it," Alex growled.

She quirked an eyebrow in his direction. "Jealous?" She couldn't believe how comfortable she felt with him now, as if time had reversed itself and they'd picked up where they'd left off.

"Insanely," he mocked.

Juliana swatted his arm playfully and gazed in the direction of the guesthouse. A forest of cedars, redwoods, spruce, and various bushes nearly obscured the structure.

Beyond the fertile landscape, a tall stone wall covered by thick, leafy ivy separated the dwelling from the estate grounds.

As they continued along the stone pathway, the fountain's glassy tinkle drifted away. Leaves and pine needles rustled in the breeze. The call of magpies joined the flirtatious cackle of the blue jays darting through the trees. The path ended, and they passed beneath an arbor mantled by a creeping wisteria vine. The blooms were long gone, but Juliana imagined how beautiful the purple mass would be in the spring.

They crossed under the archway to the other side. A mini rendition of the main house appeared before them, in its own private slice of paradise. As they entered the luxurious guesthouse, pleasure coursed through Juliana to see that the cottage replicated the décor of the main house's sitting room.

"Well, here goes nothing." She walked to the coffee table and picked up a TV remote. The moment she held it, terrible dread suffused her, crumpling her knees. Blood rushed from her face, and she recoiled, dropping the remote.

The thick, geometric-pattered rug rushed to meet her, and the world around her blackened.

CHAPTER SIXTEEN

"Jasmine, take Lisette to the house." He stared at the hot, succulent young woman kneeling on the other side of the coffee table. Her breasts overflowed her tight as sin tank top and he licked his lips. A sharp stirring in his loins prompted the lustful look he threw her way.

Lisette bent her blond head over a coloring book on the coffee table.

"Say goodbye, Lisette." Pushing out her chest, Jasmine grinned at him from across the table.

"But I wanna finish my picture," Lisette pleaded. "Please?"

Jasmine stood. "Nana wants to read you your story. Don't you want to hear how Charlotte's Web ends?"

Lisette jumped up in her excitement, scattering her crayons across the table. She skipped into his outstretched arms.

"Eskimo kiss," he said, and her petite nose rubbed against his until she giggled uncontrollably.

"Bye." Lisette jumped back and ran to the door. "Hurry, Jasmine, before Nana's too tired."

"Lisette? Remember our secret." He brought his thumb and forefinger to his lips and pulled an imaginary zipper.

She mimicked him in the perfect manner he'd taught

her and shot out the door.

Too damn gullible, Lisette was his perfect ticket out of hell.

"Jaz, shut her up. You told me she'd be as docile as a lamb." His anger bogged down the air, almost palpable to the touch. "Why don't you put your stupid child psychology class to use?"

"Baby." Jasmine reached for him. "She's just a child."

"Give her another sedative. How can I concentrate with her crying?"

"It's too soon. I'll take her outside."

Fear flowed off her as she shied away from him. Good, let her fear him.

His anger fired his lust. He could have any woman in the world. Yet, for the moment, he wanted the twenty-year-old goddess. She'd do anything for him without using her tiny brain cells to think about it first. He had her so wrapped around his dick, she wouldn't know what sucker-punched her when the time came for him to leave—without her.

Lisette's crying ceased, spinning his thoughts back to his desperate need.

"Shut the door and come here."

Jasmine nearly danced to him. His mouth found hers in a hard kiss, his tongue lashing hers, and they scrambled to stand upright. She stroked his bare chest, his nipples hardening under her hot palms. His fingers trembled as he released the buttons on her short denim shorts. He pushed the bare slip of material to her slim ankles, and she worked at releasing his throbbing erection. Their mouths pulled apart. Air was in short supply, but her lips locked onto his neck, and he cupped her full breasts in his hand, pinching her nipples the way she liked.

"Now," she screamed, panting. "Oh, yes, yes. Now!"

No time or ability to leave the hallway, he hoisted her in his arms, and her long, lithe legs wrapped around his waist. He plunged into her with enough force to split open a watermelon. She reared her head back, and her scream of pure ecstasy pulsed through his body.

He pumped in and out, each brutal thrust probing deeper and deeper. He dug his fingers into her sweet, perfect ass. Slamming Jasmine against the wall, his control shattered, and his strokes became frenzied, brutal.

"You're hurting me." Jasmine gasped for air. She tried to push him off, but his hands pinned her hips against him, against the wall.

Her legs loosened, and a deep growl emerged in him. He thrust faster, harder, touching her core. Feeling her body slam against the wall, the sounds added fuel to his raging desire.

He crushed her mouth beneath his, shoving his tongue against hers until she bit down. The metallic taste of blood filled his mouth, causing an unparalleled fury to boil inside him. Rage amplified his lust, and he thought he'd tumble over the edge before he was ready.

Hot pleasure crested as she continued to struggle against him. "Come on, baby. You like it rough. What's the problem now?" He managed to get the words out with the limited air in the hallway.

One final hammering plunge and his release came, tearing through him, one ecstatic wave after another. "Goddamn," he gasped.

He almost dropped her as he stumbled into the master bedroom. In utter exhaustion, he fell on the bed, landing on his back, Jasmine in his arms. Her struggles ceased, and her tears dried on her cheeks as she tried to catch her breath. He stroked her cheek and kissed her gently, soothing her pain.

Hoisting her off him, his hand butted against a small square object on the bed. "What the hell?" He curled his hand around the compact and lifted it up to his face. Glancing into the small mirror, he noticed his smoldering eyes. It amazed him how dilated they became after sex and how the color blackened.

Sudden apprehension startled him, and the hair on his arms stood erect. Gooseflesh spread over his slick skin. Intrusive eyes pierced him and probed his mind. His head flailed on the bed, scanning the room. Looking for someone with eyes the color of green glass.

Disconcerted, angry, he threw the compact at Jasmine. "I told you to quit leaving your shit around." He leaned over and landed a fierce kiss on her lips before rising off the bed.

His meal ticket waited in the next room. It was time to prepare his ransom note.

Sheer black fright swept through Juliana as she fought the darkened void. Part of her sought an elusive entity. The other part wanted to escape it. Her eyes locked on another pair of eyes.

Eyes the color of charcoal.

She yanked her gaze away from the dark, unfathomable eyes, and the foreign entity followed her gaze. Darkened gray eyes penetrated all thought, digging deep to familiarize itself with her.

Juliana's mind refused to settle on any lucid thought. From a distant place, a familiar voice called to her. A driving need guided her closer to the voice, knowing she'd find comfort when she reached her destination.

The strange eyes in her head vanished.

Juliana woke frantic, bound in Alex's arms. He cradled her on an unfamiliar sage-colored couch, whispering words she could hear but not comprehend.

Horror and disgust built pyramid-style inside her.

"No," she moaned. "Not one of these connections." Her stomach heaved. "Oh, no." Juliana cupped her hand to her mouth and struggled out of Alex's arms. "I'm gonna be sick."

After purging her stomach, if not the revolting vision, Juliana let Alex carry her away from the sink, out onto the patio. He gently set her on a lounge chair, and the fragrant shadowed garden renewed her flagging energy.

To stop the world from revolving around her, she dropped her head between her knees. "See if there's a soda in the fridge. It'll settle my stomach." She had to concentrate to drag her head back down to Earth, to keep her stomach in place. Counting to ten hardly helped, nor did the deep inhalations of the cleansing air.

Alex returned in a flash. "Here, sweetheart."

He squatted in front of her, tenderly smoothing down her hair as if she were the teenager he'd loved all those years ago. Front to back, front to back. The motion lulled her, and his touch continued to revive her. She raised her head, heedless of the tears dripping from her eyes.

Alex lifted the can of soda to her lips, and she drank several sips before surfacing for air.

"How long was I out?" The sudden changes in her ESP freaked her out. Twice in two days. Both times, Alex was there to catch her before she kissed the floor.

"A few minutes. How do you feel?" He pulled her into his arms and wrapped his muscular body around her like a down comforter on a stormy night.

"Better." She leaned her head on his chest, closed her eyes. Her head throbbed. She pressed her fingertips to her temples and massaged them.

The visions emerged in a gush. *Oh, my God!* "Jasmine," Juliana said in a strangled voice and bolted upright. "She *is* implicated. *He's* been here with her *and*

Lisette."

Alex disentangled from her and rose from the lounge, his face dark and dangerous. "Are you sure?"

"Positive."

"Was it Bremley?" he demanded, hands clenching and unclenching.

Juliana shook her head. "I don't think so." A shudder convulsed her. "God, Alex, I don't know. I still can't place him." She dropped her face in her hands and rubbed her forehead.

Alex called James. "Get over to Jasmine Webley's house. She's an accomplice. Bring her in for questioning. I'll explain later."

He clicked off the phone and clasped Juliana's hand. "You okay?"

"Give me a minute." She managed a wan smile. Leaning back, she savored the aromatic roses fringing the patio.

Twilight gray eyes haunted her. Why did she have the inescapable sense of those eyes following her? She'd never experienced such a phenomenon in her life.

Worry etching his face, Alex knelt level with her. "Is this normal?"

"Not these day visions or the fainting." *Juliana Westwood calling Doc Brian. Beam me up.*

A pair of chattering squirrels scrambled up a nearby pine tree, startling the blue jays into flight. She watched the carefree play, wishing she could fly away on the wind. "Headaches and nausea are normal after an intense dream."

Alex stroked her hair. "Damn. How can you stand it?"

"It doesn't get easier." His concern was so sweet, she blinked back tears. God, how she loved him. Needed him. Wanted him.

You never stopped loving him, you fool. The

undeniable truth remained, and she didn't know if she could let him go when the time came. *Think about Alex the cop*, she admonished herself.

Anxiety carved every square inch of his face. His hand fell away from her cheek and rested heavily on her thigh. He waited while she gathered her thoughts.

"What's weird is that I saw two distinct visions. One occurred here in the past, and the other appeared real-time, at what's probably the kidnapper's current location."

She gave Alex the gist of the visions. Well, most of it. She still couldn't figure out how she saw the eyes in her head. Alex most certainly wouldn't understand.

"Now we have a little more to go on." Grim determination framed his voice.

"These day visions are different from my usual night dreams, where my mind opens and lets the dreams in and out." Tilting her head, she squinted at Alex. "These were more intense. My mind was forced open and yanked into his head against my will."

"They're real, right?" Not a hint of skepticism appeared in his voice. He'd come a long way in a mere couple of days.

"Without a doubt."

Relief dropped his shoulders a fraction. She knew it had to be devastating to learn that Lisette had fostered a friendly relationship with the kidnapper prior to her abduction. As much as Juliana softened the words, she wondered if he'd implode at the implication that the kidnapper may have touched Lisette in an inappropriate manner. But the kidnapper's thoughts didn't stray in a sexual direction. Juliana was positive.

She recognized the kidnapper's intent as unmistakably as she'd felt him buried deep inside Jasmine. His lust and anger coursed like acid through her intestines. She rocked back and forth, fighting the nausea that threatened her again.

"Jewel?" Alex caught her into his arms. "Is there more?"

Would he believe her if she told him? Or would he treat her like a pariah?

She shielded her eyes from the sun filtering through the trees. "It's not important."

"I want to know *everything*," he demanded. "We're in this together. You're not suffering alone any longer." Alex pulled her into an airtight embrace, his face buried in her hair. "Tell me. Don't hold back now." His voice cracked.

The afternoon sun shifted behind the trees, lengthening the shadows on the patio, stretching the moment and pushing them apart.

"Alex, it's—" It didn't matter what he thought. It would simply make life easier to walk away once they solved the case. Silently, she counted to ten and the words tumbled out in a low voice. "I felt everything he did. As if I were . . . him."

Alex's body tensed. His head tipped back sharply, confusion playing havoc on his dour expression. "I don't understand."

"His anger, his lust, every thrust as he . . . made love to Jasmine." Tears renewed their assault on her face. She couldn't bear witness to the shock on his face, as if she'd confessed to killing his niece. If he doubted what kind of freak she was, he knew for sure now.

He hid his face in her neck, his arms painfully tightening around her.

The birds and the squirrels frolicked and chatted merrily around them, as if all were right in their skewed fantasy world.

CHAPTER SEVENTEEN

Bremley startled Alex and Juliana a few minutes later. The butler cleared his throat, presumably in embarrassment or derision. *Who could tell from the perpetual snooty, shit-eating look on his face?* His voice was solicitous, devoid of his earlier haughtiness. "Is everything to your satisfaction, Lieutenant?"

Alex drew apart from Juliana. "I want you and the Chambers to meet me in the study in five minutes." He slashed his hand through the air dismissively.

Stiff-backed, Bremley nodded and strode away.

Alex helped Juliana stand, as if she were a glass egg. His tender concern quickened her insides.

She loved it.

Hated it.

"Can you walk?" he asked as she took his hand in her clasp.

"My legs aren't broken." She smiled, her vitality returning with every breath. "I need to wash my face, rinse my mouth." She glanced warily at the cottage.

"You want to go to the main house?" Alex twisted the gold filigree ring on her finger.

"No. It's okay."

"Give me the word and we'll be out fast enough to spin

your head."

She groaned. "That's the last thing I need right now, thank you very much." His face reddened beneath his deep tan. Another smile tugged at her lips.

"Anytime you want, just tell me what an idiot I am."

"Never."

Alex's warm palm on her back reassured, lending her courage to walk through the guesthouse to the bathroom. He blocked the doorway, eyeing her every move. Both relief and nervousness nagged at her. She wet a washcloth with cold water and gazed into the mirror.

Steel gray eyes returned her stare before turning emerald in her mirror image. Juliana dropped the washcloth and gripped the vanity edge. What in the world? A thought clicked in her mind. The harder she tried to ignore the truth, the more it persisted, until terrifying realization slugged her. The dark gray eyes had locked with Juliana's in a small compact mirror.

"No. It can't be." She shook her head to scatter the frightening conclusion.

"What?" Alex's face whitened.

"Ridiculous." Her unnatural shrill laugh surprised her.

He placed gentle hands on her shoulders and swiveled her around to face him. "Make a deal with me." His expression turned dark, formidable. "I don't want you holding anything back. I don't care how ridiculous, how unimportant, how weird, or how much you think it will hurt me. Okay?" He tapped his index finger on her shoulder after each syllable.

She pulled away from him and faced the mirror again. Apprehension trounced her. Relenting, she said, "He saw my eyes."

Alex's mouth dropped open as he stared at her reflection in the mirror. "You're joking, right?" He fingered the strap of his shoulder harness.

"I told you it was absurd." Was it? "The kidnapper was looking for someone—someone with green eyes."

Alex's face wiped slate clean, giving nothing away. "What the hell? Has that ever happened to you?"

"Nothing about this case is normal." A loud groan of frustration slipped out as she dipped the washcloth in the cold stream of water.

"Maybe you ought to call your doctor pal." Concern and unease riddled the suggestion.

"You a mind reader now?"

A tentative smile flickered across his face before she covered her own with the wet cloth.

She quickly finished and they left the cottage. A distant tension hummed between them. When he stopped her at the archway leading back to the mansion grounds, he wrapped his arms around her waist, pulling her close. She relished the feel of him, her breasts flattened against his chest, tingling. He tilted her face up and cupped her cheeks. His mouth met hers in a gentle, languorous kiss that left no doubts about what he really believed.

Juliana braced herself against his chest as if to push him away, but he zapped what little strength she possessed. Her body awakened at his touch. His lips began to melt away the long, lonely years of heartache. She was powerless to stop him.

Defenseless to stop his tongue from tangling in a sensuous tango with hers. Defenseless to stop the aching need to submit to his will.

To yield to her own will.

Breathless, Alex broke off the kiss. A satisfied twinkle in his eyes robbed her of what little sanity remained. He grabbed her hand and led her away from the magical moment.

❧

Alex and Juliana left the Chamber estate with Jasmine's placement agency's contact information and little else. The Chambers and staff weren't aware of any mystery man. A back entrance to the estate existed, but only those who knew the electronic code could get through the gate.

Alex deftly evaded Grantham's probing into what evidence the police had obtained against Jasmine. Grantham blustered, but received no satisfaction. Samantha emphatically defended Jasmine. Bremley maintained his stoicism, providing useless answers to Alex's questions.

Juliana used her telepathy to gain entrance to Samantha's and Bremley's minds. She captured no useful thoughts in either. She stared hard into Bremley's dark, shifting eyes. But there was no recognition—even though his unsettling gray eyes were similar to the pair in her visions. Grantham's thoughts remained sheltered behind a solid fortress.

They drove away from the estate, and Juliana assured Alex that Grantham gave no sign he recognized her banging against the gates in his mind.

They settled in Alex's office, her hand securely in his clasp. After what happened at the cottage, he didn't think he could let her out of his sight, away from his touch. The craving to care for and protect her burned hot in his core.

"Where's Jasmine?" Alex demanded the moment James crossed the threshold. His muscles coiled under the tension of self-control as he wrestled to drive out his seething rage and helplessness.

Juliana lifted his chin with her free hand. "Look at me."

His eyes met the serene liquid jewels and his fury subsided. *How the hell does she do that?*

Ignoring James' impatient tapping on the doorframe, Alex kissed her palm. He released her and approached James.

"We didn't reach her in time," James said. "She gave us the slip."

"Son of a bitch." Alex pounded a fist on the wall beside James' head. "Is she on the run?"

James' averted his gaze. "I've issued an APB as a person of interest. We're watching her place twenty-four-seven."

⊗⅁⅄⊗

Standing in Juliana's foyer later that evening, uneasiness settled between Juliana and Alex. The sun dipped, angling gold through the wide open door.

"Maybe I'll see you tomorrow." She didn't know what else to say. They'd reached a turning point, and she feared what the next bend would bring.

"You'll see me tonight," he challenged, leaving little room for argument. His gaze held hers with a frightening intensity.

"You don't need to fix the porch light. I'll get it fixed." *Stupid, stupid, stupid. You really don't think that's what he meant, do you?* Their kiss under the arbor still created bedlam with her emotions.

"You didn't think I'd leave you alone after today, did you?" His low tone was challenging and sensual at once.

Juliana didn't know if she should be thrilled or irritated. He moved closer, until his face was a hair's breadth away.

"It's not necessary," she replied. "I've handled myself quite well for twelve years." It touched her deeply that he wanted to help chase away the monsters in her mind. But she needed the distance. Needed to sort through what was happening to her, with the case, with her feelings for Alex.

Alex's mouth caught hers in a hard, passionate kiss. Her body betrayed her when her arms wrapped around his shoulders, pulling him solidly against her. After the long and thorough kiss ended, they remained in each other's arms, breathless, bodies molded together as if made for one another.

She tipped her head back and studied his face. "Go home. Get some sleep tonight." He released her, backing away, and scrubbed at his scar. "You won't sleep, will you?"

"What do you think?"

Juliana stepped to the bombe chest and pulled out a spare house key from the top drawer. She handed it to a bewildered Alex. He glanced at the key, but didn't touch it.

"Take it." She pushed the brass key into his palm and wrapped his fingers around it.

He pocketed the key and brushed his lips over hers. Wordlessly, he left her standing in the foyer. A sense of finality engulfed her as she pushed the door closed.

Juliana Westwood has taken leave of her senses. She walked determinedly toward the phone to call Doc Brian. To her disappointment, his wife informed her that he was on a weeklong fishing trip deep in the Oregon woods, no phones, no electricity. He wouldn't return home until next weekend.

A quick search through a box in her office produced several research papers written by Dr. Brian Miller. She carried them into the kitchen and tossed them on the table.

Exhaustion and hunger wore her out. If she didn't eat, she'd never be able to climb the stairs to the bed calling her name. She was ravenous enough to eat a sixteen-ounce porterhouse steak. Unfortunately, her refrigerator was as bare as Old Mother Hubbard's cupboard, and she didn't feel like eating a crappy frozen dinner. Reluctantly, Juliana buried her appetite in a bowl of canned vegetable beef soup and Doc Brian's research reports.

Brian's research dipped deeper into telepathic connections and the dangers of forced mind-linking. A long while later, satiated and troubled by what she read, she trudged upstairs and crawled into bed, sinking her weary body onto the plush mattress.

But sleep wouldn't grant her an audience and her thoughts wandered in a maze. They wound and curved their way with heedless abandon around the ultimate finish line.

Alex MacKenzie. And what he was doing to her.

Her heart accelerated at the memory of his body protecting, comforting, his lips molded to hers. There was no turning back. No turning away.

She vibrated with an urgent need to see Alex, to touch him, to smell him, to hear him breathe. She shouldn't feel that way. Her plate was too full. She'd learned to live her life with a famine of trust, to enjoy life and her freedom alone, to rely on no one. Reluctantly, she'd decided years ago to never let herself get close to any other man, allowing no attraction to build with another.

How could she push Alex away when deep inside, she didn't want to? How could she convince him that life with a psychic would torture him, when she didn't know any more?

Cooperation between her heart and head had vanished when she'd first come face-to-face with Alex at the SJPD.

Her mind flooded her with 'what ifs'. When JB snuggled onto her stomach, seeking attention like a newborn, Juliana finally let her mind drift to nothingness and fall asleep.

CHAPTER EIGHTEEN

The closed blinds muted the lights of downtown. Even with his office door open, the squad room was subdued for a Sunday night. Alex and James scoured case notes while waiting for Captain Hayes, who'd demanded an update on their investigation. Alex knew he'd have to reveal his source to Hayes. Experience proved his superior wouldn't dole out a free ride forever.

When Hayes strode into the office, his eyes flitted from James to Alex. "Well, gentlemen, time to ante up."

James shut the door. Alex eased his hip on the desk and faced his boss.

No taller than five-nine and two hundred pounds of solid muscle, intimidation was Hayes' forte. Freckles on his dark leathery arms and face gave testimony to long hours in the sun. On the brink of sixty, he was street-hardened, and it showed in his weathered face.

Hayes dug his hands in his front pockets. "You have two sets of potential suspects on the run and no concrete evidence against either."

"At least we have suspects." James crossed the room and stood with his back to the window.

Hayes flashed James his trademark icy stare.

"This stays in this room." Alex tossed a defiant glance

at Hayes and received a curt nod in return.

"Spill it." Hayes folded his arms over his barrel chest, his legs spread wide in an impatient stance. "I have a statement to deliver to the press in a half hour."

"We have a psychic working the case." Alex winced, expecting the worst. He tapped a letter opener on the desk before tossing it aside.

Hayes belted out a sardonic laugh. "You, MacKenzie, working with a psychic? Now I've heard everything."

"I'm glad I could provide you some amusement."

When he realized Alex was serious, Hayes sobered quickly. "Give me the goods."

Alex briefed the Captain on Juliana's involvement without divulging their personal relationship.

"Let me get this straight." Hayes unfolded his arms, resting a foot on the visitor chair. "The babysitter's doing the guy who snatched Lisette. Supposedly she's a pawn in his trap to acquire the Chamber pot of gold. You expect a ransom demand any day. And you can't identify the kidnapper." He paused, looking from James to Alex. "Does that sum up your psychic's visions?"

After Alex's affirmative nod, Hayes continued, "The neighbors are incommunicado and have a room set up for a girl Lisette's age."

A knock sounded at the door, and it opened before anyone could respond. Sterling slid an urgent file through to James.

James scanned the contents. "Hang on." He raised his hand, shock paling his freckles. "Sharon and Matthew Douglas were booked on a flight to Romania yesterday. Three seats reserved. One's registered for a child."

"Romania?" Alex's spine stiffened as he slid off the desk and straightened to his full height. If Juliana was wrong and the Douglases had abducted Lisette . . . Fear dropped him in his chair. "Tell me it's a misprint."

"Sorry, man." James slapped the file on the desk. "I can't believe this shit."

With sausage-thick fingers, Hayes snatched the report from James. "The airline hasn't confirmed if the seats were filled. Get on it, O'Malley. Meanwhile, I can feed the Douglases to the press. We can keep your source hidden."

James raced off, giving Hayes the opportunity to grill Alex. "Who is she?"

Anxious fatigue burrowed into Alex. "Juliana Westwood, a financial planner by trade."

"That's not what I meant. Who is she to *you*?"

Alex knew Hayes had made him. He sighed, gave in—to a degree. "An old friend of the family. Recently moved back here from New York. NYPD used her extensively. We have references."

Hayes threw Alex another skeptical, impatient look.

"Cap, don't push it."

"You better know what you're doing, MacKenzie. I'd hate to see you compromise your ethics. And I'd hate to put you on the beach." Hayes dropped his foot to the floor with a loud smack and backed toward the door. "Lisette's one of our own. I'll be damned if I'll let her get the shaft. I want a full report in a sealed envelope on my desk before you leave."

Like he'd compromise anything to save his niece. Alex nodded. "Thank you."

Hayes hesitated at the door, his eyes softening. His tone held none of his usual brashness. "Alex, we'll find her. You can count on it."

The Captain left Alex alone with his thoughts. Apprehension etched canals on his forehead deep enough to feel to the bone. The urge to strike out prevailed over the dread floating like a glacier in his gut. If that bastard so much as hurts a hair on Lisette's head . . .

"Hey, man." James jogged back into the office.

"Airline's working on a final manifest for the flight out of SFO."

Alex waved James' words off with a razor-sharp flick of his hand. "They don't have her. Juliana's positive."

James rolled his eyes. "I'm not giving up on them."

"I'm not asking you to."

"You are in deep," James said in a mild tone. He turned a chair around and straddled it.

The glower Alex pinned on James could have shrunken heads on a lesser man. "Shut the hell up." He heaved back from the desk. He didn't need a lecture from his conscience in the guise of James O'Malley.

"You can't imagine what she goes through when she has those visions. She gets sick, puking her guts out." He reached in his desk drawer for a roll of antacids and popped a couple in his mouth. Grimacing, he threw the roll on his desk for easy access. "She's chasing this bastard in her mind, seeing what he sees, feeling what he feels."

"Bad, huh?"

Alex scratched his scar. Reluctantly, he forced her to the back of his mind. "Give me an update."

James shoved his tablet in front of Alex. "We'll have a manifest in a few hours. Short of rousing the airline's CEO or threatening a national security breach, they won't move any faster." He tapped the screen. "Here's the intel on your Scottish keychain. It's a custom order item. Each seller should have records of any buyers."

Optimism sparked inside Alex. He greedily seized the file. Celtic Creations, as evidenced by the two intertwined 'Cs' engraved on the flipside of the keychain, had created it. The file contained a short list of North American sellers.

"Give the list to Sterling."

"Already on it."

Alex pushed the tablet into the clutter littering his desk. "Anything on a ransom?"

"I have a feeling Chamber will receive the ransom demand and keep his mouth zipped."

"I want twenty-four-seven surveillance on them, including Bremley."

"Already done."

"Hayes wants a full report on our mystery source. I'm going to check in on Andrea. You'll be there?"

"Yeah." A hangdog look skittered across James' face. He rifled the file pages. "I know we haven't talked—"

"Save it." Alex smiled wryly. "What you two do on your own time is your business." Andrea's infatuation with James spanned months. How could he not know, when every weekend he'd spent with his sister, she'd made a point to invite James? "I'm glad you're there for her. I sure as hell haven't been."

James rose and turned the chair around. "She gets that you're tied up with the case and busy working with Juliana."

"I'll never hear the end of it later on. You don't know my sister as well as you think you do."

"No, man, but I'm getting there." James gave Alex a mock salute and left him to his own internal battles.

Alex felt secure leaving Andrea in James' capable hands and leaving the office. At least because of this mess, his twin and James had revealed their attraction to one another. And he wouldn't have to worry about the next guy in Lisette's life, as long as they found her. He parked his SUV in Juliana's driveway and flung the morbid thought out of his mind.

An obsessive need to possess her in every way surged through him. He wondered how she'd managed to seep under his skin so fast after all these years. But then, she'd never really left his heart to begin with.

The dark porch gave brief rise to Alex's ire. Yet the broken light didn't quell the anticipation to see and touch Juliana. He slipped through the front door, locking it behind him. Soft light drew him into the empty family room. He became painfully aware of the pillow and blanket stacked neatly on the couch, as welcome as an iceberg.

A foray into the kitchen produced a smile when he found a six-pack of beer in the fridge. A couple of swigs of brew hit his empty stomach like a lead weight. The vending machine sandwich he'd choked down at lunch hadn't sat well in his stomach. He set the half-full bottle on the granite counter; a loud clink filled the still house. If he finished the beer, it would expand the inferno devouring his insides.

His real hunger was for Juliana.

The pain of her disappearance had receded like footsteps in a blizzard, leaving behind only memories of love, and none of the bullshit of her disappearance and the aftermath. Something bottomless and powerful within him wanted to make up for the hurt and disappointment she'd suffered during her time away.

The memory of her in his arms earlier created a painful tightening in his groin. The intense feelings exceeded any reaction he'd ever felt for another woman. It frightened and exhilarated him at the same time.

Alex unbuttoned his jeans to lessen the pressure. He slipped up the stairs into Juliana's bedroom. The bedside light spilled a muted radiance across the bed, across the inviting body within. He pulled off his shoulder harness and set his gun on the night table. Only then did he allow his eyes to indulge the fantasies overriding all other thought.

Alex's gaze devoured her luscious body, uncovered and clad in a lacey camisole top. Silky shorts bared her slender legs. Her blonde hair fanned out around her head in a halo of sunshine. His breathing grew ragged, and he fought the desire to blanket her body with his. The one functioning cell in his brain screamed at him to slow down.

Juliana's eyes fluttered open and widened briefly in terror. "Alex!" she gasped. "You nearly scared me to death." She rose on her elbows, pulling the sheet up to her breasts.

"Sorry." He eased onto the bed beside her, flat hands braced on either side of her shoulders, pinning her in position. "Your light was on. I thought you'd be awake."

She averted her eyes and smoothed the sheet over her stomach.

He narrowed his eyes. "What's wrong?"

She lifted her gaze to his face. "No one else knows what it's like to have murderers and kidnappers in my head. It feels the same to wake up to someone staring at me."

He'd kick himself if he could reach his ass. "No one knows, except maybe a homicide cop?"

"Maybe," she conceded with a tiny smile. "Now you know why I like having a safety net around me. Even though it's a false sense of security."

Leaning in, he tightened his arms around her. "And the lights?" Her clean, fresh scent assaulted his senses. He breathed deeply, filling his soul with her, with life. With everything he'd missed for twelve years.

She hedged, her face flushed pink.

"Are you afraid of the dark?" She seemed so strong and fearless, despite everything. He wanted to protect her from all the bad things in her life. Forever.

"I was locked in dark rooms at the Institute." Juliana continued to iron the bedcovers with her palms.

Alex laid a finger against her mouth and, with a

featherlike caress, brushed her lips. His gaze strayed momentarily to the decimated scarf ring in the corner of the room where he'd tossed it the night before. "Let me be your safety net," he whispered.

Her plum lips puckered. Freckles dotted her flushed cheeks, and he traced his index finger over them.

Juliana grinned. "You're impossible."

"You used to like that about me." He caressed her face one last time, then his fingers fluttered to her neck. He felt her body tremble beneath him. "Just let me hold you, okay?"

"Is that all you want?" she asked, eyes twinkling.

"I want all of you. But, I think that's more than you're willing to give me right now."

"Alex," she said with no real insistence.

He continued to stroke her neck, fascinated as her emerald eyes darkened and lightened as they shifted from one emotion to another, ranging from fear to desire.

"I can't . . . we can't. I won't lead you on." She rested her small hands on his arms as if to push him away.

"You're not." He slid his hands back to the bed, cocooning her within his arms. Not touching, even though they begged to stroke every inch of her. "I'll sleep on the couch. I got the hint."

Her shy smile squeezed his heart. Without another thought, he lowered his head and seized her lips in a passionate kiss, exploding the firestorm within. Mouth molded onto his, her arms wound around his neck. She clung to him as if she never wanted to let him go.

He pressed the length of his body to hers, a harsh groan escaping him. Heat from her body radiated through his jeans, causing his erection to throb. Like a man starved for her taste, yearning to unearth a long-buried passion, he kissed her.

They couldn't savor enough of each other. Couldn't get

close enough. Couldn't satiate the long-smoldering flames. He'd die if she pushed him away. His body hummed and quaked with an all-consuming need. Fighting himself before he proceeded too far to stop, he freed his mouth from hers and forced frayed words out. "Tell me to stop."

In a breathy whisper, Juliana said, "I can't."

"Tell me what you want," he demanded harshly, eyes slivered.

"You. Here. Now." Her fingers delved into his hair and she pulled his mouth back to hers.

Alex struggled against an urge that paralyzed his every thought and emotion. He'd wanted Juliana forever, and she offered herself to him in ways he'd only dreamed. The need to have her overwhelmed him. The hunger devastated his forced calm.

Ending the kiss, she pushed him up and tugged off her camisole. He sucked in his breath, motionless, mesmerized. She reached tentative fingers to the hem of his shirt and helped him pull it over his head. Her touch scorched his already inflamed skin.

His gaze scanned the perfection of her near-naked body, painting a blush on her cheeks. "Touch me," she whispered as she settled back on the bed.

Alex caressed her face and slid his hands into the waterfall of her hair. His body trembled as hers quivered.

"Goddamn. You're so beautiful." Awe roughened his voice. He claimed her mouth in another possessive kiss, and Juliana pressed herself against him, intensifying their kiss. Flesh to flesh, tantalizing, searing. She held nothing back, and he wanted it all and more. For a brief second, reason entered his mind again. He tore his mouth from hers, his eyes heavy. Desire suffused her face. But he needed to hear the words again before he crossed the line of no return.

"Are you sure?" He held his breath, his nerve endings

aching with his need. He didn't think such a passion could exist, but it did. It frightened him, awed him, thrilled him.

"Yes." Love and desire made up her face.

Slowly, he drew Juliana's silky shorts off, lightly stroking her smooth, tanned legs. Then he pushed his own pants down and Juliana's languid eyes raked over his body with greedy deliberation. A growl escaped him.

Alex caressed every inch of her, leaving a blazing trail of kisses across her skin. They sank into each other's eyes, and he needed no further encouragement. Juliana shuddered as he kneed her legs apart. Alex's mouth covered hers, and they caught each other's cries of pleasure as he slid into her, merging as one with each slick stroke. Tangling his fingers in her hair, he couldn't imagine a more exquisite woman or a more extraordinary heart than the one beating so wildly beneath him. All reason fled as Alex lost himself in his jewel.

They slipped into a slow, hot rhythm, building energy between them. Juliana stroked his back, trickling fingers down to knead his butt, nails biting into his skin. Gently parting her mouth with his tongue, he kissed her, filling himself with the minty taste of her mouth. Moaning, she deepened the kiss, her teeth scraping his tongue. Their mouths separated, she drew in a deep, shaky breath, and he trembled, thrusting harder and faster. Her lips and tongue explored his neck, and lightning bolts of sensation ignited across his skin.

Writhing beneath him, she whispered his name between kisses, and the heat of her breath seared his skin. The thrill of hearing his name on her lips drove him higher and higher into frenzied excitement. Her petal-soft skin felt like a blanket of velvet soothing his scorched skin, firing his passion.

Juliana bit his neck lightly as her back arched,

muffling a sharp cry. She lifted her head, her body quivering and burning against his. "Alex. God, Alex. Alex," she panted out. "If you stop, I'll kill you."

The cadence of her voice dove deep into his heart, resonating down to his soul, driving him beyond the door of control. Alex lifted her head and whispered, "No. I'm not God. But you're mine." Groaning his pleasure into her mouth, he ground himself deep inside her. "You're mine, always and forever."

When the thunderous wave rolled through him, she cried out, bucking against his hips as she climaxed. He convulsed one last time, a low roar in his throat.

He had come home and captured the other half of his soul. Still cloaked inside Juliana, Alex gripped her in an unyielding embrace as if afraid she'd disappear. They rolled onto their sides without losing hold. Shattered, he never dreamed it could be like that with anyone.

A frown flashed across Juliana's face, and an arrow nicked his heart.

"Are you sorry?" She'd branded his soul with her passion. Already he ached with renewed need, a hunger only she could satisfy.

As she caressed his face, he stroked her back, enjoying the feel of her moist, fevered skin against his rougher fingers.

"I had no idea—" Her face mirrored the incredulity his own must have betrayed. "Aren't you glad we waited?"

"If I'd known making love with you would be this spectacular, I wouldn't have waited until prom night."

"Alex." She expelled a tiny breath through her swollen lips, and he wished he could kiss her doubts away.

"I know." He sighed. "No promises. No regrets."

Slow and seductive, Alex showed her again and again how perfect it was between them. And he gave her no chance to kill him as she'd earlier threatened.

CHAPTER NINETEEN

Juliana was dreaming of Alex's arms wrapped around her. Happiness meandered through her like flashes of sunshine at her nerve endings. She felt safe, secure, and loved like never before. No demons ravaged her mind with Alex holding them at bay. No killers and kidnappers infringed upon her sanity. Simply unsullied, idyllic heaven.

"Jewel." A whisper intruded into her mind. "You awake?" The voice grew insistent.

"Hmmm," she murmured, not ready to surrender the marvelous dream.

A warm nibble on her earlobe tickled her senses awake.

Her eyelids fluttered open, and she faced Alex, a secretive smile on his face. Startled, she realized the dream was real. The light down of his chest hair tickled her breasts, generating a delicious pulsing sensation in her womb. She settled back to enjoy his bare flesh against hers.

Juliana wanted to savor the moment for as long as possible. It would be the last time she would feel such bliss. Fear of losing herself in him gnawed at her. But she'd had to taste him at least once since it was all she'd dreamed of during their long separation. *One kiss, one touch, one night. It's all she wants to last her forever.*

"No bad dreams?"

"Ummm, no." She reveled in the nightmare-free night.

"Good." He kissed her neck, his stubble tickling her sensitive skin.

"It's good and bad." She sighed. "I mean, I hate having them, but I wanted another chance to see him, another clue."

"I know, baby. Me too." Alex kissed her temple. "I need to go home and shower, get this day underway."

"A cold shower, I suspect."

"Don't even ask." Teeth nipped at her ear. "Hey, curious, but when did you get a tattoo? You always hated them."

Juliana craned her neck to glimpse the small Celtic trinity knot tangled in a heart tattoo on her left shoulder. "Too much to drink celebrating my college graduation. My two girlfriends and I all got a tattoo that night." She laughed. "Dumb, huh?"

"I thought you weren't part of the Psychics Guild."

She frowned. "I'm not."

"That's their logo."

"Really? I had no idea." Eyes narrowed, Juliana traced the tattoo. "It called to me in the tattoo catalog. The artist said it fit my type. I was too drunk to ask what he meant."

"What does it mean for you, if you don't mind me asking?" Alex clasped her hand, stilling her fingers on the tattoo.

Her face flushed. "The trinity. My mind, body, and soul. I wanted to always remember."

"Me?"

She dipped her head. "Yes. Captured by your heart."

Alex leaned over and kissed the tattoo, his lips soft

and warm, so sensual, she wanted to melt into his kiss.

"Alex?" She cupped his face, making him look at her. "Did you ever try to find me after I left?" She'd wondered for a long time. Knowing her father, he'd probably done his damnedest to bury all traces of her whereabouts. Hell, as far as her father was concerned, he probably even denied he'd had a daughter.

"Hell, yes." Alex eased up on his elbow and rested his head on his palm. "I spent months searching for you. I even broke into your father's house, looking for clues." He smoothed his hand over her bare arm, leaving her skin tingling. "I harassed him so much, he had me arrested."

"What? No way!" Dismay swabbed at her insides, dampening her joy.

He rolled away from her and leaned back against the pillows. "He never pressed charges. Basically, he blackmailed me. Told me to give it up or he'd have me arrested for breaking and entering, grand theft, and felony assault. Not that I assaulted him."

"And you listened to him?" Her father had never intimidated Alex. She sat on her heels, covering her ravished naked body with the sheet. The scent of Alex on her skin created a disconcerting heady sensation she wanted to both escape from and wallow in.

"You know me better than that." He snorted. "I wised up and steered clear of him, kept searching. Eventually your trail disappeared."

"What made you decide to become a cop?" Another question burning a hole in her curiosity.

"Oddly enough, it was the experience with your father." Alex grimaced ruefully. "I guess I should've thanked him."

"I wouldn't go that far." She could barely thank the man for bringing her into the world.

"Yeah, well, if I hadn't been arrested, the police and

their power wouldn't have fascinated me." A wicked grin gave life to his pale, lined face. "And I thought it looked cool to carry a gun."

Juliana eyed the offensive weapon on her night table. Discomfort spread a taint over her skin, sullying the glow of the exquisite night. She pushed back the intruding memories. "Cool is a new electronic gadget."

"Not to an eighteen-year-old boy looking for his way in the world." He laughed and, in trademark style, raked a hand through his bed-tousled hair. "My baseball coach at State was an ex-cop, my mentor. He coached me on the good, the bad, and the ugly about being a cop. But I was hooked. I was completing my criminal justice degree when SJPD recruited me."

"You love being a cop, don't you?" He nodded, and she caressed his scar. The scar's uneven, pale edge frightened her. The idea of anyone marring his otherwise perfect face turned her fingernails into daggers.

Alex caught her hand and twisted the filigree ring on her finger. "What happened to the emerald?"

Guilt and grief flooded her. Alex had given her an emerald ring a month after they'd started dating. She examined the gold ring—a poor substitute. "The Institute confiscated my belongings and sent everything to my father. I never saw it again."

Anger creased Alex's brow. "He probably threw it away."

She shrugged slightly. "It wasn't among his belongings."

He settled her palm over his heart, his hand holding hers hostage, and leaned forward. They shared a sensuous kiss, and her insides purred like a kitten. When they drew apart, she sensed a part of herself still clinging to him. Reluctantly, she eased away and watched him climb out of bed.

"I need to go, before I start something I can't finish."

Leisurely, her gaze traveled his magnificent naked form from his knees upwards. *How would I ever forsake him?*

"What's on your agenda today?" he asked.

Reality returned with a vengeance. Wrinkling her nose, she replied, "Nicholas Hastings, Ned Kraven, other clients."

"Should I be jealous?"

"Insanely."

His rich baritone laugh was infectious and lightened her movements. It pleased her to find him in a good mood, at least for a few moments.

Alex gathered his clothes scattered around the room. While he dressed, she climbed out of bed, heedless of her nakedness. He'd seen her naked twelve years ago, and it was as if time had stood still and they harbored no awkwardness. Sore and sticky, the smell of him lingered on her skin, that heady mixture of designer cologne, sex, and raw male.

She belted her satin robe and turned to face him. His eyes arrested hers, dark and fiery. Two steps and his hands cupped her face, lips pressed to hers in a hard, possessive kiss.

"Got . . . to . . . go," he said between kisses. He laid a final peck on the tip of her nose.

"No time for coffee?" She arched her eyebrows.

He smiled wide and drawled, "Not if you're the cream."

She laughed. "Goodbye, Lieutenant."

He snatched his gun and spun on his heel. Caution erased the naked desire on his face. "I have leads to follow up on." He hesitated as if undecided. "Are you available later if I need you?"

"Without a doubt." Gathering her hair behind her

head, she held it off her neck, then let it fall down her back. "I already planned to clear my schedule for the week."

Alex strapped on his shoulder holster, appraising her. "You'd do that?" Gratitude turned his tone tender.

"I have a light load while I build my practice. Not all my New York clients wanted a California-based financial planner, despite the Internet."

Alex winked and walked away, leaving Juliana adrift in a sea of swirling emotions.

Making love with Alex had been intense, incredible. Long years of anticipation and frustration convened in a night so powerful, she'd never forget it. Wondrous, indefinable sensations had rocked her body and soul. She still tingled and pulsed from his touch, from the whispered words of desire that had carried them toward one summit after another throughout the early morning hours.

A delicate shiver inundated her, renewing an exquisite throbbing for his touch. She'd savor the night forever and cherish it alongside her other memories of Alex.

⊂ℛℬ∽

Juliana arrived at work, hoping Marie had finished preparing the files she'd e-mailed her last night. She was still old school, preferring certain items to be printed out for her hard copy files. Fumbling with the doorknob, she closed the door behind her and smiled at her assistant. "Hello, Marie. Did you have a good weekend?"

Marie had brought in fresh-cut roses from her garden and was arranging them around the reception room. "Hey. Same old, same old." Marie returned to her desk and held out a stack of folders for Juliana to take. "Looks like you were busy this weekend."

Juliana juggled the files in one arm and glanced at her watch. "I need you to clear my schedule after this morning for the week." She peered over Marie's head at the calendar on the monitor. "Reschedule any new clients or refer them to Phil Siebert upstairs if they can't wait."

Marie's brows lifted as her smile faded. "What's going on?"

"I need a few days for a personal matter. Can you hold the fort?"

"Sure." Crestfallen when Juliana didn't elaborate, the expression on Marie's face shifted back to business. "Don't forget, I'm taking the light rail during the week and leaving my car here. So my schedule will shift."

"Glad you reminded me." Juliana crossed the reception area.

"The janitors left the door unlocked again."

Juliana halted in her doorway. "Again?" The third time in the two weeks she'd been a tenant. Marie had complained to the management office, and they'd assured her it wouldn't happen again.

"I already called and ragged on them." Marie consulted her smartphone.

"Maybe it's time I raised bloody hell," Juliana muttered, straightening the teetering files in her arms. "Hold my calls. I need fifteen minutes of prep time." She smiled gratefully at her assistant. "Thanks."

Her solo practice as a financial planner didn't exactly abet crime solving. But with a promising assistant such as Marie, she'd be able to manage her time successfully.

She strode into her office, shut the door with a solid thump, and twisted the lock. After settling at her desk, she rummaged inside her purse for the evidence bag containing the Scottish keychain. Alex would freak once he realized she still had it. She'd deliberately neglected to return the evidence to him. Nor had he remembered to ask for it.

She stuck a tentative thumb and index finger inside the little bag. Fear wove a rope through her, but determination hastily knotted it off. Easing the gold piece out of the bag, an immediate sense of disgust hit her. The kidnapper's mind quickly reached out for hers. The weak strand was like a lightning storm on the verge of blinking out. Then the tempest strengthened and hit her full force like a hammer upside the head.

Her grip faltered, and the medallion dropped on her palm, burning her skin. It was easy to ignore the fiery sensation when her head began to pound. She closed her eyes, and the room misted, everything fading to black.

"Soon, my beautiful specter." He leaned back on the black sofa, wearing only sweat-darkened shorts. His muscles pulsated from his grueling workout. The cushy leather sofa was a balm to his sore body. He flexed his biceps and rubbed his rock-hard abs. Jasmine loved his well-muscled body as much as he loved her touching it.

A few more days and his plan would reach fruition. Excitement surged through him and awakened an arousal so hard he didn't think he could wait for Jasmine's return. His mind reeled in a dizzy array of anger. Jasmine had almost blown it. The police were on alert. And like a dimwit, she didn't know how it had happened. The need to punish her radiated through his arousal. Maybe he'd kill her after he finished with her. His humorless laughed sounded raspy.

Fingering the silky-smooth material on his lap, he lifted it to his nose. He inhaled the clean, fruity fragrance of Jasmine's perfume. Anger fueled his desire, but he ignored his bucking erection.

The closed blinds and drapes darkened the room. No

lights, no prying eyes. He spread the satin teddy reverently over his groin. He fumbled on the sofa until his fingers bit into the cold, hard gun. Lifting the Glock, he caressed the barrel. The grin never left his face. He didn't object to using the gun to achieve his goals. After all, he'd learned from the master. He stroked the barrel along his chiseled cheekbone. Shifting the gun lower, he stroked his erection.

Edginess flitted across his mind. Every muscle froze.

Jewel-green eyes joined him in the room.

He drew the gun into position and flicked on the end table lamp. His gaze scanned the room before resting on the antique wall mirror across from him.

Instead of his gray-eyed gaze, the mirror reflected familiar green eyes.

As sudden as their arrival, the eyes winked out. But not before terror gripped the green sea of light flooding his mind.

CHAPTER TWENTY

James greeted Alex in his office doorway, excitement burning across James' face, leaving his footsteps jumpy.

"Tell me you've found Jasmine?" Alex asked as he shoved past his friend.

"I received a call from Sharon Douglas' mother, Elena Havenhurst." James yanked a chair around and dropped into it. "Sharon and Matthew flew to Romania to adopt an orphan. They bought three round-trip tickets, one outbound seat empty. Round-trip tickets were cheaper than one-way."

Alex heaved a breath of unadulterated relief. "Explains why Juliana insisted they weren't involved."

"Tell it to the press." Frustration stained James' gaunt face, replacing his momentary excitement. He didn't look like he'd slept any more than Alex had the last few days.

"Nobody better tell that to the press." Alex worked his way to his chair behind the desk and slunk down in it. "Has a new press release been issued about the Douglases?"

"Yeah. They'll dog us for more, though."

Alex drummed his fingers on his desk-pad. "When there's a story to give, they'll get one. Until then, they can take their recorders and shove—"

"Hey, man." James held up his hands, palms out. "I'm with you on this. Don't shoot the messenger."

"Sorry." Alex rubbed his itching scar.

An expectant stillness invaded the room, almost sucking out the air. James looked pointedly at Alex. "Shelby's on the prowl. Don't let your guard down."

"I never do." Anger simmered below the surface as he waited for James to unload his mind. "Cough it up."

James took his time stretching out his long legs, crossing his ankles. Settled, he raised his head. "Shelby wears a size ten and a half shoe. We've bagged a pair of athletic shoes from his locker, an exact match to the print outside Lisette's window. His weight also matches forensics' evidence."

∽♥∾

Terror impaled Juliana. Her body slammed against the chair as if a gale force wind had blown her back. The impact shook her into full consciousness, and she clutched her aching head, rocking back and forth. A wave of nausea arrived to settle the score.

Quickly, she popped a couple of antacid tablets in her mouth, from the roll she'd nicked off Alex's desk. Leaning back, she closed her eyes, hoping to salvage her threadbare nerves. No longer clutched in her hand, the keychain lay on the floor underneath her desk. Too spent to reach down and pick it up, she concentrated on the vision.

He'd seen her eyes again. Shuddering, the images replayed in her mind. The gray eyes created an intense fear. It took everything she possessed to simply breathe through the mad thumping of her heart. *Why is this happening? How did I become so unlucky as to tap into this lunatic's mind? Who the hell is he?*

She had to call Alex. His anger was the least of her worries. She had a duty to help the best way she knew how, and that's what she'd done.

The intercom buzzed, startling her. Marie's voice announced, "Nicholas Hastings can't make his appointment. He'll drop by later to sign the papers."

Relieved, Juliana punched the speaker button. "Did you tell him I'll be out?"

"Yes." Marie chuckled. "He said he expects to see you next Saturday, dinner with his friends. He'll call you with details." Another phone line rang. "I need to answer that." The intercom connection dropped.

Hastings' invitation offered her a foot up in California, but she was too conflicted now to think of building her practice. She gnawed on her lower lip. Tomorrow. She'd think about it then.

The pounding in her skull worsened, and she downed a couple pain relievers. She stared at the moonlit ocean scene depicted in the oil painting across the spacious office. A stalwart lighthouse flashed a welcoming beacon to endless inhospitable waters. Mighty waves crashed upon the beach. The windswept sea grass populating the sand dunes confirmed the onslaught of the oncoming storm. A storm that threatened to smother the light and inflict havoc upon her body. Lost in the panoramic scene, Juliana had a sudden feeling of displacement. She swung her gaze away from the mesmerizing painting and forced her concentration onto the here and now.

A call into her voicemail produced two messages from Alex. The first one thanked her for last night. Heat rushed to her cheeks at his heartfelt words, and the implications—him, his body—wrapped around her, the feel of his lips on hers, a return to old times, the two of them inseparable. His second message reminded her that the keychain still lay on the floor. He remembered she had it.

Tentatively, she retrieved the gold medallion. It rested silent and harmless on her palm. No pinprick of evil touched her mind. She thrust the broken keychain into the evidence bag and shoved the bag into her purse.

She dialed Alex's cell, and he answered on the first ring. "Alex, it's Juliana."

"I'd recognize your voice a million miles away. Not to mention your name flashing across my screen." His sensual tone illuminated a ray of sunshine in her heart. "What's up?"

"The kidnapper, that's what."

"Tell me more." Alex's tone turned brusque and the lover took a backseat to business.

"I have your keychain. In fact," she proceeded into the eye of the storm, "I experienced a vision from it. It definitely belonged to—"

"What?" Alex roared. "Alone? Where are you?"

"I'm okay. I'm at work," she said with as much annoyance as she could rally in her voice. Hurrying on, she halted his response. "I've had visions for a heck of a long time without you, Lieutenant. I think I can manage them just fine."

"Not these kinds of visions," he yelled. The sound of things flying and hitting walls crashed through the speaker. "You've only experienced dreams when you're asleep. Kind of hard to faint to the ground if you're already in bed."

He did have a point, but she wasn't ready to concede. "Give me a break, Alex. I was sitting down. You don't need to hold my hand."

"No? Just your head while you puke your breakfast into the trash can?"

She winced—the truth stung. "Lieutenant, listen to me and listen good." She tapped her fingernails on the glass desktop. "I've lived a long time alone, through one nightmare crime after another. I don't need you, or any man for that matter, telling me how to run my life."

He sighed heavily, as if he was heaving his last breath into the phone. A long moment of silence draped prickly curtains around her.

"Fine," he said sourly.

"Would you like to hear what I saw, or would you like to continue your losing battle?"

He groaned. "Alright. What did you see?"

She knew she couldn't tell him everything she saw or felt, or he'd go off again. If only he weren't Lisette's uncle.

"The kidnapper appeared to be in his living room. It was dark. The vision made me recall the night of the kidnapping. I remembered the vividness of the stars, how bright the moon was." Closing her eyes brought the details alive. "The house is dark, not only the inside. Outside too. No outside lights. No streetlights, no neighboring house lights."

"He's in the country," Alex said matter-of-factly.

"That's what I think."

"What else?" Excitement now filled his voice.

She opened her eyes and stared at her email inbox, seeing nothing but the screen light burning into her retinas. "He has a gun, a nine-millimeter Glock."

"Shit." Alex thumped his fist against something hard. "You saw enough detail to distinguish the brand?"

"I can recognize a Glock." *Don't go there, please.* "You carry one." She brushed her budding apprehension aside.

"What's he doing with it?" He spit the words out slow and cool.

Juliana could tell that his coolness was deliberate, as if speaking through clenched teeth.

"He was fondling it." And himself. She once again felt the kidnapper's lust, and more. He hungered for power, revenge, money and, of course, Jasmine. And another emotion that escaped and confused her.

She related the rest of the vision, absently filtering through her emails, not comprehending them.

After a lull in the retelling, Alex asked, "Anything else?"

"That's it," she hedged.

"He saw your eyes again, didn't he?" he barked, not even teasing at a question.

She flinched. No use dodging. The whole eye thing freaked her out. "Yes."

"Damn it, Jewel. How can he see you? None of this makes sense."

She envisioned Alex's fear and frustration, his hands skimming through his hair and rubbing his scar.

"And my delving into his mind, feeling his emotions does?" She avoided mentioning her discovery from Doc Brian's research materials. "Trust my instincts." She glanced at her watch. "Got to go. I have a million things to wrap up."

"We're not through with this conversation."

"Sure, whatever. Call me later." Clicking off her cell, she provided him no opportunity to respond.

Like hell she'd sit on her laurels and wait for the kidnapper to connect with her. She had a *tête-à-tête* to attend where the short list of invited guests numbered two—the kidnapper and Juliana Westwood's mind.

CR80

It was too easy to cajole stiff-necked Bremley into allowing her onto the estate grounds without flashing a badge. Her playful machinations yesterday hadn't gone to waste. But she couldn't discard the heebie-jeebies erupting inside whenever she was around him, or the skin eating gooseflesh scattering across her body.

After a nod of approval at her BMW, Bremley pointed out a shortcut to the guesthouse. Fully prepared, she arrived at the cottage, her stomach coated with antacids and an unopened can of ginger ale clasped in her hands. Tools of the trade.

Juliana hesitated before she touched the door handle. She forced an inner peace to rise and conquer her fears. If her psychic abilities now included touch telepathy, she'd have to work with the skill, and open her mind to the psychic connection, on her terms. Focusing her mind, she settled on the single thought allaying her trepidation.

Alex. The memory of his hands caressing every inch of her body, followed by his mouth.

The thoughts filled her with energy, strength. At a tenuous peace with herself and her surroundings, she entered the cottage. With a pang of doubt, she tied her thoughts of Alex to the outskirts of her mind. She wasn't sure if her plan would work, but it was worth a shot.

Juliana recalled one of Doc Brian's favorite phrases: "You can't see if you don't look." And look she would. His advice had never failed her.

The crime lab technicians had performed their magic after her vision yesterday. Confident she wouldn't contaminate any evidence, she slowly surveyed the room, scanning for items *he* might have touched. She'd treat objects to the touch test once she finished eyeballing the rooms. Unfortunately, she knew the master bedroom was the key. The kidnapper and Jasmine were eager and voracious sex partners. They would've made full use of the bed.

Looming dread followed her measured steps into the master bedroom. A pastel floral motif decorated the cheerful room from the thick, luxurious jacquard comforter on the queen bed to the wallpaper. The room festered with his touch. The air sizzled with his presence. She didn't need to touch anything to feel him there.

The sensation that she wasn't alone flowed over her like cooling lava. She couldn't shake off the overshadowing evil. The vision worked its way through her, searching for a crevice in her mind to crack open. In a moment of near panic, Juliana eyed the bed. The bed was the perfect spot to experience the vision assailing her from all four corners of the room.

Great place to pass out. The dim thought would've made her laugh in another lifetime.

Reconciled, she climbed on top of the elevated bed and stretched out in the center. She ironed the comforter with her hands to feel as much of him as possible. The vision came fast and furious. Pain seared her head. Rage slammed against the pit of her stomach. The bright and airy room became a cold, inky cavern.

"Lisette, be a good girl and eat. I made it the way you like." With one knee on the bed, he coaxed her to take the bowl of cereal. He'd finally bent her to his will, reducing her to a rag doll. She no longer needed a sedative. But why was she resisting him now?*

Lisette sat listlessly on the corner of the bed against the wall, as far away from him as possible. "Where's Jasmine?" Her voice trembled.

"Out."

Anticipation for Jasmine's return burned hot inside him. She should have transferred the note to the courier by now. They should have received the ransom at that stupid relic they called a house. The house that should burn to the ground with its occupants inside, to melt and wither away into a pile of ashes.

He granted them a favor by merely asking for money. They deserved so much more. Maybe, after securing the money, a small spark strategically placed . . .

A grim set to his mouth, he struck the thought from his head. Leaning closer to Lisette, the bed jiggled under him. He almost upended the bowl of soggy cereal on his freshly laundered pants. Lisette glued herself even tighter to the corner, cringing like a leach against the wall.

"Take the bowl and EAT!" No one could ever say he mistreated her by not feeding her.

His patience stretched thinner than a condom. Damn it, Jasmine, where are you? *The mere thought of her made him so hot. His erection was instantaneous, hard, aching. He wanted out of the stifling room before he lost his self-restraint.*

Why is the brat disobeying me?

"This is the last time I tell you to take the bowl!" Teeth clenched, he thrust the cereal at her the same time she reached for it. The bowl flipped, strewing soaked cereal and milk across the bedspread and splashing his khaki pants.

A heat-wave of fury deluged him. He struggled to remain cool-headed. He couldn't let her see him lose control, even though he wanted to spank the shit out of her.

Rising from the bed, he spoke through gritted teeth, "Put the cereal back in the bowl, and eat every bite. If the bowl isn't clean, you will be punished." He backed out of the room.

She averted her eyes and started sopping up the soggy mass.

She knew he was master. A jolt of smugness sent another stream of desire to his groin.

He locked the door behind him and shoved the key in his pants pocket. His hand brushed against his hardness, his anger having stoked his arousal. If Jasmine didn't arrive soon, he would have no choice but to take matters

*into his own hands. Literally. He grimaced at the thought.
As he unbuttoned his trousers to relieve the pressure, the
sound of the garage door opening transformed his mood.
Exhilaration swelled inside him, ready to burst forth like
a breached dam.*

*He jogged through the kitchen into the garage.
Jasmine's lame, matronly librarian costume didn't detract
from his desire. With excitement painting her face, the
body of Venus under the dowdy clothes, she looked enticing
even through her thick nerd glasses.*

*"Worked like a charm." She giggled and ran toward
him, bouncing on her toes.*

*"Tell me everything." He pulled off her fake glasses and
yanked off the short black wig, freeing the sun-drenched
blonde tresses.*

*"I met the courier as planned at the grocery store
parking lot. I gave him the envelope and the money." She
gloated, a feral grin on her face.*

*"Then I followed him to the Chamber estate and
parked behind the neighbor's bushes. The courier had to
wait for some stupid beemer. Anyway, he dropped the
envelope in the mail slot, hit the intercom and he was
gone. It was way too perfect." She clapped her hands like a
child.*

*He grinned as relief barreled through him. "Come here.
I have a big present for you." He shoved her against the
shiny black convertible.*

*"Now? In the garage? You must be happy," she cooed.
Her nimble fingers began peeling off his pants. "Don't be
so rough this time." She pouted.*

*Ignoring her, he gazed into the convertible's rearview
mirror.*

*Sunlight streamed through the wide garage door,
giving him a clear view of the jeweled green eyes studying
him. They startled him for a split second. Familiar with*

them now, he knew another person had linked to his mind.

Stark terror seized the green eyes while they probed his mind, searched through his eyes, left footprints on his brain. They watched him, his moves, his actions.

Soon he would know the identity of the evasive psychic.

"Baby, what's wrong?" Jasmine stroked him, back and forth. Her magic fingers quelled his quick flash of anger.

He wrenched his gaze from the mirror, but the consuming sense of intrusion remained. He treated his gaze to Jasmine and returned to his original course. The green eyes that had haunted him for days continued their excursion deeper into his mind.

"You want to see something? Well, see this." Desire muffled his voice. Roughly, he raked up Jasmine's long skirt.

The elusive eyes blinked out of his mind.

CHAPTER TWENTY-ONE

Alex assigned another round-the-clock tail on Shelby. But he wasn't ready to tip his hand, not without more than the circumstantial evidence provided by the shoes. The footprint could belong to any number of people, including Bremley. The idea that Jasmine was in collusion with Shelby grazed Alex's mind. If Shelby were responsible, he would convict himself under Alex's watch. He was an idiot waiting to get caught.

He dialed the phone number scrawled on the scrap of paper in his hands and settled into his chair. After the third ring, the pleasant voice of an older woman greeted him.

"Dr. Brian Miller, please."

"Just your luck, he's home early." She called for Brian in the background. Rustling and muffled voices preceded the doctor's voice on the line.

Out of breath, Miller greeted him, and they made their introductions.

"Are you the Dr. Miller who treated Juliana Westwood in New York?"

"Yes. Is she okay?" Miller's worried voice carried through the phone. "She tried to contact me last night—"

"She's not hurt," Alex cut in. "She's assisting me on an

abduction case."

"We heard about the case up here. We're praying for the girl's safe return."

Alex crumpled several old messages and tossed them in the trash. "She's my niece."

"I'm sorry for your troubles, son."

"Thanks." Alex hesitated a beat. "Dr. Miller, I have a few questions."

"I suppose you want to know if Juliana's ESP abilities are legitimate."

He winced. "We're beyond that."

"Great. I assume she's helping out, stubborn and tenacious as usual?"

"You could say that." Alex laughed, somber and wooden. "You said she tried to call you last night?"

"We never connected. I was on a fishing trip, but lost a tussle with a poison ivy bush and came home early." He sighed and chuckled.

"Ouch." Alex scratched a sympathy itch on his forearm.

"Son, tell me what's bothering you, and I'll tell you if I can help. You understand doctor-patient privilege?"

"I'm aware." Alex had hoped the doctor might forget the privilege for a few minutes.

"Here's the scenario." Alex told the doctor what he knew about Juliana's ESP.

"You're on the right track," said Miller. "Every brain emits electrical currents. Some currents are stronger than others and transmit farther. Certain people, like Juliana, are more adept at drawing in those currents, acting as a conduit. Picture in your mind various magnetic strengths, and then picture the biggest and strongest magnet of the bunch. That would be Juliana. She's the strongest receptor I've ever encountered." Miller paused. "Are you following me?"

"Yes." Alex shoved back from his desk, the phone cord stretched taut. A knock sounded at his door. Before he could answer, the door opened and a clerk waved another stack of messages at him. He shot her a look of disgust he didn't feel. She grinned, stuck them on his dartboard and retreated.

Miller continued, "She can receive thoughts and emotions, depending on the strength and abilities of the transmitter. Usually happens when the person's in a heightened emotional or agitated state. That's why she's good at connecting with criminals."

"Right. She's connected to this bastard through whatever channel he's transmitting his bullshit on." Animosity exploded through Alex's voice.

Miller clucked like a mother hen. "Juliana's done this many times. She knows what she's doing. Why don't you tell me what's really going on? Better yet, tell me why you're so worried."

The doctor was an astute receptor himself. "Juliana and I go way back. She's a close friend."

Silence hit the other end of the phone. Alex rose and stared at the Scottish castle poster on his wall. He could swear the line went dead. "Dr. Miller?"

"I remember you now. You're the young man Juliana left behind in California all those years ago."

Alex froze. "She mentioned me?" Was that good or bad?

"Let's just say your name came up." Miller chuckled. "I take it the case has thrown you two together?"

"Yes." Alex dug his hand in his pocket, pulled out another roll of antacids and rolled it between his fingers. "Juliana's having visions after she touches something the perp's touched."

"Whoa there, son." A stony trace deepened Miller's voice. "She never experienced touch telepathy in any of her previous cases. Tell me everything you saw."

He described both episodes he'd witnessed, including her rendition of the vision in her office. Miller's clucking on the phone disturbed Alex as much as the retelling.

Alex succumbed to massaging his twitching scar, making it itch even worse. "Doc, here's the clincher, and this bothers me the most. Juliana thinks the perp can see her." He paused. "She's seen his eyes, feels him watching while she's in his head. He knows her eyes are green; he's seen them in his mind."

Another long hush met his words. Alex waited for Miller to speak.

"Lieutenant, I'll say this straight out. She's moving into dangerous territory. This perp obviously has a deep connection with his own psychic ability. In time, he will identify her, as she will eventually identify him."

Alex didn't want to hear that. It depicted the worst possible scenario. His gut clenched, unabated, laughing at the antacids. "First one to the finish line wins the race?"

"In so many words."

"How can I stop him?"

"Short of locking her in a cage or denying access to the deviant's mind, you can't."

Trepidation spread through Alex like a slow cancer. He was caught in a catch-22. On one hand, he was desperate to find Lisette, and Juliana was the key to unlocking the mystery. On the other, if he let Juliana help him, she lived in danger from exposing herself to the kidnapper.

Let her? Who was he kidding? He couldn't stop her. Her escapade that morning proved it.

"Alex?" Miller's voice hauled him back to the present. "You can't stop her or the perp. But there's a way you can protect her, to keep her from being pulled into his mind too deeply."

"I'll do anything," Alex replied, his desperation causing him to knock his forehead against the window.

"Don't let her be alone in situations where she invokes the visions. Since she passes into a dream state, she needs someone to wake her, to back her out of his mind. Someone she trusts, who she cares enough about to bring her back. Can *you* do that?"

Despite the amazing night they'd spent together, Juliana's feelings about their relationship were a mystery. He knew she wasn't ready. Regardless, no other choice existed.

Unequivocally certain, he answered, "I can do it."

"Good. Here's what I want you to do." Miller explained the tasks, then added a final admonition. "Whatever you do, don't leave her alone."

Alex jotted notes on his desk pad. A feeling of impending doom seeped into his core. What if he couldn't do what the doctor mandated? What if he lost her in the process?

"Alex, you can do it." Miller interjected.

Alex drew in a deep fortifying breath and voiced his final thoughts. "I'm confused. I think Juliana explained it to me." Deep in thought, he stroked his chin. "Why doesn't she need someone to pull her out of her nighttime dreams?"

"While asleep, her mind searches for others, so to speak. This perp's own psychic waves are strong. When she experiences a touch telepathy episode, he uses the equivalent of a crowbar to pry open her mind. He sucks her into his mind, forcefully. It may or may not be deliberate on his part."

"Shit." Alex groaned and slammed his fist on the desk. "Why the hell does she pass out?"

"It's a protective mechanism her body takes. The kidnapper's thoughts and emotions overwhelm her. She's better off asleep. Does she still suffer from the headaches?"

"And nausea." Alex glanced absently at the clock over the door. His race against Father Time crashed into him, pounding his heart into dust. His next question rushed out. "Tell me about the Westwood family curse. She has a half-assed idea that she's going crazy."

Miller laughed. "It will never happen to Juliana. She's too smart, too strong. Ask her about it later. As for the telepathy, she controls herself well, but it could cause problems."

"I don't have issues there." Alex grinned. "She'll be pissed we talked, doc."

"We have to do what we must to protect the ones we love."

Love? Was he so transparent?

Miller laughed as if he'd read Alex's mind. "I always knew you two belonged together." A hint of conspiracy framed his words. "But any man Juliana lets close will need a thick skin."

"Like a homicide cop?" The words tumbled out.

"Son, you stole the words right out of my mouth."

The grin faded as one final thought occurred to Alex. Fear clutched his heart and squashed it. "What happens if she goes in too deep and I can't reach her?"

He listened to the doctor's grim answer before they said their goodbyes. He dialed Juliana's cell, office, and home phones and reached her voicemail at all three. He left messages for her to call and slammed down his phone.

Swiveling his chair around, he stared out the window. The morning's overcast had dissipated, leaving a molten gold sun in its wake. But the beautiful August morning did little to assuage the alarm bells ringing inside him.

"Sweetheart, where the hell are you?" No sooner did the words escape than cold reality whacked him.

CHAPTER TWENTY-TWO

A shimmer of sunlight penetrated the fog in Juliana's mind. Alex's face floated into view. She clung to the vision, trying to see him through the haze. His bright blue eyes beckoned, lighting the path to full awareness. She reached out, clutching at the air between them. The draw of love conquered the murk tugging her in the opposite direction. Her fingers found solid form and connected with the now-familiar scar on his face.

From a narrow distance, his voice called her name. "Come back to me, sweetheart," were the words that brought her fully into her own mind. Alex anchored her to his chest. Warmth flowed into her, melting the frigid evil.

She struggled to open her eyelids, but it was as if cement glued them down. Ultimately, her efforts prevailed and she blearily gazed upon Alex's gorgeous face.

The crinkles at the corner of his eyes didn't mask the anxiety paling his skin. "Going to get sick on me?"

She shook her head. "How did—"

His mouth fell on hers, silencing her. His kiss was demanding, yet ardent, seeking to chase the shadows out of her mind.

As quickly as his mouth descended, he wrenched it off

hers. Uncertainty camouflaged his face as he fixated on her. "You forgot your ginger ale."

Gently, he laid her back on the bed and positioned a plump pillow beneath her head. He grabbed the soda off the night table—the soda she'd left in the living room.

A few sips diminished the pinprick of nausea. Her heartbeat steadied as she examined Alex. His face was a rock garden of worry.

"How did you know I was here?"

Silent and welcome, he scooped her up and carried her outside into the tree-shrouded yard. His arms were safe, secure, revitalizing. Juliana breathed in deeply of the pine-fragrant air. Alex set her gently on the lounge chair and regarded her with equal parts distress and annoyance.

"After the stunt you pulled with the keychain, I had a feeling this was your next stop." His face transformed into the hard, unreadable cop face.

"Glad to hear our police force has such intelligence in its upper ranks," she teased wanly, savoring the warm breeze caressing her bare skin.

A scowl crossed his face, turned his mouth down. "Tell me what you saw before you forget."

"I don't forget." She pounded her fist on her thigh.

He towered over her, blocking the sun. "Then, tell me while it's fresh." He cocked an eyebrow.

Alex really was upset with her for working on her own initiative. *He should thank me.* Sighing, she let the matter drop. For now. The dream was too important to waste another second.

"A courier showed up with the ransom note after I arrived." Juliana absently twisted the ring on her finger. "Jasmine facilitated the handoff to the courier, then followed him to ensure the drop was completed. I didn't see any of that, just her telling the kidnapper about it."

Alex's stony façade crumbled. Excitement and expectation rebuilt it. "Finally." He hunkered down on his heels before her. "How long have you been here?"

She wanted to caress his face, but balled her hands on her stomach to resist. She glanced at her watch. "About a half-hour."

"Did you get a better look at him?"

"I only saw his eyes again. He was in his usual state of anger, excitement, arousal." The last word trailed away.

"What else?"

Juliana refused to dwell on how the dream made her feel sick, dirty, disgusted. "He drives a black convertible Jaguar. I couldn't distinguish the model. It looked sporty, new."

Alex forced her to relate every detail, regardless of how trivial it appeared. She assured him Lisette was okay—withdrawn and sullen, but alive, unharmed.

When she attempted to stand, he laid a light hand on her shoulder and pressed her down.

"You're not going anywhere," he commanded harshly.

Her eyebrows arched up. "Excuse me?"

"You'll wait here while I go up to the house. Then we'll have a little chat while I drive you home."

"I'm going with you to the house. And I have my own car, thank you very much." She pulled her braid in front of her shoulders and fingered the loose strands at the end.

"I don't have time for this now, Juliana." He met her defiant stare with his own.

An awkward silence embraced them. Ending the heavy stillness, he said tenderly, "Please do as I ask. If I need you, I'll send your pal Bremley to fetch you. Agreed?"

Various emotions barraged her chest. Alex was on the offensive, and she didn't know what to make of it. At the moment, she needed to relax, regain her composure. "Yes sir, Lieutenant." *For now.*

He patted her head as if she were a dog and rushed off.

"Good girl, Spot. Have a biscuit," she muttered as his long-legged stride carried him away from the cottage.

CRBSO

Bremley ushered Alex into the family room. The butler appeared agitated, but tried to hide it in his hasty retreat to find Samantha.

They had a ransom note and Grantham Chamber wasn't home to intercept it. Lady Luck dallied on his side, and her name was Juliana.

He was still annoyed with her. If she'd informed him of her plans, he could've helped her. Or stopped her. *Stopped her? Then what? You'd be sitting on your ass, waiting for a shred of evidence to filter its way into the PD.*

He couldn't stop her from invoking the visions any more than he could stop the nighttime dreams. Would he have prevented her from invoking a vision a second time when so much depended on them? It devastated him to watch that bastard attack her, not to mention lay his hands on his niece. He couldn't protect Juliana from the evil within her mind. But he wouldn't let her fall into the trap alone. Not now, not ever.

"Alex." Samantha rushed into the room, no more and no less distressed than his previous visits. "Any news?" Her vigilant gaze darted to Bremley guarding the doorway.

"You tell me."

"Whatever do you mean?" She twined her fingers in her pearl necklace.

"I think you know."

"Grant's on his way home." Her voice shook. "If you'd like to wait—"

"Where. Is. It?" Alex advanced toward her, towering over her petite frame. "Withholding evidence is a criminal offense."

"MacKenzie! I'll have your badge if you continue to harass my family." Grantham's arrogant, booming voice preceded him into the room.

Alex wheeled around to face Grantham. "The ransom note was delivered a half hour ago. Fork it over, or I'll obtain a search warrant and slap an obstruction of justice charge on you." Alex knew the threats were thinly veiled. Grantham's clout and money could buy his way out of almost any trouble.

To Alex's surprise, Grantham crumbled like a landslide. His eyes sunk and deep worry lines wrinkled his brow. He looked closer to eighty years old than sixty. Dazed, he draped his arm around Samantha's waist as if seeking a brace.

"Where is the message?" Grantham asked her in defeat.

She inclined her head at the butler. Bremley fished the courier's envelope from the roll-top desk beside him. He handed the slim package to Alex, his eyes dark as he also handed Alex a withering glare.

"How did you know?" Grantham asked. "Who's watching us?" He guided Samantha to the couch where they both sagged into its cold depths. "Need I be concerned about evidence you've obtained?"

Grantham's voice no longer held any rancor. Something had finally pierced his thick veneer. Alex vaguely wondered if a heart might actually exist inside the old man's body.

"You don't need a lawyer. Yet."

Alex pulled a pair of latex gloves out of his pocket and tugged them on. He slipped the ransom note out of the cardboard envelope. His pulse quickened. The cloying scent of Samantha's flowery perfume almost uprooted his stomach. Swallowing the bile in his throat, he unfolded the sheet of white printer paper.

In a generic printer font, the message read:

"If you want to see your granddaughter again, gather five million dollars in unmarked and non-sequential bills. You have forty-eight hours from the time of delivery of this letter to have the cash ready.

Twenty-four hours after receipt of this letter, you'll receive further instructions for a drop-off location to occur twenty-four hours later. Grantham Chamber, driven by Bremley, will be instructed to appear alone at the drop-off site."

It was no less and no more than Alex expected.

He showed the note to Samantha and Grantham, not releasing it from his gloved hands. Grantham rose from the couch and shuffled to the floor-to-ceiling windows overlooking the back gardens. He slowly turned around to face Alex. Tears trickled down Samantha's face. From relief, remorse or fear, Alex didn't know, didn't care.

Alex's fiery gaze landed on Grantham. "Who has it out for you so bad that they'd kidnap your granddaughter and demand such an outrageous sum?"

"MacKenzie, I don't appreciate your implication." Grantham's attempt at a scowl fell short. "Would you like to know about every business deal I've been involved in?"

"Not unless you think one of the parties has a vendetta against you or your family. You should've

stopping in front of Grantham. "Can you raise the money?"

He cocked his head to the side. "You're not seriously thinking I'm to abide by this extortion? Or play delivery boy?" Wrath flickered across Grantham's pallid face.

"To save my niece, damn straight I am." Alex stared him down. He folded the courier envelope with deliberate care. "Can you raise the money?"

"I'm not certain." Grantham spun away. "He doesn't give me much time. What if he takes the money and doesn't release Lisette?"

"Get the money and let me catch the bastard." Why was the man being so stubborn? Wasn't his granddaughter's life worth it? Alex wanted to beat common sense into the man.

Grantham nodded slowly.

Alex's blood boiled, although he didn't show it as he shifted into fifth gear. He called the PD and ordered a wiretap on the Chambers' phone, and alerted James to prepare for a long night of strategizing.

Securing the ransom note in the envelope, he strode off to collect his wayward psychic.

CHAPTER TWENTY-THREE

Juliana waited in the gardens, not so much to obey Alex, but to glean details about the ransom. Faint tinkling sounds from the water fountain drifted to her. She desperately wished she could laze forever in the serene gardens. She'd barely closed her eyes to soak up the sun when Alex's footsteps drew near.

"You were right," he announced. "Let's go." He barely slowed down.

"How much? How long?" Juliana jumped off the lounge, lengthening her steps to match his stride on the flagstone path. They rushed toward their cars until he slowed to adjust his stride to hers.

"Five mil, forty-eight hours."

"Can they raise the money?"

Alex halted in front of his SUV parked beside her car. "He's working on it. We'll come back later for your car."

"Afraid not. I need my car." The fire in his eyes didn't bode well for her.

"Why, Juliana?" Alex stepped closer, dominating the space around her. "So you can pull another stunt like this? I don't have time to talk to you later. Get in so we can talk now."

tender squeeze.

"Please, Juliana, I want you safe." His face softened. "I don't want you running off half-cocked and getting into trouble."

"I'm not getting into trouble." She stamped her sandal on the pavers.

Alex studied the ground, then lifted his head. His mouth quivered slightly. "I spoke to Dr. Miller this morning."

Juliana rolled her eyes and released his arm. "Doc's on a fishing trip."

"He came home early."

Alex spoke to Brian? How dare he?

"Where are we going?" She narrowed angry eyes. How much of what she'd read last night did Alex now know?

"I'll drop you off at home. Then I'm going to the station." He lowered his head and added menacingly, "No half-assed ideas about pulling another fainting spell in Lisette's bedroom."

Her tongue snuck out before she could stop the childish action. Her foolish gesture caused him to laugh, vanquishing the sourpuss look from his face.

"Don't do that unless you intend to use it." He smoothed a loose tendril of hair from her face, tucking it behind her ear, his touch burning her lobe.

"Taking Comic 101 classes now?" She jerked away. "Let's go."

They were zooming off the estate property by the time Juliana gathered the nerve to ask, "So what did Brian say?"

"That you're treading in deep water and could drown without a lifejacket." Alex's biceps coiled.

"I'm doing this for Lisette." Juliana snagged the kitten beanbag off the dash and stroked the silky fur. The toy assuaged the assorted emotions fighting for purchase inside her.

"I know and I appreciate that more than I can say. We'll deal with it." His voice thickened. "I lost you once. It won't happen again."

Alex's admission sent remorse cresting over her. "Alex, we've discussed that."

"Don't remind me." His knuckles whitened on the steering wheel. "No promises. I get it." Alex swung the vehicle onto the highway and punched the gas pedal.

Firmly, she shoved her thoughts of last night out of her mind. "Tell me what Brian said." *I can't believe Alex went behind my back and called Doc!* Getting angry at him over it would shut him down, so she took the path of least resistance to get answers.

"He said if you didn't have me with you to pull you back, you could, number one, reveal yourself completely to the bastard. Number two, lose yourself in his mind and never regain consciousness." His face turned as white as his knuckles gripping the steering wheel as he added, "You could even wind up dead."

"Alex—"

"Please. Not without me."

The please undid her, unraveling all her anger and annoyance. "Okay. I won't." Juliana stretched across the console and stroked his cheek. He caught her wrist and pressed a sizzling kiss in the center of her palm. An intense flare of heat jolted through her.

Frightened by Dr. Miller's research, she thought if her mind latched onto Alex, she could endure the visions on her own. It had worked for others, according to Dr. Miller. But the experiences in the cottage scared her to death. She didn't know if Alex in the flesh pulled her out of the kidnapper's mind, or if her subconscious did. And would it work again, even if the kidnapper's pull grew stronger?

CRSO

Alex fingered the keychain as he strode toward the back entrance to the PD. His dread shadowed him like a stalker. He feared leaving Juliana alone. Feared what she might do despite her promises to the contrary. He hoped he got through her thick skull. If she attempted to invoke another vision without him, he didn't think she'd come away unscathed.

Damn it! It was the most crucial case of his life, and he couldn't solve it without her. Alex felt the twin pulls of Lisette and Juliana, and it plagued his every second, every move. He had to trust that Juliana knew what she was doing. It didn't mean he had to like it. As long as she played by his and her doctor's rules.

An inner torment gnawed at his stomach, inching upward. He hardened his heart against the invasion. It was far easier to turn the investigation into a strictly police matter. Otherwise, his tightly-roped emotions would sink him into the black muck threatening to engulf him completely. At that point, he was only in it up to his knees.

Smoke enveloped the city—a typical summer, with grass and forest fires raging throughout the state. The haze echoed the avalanche of emotions crushing him since Juliana had walked back into his life, which then intensified when that monster snatched Lisette. He prayed he wouldn't have to sacrifice Juliana's life to save Lisette.

Nothing mattered more to him than chasing the shadows away from Lisette and out of Juliana's mind like the refreshing breeze chasing the suffocating smoke back toward the foothills.

As soon as the war room cleared, Alex gave James a nutshell version of Juliana's latest visions.

"So we got a ransom note." James ignored the thunderous glare Alex nailed on him. "We'll handle it."

The stench of stale coffee churned Alex's gut. He prowled around the large conference table scattered with files, charts, and evidence. "We'll be screwed if the entire PD crawls up this guy's ass. Can't take the chance."

"We finalize our strategy after we receive the drop-off instructions." James marked a timeline on a whiteboard.

"He won't leave Lisette at the drop-off."

"You don't know that."

Alex slammed a chair against the wall. It bounced and crashed against the steel-legged table, landing upright as if to mock him. The sight jolted sense into him and he checked his anger before he spoke. "A smart kidnapper will get the money before releasing the victim."

"We'll have every conceivable escape route under survellaince. We'll tail him." James capped the pen and turned around. "Nothing's gonna go wrong."

"Easy for you to say. She's not your niece," Alex barked. James scowled, but Alex was in no mood to sweeten his words.

"No, I'm not her uncle." James threw the marker on the table. "Doesn't mean I don't love her."

Alex shot James a mad-dog glare, but cushioned his expression after witnessing James' distress. He stopped pacing and sank into a chair. "Update me on the other leads."

"We've confirmed that the Douglases are in Romania adopting a child." James jangled keys in his pocket. "They return on Wednesday." He picked up a folder from the table and reviewed the contents. "The customer lists from the Celtic jewelry vendors are trickling in. A few aren't well-organized and lists are incomplete. The item was popular. Campbell's a massive clan. But we're honing the

to another page. "Your research on Grant Chamber, the oldest son, pans out. He's definitely in Barcelona."

Alex scanned the duplicate list of Celtic stores. "Shelby?"

"Still have a tail on him. His place is staked out. Nothing yet."

Alex shoved back from the table. "What about Bremley and the Chambers?"

James slid a file across the table toward him. "See for yourself. No unusual activity."

Alex ignored the folder. "Anything on the Jag?" A muscle throbbed in his arm, matching his pulsing scar. He rubbed his arm, wishing he could soothe his other aches and pains.

"We've pulled a list of dealers within a hundred-mile radius. We're researching customer lists of black sport convertibles for the last five model years. If the perp has that kind of taste or money, he probably bought it new."

"Makes you wonder about the ransom." Alex curled his hands into balls on the chair arms. The investigation efforts devoured time they didn't have.

"We'll have final lists on the Jag by end of day."

"Where's Jasmine?" Alex stood and paced, halted mid-stride before a flip-chart. Suspect names and probability statistics covered the top sheet in multi-colored inks.

"No luck." James scanned his notes. "We tracked down her parents in Boston. They haven't heard from her in a month. Jasmine followed her boyfriend to San Francisco last year, then he dumped her. She enrolled at State in a child development program, of all things." James pulled at his shirt collar, loosening his tie. "She kept regular contact with her mom until a month ago. Her mom's worried."

"Did she mention anything to her parents about a new boyfriend?"

"No. Her mother said Jasmine's been tight-lipped about her life for the last couple of months." James slammed his notepad on the desk, his frustration evident as an empty coffee mug rolled to the floor unimpeded. He kicked it under the table.

After he wrapped up with James, Alex stepped out into the cool night. The coastal breeze had chased away the smoky haze, invigorating him.

On his way home, he detoured to update Andrea on the case. His sister was inconsolable. He made her take a sedative before she stormed out into the night in her own pursuit to find and kill the bastard who took her only child.

Tears dried on her cheeks as she lay on the couch, her head in his lap. It shredded his insides to view the havoc the kidnapping inflicted on her. Life had been hard on both of them. They couldn't afford any more grief, any more losses.

Alex thought himself immune to love's tribulations. He'd deliberately deadened his heart against loss when Juliana had vanished. But her reappearance awakened him as if he'd been reincarnated. Her return changed everything.

Up to that point, Alex had survived homicide police work with cold detachment, identical to the way he treated the women who'd tried their hardest to get close to him, to get him to open up. He dated few women, neither loving nor trusting any of them. He never wanted the pain of loving one who'd leave him again. Instead, he buried himself in his work and gave his love and attention to Andrea and Lisette.

And he felt like he was failing them now, at a time when his heart was more alive than ever.

A new kind of anguish ripped across his awakened

ached fiercely to hold her close, to ensure she was safe. Alex waited for James' arrival before he set off for the one place that gave him pleasure, escape.

The short drive to Juliana's house was interminable. The Mediterranean house loomed in the dark. Soft light seeped through the downstairs blinds, summoning him. The porch was dark and ghostly, the deadbolt stiff. He made a mental note to exert official pressure on the builder.

The rousing in his groin intensified as he took the stairs to the second floor two at a time. He scowled at the scattered nightlights and the reason for their existence. He wanted to replace the light and never let Juliana fear the dark again.

"Jewel," Alex whispered, entering her bedroom. Longing increased inside him as he studied her angelic face, the halo of blonde hair arrayed across the pillow. He didn't want to frighten her again and kept his distance.

"Alex?" Her eyes flickered, opened.

"Expecting someone else?" He crossed the room and perched next to her on the bed. He trailed his fingers up her arm and rested them on the side of her neck. Petal-soft skin and her intoxicating floral scent intensified his arousal. His eyes roved boldly and lazily over her half-exposed breasts.

"I'm not used to men sneaking into my bedroom." She offered a shy smile.

"Get used to it." Wistfulness toyed with his tone.

Her face darkened as she sat up and leaned against the heavily carved headboard.

Scooting closer to her, he took her hand in his. "Don't give me that look. And don't say another word about it."

She appeared to struggle within herself, ready to argue. "Anything new on the case?" she asked, diverting her struggles.

Alex shrugged out of his shoulder harness, checked the safety catch on his revolver, and set it on the night table. Despite the widening of Juliana's eyes, he stripped down to his skivvies while he updated her on the case.

Stretching out on the bed, he rolled on his side facing her. "Thank you." He brought her hand to his lips and kissed her palm. Her delightful shudder added firewood to his igniting desire. "We wouldn't have made it this far if not for you." He combed through her golden tresses. Her hair felt like live silk on his skin.

"You don't have to thank me." Juliana settled on her side alongside him and traced his scar.

He burned from her touch. "You suffer, and you want no thanks?" His fingers grazed her arm, goosebumps rising in the aftermath. "You're amazing." Her hand moved to the back of his head, burrowing softly into his hair. "How are you feeling?"

"Better, now that you're here." She gave him another shy smile, then tugged his face to meet her mouth in a fervent kiss. He tasted mint on her sweet breath. And he tasted a deep hunger, a consuming desire he was powerless to deny.

The kiss was all the invitation he needed. Not another word was spoken while they rediscovered how well they fit together, how much a part of one the other was.

CRSO

Snuggling into Alex's arms, Juliana's mind wandered into dangerous territory and how right her life felt in his strong embrace. She'd discovered a half of herself previously buried with her past. She clutched him to her and held on, afraid to let go. No worries reared up while his presence chased away the dark that had held her in

relationship with him. He made it effortless as if no time had elapsed since they'd been together. But old and new doubts plagued her, unrelenting.

Loving Alex was both the easiest and the most difficult thing she'd ever experienced.

Tears glided down her face. She couldn't just walk away after they found Lisette. They had to give it a shot and see where it led. If she didn't, she'd never forgive herself for this second chance. If he could live with a psychic and trust her abilities to block out his thoughts, she'd surrender to their love. She should just go with the flow for now. Shouldn't she? Thinking Alex asleep, she was startled when his voice interrupted her thoughts.

"Jewel, what's wrong?" He lifted his head to peer into her face, but she buried it in the hollow of his shoulder.

"Nothing." To her dismay, her voice splintered. "I'm just confused. About you, me." She'd vowed to herself earlier that there would be no more secrets, no more hiding.

"Don't." His voice was satin-smooth. "Just go with it. Leave the past behind."

"I'm trying." Her arms tightened around him. "I have too much baggage. You've seen who I am."

"Stop." Lifting her chin, he kissed her forehead, locked gazes as if she'd disappear if he turned away. The moon cast an incandescent glow in the room, and his eyes sparkled with desire and something more. Something exciting and lethal. Something like love. "Don't you understand how much I want you? All of you. Just the way you are."

"Oh, Alex." Hot tears of joy and sorrow dropped on his chest.

"Shhh." He brushed another kiss on her forehead. "Did you mean the inscription in the book?"

The question caught her off-guard. How could he not

know she meant every word? "I wouldn't be here with you now if I didn't."

"Okay then. Let me hold you, keep you safe." Not even a doubt could slither between them as he held her tight to him.

Wanting to change the subject and learn more about Alex's life, she asked, "Tell me about Lisette. What's she like?"

Tension hummed through Alex and his muscles stiffened. She smoothed her hands over his back, leveling his anguish. She pressed kisses on the hollow between his throat and collarbone until he relaxed.

"She's smart, beautiful, open, trusting." His voice roughened. "She's talkative, inquisitive, sometimes too much." Alex shifted the pillows to lean against the headboard and gently pulled Juliana against his chest. "She loves everyone and everything. Animals, insects, lizards. You name it, she's not afraid of it."

"She sounds wonderful. From the pictures I've seen, she's going to be a knockout."

"Yeah, with more of Ethan's features than Andrea's."

Juliana heard a touch of irritation in his voice. Maybe talking about Lisette wasn't such a great idea.

"If I recall from high school, Ethan wasn't such a bad looking guy." She trailed a finger across his chest, feeling the heat where her touch inflamed his skin.

Alex groaned. "I'd spank you if I had the energy."

"Promises, promises." Seductively, she planted kisses along his throat and jaw, giving in to temptation. "Do you have a little energy left?"

Her hand reached lower, and he sucked in a sharp breath. "Enough."

CHAPTER TWENTY-FOUR

The moon waned around the edges. Waiting in anticipation, he stared at the luminescent globe through the wall of windows, the darkness a backdrop calming him. A smug grin kicked up his lips as he remembered the night he'd kidnapped Lisette, how the moon became his friend rather than his betrayer.

Anger had seethed in him all day as the green-jeweled eyes became more than a mere annoyance. They haunted him, chilled him. He knew another mind had entered his own, watched him, and sought his identity. Wanting to destroy him, like others had tried, to no avail. Soon the world would give him the notice due him. And they would pay for it.

He gripped the bottle of whiskey and knocked back a healthy swig. The leather couch cooled the flush prickling his naked body and the heat rising from the alcohol. First things first—he needed to uncover the enigma behind the jeweled eyes.

"Where are you tonight, my beauty? Come out, come out, wherever you are."

Minutes ticked by. Nothing.

He closed his eyes, tipping his head back against the couch. Two more days, and he was home free. Free to leave behind the world that shunned him. Free to return to the world that welcomed him with open arms.

Anticipation flowed through him like a river of melting gold, cresting in his groin with an overpowering need for release. "Jasmine, where the hell are you?"

"Jasmine," he called again. His need and excitement flickered hotter in his veins. He lurched off the couch and dropped the bottle, spilling the amber liquid on the rug. The smell of Scotch whiskey permeated the air. "Shit." He stumbled down the hall until he stood in the open doorway to the captive's room.

Lisette stared at him, horror in her eyes.

He belched and choked out a derisive laugh. "What's the matter, little girl, haven't you ever seen a grown man naked?"

Jasmine jumped off the bed, tossing aside the book she was reading to Lisette. The reproachful expression on her face was almost comical. She blocked Lisette's view with her body. "What are you doing?"

"I need you, now!" Anger replaced his excitement, his lust reaching another summit.

Green eyes bored into him. A slow grin extended his mouth. He didn't taunt the eyes or fear them this time. Instead, he let them roam at will, falling into his trap.

He grabbed Jasmine's arm, tugged her out of the room, and hauled the door shut with a bang. He yanked open her satin robe, her body naked underneath. Filling his hands with her round ass, he lifted her off the floor as she hooked her legs around his hips. He kissed her, biting her lips, grinding his mouth hard against her. Whimpering, she tried to turn her face away from him. But he forced her mouth open, his tongue demanding entrance and lashing around her quivering tongue. The spicy taste of her tequila-laced mouth incited him further.

a desert. A gasp erupted from her, and he swallowed it as he continued to ravish her mouth. The green eyes watched with a fusion of fear and horror. Hammering into Jasmine with abandon, he paid her little heed when she began whimpering. Growling like an angry bear, he came in a fierce explosion, bringing her completion fast in his wake.

Breathless and satiated, he realized Jasmine wasn't responsible for his exquisite release.

It was the woman with green-jeweled eyes. A blonde. Haze still shrouded her other features, but her hair was unmistakably blonde.

CR80

Juliana's moaning and thrashing jerked Alex out of a sound sleep. He gripped her arms and shook her gently. "Juliana, wake up."

His heart beat an erratic, guarded tempo. A vision had trapped her, and he couldn't wake her. He knew she was inside that bastard's mind. Her skin was clammy, and she panted as if she ran for her life. Hatred accompanied his intense craving to put that bastard in front of a firing squad.

"Sweetheart, I'm here. You're safe." He rained kisses from her forehead to her chin, trying to erase the vision's impact from her ravaged face.

"Please, Jewel. I love you, I need you." The words came unbidden. He felt glad to voice his mind and heart, even though she might not remember it after she awoke.

Her eyes flew open and her gaze latched onto Alex's face. Violent trembling seized her, and he enfolded her into the security of his body.

Alex's lips lingered on her forehead, willing her pain away. "Say something so I know you're okay."

She tried to push him away. "I'm sick."

In a repeat of yesterday, he picked her up, barely cognizant of her naked skin against his own. Gently, he settled her on a towel on the bathroom floor. Holding her hair in a ponytail, he rubbed her shoulders while she knelt over the toilet. Dry heaves purged the nightmare from her system. Spent, Juliana sat back on her heels and gulped in draughts of air.

A raging river of worry flowed through him. "Will you be okay while I get you a soda?"

She nodded listlessly, her elbows balanced on the closed toilet lid. He yanked a purple robe off the hook on the door and draped the satin around her tense shoulders. As if the hounds of hell were after him, he sprinted away and returned with his hands full. A reflective silence surrounded her as she accepted the soda and aspirin.

When he bent to help her stand, she brushed him away. "Leave me alone for a few minutes." Her voice was savage, raw.

"Not done?"

Her face remained lowered. "Alex, please, just go."

"Come back to bed 'til you feel better." Was the dream so awful? Was she afraid to tell him what she saw? Was Lisette okay?

"No."

"Jewel, why are you resisting?" he demanded.

She slurped soda and downed two aspirin. "He knows I'm a woman with blonde hair."

Fear filled every cell of Alex's body. With brute strength, he shoved the raw emotions inside, refusing to allow Juliana to witness his vulnerabilities lest he join her misery.

Finally, she let him pick her up. Cradling her to his chest, he carried her to the bed and wrapped the comforter around them.

down her cheek.

Juliana wound her arms around his neck and told him every detail.

Fury joined his fear and turned his insides into black ice. He wanted to torture then destroy that beast for everything he'd done to Lisette, for even walking the face of the planet. What kind of sick bastard had no clue how to act in front of a child? Hot rage seethed inside him. Only Juliana's touch kept it in check, kept him from going postal.

Nothing had prepared him for the lunatic's substitution of Juliana while engaged in sex with Jasmine either. Trembling, he rested his lips on her forehead and tightened his arms around her until his trembling became one with hers.

Slowly, she lifted her head and eased back. "Look at me long and hard. And tell me," her voice caught, "why you want to stay with me."

"Because I need you and you need me." Tenderly, Alex caught her face between both hands and kissed her hard, unrelenting at first. The joining of lips turned into a kiss of need and of a soul-deep passion.

Juliana didn't question him further.

CR80

A short time later, a possessive arm wrapped around Juliana's waist, Alex led her into Andrea's condominium. Andrea greeted them with hugs and a forced but warm smile. Alex gave Juliana a quick kiss and a stern admonition to keep out of Lisette's room and stay put until he returned. His concern soaked her in warmth. She didn't mind his control, as she was too confused and exhausted to fight it. Besides, he was right.

As soon as Alex closed the front door, leaving them

alone to visit, Andrea began fidgeting with her watchband. She gave Juliana a tremulous smile. "Would you like something to eat, drink?"

"Cold water sounds good." Uneasy and shy, Juliana set her purse on the coffee table and glanced toward the back of the condo. "I'll get it. Let me do something for you."

"Juliana! You're already doing so much." Andrea laid a warm hand on Juliana's arm. "I can't even imagine what you're going through now, or what you've gone through."

How much had Alex told Andrea about the past twelve years? "I've learned to live with it." Juliana offered her old friend her own timid smile. "Now what would you like to drink?"

As Juliana walked toward the kitchen, she spied a familiar brown envelope and stopped short. Her life lay on the kitchen table as if on parade. Andrea knew everything. Uncertain relief walked a fine line down Juliana's back. At least she wouldn't have to repeat it all.

From behind her, Andrea said, "Alex told me. I hope you don't mind."

"I'm glad." Juliana chewed on her lower lip and spun around to face Andrea. "You're not mad at me for not returning home sooner?"

"To face your father?" She snorted. "No way. But we could've helped you."

"I had to learn to live with this on my own." Juliana hitched her hands in the pockets of her denim shorts and shrugged. "No one likes being around a telepath."

"You didn't need to worry about us." Andrea crossed her arms. Her mouth opened as if to speak and then closed, her face coloring.

"I wish." Wistfulness creased Juliana's heart. Her gaze drifted to the grape ivy hanging in the corner of the

"You don't understand, Juliana." Andrea closed the distance between them, her face stained scarlet. "Alex and I have a deeper connection than most twins."

Juliana's eyes widened half in anticipation, half in dread. "What?"

"Didn't you ever wonder how we used to communicate without talking to one another?"

"I chalked it up to your closeness with each other." A strange feeling seized hold of Juliana.

"After our father left, we figured out how easy it was to communicate without anyone else knowing." Andrea smoothed back her hair. "In the last few years, we've even learned how to block our thoughts from one another."

Shocked, Juliana's mouth gaped open. Alex knew how to block telepathy? Could he read her mind too?

As if reading her thoughts, Andrea said, "We can't read other people's minds, if that's what you're wondering."

"I had no idea." Juliana sagged onto the nearest dining room chair. "My doctor mentioned that some twins have limited ESP. But I never imagined you two did."

"By the time you met us, we had pretty much quit reading each other. You know, for privacy." Andrea began to gather the articles strewn across the table.

Juliana sat in stunned contemplation. Why the hell hadn't Alex told her he possessed the ability to block her telepathy? He knew telepathy and its ramifications was a big part of the Westwood curse! Hope edged her excitement, a hope she dared not dwell on.

"I think you could use that water." Andrea grinned and rushed into the kitchen, returning with two bottles of ice water. "I'm so glad you're home. I missed you so much. Alex might not ever admit it, but he never gave up hope that you'd return."

"Could've fooled me." Juliana grimaced as she opened

the cold bottle. "If he had access to the daggers his eyes flung at me that first day at the PD, I wouldn't be here now."

"Can you blame him for the initial shock?"

"No." Juliana guzzled half the water to quench the arid desert in her mouth. "A cannon could've ripped through me and it wouldn't have surprised me more. I never expected to find Alex working as a cop, of all things."

Andrea shrugged. "It suits him."

Juliana always knew he'd succeed in life despite his upbringing in a poor, broken family—or in spite of it. He possessed the eagerness, the drive. She loved that about him.

"Yes, it does." With a dismissive wave of her hand, she said, "Forget about that, Andrea." Alex was a subject she'd dissect later. Juliana rose and pushed in the chair. "Tell me how you're doing."

"I'm okay, I guess." Andrea finger-combed her shoulder-length hair. The gesture reminded Juliana so much of Alex, when his hair had been longer. "But I'd rather talk about anything else."

Curiosity burned in Juliana, and she couldn't resist asking, "Tell me how in the world you and Ethan Chamber wound up together."

Andrea slivered her eyes. She motioned for Juliana to follow her into the cozy living room.

The cinnamon and apple aroma filling the air from a potpourri dish on the coffee table evoked memories of the candles Juliana's mother scattered around her childhood home. So many memories had crashed back over the last few days. Some good, some bad. All made up a past she couldn't deny. Despite the circumstances, being there with Andrea was comfortable, promising that future

Andrea sat on the couch, pulled up her knees, and hooked her arms around them. "I'll give you the peapod version. You already know what a crush I had on him in high school."

Juliana snuggled into the recliner facing the couch. "Yeah, you and every other girl but me." Alex was the only one Juliana had ever wanted.

"A year after graduation, I met him at a party. We dated. I got pregnant. Stupid condom broke."

A pained expression flicked across Andrea's face. "His father was ticked off at him, but Ethan loved to rebel. We did the right thing and got married." Andrea glanced at the crystal framed wedding photo on top of the TV. "Of course, I was crazy in love with him. We were excited about the baby." She hesitated, her voice lowered. "But I lost her in the fifth month."

Juliana sent her friend a sympathetic look. "I'm so sorry."

"It was a bad year." Andrea gulped her water. "First the baby, then Mom died."

Juliana flinched, knowing how it felt to lose a mother. She lifted a picture of Ethan, Andrea, and baby Lisette off the small table beside her chair and studied it.

Andrea continued, "We stayed married. I loved him, and in his own way, he loved me. But things worsened. He did everything possible to defy his father, who constantly bullied him. 'Go to business school. Come work at GC Media, dump that white trash wife.'" Andrea waved her arms around as if to dispel Grantham Chamber's image. "Ethan wanted none of it. He was determined to follow in his brother's footsteps and get away from his father as fast as he could."

Andrea rubbed her eyes. "Anyway, he started drinking and doing drugs. He'd clean up for a while. Then the pattern would repeat." A tear skated down her cheek and she brushed it aside. "I wound up pregnant with Lisette during one of the lucid times. She's the only good to come from our marriage.

"Lisette worshipped her father, even though he wasn't around much. I guess I hung in there for her. One day, I got a knock on the door." Her mouth tightened in a grim line. "The police. Ethan had OD'd at a party the night before."

Juliana returned the picture and crossed the room to sit next to Andrea. A stab of guilt pierced her chest. She wished she'd been there for Andrea during her troubled times.

"In hindsight, I was young, stupid, hoping his family would accept me." Andrea clasped Juliana's hand. "Lisette made it all worthwhile, though."

"She's beautiful." Photographs of Lisette peppered the homey condo. With her blonde hair, her looks favored Ethan, yet with Andrea and Alex's eyes.

In renewed friendship, they spent the afternoon reminiscing about high school and the last twelve years. Andrea brought out photo albums, and they were both misty-eyed by the time they flipped the final page.

They ordered a pizza and turned on the TV to watch the evening news. It wasn't long before the news centered on the abduction. "San Jose Police are continuing their search for Lisette Chamber and suspect Jasmine Webley. New evidence has come to our attention that the SJPD are following a trail of evidence brought to them by professed psychic Juliana Westwood—"

The newswoman's voice faded away. A buzzing began in Juliana's head. She willed herself to concentrate on the news report, but stars wavered in a haze before her.

"A successful financial planner, Ms. Westwood, recently relocated to San Jose from New York where she

Our SJPD source informs us that Ms. Westwood has provided false leads, including accusations that Grantham Chamber may have abducted his own grandchild."

Juliana existed in a dream world, far, far away, where real life and nightmares overlapped. A white-hot rage threatened to choke the stagnant air out of her lungs.

Chilling memories of the last time the press got wind of her psychic abilities dominated all other thought.

CHAPTER TWENTY-FIVE

Evidence, charts, and fast-food wrappers cluttered the war room. Team members entered and exited. Alex waited for the room to empty before divulging Juliana's latest vision to James.

"Lisette's still alive. I feel it. Juliana sees it," Alex concluded. He sipped his coffee and grimaced at the stone-cold brew. He tossed the cup in the trashcan, splashing coffee on the floor. The aroma battled with the persistent reek of leftover hamburgers gone cold.

"Don't disclose the decoy plan to anyone until we work it out." The door opened and Alex turned around, startled by Juliana's silhouette in the doorway.

The heated glare and condemnation on her face sent a bolt of lightning through him. A handful of wary police personnel followed her stormy path through the PD. Someone recognized her enough to let her inside, but obviously didn't trust the murderous gleam in her eyes.

James swiveled in his seat and jumped up to tug Juliana into the room and Alex chased everyone away.

"What have you done?" she spat out, her eyes a roiling sea of darkening green.

"Jewel." Alex gripped her upper arms and rubbed

a steel beam.

"Don't touch me." She wrenched away, her back against the door.

He stepped closer, but didn't attempt to touch her again. With the fury in her eyes, he wasn't sure she wouldn't use her manicured claws on him. "What's wrong?"

"As if you don't know."

"Sweetheart." His scar started to twitch, and he absently rubbed it in his confusion. "Tell me—"

"Don't 'sweetheart' me, Lieutenant MacKenzie. I put my life in your hands, and look what happened," she sputtered. "You're one puppet-master who can find himself another puppet."

Alex darted a bewildered glance at James and received a wide-eyed shrug in return. Alex gestured to Juliana and then a chair. "Sit and tell me what's going on." He reached for her hand, but she hid it behind her. The freckles on her nose disappeared in her crimson rage.

"You promised." She choked on a sob. "It's all over the news."

"I'll check it out." James shot out the back door, as if he couldn't escape the tigress fast enough.

Alex eased closer to Juliana. "What's in the news? We've been locked in here all afternoon." His mind reeled with crazy ideas of using Juliana's telepathy to catch the kidnapper. A faint brush against his mind startled him, but he ignored it and gave his full attention to Juliana.

Shock crossed her face. Strangled words stumbled out. "You're going to use me and my ESP as a decoy to distract the kidnapper? Is that why you spilled—"

His thoughts punched him in the gut. He searched for a plausible explanation. How could he defend his own thoughts? He didn't even have a plan fully fleshed out. Not that she'd believe him in her current frame of mind.

"You're right. I wouldn't believe you. That trip ended an hour ago." She folded her arms across her chest.

"Stop, Jewel. Let me explain." Alex reached toward her, but her fiery eyes warned him to back off. Reluctantly, he dropped his arms to his side, his hands dangling uselessly when he wanted to be touching her, soothing her anger and confusion. Whatever had happened was bad. Real bad.

"Don't ever call me Jewel again, Lieutenant. You no longer have such privileges."

The words sliced through his heart.

James jogged back into the room. "Man, you're not gonna believe it. Juliana's been ID'd as our source. It's not good. The press says she's given us false leads and we're bumbling around like idiots."

"Shit." Alex shoved a whiteboard covered in scrawled tactical solutions out of her view. No need for her to see more strategy he'd discarded as dangerous. He landed a hard look on Juliana. "You don't think—"

"Tell me what a decoy's supposed to think." Lines of pain mingled with the anger on her face. She pivoted toward James. "James, I'll call you if I happen to have any more dreams. But from past experiences, now that I have to fear for my own life, the dreams won't come back."

She reached behind her for the doorknob. Alex caught her arm, tried to force her around. But she yanked away and he reluctantly released her, hands in the air in surrender.

He had to make her understand. "Please sit. Let me explain."

"Let me tell you something, *Lieutenant.*" Juliana shook her head. "The last time I was exposed as a psychic, I was kidnapped and held hostage with a nine-millimeter Glock in my face for two days." She wrapped her arms

people, three of them his own family members. I barely escaped with my life after almost being gunned down by the maniac and the NYPD in a SWAT standoff."

Alex stiffened, his muscles corded. "I'll place 'round-the-clock guard on you. Just listen to me."

"Don't do me any favors," she spat out. "Two topnotch policemen had guarded me, and neither one of them survived. I no longer trust that you have my best interests at heart." Eyes narrowed, she pushed back the tangle of hair pulled loose from her braid. "Well, 'heart' never entered the picture, did it? I guess I can't blame you. I hope the last couple of nights paid you back for the twelve years I was away having fun. Because that's all you're getting. I hope to hell it was worth it." She flung open the door and raced into the hallway.

"Jewel," he shouted.

"I'll put Sterling on her." James grabbed the phone as Alex darted after Juliana.

He was damned if he'd let her out of his sight. "Juliana!" She reached the door in the front lobby. "Stop," he bellowed. To Alex's surprise, she halted and turned to glare at him.

The usual squad room clamor fell to a deafening silence. Several uniformed officers surrounded Juliana. Alex motioned them to back off. They complied, wary eyes trained on Juliana, fingers twitching at their holsters.

"Lieutenant, I've said all I care to say to you. Spend your time on the bad leads I gave you." Juliana swiped at the tears on her cheeks. "Then go to hell."

Chatter swelled among the onlookers. Alex ignored it, focusing on Juliana.

"Juliana, I didn't leak it to the press."

"Save it." She rubbed her palms on her shorts, her eyes scanning the faces around her. "Deny that you were thinking of using me as a decoy."

What he saw on her face cut him to the bone. Betrayal. Fear. Destroyed trust.

"No, sweetheart. It's not true." He itched to touch her, but kept his arms pasted to his sides, afraid to reach out. "Stay here. I can keep you safe."

"Safe? You can't even keep your sources safe." She spun toward the door again. "Don't follow me. Don't even come near me."

The words were pure poison, dripping straight into his heart.

James grabbed Alex's arm, stopping him from following her.

"I have to go after her." Despair and fear towered up Alex's back.

"We need you here. Let her go. She'll be okay." James shouted for Sterling.

The crowd around them dispersed, police personnel returning to their duties. The din increased as the activity level returned to normal.

Juliana walked into the hornet's nest at the bottom of the concrete steps. Alex shouted out a demand for uniformed officers to clear a path for her and to hold off the reporters.

"Sterling," James yelled again. "Shadow her. I want a team of twenty-four hour protection on her."

"Yes, sir." Sterling jetted out the door.

The young uniformed officer caught up to Juliana and followed a few steps behind. One of the PD's best new recruits, he'd keep her safe. Alex had to trust in that. Not like he had a hell of a choice.

He shot scathing glances around the room as he and James passed through the squad room, heading to his office. Strung so tight, he couldn't even clench his fists. One swipe of his arm and half the items on his desk sailed

James closed the door and leaned against it. "Let her calm down, then go talk to her."

"Who the hell was it?" Alex sagged into the nearest chair. Three people at the PD knew about Juliana's ESP. Two were in his office. The third was Captain Hayes.

But a potential fourth person would try anything to seek vengeance against Alex.

Chad Shelby. The bastard must have intercepted Alex's reports to Captain Hayes. How else had he found out? Had he sneaked into Alex's office and computer? *Fuck.* If Shelby was responsible for the leak, he'd have that asshole's balls delivered to IA in a paper sack. He could try to ruin Alex's career all he wanted, but he went beyond twisted by involving innocent people and putting his niece in more danger.

The memory of Juliana's face and her cutting words seared into his mind. He'd failed to guard his thoughts when she'd stormed into the war room. He'd have a hell of a time explaining the idea they'd cooked up, if she ever gave him the chance.

To hear about her kidnapping and attempted murder in New York nearly drove him insane. He couldn't lose her again. The possibility swept cold dread through him before turning to a scorching rage.

James rapped the table and coughed loudly, diverting his attention.

Son of a bitch, he didn't have time for this shit, not when Lisette was in the hands of a maniac.

❧❧

Juliana punched the gas pedal of the car she'd borrowed from Andrea. A cop followed in an unmarked vehicle, and she didn't care that she raced twenty miles over the speed limit. Hysterical laughter exploded from her compressed lips. "I'm in this mess because of them!"

Her laughter quickly evolved into a chilling calm, enough to clear her mind, to stay one pace ahead of the kidnapper. He knew she existed. Three times now, he'd seen her—the last episode more revealing than the previous dreams. With a definite feeling of blind destiny, she knew he wasn't far behind.

The police cruiser closed the distance on her tail. She needed to lose it fast. They'd hamper her or haul her back to the PD and charge her with some stupid infraction to justify holding her. The SJPD couldn't keep her safe. She'd be better off on the run, hiding out, working from a distance.

A skewer of pain rendered her heart numb. How could Alex have let this happen? She'd trusted him to keep her identity hidden, not to use her as a decoy. How dare he?

She banged her hand on the steering wheel. "What a fool I am." Undeniably in love with a man who'd used her and betrayed her. The last two nights should never have happened. Alex should never have happened.

A sleek sports car cut in front of her. She narrowly avoided crashing into it. Shaking off the mental cobwebs, she concentrated on her driving and a solid plan. Clutching the steering wheel, she zigzagged in and out of traffic. The police car maintained a discreet distance, like a tick on a dog she couldn't shake.

Her office tower came into view, and a light bulb blinked on in her head. Marie was using the county transit system during the week to save on gas. She left her car at the office to run errands during the day. The car was in the back tenant parking lot, spare keys in her desk. The imbecile cops would never catch on, not before Juliana was long gone. A sigh of satisfaction escaped her pursed lips.

the customer lot in front. The cop car caught up, but veered to the left in the parking lot, never losing sight of her.

Juliana nonchalantly locked the car and sauntered into the building through the front door. She maintained an air of composure despite the anvil weighing her down.

The elevator ride to the fourteenth floor was interminable. She caught sight of her ashen face in a beveled mirror panel and blanched. Unrecognizable murky pools of green stared her down. She hated the terror in her eyes and jerked her gaze to the elevator doors as the fourteenth floor dinged its arrival. A few steps, and she faced her office door. The key slipped into the lock with no resistance.

"Damn cleaning crew," she muttered. This was the fourth time in recent weeks they'd neglected to lock the door behind them.

An empty suite greeted her. A hasty search of Marie's desk produced the spare car keys. She jotted a quick note that she'd call Marie and left it, along with Andrea's car keys, in Marie's desk.

Not wanting to chance using the elevator and being seen in the front lobby, Juliana headed toward the back staircase. Breathless and fourteen sets of stairs later, she ran out the back lobby door. A quick scan around the rear of the office tower, a brisk walk, and she settled into Marie's economy coupe.

Clueless idiot cops. Juliana laughed mirthlessly.

No one followed her as she zigzagged through the busy downtown streets. She maintained the speed limit to avoid undue notice. Periodically, she checked her rearview mirror. Even in the twilight, she detected no car following her for any consistent distance. Relief settled her heartbeat to a normal rhythm.

Her cell rang several times. Certain the calls were

from Alex, she clicked off the phone and tossed it in her purse. She turned the radio on and found a classic rock station. But not even her favorite music stopped her from caving in with thoughts of Alex. She couldn't believe she'd fallen right into his web. In her own bed, no less.

At least he'd made it easier for her to walk away and pretend the last week had never happened. If she couldn't trust him not to let crucial information out of his hands, how could she trust him with her heart? The price of his betrayal eclipsed anything she'd ever experienced because she loved him to the bottom of her soul. Just that morning, she'd decided to let their relationship run its course, despite her original plan to end it. *Now what?*

Juliana maneuvered the car onto the expressway. The small engine groaned under her lead foot. Another glance in the mirror assured her she wasn't being followed, and she let up on the accelerator.

She was beginning to need Alex, and she wanted him more than anything or anyone. It felt so right to wake up in his arms, to have him pull her out of her nightmares. To chase the evil from her mind. To keep her safe from the dark. To chase away the shadows always haunting her.

She loved his smile, his laughter, his sense of humor. She loved to drown in his lake-blue eyes. She loved his tough macho act and the loving, sensitive man who bought trinkets for his niece and cared for his widowed sister.

Alex even had the ability to block his mind from telepathic intrusions. It proved they were meant to find one another again and rekindle the love denied them by her father, by her heritage.

The exit she needed came quicker than anticipated. She crossed a lane and zipped off the expressway. A car

recklessness.

Tears blinded her, and the car drifted to the left. Quickly, she swung the steering wheel to the right. The overcompensation almost caused her to sideswipe a parked van. Juliana brushed away the tears, but more raced to replace them. Pulling off the road, she slammed on the brakes, rocking the vehicle to a stop. The seatbelt locked against her chest, pinning her to the seat.

Deep sobs racked her from head to toe.

CHAPTER TWENTY-SIX

"Where's Juliana?" Alex barked at James as he slammed into his office. The door hit the wall and the wall clock clattered to the floor in pieces.

He'd just scoured the administration complex only to find Shelby missing. The police tails had lost the asshole hours ago. He booted the plastic clock face, and it scudded under his desk, clanged off the far wall, and rested against a desk leg.

"Sterling tailed her to her office. She's parked out front. A second officer just arrived on the scene."

Apprehension ran roughshod over Alex's fury. He glanced at his watch. "What the hell is she doing at her office after nine?"

The phone buzzed and James snatched it up. Alex resumed his predatory pacing. He mentally kicked himself for toying with the idea of using Juliana at the ransom drop-off. She'd obviously only picked up part of his thoughts and had been too distraught to read the rest before he threw up his mental shield. She would've remained safe, while he used a decoy in a blonde wig. He'd die first before he let any harm come to Juliana.

"Alex. You listening?"

"We have a match on the Jag and keychain. We're tracking addresses now." James shoved a notepad at Alex. One name was written across the pad.

Nicholas Hastings.

"Son of a bitch." A cold knife of fear carved up Alex's gut. "He's a client of Juliana's." Hastings knew where Juliana worked.

"A client?" James looked askance at Alex. "She didn't recognize him from her dreams?"

Alex bolted for the door, James hot on his heels.

"She never saw his face, only his eyes."

"O'Malley! Westwood gave Sterling the slip." The shout rang out as soon as they hit the squad room.

James collided into Alex, nearly toppling them both to the floor.

"Son of a bitch!" Alex roared as he spun around. "How the hell did she slip through your fingers?"

Team member Detective Gilbert approached Alex. "Sterling believes she went out the back. The janitors let Sterling inside her office. She borrowed her secretary's car and took off."

"Find the make and model, issue an APB." Alex tightened his gun harness and clipped his cell to his belt. "When you obtain a solid address on Hastings, call it in to me. The house we're looking for is in the country, probably not too far outside city limits."

"Yes, sir." Gilbert hustled off.

"I should've gone after her myself." Alex and James set off at a jog toward the parking lot.

"You can't do everything." James pulled his car keys out, a step ahead of Alex. "Lisette's your first priority."

"And I vowed to protect Juliana." The words stuck in his throat.

"You didn't know this would happen."

Alex halted at his SUV, gripping his keys so hard they

dug painfully into his palm. "I should have, with Shelby on a rampage."

"We'll find her." James tossed his keys in a cup holder, slid into the passenger seat, then plunked the red flashing light on the dash.

Alex shot a hard look at James as he started the engine. "I'll kill him if he lays a finger on her."

"Don't go homicidal on me, man."

"Do you love my sister and my niece?" Alex asked through gritted teeth.

James didn't hesitate. "You know I do."

He swerved the SUV into traffic and gunned the gas pedal. "What would you do if your girlfriend and niece were held captive by a madman who had a hard-on the size of Florida?"

"I'd kill him."

⊂ଷଛଠ

Juliana peered through the etched glass in her front door. The house appeared undisturbed, at least from her limited view. The kidnapper probably didn't know where she lived. Yet. Her phone number and address were unlisted. No one followed her. Yet she couldn't shake the feeling of ants crawling up her spine as if she were being watched.

The deadbolt gave her difficulty, as usual. She slipped into the darkened foyer, leaving the lights off. Ice filled her veins as her fear of the dark threatened to suffocate her. Strategically placed nightlights offered a faint glow, which eased the shadowed corners, but not enough to erase her panic.

The ants continued their relentless advance, but she willed herself to move. She raced up the stairs into her

First things first. She scurried to the bed and fumbled underneath it until she felt hard steel.

Juliana set the loaded gun on the dresser and quickly changed into jeans and running shoes. The gun became her final accessory as she shoved it into the waistband of her jeans on her left hip, covering it with her hoodie. The weapon's coldness penetrated her T-shirt to her skin, and she quaked from more than the cold.

An overnight bag was lodged on the top shelf of her closet, and she yanked it down. Haphazardly, she packed clothes and toiletries for several days of living incognito. Winded, she spun toward the open doorway. JB streaked into the room and leaped on the bed. His fur stood straight up as if he'd stuck his paw in a light socket.

"There you are." She bent to scoop him off the bed, and he hissed like a cornered rattlesnake. "Don't start with me, buster." She snatched up her bag and spun around.

Her blood froze, rooting her feet to the floor.

JB wasn't hissing at her, but at the blond intruder.

Amused gray eyes fixated on her.

Juliana's heart hammered in her ribcage as she stared at the motionless man filling the doorway, blocking her escape. His eyes were similar to the gray eyes that haunted her dreams. Yet nothing else about him was familiar, not even an internal psychic awareness. Confusion and fear paralyzed her completely before JB scrambled in her arms. She released him, and he leaped to the floor. Instinctively, she dropped the overnight bag and grabbed for the gun at her waist.

As precise as a trained gunman, the intruder pulled a revolver from a shoulder holster underneath his coat. He beat Juliana to the draw. "I wouldn't if I were you." The man grinned.

Gun gripped in her hand, she didn't shift a muscle. From the corner of her eye, she saw JB turn traitor and dive under the bed.

Sweat dampened the man's face, and she sensed his excitement, smelled it in the air. The odor revolted her, and she breathed through her mouth in order to control her terror. Frantically, she tried to devise a plan, her thoughts whipping about in her head.

"What do you want?" she challenged him, stalling.

"Does it matter?" His speculative gaze swept up and down her frame.

Normally, she sensed evil when faced with one of her dream criminals. But she didn't feel it with this guy. She felt threatened, but no malicious psychic connection. Confusion tightened its painful grip on her shoulders, pinching and deadening.

Surely the police knew she'd given them the slip by now. Wouldn't they track her at home? She could hope, but couldn't count on it. Her mind whirled a thousand miles a minute, and she wasn't ready to thrust her telepathic block off to read his mind and determine his identity. She had to keep him placated and talking, delaying him for as long as possible.

Juliana choked back her fear. "You're not the kidnapper." Stepping back, her gaze didn't waver off his face.

"Do I look like the sort who'd snatch a child from under her mother's nose?" He smiled and leaned his shoulder against the doorframe.

"What do you want?"

"We have a mutual acquaintance, Ms. Westwood. Although I believe he's more than an acquaintance to you."

The holster, the precision with the gun, the suit. *Shit!* Shelby from Internal Affairs? "You're from IA?"

"Aren't you a smart bitch?" His eyes narrowed in

under him.

Pushing away her telepathic block, she let his thoughts prove her right. His mind barraged her with his smugness, from stealing Alex's report off Captain Hayes' desk to revealing her identity to Channel 10 news.

Thank God. Alex hadn't exposed her. How could she have even believed it for one second?

She gave a silent prayer that she could read the intruder. The ability would give her an advantage. But his next thoughts gelled her knees, and she fought to remain standing and coherent.

He intended to rape her. Then kill her.

"Slowly set the gun on the floor and slide it under the bed." He leveled his weapon at her heart.

She was no match for a gun-toting mad cop. Keeping an eye on him, she laid the gun on the carpet. As it slid away from her hand, her heart skipped several anxious beats.

Straightening, she focused on his thoughts, his emotions. She gleaned a depraved lust, not necessarily for her, but for a deep-seated revenge. His desire drove his actions and thoughts. He wanted Alex to pay. He even wished he'd had the forethought to kidnap Lisette. Underneath it all, Juliana sensed hesitancy. She latched onto that pebble.

"You're the psychic calling the shots?" He cocked his head and eyed her appraisingly, his look traveling to a leer. "I bet MacKenzie loved having you beside him while chasing clues to his niece's kidnapper."

Juliana cringed at the direction his thoughts veered, her knees nearly losing their feeble hold. He really meant to rape her. *Oh, no, no,* she wailed silently. Where were the police? Frantic, she attempted to call out to Alex with her mind, but emptiness met her. She suspected he held no ability to read anyone but his sister, and likely only from close range.

"Please, you don't want to do this. Why go to all this trouble?" Juliana backed up until the back of her knees butted against the bed, her arms locked to her sides. "I'll give you whatever you want. Just let me go and we keep this between us."

"What I want is for you to take off your clothes and lie on the bed." Excitement gleamed bright in his eyes. He dug a small packet out of his coat pocket and tossed it on the bed. The neon-green condom contrasted sharply with the eggplant-purple and gold comforter. "I'm going to show you how a real man can satisfy you. Then we'll talk about what else you can give me."

His thoughts scurried all over the map. He honestly held Alex responsible for his fiancée's death and his demotion.

"Look, I have a trust fund."

He waved the gun at her. "Clothes off." He shut the door and advanced into the room. "By the way, you might want to fix the deadbolt on your front door."

Fix it? How could she fix it if she were dead? "You can rot in hell." The words slipped out.

A crazed laugh shook his shoulders, the sound resonating in Juliana's ears. "You should thank me for giving you your fifteen minutes of fame today." Pointing the gun at her heart, he demanded again, "Take them off."

Juliana slowly untied and slipped off her shoes. Her hands shook as she shrugged her jacket onto the floor. While she unbuttoned her jeans, she glanced surreptitiously around the room. A nail file on her night table captured her attention.

Shelby practically drooled when she kicked off her pants, leaving her underwear on. Her gaze skimmed the

Panic slammed her. Tears welled in her eyes. "Please don't. I'll give you anything else. The police will be here any minute." *What am I saying? He's the freaking police. Get a grip and think.*

Perspiration dotted his forehead. He tugged at the neck of his shirt, loosening his tie, unbuttoning the top buttons. "Don't count on it. With MacKenzie primary, they couldn't find their way out of a beer bottle."

She prattled on to catch him off-guard. "What do you have against Alex?"

In three long strides, he stood in front of her. With the gun in one hand and a crimson, savage glare on his face, he pushed her onto the bed.

Falling backward gave her a slight advantage. She kicked out with all her strength and caught him on the thigh, inches short of her target, the hard evidence of his intent.

Howling, he lunged for her. Fully on top of her now, he pinned her to the bed. He shoved the gun against her temple and screamed at her, "Knock it off, bitch, or I'll drill another eye in your face." Fury twisted his features into a deranged mask.

Juliana ceased struggling. Fighting back the sour malevolence wedged in her throat, she breathed in his ashtray-stinking breath. While he worked at his zipper, she furtively inched her hand along the bed, reaching for the night table.

But she was several feet too short. Terror immobilized her with the gun barrel jammed into her skull. "I'll cooperate. Just don't hurt me."

"Hurt you?" He stopped his movements and stared at her as if she'd lost her mind. "I'm going to make you feel so good, you'll beg for more."

"Okay." She swallowed the bitterness in her mouth. "Can we move up to the pillows and get more comfortable?"

"Now that's more like it." He made no move to slide up the bed, and continued his one-handed struggles with his pants while his vile body smothered and pinned her to the bed.

Eyes closed to block the horror, she prayed in silence. Seconds crawled by, and it felt like forever. She didn't know how long she lay there while he fumbled with his clothes before a sound near the door caught her attention.

As if in answer to her prayers, Juliana heard the blunt strike of something solid hitting skin and bones. The intruder's movements ceased, and his heavy body slumped like dead weight on top of her. The gun dropped on the mattress beside her ear, the barrel pointed at the headboard.

Relief surged through her, and she cried out, "Alex?"

She peeped around the unconscious man obscuring her vision. To her hopeless terror, she came face-to-face with her dream man.

CHAPTER TWENTY-SEVEN

"You!" she gasped, tensing beneath Shelby's weight. The new intruder's mind flooded hers, and his thoughts nearly knocked her senseless from the brutal torrent.

As sudden as the dream man's thoughts surged into her mind, they vanished. The stench of cigarettes and sweat impaled her to the satin and velvet comforter. She struggled to push the loathsome body off her, but he was too heavy and her arms weren't cooperating with her head. Helplessness polarized her into the mercy of the man towering above her. A man she'd pegged completely wrong from day one. A man who'd fooled every instinct within her.

"Hello Juliana. It's nice to see you again." His mouth widened in an arrogant smile. "You're in somewhat of a quandary, I see." He waved the nine-millimeter at the inert form nailing her to the bed, then swiped the barrel on the intruder's pant leg. A trace of crimson stained the khaki trousers. "Do you like rough sex, or does he?"

Nicholas Hastings? With gray eyes?

"*You* abducted Lisette Chamber?" The sound of her voice came from far away as her mind and body retreated into frozen shock.

Nicholas prodded Shelby with his gun and peered over

the man's inert body into Juliana's face. "Correct you are." An indescribable challenge glittered in his eyes. "You guard your thoughts well, Juliana. Much better than I, it seems. I never imagined I'd meet someone who could penetrate my mind from miles away. Or at all."

He shook his head in mock sorrow, then shoved the blond man off Juliana to the opposite side of the bed. The oppressive weight gone, her breathing steadied, although her heart continued to thump in her ears.

How had these two men moved so rapidly to subdue her? Co-conspirators? No. Shelby had his own agenda. Nicholas was quicker and smarter than she'd credited him.

He checked Shelby's pulse. "Don't worry, your boyfriend's still alive."

Juliana laughed hysterically. "He's a cop." The words bypassed the horror building inside her. "Here to protect and serve."

Why hadn't she realized the kidnapper was Nicholas Hastings? She'd socialized with him in New York. He'd sat in her office across her desk. But that man had blue eyes and a shuttered mind.

Nicholas swept an appraising look over her. "I'd love to have a piece of you myself." He pointed the gun at the vee of her thighs. "You certainly are prime real estate."

Revulsion and terror crashed into the lunacy that endangered her mind. "I'm not chattel," she said with barely restrained disgust.

"No, but you are an ends to a means." His lips curled into that charming smile she'd once found so disarming. "However, I like my partners willing."

A thimble of relief poured into her. Juliana had a fighting chance. She just needed to keep her wits intact.

"What are you going to do?" she asked tentatively, her mind as guarded as his.

"First we're getting out of here." He swung the gun at the overnight bag. "Looks like you had the same idea. I guess I should thank your cop friend for detaining you."

Stall him. Alex can't be too far behind. She realized with a start that she was counting on Alex's rescue. A short time ago, she believed he'd placed her in this precarious position. Alex would never have betrayed her. Not even if he hated her. He still had to locate his niece, if nothing else.

"How did you find me so quickly?" Goosebumps broke out over her legs as his gaze brazenly raked the length of her body.

"Did you think I wouldn't figure out who you were?"

"What?" Her voice wavered, her stomach pitched.

"Your jeweled eyes are one in a million."

"You didn't see the news?" she ventured, biting her lip.

"After I already suspected." The superior look on his face distorted his handsome features. "By the way, the janitors at your office are quite slipshod." His eyes twinkled as he shoved his free hand in his pants pocket.

Juliana couldn't stabilize her breathing, couldn't seem to take in enough air. Fog wavered in her vision.

"Get dressed." His gaze slid to her jeans puddled on the floor. "As delightful as your legs are, they might attract more attention than we need." He backed several steps away from the bed.

Juliana didn't hesitate, but her movements slowed. As much as she hated the intense shimmer in his eyes and her own exposure, she needed to stall him.

"Hurry up, Juliana," he snarled as he leaned against the dresser. He elbowed a tray of perfume bottles. They clinked together, an infinitesimal sound in the heart thuds reverberating in her ears.

Her lungs steadier, she rolled off the bed, still too far from the night table to make a play for the nail file. Legs unsteady, she tugged on her jeans and shoes. A dim thought occurred to her. She could use Nicholas to find Lisette and plan the girl's escape. As the fog dissipated, her mind began to revolve around that idea. Renewed adrenaline pumped into her veins.

Nicholas pointed the gun from the bare corner of the bedroom to her. "Stand in the corner facing me and don't move."

Juliana rushed to do his bidding and stood motionless in the corner eyeing him, leaning against the walls. Without the walls taking her weight, she feared her knees would crumple her to the floor.

Nicholas dug into Shelby's pockets and pulled out a pair of handcuffs. He rolled Shelby onto the floor and cuffed him to the bed frame. Then he stuffed the cop's revolver into the back waistband of his pants as he moved to Juliana.

"Let's go. You ahead of me." Nicholas yanked her in front of him.

She led him down the stairs, all too aware of the gun pointed at her back. Her legs cooperated with a fragment of her brain, while the rest of her mind scrambled to figure a way out of this mess.

How long could she stand having a gun leveled at her before she went stark raving mad? Once was horrible enough. A shudder ripped through her at the memory.

"Don't open your mouth until I tell you to or I'll gag you. Understand?"

Juliana nodded.

Nicholas pushed her out the front door, but hauled on her arm from behind to stop her from stepping off the dark porch.

Juliana searched the neighborhood for help. Nothing, no one. She peered down the side street of her corner lot. The dark ethereal shapes of h construction were empty, the construction workers long gone for the night. The only thing out of the ordinary was the older model muscle car parked alongside the curb at the side of her house.

Barely cognizant of her movements as he prompted her toward the two-door car, she focused all her energy inward. All she cared about now was reaching Lisette, keeping her safe from the lunatic behind her.

Nicholas duct-taped Juliana's wrists behind her back and made her scuttle crab-like into the small backseat. Then he taped her bare ankles together.

The tape for every use. Juliana managed a bleak, tight-lipped smile. He blindfolded her, but left her mouth free. He hopped in behind the wheel, pulling the door shut with a quiet snick.

The engine rumbled to life, shaking the car in a steady cadence. Nicholas turned a tight corner, the car swaying, jamming her between the backseat and the front buckets. She wedged an elbow into the front seat to shove herself back and her thoughts into action.

If she lived, she'd do everything in her power to win Alex back. He'd shown her in less than a week that life alone would be a mere existence. She didn't want to be alone any longer. She didn't want to fear the dark anymore. They'd find a way to work around her psychic burdens. If he was willing—after tonight. *Why did I drive him away? Why couldn't I just leave well enough alone for a change? Why didn't I have more faith in him and not have to rely solely on myself, as usual?*

The car hit a large pothole, jostling Juliana out of her reverie.

"You okay back there?"

Juliana wondered at the edge of concern in Nicholas' voice. "Does it matter?" she asked, trying to keep her unsteady voice from betraying her panic. The stale smell of old leather seats and dirty carpet tickled her nostrils. She fought to stifle a sneeze.

"I have no plans to hurt you. In fact, you may even decide to come along with me. I can make you a wealthy woman."

Juliana snickered. "You have it backwards."

Nicholas laughed. "Right you are, darling. My friends and I wondered how you were always on the money with your financial advice, when your associates were wrong."

Her throat felt like a fur ball had lodged in it. "You think so?" Psychic bandwidth hadn't contributed to her investment choices throughout her career. She simply possessed a knack for knowing when to get in and when to get out.

Nicholas chuckled, a sound that grated on her nerves. "I was wise to choose you as my financial advisor. It was a stroke of genius that you also tapped into my mind.

"By the way, I'll assume my investment in Altz will go off without a hitch, even with you away from the office?"

Yeah, right. The funds would sit in her escrow account until she could hand them over to the proper authorities. "Yes," she lied. "I've entered the trade." Her eyelids itched from the tightly wound scarf. Blinking didn't help. "The buy will execute first thing in the morning."

"Excellent!"

She doubted her curiosity could hurt her any further. "What insider information do you have on Altz?"

He hesitated as he turned the car onto an uneven road. She gritted her teeth against the rough jostling assaulting her side.

"A takeover bid will be announced on Friday at three times the current price. Concurrently, an announcement will be made that Altz's flagship product will be integrated into graphic chips from Silicon Valley to Siberia."

"You know this because . . .?" The lumpy seat bottom dug into her hips at every bump in the road.

"I know the venture capitalist quite well." He chuckled. "Rather intimately, we'll say."

I'd rather not. Her stomach contracted, and she fought the vertigo easing into her self-control.

"What will you do with the money?" *Keep him talking. He'll slip in either words or thoughts sooner or later.*

"You'll transfer it to my Swiss bank account. As for the rest—" He stopped suddenly, as if he realized he'd erred. "Well, you already know about the ransom note, so I won't pretend you don't. I assume the police know?"

"Did you think otherwise?"

His voice turned curt. "If you hadn't read my mind, Chamber would've done exactly what I asked. That bastard's a fool."

Did she hear regret in his voice? "What's your relationship to them?"

"You don't need to concern yourself with that."

The duct tape around her wrists tightened, stretching her skin with every jiggle. "Does it concern Lisette or her mother?"

"Of course it does." His voice held a smirk.

Juliana tried to read him telepathically, but the force of his mental and physical block sent her reeling. His emotions, everything about him, was shielded from her intuition. The padlock on his thoughts had prevented her from previously guessing his identity.

Breathing deeply and exhaling slowly, she attempted to steady her thudding heart. "I can help you if you let us go."

"Not before I get my money."

Another jolt forced a seatbelt buckle to ram into her butt. Shifting away from it, she asked, "How do you plan to get away?" *There must be a hole in his scheme somewhere.*

"Leave the planning to me." He chuckled. "You certainly are inquisitive."

"Bondage has it rewards."

Another chuckle. "Spoken like a trooper. I like that in a woman. Adaptable. Are you sure you wouldn't like to conquer the world on my arm? In my bed?"

"A zombie would be more bearable."

Gravel pinging the car's underside hinted at off-road travel.

"That's not a nice thing to say to the man who's been intimately connected to you for a week."

Yeah, nothing like having your mind linked with a sex-crazed lunatic. Slip, you bastard, slip. "So what sort of ESP do you have?"

"Who says I have ESP?"

"Now who's being witty?" If she could leverage off whatever extrasensory skills he possessed, she might stand a fireball's chance in Antarctica to get herself and Lisette out alive.

"Ms. Westwood, we've reached our destination. You'll have to put your curiosity to bed."

Brakes squealed as the car rolled to a halt. The door squeaked open, and Juliana's heart palpitated with renewed fear. She nearly fell onto the floorboards when he jerked the bucket-seat forward. He yanked the scarf and a few strands of hair off her head. Her watery eyes met an inky blackness. His long, tapered fingers lingered on her temple. She shrank back against the seat, and he chuckled that sound she now loathed.

The dark scraped along her skin, wrapping around her, suffocating her.

"You're a beautiful woman. A man would be a fool to kill you." Desire roughened his voice.

His smile iced the marrow in her bones.

She believed him foo͟l e͟n͟o͟u͟g͟h

CHAPTER TWENTY-EIGHT

Alex wanted to believe the kidnapper didn't have the balls to go after Juliana. The slow, hollow beat of his heart told him otherwise. He sensed something wrong. Seriously wrong.

He flicked off the headlights and cruised his SUV to a stop in front of Juliana's house. Neighboring lights lent faint illumination to the dark facade. The jarring stillness chilled him to the bone.

"There's Marie's car," James said. They both jumped out of the SUV.

Cursing under his breath, Alex scoped out the darkened porch. With guns drawn, they made their way to the front door. The deadbolt was loose and broken, the door unlocked. "Shit," he muttered. He should've fixed the light and lock two days ago, as he'd promised. He hoped he wouldn't live to regret it.

They slipped across the threshold and closed the door behind them with a soft snick, deafening in the stillness of the dark house.

"Take the kitchen and family room," Alex whispered, pointing to the right. "Meet me back here."

He didn't like the eerie hush of the house. His pulse quickened as he moved from room to room. Since there was no furniture in the formal living and dining rooms, he didn't need to flip on the lights. Illumination from the nightlights didn't reveal any unusual shadows. Alex crossed into Juliana's office, flicked on the light. Nothing. The bathroom and closets were empty. He moved back to the foyer where James waited.

"All clear." James pointed up the stairs.

Alex ascended the stairs slowly. "You take the left," he murmured over his shoulder.

Approaching the master bedroom, he was acutely cautious of the light angling through the partly-open door. Primed and ready, he nudged the door open with his foot.

A black ball of fur lunged for his legs.

Son of a bitch. The cat damn near startled the words out of his mouth. The fuzzy black animal rubbed against Alex's boots, purring loud enough for Alex to feel the vibrations. JB darted away and jumped onto the bed. He arched his back and hissed at the floor on the far side of the bed.

Gooseflesh rose on Alex's neck as he spotted the stuffed overnight bag on the floor. Juliana had been there, but where was she now? Dead, on the other side of the bed? The thought froze his blood. No, she was still alive. He'd feel it otherwise.

He scanned the room, slowly creeping toward the bed. Only a few seconds had passed since the cat crashed into him, but it felt like hours. He halted at the side of the bed closest to the door. Faint breathing and the rustle of fabric emerged from the other side.

Sweat beaded on his forehead despite the ice in his veins. James came up behind Alex, startling him into action. Alex pointedly waved his gun at the bed.

"She's not here," Alex said loudly. "She must have skipped out on us again." He motioned for James to skirt the bed and he climb

silent.

With trained synchronicity, Alex and James made their move. They came face to face with the immobile form of Chad Shelby and a .38 special, old school police issue.

"Drop the gun," Alex roared, training his revolver on Shelby.

"Well, well, well," Shelby croaked, pain glazing his eyes. "If it isn't lame lover-boy and his sorry sidekick." Eyelids drooped in a ghostly white face.

"Lay down the gun. Now!" Alex commanded, prepared to jump on Shelby.

Shelby made no move to comply. Given the unsteadiness of his hand and his unhealthy pallor, Alex guessed he was injured.

"Drop the gun, slide it to me." James' rigid form towered over the downed man.

Shelby's eyes closed. James seized the advantage and slammed his foot onto Shelby's open hand. Howls of agony and rage erupted from him.

Alex leaped off the bed and snatched up the dropped weapon. Both men leveled their guns on Shelby, who writhed on the floor, cradling his battered hand against his chest.

"Where is she?" Alex asked through gritted teeth.

"Who?" Shelby taunted, pain muffling his voice.

"Game's over." James raised a foot, poised to kick Shelby again.

Shelby attempted to roll away, but his handcuff leash stopped him. "I came here to protect your source." His Adam's apple bobbed. "You were stupid enough to leak her name to the press."

Incredulity siphoned the blood from Alex's face. "Are you insane?" He steadied his gun, closing the distance between the barrel and the asshole's damp, pasty face.

"Tell me where she is or I'll blow your fucking brains out. I'm pissed enough to do it." His gaze remained fixed on Shelby's disgusting face. "How 'bout it, James, self-defense?"

"Shelby pulled a gun on MacKenzie, fired, missed. MacKenzie shot back in self-defense, bullet pointblank between the eyes," James mocked as though reporting to his superior officer. "I saw it happen, Captain."

Alex cocked his weapon. "A bullet hole in the ceiling will prove you shot first."

The acrid odor of fear drifted up from the floor. James leveled his foot over Shelby's cuffed wrist, and began easing it down. Sweat dripped off Shelby's face as he convulsed into sobs. "I didn't do anything."

"What happened?" Alex growled.

Composing himself, Shelby sniveled through his words. "I came here to talk to Westwood about your case. She was in a hurry and asked me to come up here." His voice cracked. "Someone hit me on the back of the head. Next thing I know, you two showed up."

Alex knew Juliana wouldn't have let Shelby inside, not in her state of mind. He inched his weapon closer to Shelby's head. "Tell me the truth, you lying piece of shit." The gun barrel dented the furrows on Shelby's sweaty forehead.

Shelby edged away. As he did, Alex's eyes shifted to the man's open pants. And his exposed genitals.

Alex jerked up as if electrocuted. Sweltering fury forced him to stumble forward a half-step before he rested the gun barrel on Shelby's withered penis.

CRSO

Nicholas sliced the duct tape from Juliana's ankles and guided her th

He followed on her heels, the gun aimed at her back.

She hesitated at the expansive hedge of ten-foot-high oleander bushes. The sight and smell of the flowers produced a pandemonium of emotions. Nicholas gripped her arm with one hand while he spread branches to reveal a hidden pathway. He hauled her behind him to the other side. Shivering, she shook her hair to rid it of leaves and debris, wishing she could shake him off as easily. Never would she smell or see oleanders again without remembering that night.

"Walk toward the house."

A large shadowy shape loomed to her left. The darkness closed in on her, and the glow peeking through the blinds of one window was her only light. She peered into the darkness trying to discern her whereabouts, but it was just too dark. She guessed they'd driven for twenty minutes, bringing them into one of San Jose's nearby rural areas.

Juliana picked her way toward the house over the uneven gravel. Nicholas didn't rush her. Gratitude for the small concession made only a tiny dent in her mind. At his direction, she entered the back door, startled to bump into Jasmine.

Pure hatred turned the beautiful blonde babysitter into an ugly shrew.

"Nicky, what's going on?" She crossed her arms under her voluptuous breasts and glowered at Juliana.

"Shut up, Jaz." He turned domineering eyes on Jasmine, forcing her to drop her gaze to her feet. "Give me the key."

Jasmine pursed her lips as she dug a key out of her tiny shorts.

Prodding Juliana with the gun, he led her down a dim hallway. "Last chance to use the bathroom."

"What a nice guy," she blurted out.

"I wouldn't go that far." A small smiled tugged at his lips. "What do they say about nice guys?" His once-charming smile widened.

Anger rippled through her, but she suppressed it in her voice. "Can you untie my hands?"

"Certainly. I wouldn't want you to soil your designer jeans." He jerked open his pocketknife and cut the tape.

After she finished her business, she explored the bare, windowless bathroom only to find nothing to help her. Time cut short when Nicholas pushed the door open, seized her arm, and nudged her toward the last doorway at the end of the hallway. Without loosening his grip, he pocketed his gun and unlocked the door, then shoved her inside the weakly lit room. The lock clicking into place lent a certain finality to the night.

Panic rioted within Juliana, her heart racing, perspiration forming between her breasts. She hated being locked up almost as much as she hated the dark. A small lamp burned on the otherwise bare dresser. The same lamp and dresser from her dreams. Terror clutched her insides in a controlling fist and refused to let go, until she heard a childlike cry.

Juliana whirled toward the bunk beds dominating the right half of the room. She forced a reassuring control to her voice. "Lisette?"

"Yes. Who are you?" Lisette asked in a small, trembling voice. She scrambled to the far corner of the lower bunk.

Juliana kept her distance to avoid frightening the girl further. "I'm Juliana, honey. I'm a friend of your Mom and Uncle Alex. I'm here to help you." Despite the tangled blonde hair, the fear ravaging her face, the girl was a beautiful sight.

"You know my Mommy and Uncle Alex?" Awe chased away her fear.

"Yes, I do. Can I sit with you?" Juliana's neutral voice masked her inner turmoil, but she began to gather her wits and strength.

The small room closed in on her like a coffin. Whimsical animated characters danced on the walls. Meant to portray a magical place in all its fun and wonderment, no such enchantments abounded in her prison.

"Okay." Lisette hugged her stuffed bunny to her chest.

Juliana eased down on the bottom bunk, giving Lisette space in her own little corner. "I won't hurt you, honey. Why don't you sit beside me?"

Lisette shook her head, her eyes riveted on Juliana's face.

"I've known your Mommy and Uncle Alex for a long time. I think they would want us to become friends." She smiled at Lisette and held her hand out to her. "Would you like that?"

The six-year-old frowned. "How come I never saw you before?"

Juliana dropped her arm and gripped the dragonfly-covered comforter to still her trembling. "I've been away for a long time, in New York. Have you heard of New York, where the Statue of Liberty is?"

Lisette shook her head again.

"I'll show you a picture of it after we get home." False cheer widened her smile.

A lone tear trickled down Lisette's pale cheek. "Is my Mommy coming to get me?"

"You'll see your mom soon. Uncle Alex is looking really hard. He'll find us soon. In fact, I've been helping him to find you, and look how well I did."

It wasn't the best way of granting hope, considering she was as trapped as Lisette. But hope floats, and she wouldn't sink it yet.

Excitement sparked in Lisette's eyes. "How did you find me?"

Juliana pondered the answer as she brushed back the hair from her unraveling braid. "I dreamed about you alone, scared, and I found you through my dreams."

Lisette's eyes widened.

"Honey, why don't you try to sleep?" Juliana stood. She wanted to search the room for a way out, a weapon, or anything that would help her plight. She desperately needed to occupy her mind or she'd scare herself out of her own skin.

The expression on Lisette's face turned to an indecisive fear. "Will you stay with me?"

"I won't go anywhere. Want me to tuck you in?"

Lisette nodded, and Juliana helped her slide under the covers. She planted a light kiss on Lisette's forehead and sat next to her until her breathing slowed and steadied in sleep.

She proceeded to explore every nook and cranny of the room. To her dismay, she didn't find anything to aid escape or even provide a clue as to their location. The dresser held a couple changes of new, clean clothing for Lisette. A window, dry-walled off from the inside, hid behind the deceitful pink curtains she'd witnessed in her dream.

Nicholas Hastings had planned his coup with the efficiency of a corporate raid.

Juliana climbed up to the top bunk and stretched out. What if Alex or the police didn't rescue them before the ransom was paid? How could she get them out of there? After Nicholas received the money, would he let them go? Or would he kill them?

Thoughts flew at her. She employed all her mind control tactics to clear her head and devise a plan for all contingencies.

CHAPTER TWENTY-NINE

Alex filled the doorway of Juliana's palatial bathroom. Anger tore at his gut, ripping the adrenaline out of his system.

Uniformed officers cuffed Shelby's uninjured hand to the gurney before the paramedics wheeled him out. There was no sympathy amongst the cops on site. For one cop to turn on another was akin to turning against the entire police force.

The forensics team had arrived moments ago and the once-lonely house now crawled with police personnel.

"Lieutenant, you're up." The call from downstairs sifted through Alex's thoughts.

Footsteps heavy, he descended the stairs. The house glowed like a Christmas village, reminding him of Juliana's fear of the dark and her craving for light, like a rose in bloom. He entered the kitchen where Lieutenant Malcolm Crane from IA waited. A straight shooter, Crane was the only one in IA Alex held in high regard. The man detested Shelby more than Alex did. He'd led the year-long improper behavior investigation against Shelby. Tonight's debacle would kill Shelby's law enforcement career.

"Alex." Crane shook his hand in a firm grip. "I

understand you have a personal relationship with Ms. Westwood?" Alex nodded. "I'll make this as painless as possible. However, you'll have to give me the goods on what occurred tonight to the best of your ability."

Veiled significance overshadowed his last few words. Crane would believe whatever Alex told him, whether true or not. Alex had no doubt that Crane would back him up and not play to his own agenda.

Muted sounds from the forensics team filtered through the doorway. Alex glanced around the kitchen, remembering the last time he'd been there. Juliana had stood before him, her unbound hair shining like golden sunshine. Her radiance illuminated the kitchen, bringing life to the otherwise sterile environment. Even with all the lights burning, the room felt bereft without her presence. Alex turned to the dining table and kept his gaze from drifting, his mind from remembering.

He sat down, feeling pummeled from head to toe. His gaze landed on the .38 revolver resting on the cherry-wood table. It wasn't standard police issue. He frowned, confused. "That's not Shelby's gun."

"It's registered to Ms. Westwood." Crane swiped his finger across his tablet to a blank page, and using a stylus he scrawled Alex's name at the top. "What happened here?"

A fresh surge of mixed emotions rolled through him. Palming his antacids, Alex popped the last two in his mouth to dampen the incessant inferno in his gut. With forced professionalism, he gave his statement. Halfway through, his voice broke, his fists clenched on top of his thighs.

"Do you need a minute?" Crane strode to the counter, leaned over it for a couple of seconds before turning back around, his expression commiserate.

Alex shook his head.

control. Through clenched teeth he continued, "Shelby admitted to an attempted rape of Ms. Westwood. During his pursuit of the act, an unknown assailant approached from behind and knocked him out. It was the last he remembered until O'Malley and I appeared on the scene." Alex crossed his arms over his chest, his rage stretching his muscles taut. "I called for backup. We searched the house and grounds, but didn't locate Ms. Westwood."

"Okay. Your story ties with O'Malley's." Crane closed his tablet cover, and patted Alex's shoulder, his hand heavy. "You're free to go. Get some rest."

"Rest?" Alex scowled, scrubbing the back of his neck.

"What good are you to your niece and your girl if you can't function?" Crane leaned toward Alex, his expression inflexible, persistent. "O'Malley advised me that the address leads on Hastings are false. Officers are working around the clock. Uniforms are interviewing Ms. Westwood's neighbors, and we have an APB out on her. What more can you accomplish tonight?"

Alex stood and beat a fist on the table. "I can't stop now."

"O'Malley," Crane yelled through the arched doorway. "Take MacKenzie home. Tie him down if you have to."

Alex opened his mouth to argue, but he realized Crane was right. If he didn't crash, he'd start making mistakes that could destroy people he loved, family members who needed him, and the woman he cherished.

James prodded Alex toward the foyer. As he approached the front door, his gaze rested on the defective deadbolt. He knew the kidnapper had abducted her. She wouldn't have left the house unlocked, her purse and keys scattered on the bombe chest.

It was hell worrying about Lisette and the things that bastard was doing to her. Add to that the thought of the kidnapper touching Juliana. Fists tightening, his knuckles knotted white. If he could reverse time, he'd trade reuniting with Juliana for keeping her and Lisette safe.

Once he found Juliana, he'd never let her go, even if he had to handcuff her to his bed. He vowed to bring her back. No matter what. And to convince her they were meant to be together. No matter what.

He had twelve long years to make up for and a lifetime to love her the way she deserved.

CRSO

Juliana jerked upright, awakened by a thump, and unsure of her whereabouts. A few blurry seconds passed before the events of the previous day crashed into her. A consuming heaviness anchored her to the bed. But with firm determination, she shrugged off the feelings. She wouldn't yield yet. Not while her body contained a teaspoon of breath and certainly not while Lisette needed her.

She'd worked out a couple plans of action during the night while she lay listening to the house settling. The lack of a window or city streets outside made for a quiet night, but didn't serve to buck up her fraught nerves.

Languid with exhaustion, she climbed down from the bunk and sat on the edge of the bottom bed, watching Lisette sleep. Juliana finger-combed her tousled hair and proceeded to re-braid it as best she could. *Would Alex and I have a daughter as beautiful as Lisette?* The unexpected thought shook her soul, shattered her reservations about Alex.

Would she get out alive to have a life with Alex? Would he want her? Were her dreams just fantasies? *No!* She refused to think negatively. If she continued believing

wanted him with an intensity she could no longer deny. He'd awakened her and fulfilled her entirely, the missing link on her chain of happiness. Her soul was only half-alive without him. It was useless to deny her feelings any longer.

Lisette whimpered in her sleep. Juliana reached over to push the knotted hair off the girl's face. Lisette's eyes flew open, round with fear before recognition brightened the familiar azure gaze.

"It's okay, honey," Juliana murmured.

"You're still here," Lisette whispered, a smile crinkling the corners of her mouth.

"Of course." Juliana rubbed Lisette's arm tenderly. "I said I would stay with you."

"Will Uncle Alex find us today?" Lisette climbed out from under the covers, her bunny clutched in her arms. She sat next to Juliana as if they were lifelong friends.

"I hope so." The clean sweatpants and yellow T-shirt Lisette wore reassured her. At least Nicholas was taking care of her. "Would you like me to fix your hair?"

"Can you braid it like yours?" Lisette smiled shyly, as if she'd asked for the moon.

Juliana nodded. "You'll look like a princess with your hair braided."

Just as she finished tying Lisette's braid with a strip of cloth, the lock on the door clicked. She pulled Lisette onto her lap and hugged her close.

Nicholas kicked the door open, balancing a tray of cereal, milk, and coffee. "I see you're making friends."

The rich aroma of steaming coffee filled the stuffy bedroom. Sweet, heavenly coffee. Juliana would even dare to drink the ambrosia straight black. How considerate of the bastard.

He held the tray toward her without moving from the doorway. "Bathroom breaks. You first, Lisette."

Juliana looked into his deep blue eyes. Her suspicions panned out. He wore colored contact lenses.

"Juliana, come with me." Lisette turned plaintive eyes on her.

She hated to deny Lisette, but she wanted a moment alone with Nicholas. "I'll be right here. Be a brave girl and go by yourself." She set the breakfast tray on the dresser. "Okay?"

Jasmine materialized behind Nicholas, grabbed Lisette's arm with a talon-like hand, and tugged her into the hallway.

Time to set Plan A in motion. Guardedly, Juliana watched Nicholas in the doorway while he waited for Lisette to return.

She colored her voice in neutral shades, despite the rainbow of emotions inside her. "Nicholas, let Jasmine drive Lisette into town and release her. You can keep me as your hostage. I'll do whatever you want. But let her go."

Nicholas leaned his shoulder into the doorframe and crossed his arms and ankles. He studied her face, a slow smile stretching across his. "I don't think so. You two make for a more enticing payday together."

Juliana twisted her filigree ring round and round her finger. "You're going to ask for more money?"

"You're a package deal now." His eyes twinkled, his smile widened to a grin. "I'm sure you have plenty of money from your father's estate to pay Chamber back several times over."

Juliana blinked rapidly, stunned, unable to hide her surprise or pull her jaw off the floor.

"Your father was well-known." Nicholas uncrossed his ankles, reached behind his back, and drew his gun. "Anyone dabbling in the high-tech world knows of your

Juliana gripped a bedpost, the pine solid beneath her palm. Thinking fast, she said, "Then take both of us into town. I'll get you the money. You can leave us and go your merry way." Her mind was a crazy blend of hope and fear.

"How will you raise ten million in cash in one shot?" Nicholas rubbed the gun's barrel, then slid it into the back waistband of his pants.

Juliana barely resisted staring at his crotch, the last place she saw him rub the gun. Disgust twisted inside her, and she averted her gaze.

Ten million? Juliana gave a small shrug. "I have a safety deposit box with bearer bonds worth five million dollars. It's yours if you let us both go. Today. Alive."

Intrigue flickered in his eyes before distrust shadowed them.

She did have bearer bonds—eight million dollars' worth. Bearer bonds transferred from one person to another without the necessity for formal transfers of ownership. The bonds meant nothing to her. She never wanted her father's money. She'd wondered why he left his entire estate to her. As if money could replace love or the years she'd lost.

What was Nicholas Hastings' goal? What did the Chambers ever do to him? What was he replacing with the money?

He narrowed his eyes. "I'll have to think on your tempting proposal."

Juliana dug her nails deeper into the bedpost and pressed her final point. "It's the only way you'll escape without police involvement, and you know it."

"Shhh," he said when Jasmine and Lisette stepped into the hallway. "Your turn. Keep the door ajar."

What did he think she'd do? Tunnel out with the bar of soap? Or write SOS on the nonexistent window with toothpaste? Maybe the perv simply liked watching.

As she eased by Nicholas, he moved closer, almost pinning her to the doorframe. He brushed his fingers across her cheek, intimate and provocative. She cringed inwardly before he eased back and allowed her to slip past.

CHAPTER THIRTY

The phone's loud ringing woke Alex as the stars dissolved in a gray cloudless dawn.

He leaped out of bed and snatched the cordless in one flowing motion. "MacKenzie." His deep voice rasped with sleep, and his mouth felt like chalk dust coated it.

Shock iced his spine as Sterling's words sunk in. He threw the phone on the disheveled bed, and stomped on the clothes strewn across the floor to reach the door. "James!"

"What the—" James groaned as he stumbled out of his bedroom across the hall, knuckling his eyes.

Excitement and adrenaline fully revived Alex. "We traced the Jaguar purchase to the Chambers' address."

"No shit?" Awe rounded James' eyes. "Who was it?"

"We'll find out. Someone paid cash for the car. The DMV papers were mailed to the mansion in Samantha's name."

Less than an hour later, Grantham Chamber joined Alex and James in the den.

"You're out early, MacKenzie, O'Malley." Grantham, dressed for a business day, looked fresh despite the early hour. "Have you found my granddaughter yet?"

The smell of whiskey-laced coffee hung over the room,

turning Alex's stomach.

With no attempt at pretenses, he asked, "Who's Nicholas Hastings?"

Nonplussed, Grantham replied, "I'm not familiar with the name."

"How about your wife? Where is she?" Alex strode toward the door. "Never mind. I'll find her myself."

"MacKenzie! Stop right there."

"Get your wife. Now!" Alex halted in the doorway, his back to Grantham, eyes drawn to the wide staircase.

The sight of Samantha Chamber slumped at the bottom of the curved stairwell, heaving with sobs, riveted him.

Grantham pushed past Alex and hurried to his wife. "Samantha, take control of yourself. What is the meaning of this?" He crouched down and shook her shoulders.

Her bleary eyes caught Alex's gaze. He recognized sorrow in them, and unmistakable guilt.

Alex asked softly, "Who is Nicholas Hastings?"

"Samantha." Grantham released his wife, looming over her. "Tell me you don't know whom they're referring to."

"No. I can't hide it any longer." She clutched her stomach with one hand and buried her face in the other. "It's tearing me apart."

"What the hell are you referring to? Is he one of your Hastings relatives?"

Defeat on Samantha's face confirmed research Alex had uncovered as James drove them to the estate that morning. Hastings was Samantha's mother's maiden name.

Alex crossed the room and stood before Grantham. The man's arrogant face was impenetrable. He waited, watching the scene unfold and the evidence to fall at his

Samantha's sobs subsided as she shoved at Grantham. "It's your fault, Grant. If you hadn't run him off, he wouldn't have resorted to—" Sudden anger and loathing glinted in her watery eyes.

"Resorted to what?" Grantham narrowed his eyes at his wife. "Samantha!" He gripped her shoulder with a claw-like hand. "Speak to me."

"Who. Is. He?" Alex asked once more.

"It's Grant. Our oldest son." Samantha pushed up from the stairs, dislodging Grantham's hands. "Nicholas is his middle name. Hastings is my mother's maiden name." She heaved a loaded sigh. "Tell me what he's done."

Alex carried little compassion for Samantha and her guilt. "He's the kidnapper." A glacial chill entered his voice. "We think he's also holding Juliana Westwood."

The color drained from Samantha's face. She grasped the carved-wood banister as if to keep from falling. "No, no, no. You're wrong. Grant's incapable—"

James barred a distraught Bremley from entering the room. "Who's wrong?" James interjected sarcastically, scowling at Bremley's attempt to push past him.

"Impossible. The kidnapper can't be Grant." Dazed, Samantha stared at Alex.

Grantham sagged onto the stairs, leaning his head against the newel post, his face slack, his complexion ashen. "Who's Juliana?"

Alex stood immobile, his legs spread defiantly, and folded his arms across his chest. "The psychic working the case."

James crossed the room, glaring at Grantham. "We have proof your son's implicated."

"Right now, we need his address," Alex demanded. "Where does he live?"

"He lives in Monte Carlo." Grantham spoke in a

faraway voice. "Or Barcelona."

"No, he lives in the San Jose area." Alex stepped toward Samantha's sitting room. He halted and flung a glance over his shoulder. "He's been screwing Jasmine in your guest house while befriending Lisette."

Samantha's hand flew to her heart. "Oh, God. He warned me he'd take drastic measures against the corporation if I didn't give him more money. But kidnapping?"

"Money? You've been giving him money?" The "m" word sprinkled life back into Grantham. His back stiffened as he swung his head toward Samantha.

Her spine sprang taut and she met his glare. "You did this to him, Grant. He hates us because of you." Her eyes hardened into diamonds.

Defeat slumped Grant against the banister again. "What did you give him?"

"My trust fund." She turned away. "I bought him a car and recently gave him a million dollars." Samantha walked to Alex, arms clutched across her breasts. "I thought it would tide him over for a while until I could figure out what to do."

"Do you have his address?" Alex asked.

Her strong, familiar perfume caused bile to rise in his throat. Honeysuckle. He recoiled inwardly as a puzzle piece tumbled into place. Juliana knew that Nicholas hated honeysuckle from her vision. He swallowed hard, not dragging his gaze off Samantha.

"Alex, tell me you won't hurt him." She reached a hand toward him, but he stepped back as if she harbored the plague. "Please," Samantha pleaded.

Alex couldn't promise her that. Nor could he promise her they wouldn't charge her with conspiracy. "Give me his address."

ago," she replied. "It's on several acres of land. I think I have the street name." Samantha brushed past Alex into the sitting room.

The cloying honeysuckle scent enveloped Alex, and he breathed through his mouth to avoid the stench. Alex and James followed her into the room.

She leafed through an old-fashioned leather day planner. "He was going to straighten out his life. Quit gambling and make amends with his father. I assumed he was taking his time, and I didn't pressure him." She stopped scanning the calendar on a week in February.

"Here it is. Lochhaven Drive. It's a house on five acres of fruit orchards."

James jotted down the information while Alex paced the floor in quick, short steps, itching to hit the road.

Samantha grasped Alex's arm, stopping him mid-stride. "Alex, please bring back my granddaughter."

Alex didn't think it odd she mentioned only Lisette. He sensed she knew she'd never see her son alive again.

CR&SO

Back in the war room, Alex and James poured over a county plot. Lochhaven Drive was located in a rural area outside the suburban Almaden area. Juliana's guess that the house sat in the country was dead-on.

The county recorder's office verified the end parcel belonged to Nicholas Hastings. The land included a three thousand square foot ranch house and a four-horse barn. The homestead sprawled among fruit orchards on all sides.

Why would Hastings purchase the property if he planned to leave the United States? Maybe he just figured he'd be long gone before we caught up to him. Either he was stupid or Machiavellian. Alex factored both into the equation for their plan of attack.

Sterling rushed into the room in a flurry of noise. "Gilbert reported in. No ransom call."

The call was two hours late. Alex fingered his pulsing scar with a sense of foreboding. He had the uneasy feeling that something was very wrong and that Juliana was stuck in the middle of it.

CHAPTER THIRTY-ONE

Nicholas returned an hour later and tied Juliana's wrists behind her back with a silk scarf. Although her wrists still stung from him ripping off the duct tape, the tightly wound scarf was bearable.

Silently, he led her into the living room and pressed her down on a leather couch. The large room boasted a vaulted ceiling with cobwebs hanging from the exposed beams. A black leather couch and a pair of square oak end tables barely filled the middle of the room. A gilt-framed mirror hung on the wall next to the double front door. The ornate mirror that once reflected her eyes.

Juliana slumped onto the couch, warily watching Nicholas. The man certainly lived spartanly, belying the money he flaunted in his upper Manhattan penthouse. Money was evident in the car he drove and in his designer clothing.

He crossed the room and leaned back against the mantel above a humongous rock-faced fireplace. Studying her, he said, "I've decided to accept your offer." He lifted an autographed baseball off a plinth on the mantel and palmed it reverently. Tossing it above his head, he caught it and stroked it. "With a twist. First, tell me how you propose to get into your safety deposit box without a key."

By the look on his face, a plan had already formed in his warped mind. If she played her cards right, she'd remain at least a half step ahead.

Juliana wrinkled her nose. The newer sofa smelled strongly of leather. "The key's at my house." It was still in a tiny envelope with the bank's name and address written on it. She'd never gotten around to putting it in a safer place.

Nicholas twisted around to return the baseball to its stand. She quickly surveyed the room before he faced her again, finding nothing new in her scan. "Lieutenant MacKenzie at the PD has a key to my house. Let me call him, and I'll have him drop it wherever you want." She suffered a dull ache of longing for Alex.

Silver flecks of curiosity glittered in Nicholas' eyes. "Why does MacKenzie have a key to your house?"

"It's the way the police and I operate." She gave him a vacant stare as she worked her wrists, but the tight scarf gave no quarter. "I've worked with the police before."

His mouth edged up at one corner. "No doubt."

Juliana dug her fingers between the cushion and sofa back on a hunting expedition. "If I get the bonds, you'll free us?"

Nicholas' voice dropped low and condescending. "Now why would I do that? There's another five mil at stake." He stepped away from the fireplace and approached her.

She froze her useless groping between the cushions. "You seem to know a lot about Chamber. Are you sure he cares enough about his granddaughter to—"

Fury flitted across his face before he masked it. "Don't tell me what I know. Keep your pretty little mouth shut and do as I tell you."

The flare of anger ripped an opening in his mind. She seized full advantage and eagerly glommed onto his ~~relationship with~~ Grantham Chamber would pay for in spades.

He wanted more than money. He sought revenge. *Who the hell are you, Nicholas Hastings? Why pick on a defenseless child?*

Fear for Lisette's safety mounted inside her.

Juliana sat stiff-backed on the sofa and stared out the huge picture window. The view gave way to a barren backyard, desolate except for a few scattered oaks. Two hundred feet away, beyond the immediate backyard, the oleander hedges grew in a straight line, a natural barrier from the orchards and neighboring property.

"What do you want me to do?" She tilted her head.

"You'll make the call." He closed the span between them. "Tell MacKenzie where to find the key. You'll call back later today with a drop-off location. We'll follow with further instructions on the original ransom demand. Can you remember, or should I write it down?"

Screw off. Despite his condescension and her own formulating plan, her qualms increased by the second. A sense of doom descended upon her. *Be strong. Lisette's life is at stake.* "I can remember." She battled to restrain the sarcasm in her voice.

"Excellent." He pulled her to her feet, his face inches from hers. "I'll time the call, so keep it short. And I'll be on an extension."

CRSO

"Lieutenant, line one," Sterling shouted from the hall. "Juliana Westwood."

"Trace it," James yelled.

Alex pushed past James and seized the phone from the messy war room table. He motioned for everyone but James to clear the room before he punched the speaker button.

Juliana was alive. Relief rushed through him like a balmy breeze.

"Juliana." Alex exhaled, rubbing at the muscle jerking in his jaw. "Are you okay?"

"Yes." Her voice cracked.

His heart swelled at the welcome sound of her voice. "Where are you?"

"The kidnapper has me." In a rush, she said, "Is Andrea with you?"

Andrea? Why the hell did she think Andrea was at the PD? "No. Is Lisette with you?"

"Yes. Alex, open up and let Andrea in on the investigation, so she knows Lisette's safe."

In a heartbeat, he knew where she was driving. Exhilaration pumped new endorphins into his ravaged veins.

If you can read me, say "I'm okay, but I wouldn't pass up a ginger ale," Alex told her in his thoughts. "Are you hurt?" he asked out loud.

"I'm okay. But I wouldn't pass up a ginger ale." Rushed panic flooded her voice. No other telltale sounds in the background gave her location away. "I need you to get my safety deposit key."

"Okay. Is Lisette okay?" *Say Lisette's okay, all blonde hair and blue eyes, if it's Nicholas Hastings.*

"Yes." She repeated the words and added, "The key's in my nightstand drawer."

We know where he lives. Repeat where the key is if you're at a ranch house surrounded by orchards.

"Again, the key's in a bank envelope in my nightstand drawer."

"Got it." Alex etched the information on his brain.

"I've got to go. I'll call back later today and tell you when and where to leave the ransom." Juliana spoke

The phone clicked off.

"No trace," Sterling shouted through the door.

"I didn't expect one." Alex slammed the phone down and rested his clenched fists on the table. "He knows what he's doing."

James shoved aside a tray of half-eaten sandwiches and eased a hip on the table. "What's in the box?"

"No idea." Alex strode to the door, stopping on the threshold. "Whatever it is, she's convinced him it's worth the risk."

CR&O

Alex loved her. After everything, he still loved her. She wanted to cry out with the joy that energized her and propelled her fear out of sight. But she forced herself to block her thoughts, to concentrate on Nicholas and her situation.

"You did well." Nicholas gripped her arm and led her back to the locked bedroom.

While she considered the options that had kept her awake most of the night, her curiosity bubbled to the surface. "Where's Jasmine?"

"Sleeping. I kept her busy last night," he drawled as he brought her to a halt in front of the white bedroom door. His smile might charm rampaging snakes, but it didn't fool Juliana. "Would you like to keep me busy tonight?"

"I'd rather sleep with vipers." *Get angry, you bastard.*

No such luck. He laughed instead.

Nicholas canted his head. "You *will* change your mind. I promise," he whispered, his breath hot against her ear, brushing his lips over her cheek.

His touch sent revulsion surging through her, liquefying her knees. She would have fallen without his firm grip on her arm.

"Don't bet the ranch on it." With steely resolve, she straightened and shrugged. "I'd rather die than let you touch me."

Abruptly, he pressed his soft, dry lips on her forehead in a disgustingly possessive kiss. His tangy sandalwood aftershave invaded her sinuses. The scent would have been pleasant if not for the man who wore it.

She suppressed a shudder. "I thought you only screwed willing partners."

"If I told you I'd kill Lisette if you didn't sleep with me, wouldn't you be willing?"

A renewed horror took root within her, and the blood drained from her face.

He chuckled. "That's what I thought." He kissed the tip of her nose. "You really are too beautiful to pass up."

If it meant saving Lisette. Juliana couldn't suppress another bone-jarring shudder as she felt her blood drain down to her toes.

"Nicky? What's going on?" Jasmine's shrill voice shattered the interlude as she appeared behind Nicholas. If Jasmine had claws, they'd be sharp and extended.

Perfect timing. Time for Plan B. Quickly, she wound her free arm around Nicholas' neck, seeking his lips with her own. She closed her eyes and endured the repellent kiss. As his tongue forced her lips open, she couldn't curb a reflexive gag. The kiss deepened and grew intimate. His tongue lashed against hers, his cruel lips crushing in his swelling lust. It took all the courage and mind control Juliana possessed not to push him away, not to bite down on his lips, not to bash her knee into his erection pulsing against her stomach.

After an eternity of stomach-roiling disgust, Nicholas

gaze. She splayed a trembling hand on the front of his jeans and pressed into his hard arousal. The violent urge to squeeze his life out through his penis nearly took Juliana over the precipice.

Jasmine's screeching brought him back to the present.

"Jaz! Shut the fuck up. You do *not* own me." He backhanded her across the face, slamming her against the wall. She sagged to the floor, sobs racking her shoulders.

Juliana sent Jasmine a sympathetic glance. Regardless of the girl's troubles, score one for Juliana.

"Get in there," Nicholas said harshly. He unlocked the bedroom door and shoved Juliana inside the room.

෴

"You hear that noise?" Jasmine had worked Nicholas into a lust-filled frenzy.

Hotter than ever, she was a tiger when mad. She rode him hard and deep. Twisting her head to the side, her body stiffened. His upward thrusts quickened and intensified.

"I hear something." She pursed her swollen lips.

"You hear nothing," Nicholas snapped. He squeezed her hips and pressed her down onto him.

"I'm serious." Before he could stop her, she lifted off him and ran naked to the sliding glass door in the dining room. "Don't you hear that?"

Nicholas froze. He did hear an odd noise, and he didn't like the sound of it. Leaping off the couch, he pulled his pants up and made a dash for the open door. "Of all the worst luck in Monte Carlo."

Green eyes followed him around the room while he scrambled into his clothes.

His face contorted in fury. "Juliana, I'll kill you if you do that again!"

CHAPTER THIRTY-TWO

A feather touch on Juliana's face drew her out of the distasteful dream. Lisette's tiny fingers patted her cheek. Muffled strains of Nicholas shouting urged her into full alertness. She didn't think she'd slept more than a few minutes. A dull throb began in her head.

Frightened, Lisette reached for her, and she sat up to comfort the child. The need to give solace swamped her as Lisette's little arms clung to her neck.

Monte Carlo? The name nagged at her like an old buried memory scratching for the surface.

Snuggling Lisette closer, Juliana recalled the dream. Helicopters? Could it mean the police—Alex—were on their way?

A slow smile stretched Juliana's mouth. She had attempted to read Nicholas all day with no luck. But as soon as Jasmine sheathed him, his mind opened like a cracked egg. Obviously, sex created a stronger force than his own mental blockade.

A loud banging on the door startled them, followed by Nicholas' rushed, angry voice. "Stand back." The door flew open, and he barreled in with a roll of duct tape in his

expression and unkempt appearance. She held steadfast as he bound her wrists in front of her and discreetly sighed when he left Lisette unbound.

Shrinking from the cold gray of his eyes, Juliana's mind floundered for a new escape plan. Nicholas shoved her toward the door, the nine-millimeter once again in his grip.

Lisette scrambled toward the bed. "Fluffy," she cried.

"Lisette, get over here." Nicholas banged his gun on the doorframe.

"Lisette, leave it," Juliana ground out. But Lisette managed to snag the stuffed bunny and glued herself to Juliana's side before Nicholas posed a further threat.

Jasmine entered the room, and her long fingernails bit into Juliana's arm. Juliana ignored the sting as Nicholas led them into the backyard.

Bright sunlight blinded Juliana, watering her eyes. She quickly recovered and scanned her surroundings. Orchards surrounded them, feeding the chill of desolation prickling under her skin. No help in sight. She listened intently for the helicopters from her vision, but heard nothing remotely like the whirl of blades.

The living oleander fence separated the perimeter of the yard from the nearest orchard. The thick bushes shielded the car hidden on the other side. The acrid scent of oleander blooms filled her nostrils, and she stifled a gag.

Nicholas halted at the hedge and uttered unintelligible words. He thrust the gun at Jasmine. "Hold them here." He sprinted back toward the house.

Jasmine took the gun without batting an eyelash. She backed up a couple of paces and held the nine-millimeter steady on Juliana, triumph gleaming in her eyes.

"Cut your losses now, Jasmine," Juliana said in a low voice. "I can convince the police to go easy on you if you help us escape. Free me and give me the gun."

Jasmine laughed, a tinkling, crystal sound. "Why should I? So you can have him?"

"Don't be insane. If you help me now, things will go easier on you." Lisette hugged the back of Juliana's legs, and Juliana blocked her small body completely. "I'll tell the police you were also held captive. That you helped us escape."

"They won't believe you once they find out I'm his wife." She flashed a large diamond ring on her ring finger. It glittered as it caught the bright sun.

Stunned, Juliana had never noticed the ring. God help the poor twit.

"Did he talk you into this, or did you go along willingly?" Juliana stood her ground. Wariness settling over Jasmine's face gave her away. "He said he'd marry you if you helped, didn't he?"

"So what if he did?" Jasmine's upraised arm dipped. She quickly steadied it with her free hand. "He loves me."

"He's not going to take you with him." Juliana looked askance at the idiot girl. "You know I can read his mind, right?" She'd destroy Jasmine's faith in Nicholas by the time she was done with her.

Jasmine laughed. "He'd never leave me behind. Not even for you."

"Don't fool yourself, Jasmine." The duct tape pinched her skin. She fought the urge to raise her wrists to her mouth and chew off the tape. "He's a handsome man; he can have any woman he wants. Why should he settle for you?"

Anger and jealousy flickered in Jasmine's misty eyes. *Bingo.* Juliana had hit a tender mark.

The breeze kicked up, and Jasmine's blonde hair

available was the pea gravel covering the dry ground.

Nicholas jogged back, a small nylon backpack slung over his shoulder, cutting short her time to wear Jasmine down.

"Move through the hedge." He yanked another gun from the waistband of his pants. "You first, Jasmine. Then Juliana, and keep Lisette quiet."

As Jasmine disappeared through the thick hedge, Lisette's whimpers intensified.

"No, I can't go through there," Lisette cried, clutching Juliana's legs, her bunny falling to the ground. Fear emanated from her tiny quaking arms.

"Honey, it's okay." Juliana crouched down and offered a tremulous smile to Lisette to calm her. "Pretend it's a tunnel to a magical place. I'll be with you, okay?"

Lisette gave her a nervous look of trust, then nodded. She led the little girl through the wall of leaves and pink flowers. Nicholas brought up the rear. Once on the other side, Lisette tried to pull away from Juliana.

"Fluffy," she cried. "Uncle Nick, I need my bunny," she wailed. Renewed tears spilled down her cheeks.

"Shut her up!" Glowering, Nicholas waved the gun at Juliana.

Uncle? Suddenly, Juliana recalled where she'd heard the reference to Monte Carlo. It was where Grantham Chamber's oldest son lived part-time. Shock and confusion streamed through her blood. Puzzle pieces fell into place. The ostracized oldest son, seeking revenge against his parents. A sick feeling of déjà vu quickened her heart.

No time to think further as Nicholas prodded her toward the car. Jasmine already sat in the front passenger seat. He thrust Juliana and Lisette into the cramped back and clambered into the driver's seat.

Jasmine turned to face the backseat. Her arm bobbed

as she aimed the gun at Juliana's heart. Juliana maneuvered Lisette to her left, away from direct sight of the gun. Lisette lay partially on Juliana's lap, covering her bound hands. Grim satisfaction zipped through her. She had banged a sizeable dent in Jasmine's trust. Jasmine's face was a palette of jealousy, suspicion, and anger.

Nicholas drove at a turtle's pace to avoid kicking up too much tell-tale dust. He focused on the road, paying Juliana no heed. She scanned the orchard, but row upon row of thick, leafy trees met her gaze.

Dipping her head, she whispered in Lisette's ear, "When I tell you to get on the floor, can you move really fast?" Juliana pointed to the cramped floor behind the front passenger seat.

Unshed tears pooled in Lisette's eyes. "Yes," she whispered.

"What are you two whispering about?" Jasmine adjusted her grip on the gun.

"I'm trying to calm her down." Juliana batted down the panic rioting inside her own chest. *No time to fall apart. It's not the first time you've had a gun pointed at you.*

Jasmine's head swiveled from side to side. "Can we get out of here?"

"Do you think I'm an idiot?" Nicholas rounded on her.

Well, if the nickname fits. Juliana quickly quashed her inner voice.

Was the car visible from the air through the dense canopy of trees? Where were those damn helicopters?

Stealthily, she studied Nicholas' profile in the rearview mirror. The similarities to the Chambers were visible; she'd simply never synced up the resemblance. He

belong to the spawn of the devil.

Juliana bowed her head and whispered in Lisette's ear again. Hidden behind the driver's seat, her small body shielding Juliana's hands, Lisette proceeded to peel off the tape binding Juliana's wrists.

"Juliana, what do the cops know?" Nicholas glared at her in the rearview mirror, paying no attention to Lisette.

"I don't know." Her face remained as impassive as a rock, even though pebbles zinged her insides in rebellion.

"Don't lie to me." He sneered. "You saw things in your dreams. What did you see?"

"You two, going at it constantly." She censored her words for Lisette's sake. "The kidnapping."

Nicholas hesitated as if in thought. "You saw me by the car in the garage, didn't you?"

Juliana debated lying to Nicholas, but feared his retribution. He possessed his own breed of psychic intuition, and until she knew what it was, she had to play it safe. Her mind swirled in different directions, but at that moment, she could only think of the truth.

"Yes."

"You knew Jasmine was involved?"

She cleared her throat in distaste. "Plain as day, since you couldn't keep your hands off her."

Jasmine squealed and wriggled her body suggestively, the gun dipping and swaying with each movement.

The oleanders veered to the right and Nicholas made a sharp turn. The swerve thrust Juliana against the seat back. She grabbed at Lisette's arm to keep her from rolling off her lap.

"I know you never saw me. I doubt you have that much psychic power. But you saw the car, didn't you?"

You have no inkling what power I have, asshole. "I saw a black convertible."

The car reached the end of the copse of trees. They

appeared to have dead-ended at a small hillside. But Nicholas made a sharp left turn and drove a short distance over an uneven plowed field parallel to the hillside. He approached a hidden ravine that split the hillside in half. The car crawled over small rocks and sparse undergrowth of summer-brittle weeds. The trail was marked, used by others as evidenced by assorted tire tracks. Nicholas obviously knew the route or he wouldn't attempt to drive a low-slung car over the uncertain terrain.

"Where are we going?" Juliana chanced the question. Lisette continued to pry at the tape on her wrists.

Nicholas smiled at her in the rearview mirror. "My Plan B."

His leer sent snakes slithering down her back. Could he read her mind? No, no, she denied the possibility as she beat down her escalating fear.

The doors in her mind shut tight and safely shielded her thoughts.

∞

Alex and James waited in James' truck at the street opening to Hastings' driveway. Unmarked cars bearing Sterling, Gilbert, and SWAT team members waited behind them. All potential land exits surrounding the area were blocked, and SWAT and patrolmen were posted along the hedges bordering the property. Two choppers hovered a short distance away, waiting for their signal.

The rush continued unabated inside Alex, replacing the tension that had held him hostage for days. He loved fieldwork. His intense concern for Lisette and Juliana's safety during the siege kept him more determined and

the hedge. Let's do it." The call from the SWAT leader blasted through Alex's earpiece.

"You don't have to do this." James turned to study Alex.

Alex sat iron-rod straight in the passenger seat, checking his gun for the third time. "That's my family."

Nodding, James knew better than to argue with him any further.

Three minutes after the ground team arrived at Hastings' front door, the birds would conduct a crisscross fly-by.

The driveway was a quarter-mile long, edged on both sides by meticulous rows of cypress and fruit trees beyond. A couple hundred feet from where the line of trees ended in a circular driveway, a long ranch house stood, flanked by several old oaks.

James drove as close to the house as the front yard allowed. They stopped and jumped out with guns drawn, seeking cover behind the open vehicle doors. The ranch appeared deserted, not a car in sight, not a sign of life. A blackbird's raucous cawing slashed the eerie hush that stole the air from Alex's lungs.

More adrenaline pumped through him while anxiety sought a foothold. "Watch my back." He dashed onto the porch. Vibrating with tension, he kicked in the front door and entered. The SWAT team immediately stormed the house behind him.

The house was too static. Alex knew at once. They were too late.

He moved from room to room, James covering his back. He reached the end of the hallway and entered a child's bedroom. Juliana's description fit to a tee. A sick thud resounded in his gut as he took in the small, familiar room.

He picked up the pillow from the top bunk, breathing

in Juliana's faint scent. The same scent that had lingered on his skin and shirt for the last two days.

"He held them here." Alex tossed the pillow aside.

"Looks like it." James yanked back the pink curtain to reveal the windowless wall. "Well-planned, with the walled off window and deadbolt on the door," James added as an afterthought.

Alex crossed the room and picked up Lisette's pajamas—the set he gave her for Easter. A vein of cold rage throbbed on his forehead.

"Lieutenant!" The SWAT leader ran into the house as the choppers descended upon the scene. "The place is cleared out. The Jag's in the garage."

"Shit." Alex slammed his fist against the wall.

Shouting, Sterling darted into the house. Alex spun on his heels, his eyes captivated by the familiar white object in Sterling's tan grip.

"Found this out by the flower bushes in back." Sterling extended the stuffed toy to Alex.

Alex grabbed the bunny and shook off the dust. "He's on the run. Lisette would never leave without this unless she was under pressure. And he obviously knew it helped keep her subdued." He jogged past the group and out of the abandoned house.

"Where'd you find it?" he asked the officer closest to the pink and green leafy wall. The officer pointed out the spot under the bushes where he found the stuffed animal.

Several black-uniformed men scrambled back through the hedge. "Fresh tire marks on the other side."

Alex sprinted toward the driveway. "O'Malley!"

He reached the truck the same time James jumped off the porch. As James' feet touched the ground, an explosion rocked the world around him. The house flared

debris struck the truck, slamming Alex's forehead into the steering wheel. The force bounced him back against the open door. Pain blasted through his head, and an inferno swept over him.

The last thing Alex saw as he slid to the ground was James' flying body hitting the ground face-first. Everything else vanished into a swirling abyss.

CHAPTER THIRTY-THREE

Juliana jerked as thunder boomed in the distance. Except it couldn't be thunder in a cloudless sky. She craned her neck to peer out the back window, but the hillside blocked her view. "What was that?" She twisted forward. The smile that crept across Nicholas' face in the rearview mirror stunned her.

"I just destroyed every trace of my existence, like my family always wanted," he replied, not an ounce of remorse in his voice. "If I was lucky, I took out a couple of your cop friends too." Nicholas locked gazes with Juliana in the mirror.

Jasmine gasped, her hand trembling under the weight of the gun as if the weapon weighed thirty pounds. "What?" she cried. "Where are we going to live?" Her hand dipped precariously.

Nicholas maneuvered the car onto another dirt road, leaving the hillside and shallow valley behind. Despite the dread seeping into Juliana, she forced herself to focus on Jasmine's unraveling. Lisette had managed to free enough tape on Juliana's wrist to enable her to pull the rest of the tape off without catching Nicholas' or

weren't leaving the country."

He laughed, eerily at ease with the situation. "No, I said *you* weren't."

"What?" Jasmine's wounded look turned incredulous and she sagged in the front seat.

The opportunity Juliana waited for arose, and she motioned to Lisette. Without hesitation, Lisette sank to the floor, curling into a tight ball.

Nicholas steered the car toward a tarmac road less than a hundred feet ahead.

Jasmine's face paled. The hand gripping the gun sagged to her side. "But I'm your wife. You can't leave me here."

Seizing the moment, Juliana lunged between the front bucket seats, aiming for Jasmine's neglected gun.

Nicholas roared like a lion pouncing on his kill. The car swerved sharply. He slammed the brakes so hard, the vehicle spun a one-eighty, billowing thick dust around them. Juliana flew between the front seats, her shoulder smashing against the dashboard. Her hip ground painfully on top of the gearshift, but she managed to get a grip on the gun.

Growling, she wrangled with Jasmine for possession of the weapon. Nicholas yanked on her arm and slammed Juliana's wrist down on the gearshift. A bone cracked, audible in the frenzied din. Excruciating pain shot up her arm. Her hand convulsed in agony, and she lost her grip on the gun.

For a brief moment, Nicholas' thoughts clouded her mind, his mental block flung aside. Dizziness overcame her, and she couldn't focus on her own thoughts, let alone his thoughts leaking into her mind.

"Let go of the gun, Jasmine," he snapped, his hand covering hers on the weapon's grip.

Juliana finally leveraged her head up and found

herself eye-to-eye with the barrel of the gun. Nicholas shoved her backward, and she sprawled in a heap on the rear seat. Dazed with pain, she clutched her left wrist to her chest. The blood drained from her face as she fought the nausea spinning her world out of orbit. With every ounce of effort, she thrust her thoughts away from the pain and focused on the need to keep Lisette safe. The little girl still crouched in a ball on the floor, eyes round, terrified.

Jasmine cried hysterically in the front seat.

"You try that again and I *will* kill you." Nicholas sported a scarlet mask of fury.

CR80

Alex lay flat on his back on pebbled ground. His eyelashes felt like they'd been singed off. Every inch of him burned, as though he'd walked naked in the desert sun for days. A warm, sticky substance dripped from his temple above his left eye. He raised a shaky hand and touched his forehead. Through hazy eyes, he recognized blood on his fingertips, smelled the coppery tang of it.

Had a stray bullet hit him? It took a moment to collar his memory from the haze in his mind. No bullet. He recalled the heat blast that careened into him and slid him down the side of the truck as if it had liquefied his bones.

Voices peppered the air around him. Alex tried to decipher the words through the cotton plugging his ears. He attempted to sit, but his head spun and his body refused to obey.

A voice eventually penetrated the mist in his head. "Lieutenant, don't move."

grounds. Flames engulfed the ranch house, shooting from the roof.

The acrid stench of scorched wood, tarred roof shingles, and smoldering electrical wires permeated the air as black smoke drifted skyward. Heat from the burning building raised perspiration on Alex's skin. He longed for the cool Pacific Ocean to quell the agony inside and outside his body. His gaze landed on James, perched on the truck's tailgate, fighting the hands pushing against him.

Relief rippled over Alex's agony. "James, you okay?" Blood trickled onto his left eyelid, and he smeared it off before it dripped into his eye.

James' rough voice drifted to him. "Man, I thought you were a goner."

Sterling appeared at Alex's side and pressed a cool cloth to his head. The pressure on the gash exacerbated the throbbing.

He winced but held steady. "Did everyone get out?"

"We lost one SWAT member on the ground, and there are a few injuries. Fire and EMTs have been dispatched," Sterling replied.

"Help me up." Alex pulled his knees up.

Sterling laid a heavy hand on Alex's shoulder. "You should wait until the paramedics—"

"I'm going after that SOB." Alex clutched the bottom of the truck and pulled himself upright. Sterling reluctantly assisted from the other side. He held onto Alex's arm as Alex gained his balance, ignoring the sensation of a bulldozer flattening him into the dirt. Even his hair seemed to hurt.

He ignored Sterling's protests. "James, you with me?"

James stumbled to his feet. "Don't have to ask me twice."

James appeared in better shape, so Alex let him take

the driver's seat. Alex's overwhelming need to find Lisette and Juliana battled against his aching body. His adrenaline slowly began to resurface.

Sterling called for backup while Alex crawled into the passenger seat. Dismayed, he surveyed the scene of destruction. James maneuvered the truck around debris and police officers, locating a route through the oleanders. A patrol car followed behind. The faint wail of sirens pierced the air.

Nicholas Hastings, aka Grant Chamber III, had just turned the corner into a murder one charge with special circumstances. He'd never see freedom's light—if he lived another hour.

Would they be in time to save Lisette and Juliana? Alex opened the block in his mind and searched for Juliana. He found emptiness, but he felt her presence like a cool salve on his flushed body. She was nearby.

The tire tracks made an easy trail to follow. James' four-wheel drive pickup sped through the tilled terrain effortlessly. Two hillsides formed a mini valley at the orchard's end. A faint dust cloud dissipated beyond the hill. The truck sped toward the base of the hill, unmarked cars fast on their tail.

It must be them. Alex's skin tingled from Juliana's presence. It was as if the bomb blast had unlocked his mind and forged an unconscious connection to her. He cautioned James to a stop before giving up the shield of the hillside. One of the SWAT members who tailed them jogged over to the parked truck. He pushed a map through the window.

"A road parallels the hill on the other side," the officer said. "We've blocked it at both ends."

Alex's eyes blurred, and he couldn't focus on the map.

"Another fenced-in orchard." The officer pointed at the map. "Unless there's off-road access, he's trapped. No one has come out at either end of the blockade."

"He could scale the fence and take off on foot." Alex threw the map on the seat and pulled his gun out of his shoulder holster.

"Possibly." The SWAT officer raised his hand to chest height. "It's cross-fenced, four feet tall. He can't drive a car through it."

"We'll drive out of this valley. Back us up." Alex pointed his gun out the windshield as a signal to James. "I know Hastings is out there."

James slammed the vehicle in gear and inched forward.

Alex pushed the connection in his mind. *Juliana, it's Alex*, he tried telling her telepathically. *Stall him.*

"Alex, he might be long gone." James drove closer to the opening to the valley.

Alex sensed another wave of Juliana's nearness. "It's them."

We're right behind you, Alex told Juliana in his mind.

James looked at him as if he'd lost his marbles in the bomb blast, then shrugged stiffly. "You're the boss."

CR80

Juliana, it's Alex. Stall him.

The penetrating thought startled Juliana. She masked her surprise, lest Nicholas suspect anything unusual.

We're right behind you.

Thank God, the cavalry had arrived. Her injured wrist had put a crimp in her escape plans.

Nicholas attempted to resettle Jasmine with the gun in her hands, but she resisted. Her sobbing sent shudders through Juliana, but Juliana had her own worries.

Her wrist swelled. A drum beat in her head. Close to passing out, the surging in her stomach gave her the perfect excuse for a delaying tactic.

"I'm going to be sick," she croaked. "I need to get out."

"Try again." The look on Nicholas' face could have frozen water.

"Please." She sensed her face was whiter than white. It must have caused him concern, because he stopped in a dirt lot alongside the two-lane road and opened the car door. He peeled himself out of the front seat and yanked it forward.

Pain tore through her as he tugged her from the backseat. Seizing her right arm in a brutal grip, he led her away from the car. She sank to her knees in a patch of dying tumbleweeds and emptied her stomach.

Nicholas waited patiently and handed her a mint when she finished. "I'm sorry I hurt you."

"Are you? Why?" She wiped her mouth with the back of her good hand.

"You weren't part of my plan." The shadows from a nearby oak tree darkened his face.

"Some plan," she retorted. "You hurt everyone else. Jasmine and Lisette." She tilted her head to gauge his reactions. "Her mother, her uncle. You hurt your parents, *Grant.* And yourself."

The words didn't appear to shock or sting his impassive mask. It was as if he expected them. His eyes emptied of expression. "How long have you known?"

"Since we left the house, *Uncle Nick.*" For the first time, sorrow shadowed his face, and he shuffled his feet through pebbles in the dirt. "What did they do to you?"

"My father never loved me. He never accepted me for who I was who I wanted to be," he said without emotion,

The words dipped into her battered heart. She couldn't argue with them. She'd spent a large portion of her own life living in misery, not unlike him.

His eyes looked through her. "We're a lot alike, you and me. Both orphans. Abandoned by family, never part of one. And we'll always be that way."

Juliana didn't plan to waste one more second of her life thinking she'd always be alone. Not any longer.

"You have a family." Her gaze met his troubled gray eyes. "How can you deny them?" She held her swollen left wrist in her lap.

"It doesn't matter." He pulled her to her feet. "Let's go."

Swaying, renewed agony burst in her wrist. Nicholas caught her in his arms and anchored her against his chest. The repressed pain in his taut body—the grievous injury caused by a childhood perceived without love—radiated into her. For an instant, she experienced a bone-chilling grief for childhoods that could have been. For him. For her.

Nicholas released Juliana and helped her crawl into the tight backseat. A spot of silver out the window caught Juliana's attention. With a subtle flick of her head, she spied a truck crawling around the hillside the Firebird had just left behind. James' truck. Relief swamped her. She wasn't ready to throw in the towel, but Alex's timing was perfect. Even though it was no time to relax, Juliana let a fraction of her terror and anxiety fly away on the breeze.

Nicholas leaned down to climb back into the driver's seat, giving no indication he'd seen or heard the truck.

Alex slid out of the vehicle before the wheels stopped rolling. With the door shielding him, he shot at the muscle car's back tires, flattening them. The crack of the shots reverberated inside the old car, shattering the mantle of terror.

Nicholas roared, pulled the gun from his waistband, and began shooting blindly over the top of the car from his crouch in the doorway. He reached in and ripped Juliana from the backseat, cushioning her in front of him. He wound a crushing arm around her ribcage, holding her against his trembling fury. Juliana gasped from another round of white-hot pain.

The faint whir of helicopters grew louder.

"Hold your fire!" Alex's voice roared above the escalating noise.

"Lisette, don't move," Juliana snapped at the terrified child scrunched on the floor of the car. A petrified Jasmine crumpled low in the front seat, relatively safe.

Nicholas held her left arm against her stomach. Pain raged like a wildfire within her. Once again, she forced her mind to leap beyond the bodily pain and concentrate on the scene unfolding around her. It took all the physical and mental energy she possessed.

Patrol cars surged toward them, sirens clogging the air as they raced in from both directions on the country road. The whirling of approaching helicopters charged the air.

Juliana gazed into Alex's eyes. Even from the distance, his love emanated from the vivid blue pools, lending her strength.

Where's Lisette? Alex asked in his mind.

Juliana tipped her head in the car's direction.

Is she alive?

Juliana nodded twice.

"Drop it, Hastings. You're surrounded," Alex called out.

"Do the right thing," Juliana pleaded with Nicholas,

of emotions, from fear to anguish, roiled inside her.

"If I die, you die with me." His hot breath tickled her ear. "Two orphans entered this world, and two will leave it."

"Don't." Juliana locked gazes with Alex. His eyes bored into her soul, fortifying her resolve. "I can help you."

"Release her," Alex yelled, his voice flinty and lethal. He broke eye contact, but she could feel him in her mind.

Backing against the open car door, Nicholas tightened his arm around her waist. Excruciating pain continued to spear her arm. Nicholas held the gun against her temple, and she forced herself to disregard the threat to her life.

Juliana, try to move away from him. We need a clear shot from either the front or back. Alex's voice filtered into her mind.

Don't try anything or I'll kill you. Suddenly, Nicholas' thoughts competed with Alex's, a stabbing and calming mix of relief and terror.

With enormous effort and regret, she closed her mind off from Nicholas—and from Alex. She couldn't chance leaving any type of opening to her mind in case Nicholas penetrated it.

"Nicholas, if you let us go now, I can help you." She cradled her left wrist against her stomach. "I'll talk to your parents, convince them they're wrong. Please don't do this."

"You'd help me? While I'm in jail?" He laughed derisively and bent his head to her ear again. "I'd rather die than spend the rest of my life being pitied by those people you call my parents."

"You're not a killer, so don't become one." His body pressed hard against hers, his muscles rigid. Anger and excitement radiated from the sweat soaking him.

"What would you know about that?" The sneer in his

voice was obvious.

"I know you." She gulped, fighting the fist of vertigo bullying her self-possession. "Like you said, you and I are alike."

"Then you know how they hate me." His voice lowered.

Confusion veiled Alex's face. Juliana knew he was trying to send thoughts to her blocked mind. She hated that she'd had to shut him out when he needed her most. But she couldn't take the chance, not knowing the extent of Nicholas' psychic abilities.

"They don't hate you." Juliana dropped his wrist and gave his arm a quick squeeze. "They love you." From an earlier fleeting thought she'd captured in his mind, she chanced her next question. "Didn't your mother help you with money?"

A strangled chuckle erupted in her ear. "Because I threatened her. My father would kill her if he knew."

A tendril of shock wound through her. Her perceptions were correct. "I'm sure they only want what's best for you." Deep down, she hoped her words held some truth.

Nicholas' unyielding arm loosened. He turned her around to face him, pinning her against his rock-solid chest again. She dropped her arms to her side, mindful of her broken wrist. The faint smell of gunpowder lingered. The weapon still pointed at her temple.

Dimly, Juliana wondered why her intuition told her she'd live to see another day. Nothing separated her from death, trying to ruin the life she hoped to have with Alex. Holding onto those thoughts gave her strength to let her intuition prevail.

Nicholas bumped her bad wrist and Juliana gasped in renewed pain. Uncertainty exaggerated his bleak expression. She smiled, tentatively catching him off-

thumb caressed her left breast, his hand shaking.

Exhilaration poured into her. She'd succeeded in stabbing his shallow control.

She raised her right hand to his shoulder, her fingers feathering over his neck in an intimate gesture. "I know you, Nicholas, it's not in you. You have too much to live for."

A brooding look descended over his face.

Juliana knew exactly what he wanted, needed. It had nothing to do with money. His need centered on love and acceptance. The same things absent from her life. It was mirrored in his eyes.

She traced her index finger over his lips. When he didn't stop her, she raised her mouth to his, lips touching lightly, then firmer. A shudder tore through her as she met his hunger, forcing down a gag reflex. He lowered the gun and grasped her waist. The kiss deepened and became possessive. The gun barrel, solid and cold against her buttocks, pointed at the ground.

"No!" A scream of horror erupted from Jasmine, startling them both, handing Juliana the chance she'd hoped for.

She ripped her mouth off Nicholas. With her waning strength, she pushed back from him as far as his arms allowed and slammed her knee into his groin. The contact vibrated up her thigh and pelvic area, and his arms dropped away. Without a wasted second, she scrambled out of his reach, ducking behind the car.

Swearing and moaning, he stumbled, gripping his crotch with one hand and attempting to raise the gun with the other. An incensed wail rose up his throat. "You bitch!" he screamed, falling to his knees.

The crack of a gunshot followed the cry of the madman. She flung herself to the ground and rolled under the car away from him, away from the chaos. The force of her body hitting the ground sent a new gush of searing torture up her arm. An agonizing maelstrom flooded her mind, paralyzing her. Her eyes clouded, but through the mist, she spied Nicholas on his knees. A slow red sea spread across the left side of his chest. He toppled face-forward on the dry, hard-packed earth.

Juliana's head felt as if it would explode as Nicholas' thoughts and emotions crammed inside her mind. Every thought, every emotion. A cold, dark desolation filled him. Filled her. He'd grown up in his father's shadow, never knowing how to love or be loved in return. Never accepted, never doing right.

His mind consumed hers completely. For a brief instant, she felt warm, strong arms around her, then black ink drenched the sun.

Juliana struggled through the darkness and the death trying to carry her along for a ride. An energy-force wrapped around her, dragging her away from the darkness. From far away, someone called her name.

Alex.

Pure love surrounded her, warmed her insides, and spread light in the dark corners. His need filled her and chased off the malevolence, the hellish void. All the doubts she harbored about Alex and their love vanished. The loneliness disappeared. Everything she'd ever wanted waited for her outside the abyss. She wouldn't allow herself to end up like the psycho who'd terrorized her world during the last week.

Nicholas was dying, yanking her to hell with him. Juliana fought against death's pull, sensing it inches away. She tried to call out to Alex, but no sounds came forth. Her arms and legs felt leaden, and she couldn't move her head or her eyelids. A sluggish heart thumped

Alex kept asking her to come back, telling her he loved her. That he'd never stopped loving her. That he couldn't live without her.

Final shudders jerked her body as the last vestiges of Nicholas Hastings evaporated from her mind.

"Jewel, wake up. Don't leave me."

Tepid raindrops fell on her face. Juliana brushed them away, startled when her hand obeyed her brain. She tried again to open her eyes. They twitched, fluttered, then opened wide to feast on the beloved face of the man she adored. The droplets on her face were Alex's tears.

He cradled her against his chest with one arm, wrapping Lisette close in his other arm. The three of them huddled on the ground under the gnarled oak. Juliana settled her swollen and numb wrist on her stomach. She was right where she wanted to be. No more gloom clouded her heart or her mind.

Her head ached worse than ever. Her stomach clenched, but at least she was alive to experience it. The pain didn't compare to the heartache of never seeing Alex again.

His heart glittered in his eyes as his gaze devoured her. She didn't know what to say.

"Juliana!" Excitement transformed Lisette's face. "You were right. Uncle Alex saved us."

Juliana gloried in the moment, the three of them together, safe. "Yes, he did, honey," she said in a weak voice.

Alex hugged them, blocking their view of the paramedics wrapping Nicholas in a body bag.

"Alex?" Juliana whispered.

"Shhh. All I want is to hold you both."

"Did you mean what you said yesterday? Just now?"

His expression grew quizzical before a slow smile lit his gaunt face. "Yes. I love you. I never stopped loving you."

Juliana smiled back at him and fingered the dried blood on his forehead. She lifted up and brushed her lips over the gash. "What happened?"

He pulled her tighter against him. "It doesn't matter. I'll tell you about it later."

Her wrist wedged between them, and she gasped. Renewed pain blasted her arm.

Eyes slivered, Alex searched her face. "What? What's wrong?"

"My wrist—"

Gently, he released the pressure of his embrace and eased her arm free. "Why didn't you tell me?"

She leaned her head back on his shoulder and searched his intense eyes. "Because I didn't want you to let me go."

He pressed a loving kiss on her temple. "I'll never, ever let you go, you hear me?"

CHAPTER THIRTY-FOUR

Jewel, I love you.

Juliana awoke next to Alex, his soothing voice in her head. She opened her eyes and found him watching her, his sly, sensuous smile a boon for her sore and tired body.

Wooden blinds closed out the world outside. She had no sense of the time. But she knew she lay in Alex's bedroom. Off-white walls were unadorned, save for a wrought iron framed mirror across from the bed. The light oak furniture was plain but serviceable, cluttered with various articles of clothing. A bachelor pad, plain and simple. Things would have to change.

"Hey." She caressed his face, his hair damp from a recent shower. He smelled clean, renewed, and heavenly. His smooth-shaven face was devoid of the tiredness, anxiety, and anger she'd become accustomed to the last few days.

"Hey yourself." Alex kissed her forehead and brushed his lips over hers. "Do you always crash for so long after your cases end?"

Juliana glanced at the clock. Four P.M., a day later. "I've never come so close to losing my mind in a dying man."

Alex's face darkened, his eyes slivered. "That won't

happen again."

A deep sense of relief burst inside her, and she gave way to it completely. She could have slipped into a coma, and might have died after Nicholas' mind subjugated hers. Alex had brought her back and saved her life. In more ways than one.

"Are you going to chase away all the boogiemen?" she teased, despite the seriousness of what had happened.

"Yes." Gathering her closer, he molded her against him. "Even if I have to put you under lock and key."

"Only if you're there with me."

"Nowhere else I'd rather be."

Juliana snuggled against his bare chest, her fiberglass-encased wrist resting on his hip.

He brushed the tangled hair off her face, his touch gentle, warm.

"How are Grantham and Samantha handling things? Or have you been sleeping with me the whole time?" She eyed the clean denim shorts he wore.

"With you, mostly." Alex's fingers twined in her hair. "Grantham's one broken man. That chip on his shoulder's pretty much demolished. Since Ethan and Nicholas are gone, he holds a ton of guilt for treating both his sons like crap." He wedged his knee between Juliana's legs, and she twined her legs around his.

"Samantha's trashed, but she's the one holding it together. She confirmed that Nicholas had limited, sporadic telepathic ability." He stroked her face, her neck, his heated touch leaving a feverish trail. "No charges will be filed against her. She was fooled, like Jasmine."

Juliana ran her fingers, featherlike, along Alex's arm. He caressed her back, leaving more trails of fire through the oversized T-shirt she wore—Alex's T-shirt. "Did you

out for a while." Alex sighed. "He followed her to school and seduced her into his scheme." His hand ventured beneath her shirt and continued caressing the inflamed skin of her stomach. Heat flared through her entire body, and she quivered under his exquisite touch. "Nicholas married her because he knew if things went sideways, she couldn't testify against him."

"What a waste of two lives." Juliana exhaled a small breath. Jasmine would most likely get jail time for her blind part in the crime. "Nicholas truly believed his parents owed him for the years of what he considered to be abandonment."

Nicholas told her he'd blown up his existence when he destroyed his house. Now that he *was* dead, his existence destroyed, his words had come true.

"He reached out to his father a couple of years ago, but Grantham castigated him for not fulfilling his potential as an oldest son should," Alex explained. "That's when Samantha started feeding him her trust fund."

"The well dried up, and he concocted his stupid plan." Alex's jaw clenched and loosened. "He found a look-alike and sent him on an all-expenses-paid vacation to Barcelona to make it look like he was there the whole time. The friend's in custody pending charges."

"How could he be stupid enough to register the Jag at his parents' house?"

Alex laughed grimly. "Samantha bought the damn car for him. His biggest screw-up."

"What did he do with all the money?" Juliana moved her hand to Alex's bare, muscled chest. He trembled from her touch.

"He ran up huge gambling debts in Monte Carlo." Leisurely, Alex stroked her abdomen, inching upward. "The five million from the ransom would've given him a new start. No one seems to know his plans. He told

Jasmine they'd live at the ranch house forever. She believed him."

Afraid to give in to her emotions and her arousal too hastily without knowing where they stood with one another, Juliana reluctantly removed Alex's hand from under her shirt. Things had to be right between them before she let her lust take over. She winked at his mock grimace as he moved his hand back to stroking her arm.

"She wasn't too bright, and Nicholas probably would've lost all the money if he was a chronic gambler." She reflected on the last few minutes of Nicholas' life. "I almost felt sorry for him."

Startled, he drew back. "You're kidding, right?"

"Seriously." She gave him a stern look. "He experienced real abandonment, self-esteem issues. He called himself an orphan, like me."

His eyes widened. "You're no more an orphan than I am."

She sighed. "I know."

He tightened his arms around her, her breasts pressing against his chest provocatively. "You're part of my family now. Forever."

"Oh, Alex." She kissed his chest, laying her cheek above his heart. A missing link niggled at her mind. "Hey, what about Sharon and Matthew Douglas? Why were they so evasive?"

Alex chuckled. "They didn't want to jinx their luck. They tried to adopt a little girl but it fell through. Then they got a call that a baby was available in Romania, which is what they wanted in the first place. They had to rush over there before they lost the opportunity. They were keeping it all on the downlow to avoid pity from their friends and family. With Lisette gone, they didn't

"I had a feeling it was easily explainable." The heat from his hard body warmed her from the inside out. His musky spice scent softened the edges of her ravaged mind. "Alex, were you talking to me while I slept?"

"Sort of." He laughed. "About everything under the sun."

"Most of which you didn't verbalize?" Her eyes slivered. Ecstatic, she no longer needed to shut him out of her mind. His block was effective enough that he could let her in and out at will, without her having to keep guard. It was a breath of fresh air.

He gave her a wry smile. "I guess I should've told you about the telepathy thing with Andrea."

Juliana gnawed at her lower lip. "Can you really block me from reading your mind?"

"Most of the time." He smoothed his fingers over her arm, stopping at her cast. "I'm still learning."

"Would have saved a few brain cells from worrying if I'd known." She nipped at his chest playfully.

Red spots stained his cheeks. "Sorry. I thought you'd figured it out since you're so experienced in psychic phenomena."

"I didn't have a clue. The case totally confused me. All my psychic abilities were in an uproar." Her fingers danced on his chest. "So the decoy plan didn't involve me?"

"No, sweetheart." He lifted her chin gently. "We planned to use an undercover female cop while you remained behind the scenes."

"I'm so sorry I mistrusted you." Love reflected in the liquid depths of Alex's eyes. A love she'd desperately missed over the years.

He brushed his lips over hers and smiled. "Just don't do it again, huh?"

"I won't," she whispered, caressing his scar. Staring

into each other's eyes, they were unable to shift their gazes away.

Careful not to disturb her bad arm, he grabbed a thick, unopened envelope off his headboard shelf. "I found this in your nightstand when I snagged your bank key."

"I must have stuck it in there and forgotten it. My father's probate lawyer gave me a bunch of papers." Gingerly, she edged the contents out of the envelope. Trepidation niggled at her.

The envelope contained newspaper articles of her accomplishments throughout the years in the psychic and financial communities. She set them aside on the bed. At the bottom of the pile of clippings, she found a letter addressed to her in her father's blocky handwriting. Extricating herself from Alex, Juliana propped her back against the headboard and read the letter. When she finished, she clutched it to her chest. Tears welled in the corner of her eyes.

"What is it, sweetheart?" Alex thumbed her tears away.

"I can't believe it. I never thought I'd see or hear these words from him." She shook her head, regret stabbing her. "He said he always loved me and tried to do what was best for me. He always wanted me to break away from the Westwood curse and mold my own course. He was confident and proud that I had accomplished it." Her eyes misted over, and she dropped the letter on her lap. "He was glad I'd learned to control my psychic gifts when no one else in the family ever did. He believed I broke the curse." She paused, seized Alex's hand and held on tight.

"Do you agree with him?" He squeezed her hand. Anticipation mingled with wariness in his expression.

"I think so." Juliana froze. "But I might slip. Can you

kissed her long and hard, leaving her breathless.

Glancing at the fallen letter, she said, "He was sorry for everything he did. He believed I might forgive him someday, if not thank him." She smiled ironically. "And he even said he was proud of you for the man you became."

Alex grinned wryly. "I guess the guy wasn't all bad."

Silence ensued, comfortable and safe, as Juliana reached a decision. "Will you drive me to the cemetery later?"

"I'll take you wherever you want to go."

She picked up the envelope and a small gold object fell on the bed between them. Alex scooped up the tiny gold ring.

A thrill flared in her. "My ring." Wide-eyed, Juliana studied the small emerald ring. Paranoid of her father's perpetual disdain of Alex, she'd always worn the ring on a chain around her neck.

"Looks like your father saved it." His eyes twinkled as he held the ring out to her. "Put your hand out."

Juliana extended her left hand.

"No, your right hand."

"But—"

"I have something better for that hand." Alex reached underneath his pillow and brought out a small white jewelry box along with a second envelope.

He opened the box and a stunning, brilliant ring met her gaze. "Oh, Alex!" Twin emeralds flanked a huge diamond. Celtic knots were engraved in the antique yellow and white gold band. "It's breathtaking."

She tore her eyes from the exquisite piece and gazed into Alex's vibrant face. "When did you have time to buy this?"

"It belonged to my grandmother." He lifted the ring out of the box and tossed the box aside. It sparkled in his large hands. "She passed it on to me. I always knew it was meant for you. The stones match your eyes." His voice grew husky, and he paused as if struggling with his thoughts.

The love in his eyes mesmerized her.

"Juliana, you're my heart, my soul, and I can't live without you. I *won't* live without you in my life." He raked his hands through his hair, trademark-Alex style. "Marry me." He held his breath.

Her heart sang with delight as tears coursed down her cheeks. She was home and never wanted to leave again.

Alex kissed the tears off her face, one by one.

She held no doubts. But did he know what he was getting into? "What about the cops and wives, psychics and husbands not mixing thing? Can you live with knowing who and what I am?"

He chuckled. "Who'll catch you when you pass out? Or hold your head while you puke your guts out? Bring you ginger ale?" He trailed his fingers along her bare arm, up her neck, sending tingles to her toes. "What about you? Can you live with a homicide cop, knowing who I am?"

Juliana gave him a wide smile. "I guess we were meant for each other." A bottomless peace filled her.

"No one said homicide cops and psychics don't mix," he teased. "Dr. Miller seems to think we'll be fine. He mentioned that he's been trying to get you to join the Psychics Guild for protection for a while. He's pretty sure I can handle the job now."

Rolling her eyes, she swatted his arm. "You and my doc have become quite the conspirators, I see. Maybe I will join the Guild. Like minds, commonality, and all. I might learn a thing or two."

Alex growled. "Not if it means they'll assign you one of

As though his words had released her pent up secrets, she felt a new radiant lightness. The last of the shadows had drifted away. Tilting her head, her smile widened. "I was the first one in my family to get training for my ESP. Most of my family believed all the Westwood psychics had gone crazy. But they only allowed their ESP to conquer their lives, out of ignorance."

Alex frowned and peered intently into her eyes. "You don't have any doubts, do you?"

"About going crazy?"

He winked. "That'll never happen." The look on his face mingled eagerness and tenderness. "I meant about us."

Fiery desire raced through her bloodstream. "No. I've found my true love." She caressed his cheek. "I love you with every cell of my being. Always have. Always will."

"Does that mean yes?" Eyebrows rose, and an anxious look crossed his face.

"Of course."

He slipped both rings on her fingers and laid her back down on the bed, folding her into his embrace. Juliana was reaching her arms up to link around his neck when his mouth slanted over hers. A tremor swept through her as her heart lodged in her throat. The kiss was gentle, slow, and languorous. Tongues explored, demanded, engaging fiercely. Alex's arms shook as he pulled her tighter against his warm, hard body. He made a harsh sound in his throat, and his kiss turned hot and ravenous, as if he could never get enough. Her lips demanded and possessed in response. Juliana thought she would melt at the sheer heat of the kiss.

The kiss she'd waited twelve years for—a kiss for her tired soul to melt into.

She whimpered into his mouth, and he broke away. His pupils were dilated as he drew in a sharp breath.

Gasping, she searched his face. "Alex. Wow." Her mind scrambled to form words, anything to steady her wildly beating heart. "So what's in the other envelope?"

Chuckling, he handed it to her. "I'm taking you on a long vacation."

When she peeked inside, a full itinerary and two plane tickets greeted her. They'd get their long-awaited trip to Scotland. Not that she cared what the destination was. She'd go to the far side of the galaxy with Alex.

His devastating smile erased the weariness from his face. "We can spend one of your bearer bonds." He winked and Juliana giggled. "If you have millions in bearer bonds, why are you still working?" Alex kissed her lips, her nose.

"Because I needed to fill the lonely hours." She smoothed his damp hair off his face.

"I can think of something to fill up the hours." His voice grew husky as he nuzzled her neck, stoking a growing fire inside her.

"Make love to me, Alex," she whispered.

"That's my intent." It was all he needed to hear before he gathered her close, and she twined her arms gently around his neck. The touch of his hands was unbearably tender.

Sounds of laughter from the hallway grudgingly pulled them apart.

Alex growled. Juliana laughed, and the door burst open.

"Uncle Alex, Juliana!" Lisette flew into the room and pounced on the bed, her white stuffed bunny in her hand.

Andrea and James brought up the rear. A black ball of fur streaked into the room and jumped on the bed.

"Jingle Bells!" Juliana looked at Alex incredulously. "_____ _____ here?" She picked up her cat in one arm

"Someone had to take care of the little beast. He's the one who alerted me to an intruder in your bed—" Alex coughed. "Sorry. I guess I shouldn't have mentioned it."

Juliana waved her hand as if to wipe out the horror. "It's okay. I have to face what happened."

She turned her attention to Lisette sitting beside her, excitement bubbling from every pore. "Hey, you, I'm glad to see you."

Alex flashed a disarming smile. Her heart melted to see him smile with complete happiness and love.

Lisette's curious eyes darted to the brilliant ring on Juliana's finger. "Did she say yes, Uncle Alex?"

Andrea and James crowded the doorway, arms around each other's waists, grinning.

"Did you think she wouldn't?" Alex's smile revitalized the room, her heart, her soul.

Juliana had never been happier, more loved, or more part of a family than at the moment.

DID YOU ENJOY
CHASING SHADOWS?

If you have a few moments, I'd love for you to leave a review for *CHASING SHADOWS* at your favorite online retailer or review site. Your review is greatly appreciated!

To stay up to date on Erin Richards' latest happenings, including new releases, sales, special announcements, exclusive excerpts, and giveaways, subscribe to her newsletter at: **www.erinrichards.com/connect.htm**

Read more of Juliana and Alex in the next exiting installment in the Psychic Justice Series. *TWILIGHT RISING,* available wherever eBooks are sold.

ABOUT THE AUTHOR

After lamenting the lack of young adult books to read, Erin Richards wrote her first novel at the age of eighteen hoping to shift the tide. But the only tide she shifted was moving from high school to college. Then everyday life took its toll on her writerly dreams until 2003 when she couldn't ignore the writing bug any longer. By then, she had immersed herself in reading adult fantasy and romance novels. Writing paranormal & fantasy romance was a no brainer and she went on to publish two adult romance novels. But her muse wanted to give that YA writing gig another chance, and Erin finally realized her lifelong dream of publishing a YA novel with the debut of *VIGILANTE NIGHTS*.

Erin lives in Northern California. In her spare time, she enjoys reading and re-landscaping her backyard, even though she hates digging holes...unless she's burying fictional bodies! She also confesses to a fascination with American muscle cars and reality TV.

Please visit Erin Richards online at:
www.erinrichards.com

www.ingramcontent.com/pod-product-compliance
Lightning Source LLC
Chambersburg PA
CBHW051332250626
47155CB00007B/2573